P9-CQJ-565

DEATH
QUALIFIED

DEATH
QUALIFIED
A Mystery of Chaos

Kate Wilhelm

St. Martin's Press
New York

DEATH QUALIFIED: A MYSTERY OF CHAOS. Copyright © 1991
by Kate Wilhelm. All rights reserved. Printed in the United
States of America. No part of this book may be used or
reproduced in any manner whatsoever without written
permission except in the case of brief quotations embodied
in critical articles or reviews. For information, address St.
Martin's Press, 175 Fifth Avenue, New York, N.Y. 10010.

Library of Congress Cataloging-in-Publication Data

Wilhelm, Kate.
      Death qualified : a mystery of chaos.
           p.   cm.
      ISBN 0-312-05853-5
      I. Title.
      PS3573.I434D4 1991   813'.54—dc20   90-27504

First Edition: June 1991
10 9 8 7 6 5 4 3 2 1

For Julie A. Stevens, with appreciation and affection.

*Does the flap of a butterfly's wings in Brazil
set off a tornado in Texas?*

—EDWARD N. LORENZ

DEATH
QUALIFIED

ONE

THEY ALWAYS CALLED him Tom. The maintenance crew, the doctors, everyone called him that, and although he knew it was not really his name, he responded. *Tom do this, do that. Tom come here, help with this.* Sometimes he could almost think of another name for himself, but it never seemed to finish forming in his mind. It started—a thought, an idea, an impulse to say a different name, not to look around when they said Tom—but then he was swept by terror and it vanished again. *Good morning Tom. How are you? Any more episodes, any dreams? Here's your medicine. That's a good boy. Go on to work now. See you in the morning Tom.*

He lived in a small apartment on the grounds. Sometimes he made his meals there, but most of the time he ate in the cafeteria. He had a meal ticket. *Good morning Tom. Bacon, eggs. What'll it be?* From the cafeteria to the doctor's office. From the doctor's office to the maintenance office. Out on the grounds, sometimes cleaning up in the buildings, running the waxer, or carrying out trash. He liked waxing best of the inside work, but he liked to work on the grounds best of all. Weeding, spreading mulch, riding the mower, making long, sweeping patterns in the grass that smelled like a memory. Once they made him repair some windows, and he had hated that. Looking in through the glass, like seeing into a separate world that was not his world and was not even real, had made him edgy. It was not that he was afraid of windows,

1

he had told the doctor; it was that the windows were wrong. That wasn't how it was.

Then how is it Tom? Tell me what you mean.

He couldn't tell her. He had tried to guide her hand to the windowlike shell around him, not hard like the building windows, but yielding, stretching when it had to stretch, coming back to fit snugly, but always there. He had tried to make her feel her own casing, her shell, tried to explain that it didn't have to fit so tightly. When he tried to touch her shell, she had called for someone to come, and someone had given him a shot. Yesterday. This morning. Sometime. Everything that was not right now was sometime.

They made him wash windows sometime, and they asked him if the windows were frightening. He said no. They asked him if he could see their shells. He said no. He said he didn't know what they meant. They asked him if he had a shell that could expand and contract. He said no. He said he didn't know what they meant. He was afraid of the doctor. If he told her the truth she called someone who gave him a shot. And then when he walked outside it was different. Instead of green leaves, they might be gone altogether, or there might be snow on the ground. Or it could be different in some other way that made him edgy. He never told them about the leaves' not being right.

Sometime. He woke up in front of his television, clutching a piece of paper with writing on it: *Don't take the medicine.* He threw it away.

Sometime. He woke up in a chair in his tiny living room, clutching a slip of paper: *Don't take the medicine.* He threw it away.

Sometime. He woke up clutching his hand, which was bloody. When he cleaned it he saw scratches on his palm, as if made with a pin: *Don't.*

Good morning Tom. How are you? Any more episodes? Any dreams? Here's your medicine. That's a good boy. Go on to work now. The medicine was a long red capsule in a little white paper cup, with another little cup of water by it. He put the capsule in his mouth and took a drink and walked out toward the maintenance office for his daily assignment. On the way he spat the capsule into his hand and thrust it down into his pocket.

He touched the capsule in his pocket several times. Sticky. He broke it with a touch and felt grains like fine sand in his pocket.

Tom weed out those dandelions in the daffodils. He bent over to start, but he was shaking, chilled. *Hey Tom you sick or something? Must be flu. Everyone's getting it. Go on home Tom. Pile up in bed a day or two, you'll be okay.*

Sometime. *Good morning Tom. They said you were sick so I brought your medicine over for you. You want to see the doctor?*

When she was gone he spat out the red capsule. He was shaking so hard he dropped it. No doctor. No medicine. No doctor. No medicine. No doctor. He slept.

Sometime. *Good morning Tom. Are you any better? Half the maintenance crew is down with it, whatever it is. The doctor says just rest and drink plenty of fluids and take aspirin if you feel too bad. Here's your medicine. Go on now.*

She watched so long that the sticky red capsule started to melt in his mouth and he felt the grains like sand. He coughed it out into a tissue. She backed away.

He sweated and got chilled. His heart raced, slowed, pounded. Deep whole-body spasms doubled him over with pain, and when they subsided he shook so hard he could not hold a glass, could not hold a spoon to eat the soup with. When they asked how he was he always said better. They brought food every day, and one day he picked up the bowl and drank all the soup, then drank all the milk and juice. He had not eaten for a long time.

The day he ate the soup, he realized that he was dirty, that he was unshaven, that he had not changed his clothes since. . . . He didn't know since when. He showered. At the mirror, shaving, he studied his face, the way he sometimes did. *His* face, not Tom's. When he did this, it was with great eagerness, as if maybe today that stranger face would become familiar, that stranger mouth would open and tell him something he needed to know. Blue eyes, badly bloodshot as if he had been crying. He remembered curling up on the bed

3

crying like a baby. Brown hair with a slight wave. Thin face, thin lips, sharp chin. He was well nourished, well muscled.

For a second, he thought his mirror self would tell him the other name; he almost knew it, his real name; it was there, waiting for him to say it. He opened his mouth as if to encourage that other self to speak, and the terror flashed through him, made him clutch the rim of the sink bowl and squeeze his eyes closed. When he could breathe normally again and opened his eyes again, he did not look at himself in the mirror.

He finished shaving and quickly got clean clothes on: blue jeans, undershirt, heavy sweater, socks, boots. Then he sat down on the side of his bed. He didn't know what he was supposed to do next. He began to shake, but this was only a tremor, not the wrenching spasms that he had been enduring. He waited for the shaking to pass, then got up and began to look over his apartment.

It was very small. A sofa and chair and one lamp were in the living room, and a television on a stand. Everything was brown or tan, even a shabby rug. A small kitchen with a half-size refrigerator; a three-burner stove; two tiny cabinets that held a couple of plates, a few glasses, a single cup. A tan Formica-topped table with two metal and plastic chairs took up most of the space. In the bedroom it was more of the same, barren and institutional: a single bed, a narrow chest of drawers, and a small closet that held working clothes like the ones he now wore.

And something else, he thought vaguely, but nothing more than that came. Something else. He looked in the refrigerator: milk that had gone bad, a few eggs, cheese, juice, apples. . . . Something else, he thought again.

He went back to the living room and tried the television. Three channels came in clearly, a game show, a children's show, and a show about lions. He became aware of two windows across the room, darkness beyond, and hard rain hitting the glass. He started to get up to pull down the shades, then checked himself. Tom never had noticed that he was like a fish in a bowl. He knew all about Tom, what he did,

4

how he spent his time in front of the television, falling asleep in front of it most nights, dragging himself to bed in a stupor when snow filled the screen. Never noticing if the shades were up or down. He knew all about Tom. He knew that he and Tom were the same man, and he knew his name was not Tom, and in some way he could not comprehend, he knew that Tom was not real and that he could not let anyone know he had learned this.

He forced himself to sit in front of the television, on which people were jumping up and down and screaming and hugging one another. His head was starting to ache, and his eyes burned again, but the tears were contained, and this time they were not caused by fear or pain, but by frustration because he hated the shades' being up, hated being watched from out there in the darkness, and he did not know what to do about it. His fear of the doctor was greater than his hatred of being watched.

The rain beat against the windows harder than before, swept against them by gusting winds. Sleet, he thought then. It was sleeting. The idea made him shiver. He became very still, considering, and abruptly got up and went to the bedroom, pulled a blanket off the bed, and wrapped it around himself. When he returned to the living room, he pulled down the shades. He went to the kitchen and pulled down the shade on the single window there, then did the same in the bedroom.

Someone would come with his dinner tray and find him huddled on the sofa, wrapped in a blanket, freezing. It was okay that the television sound was turned all the way down; Tom often watched it without sound. He sat with his eyes closed, the blanket ready, and he thought about Tom's routine. This week it had been different; they had brought him his food every day. He had to stop and try to think if week was the right length of time, and he realized he didn't know. He had been too sick to notice. Suddenly he knew he had not been suffering from the flu, but withdrawal. Withdrawal, he repeated silently. The red capsules. He could have died, withdrawing like that. He dismissed the thought; he

5

didn't even know what it was he had withdrawn from. A heavy-duty tranquilizer; the answer came as fast as he phrased the statement of ignorance.

Just as suddenly the thought came to him that he didn't know how long he had been Tom. He didn't know the month, the day, even what year it was. He moistened his lips, then did it again.

He was almost too startled to grab the blanket when he heard a key turning in the lock on his door. The door opened and one of the men from the cafeteria entered with the tray.

"Hey, how you doing? You pulled down the shades. Thought you'd gone out dancing or something."

"Cold," he mumbled, clutching the blanket, burying his face in it.

"Yeah. It's a mean one out there tonight. Freezing rain, sleet, snow by morning. Springtime in the Rockies." He went on through to the kitchen and returned with the lunch tray. "You stay bundled up, stay warm. See you tomorrow."

He felt his shell touch the young man, stretch to accompany him as he ran across the parking lot that separated the apartments from the dormitory cafeteria. The sleet was driving in like icicles. Inside the big building across the way the young man stopped to wipe his face with a napkin.

"Oh, Michael, glad I caught you. How is he?"

The shell almost snapped back when the doctor approached the young man. She was gray-haired, wearing a burgundy raincoat, carrying an umbrella. Her eyes were very dark, the darkest eyes he had ever seen. The most frightening eyes he had ever seen.

"Hi, Dr. Brandywine. Better, I'd say. At least he ate lunch. First time. He's freezing, all wrapped up in a blanket, watching TV. Shades all down, trying to keep out the sleet, I guess."

"Well, if he's eating, that's an improvement. This is a nasty bug going around."

Michael left for the cafeteria, and she looked the other way and called, "Are you coming, Herbert?"

The man who joined her was tall and overweight with white hair and light blue eyes—Dr. Margolis. He was grinning. "I heard what he said. Too bad. Better luck next time."

6

"Oh, stop. That isn't funny."

He laughed. He had on a raincoat and now pulled a hat from his pocket and pushed it into shape, jammed it on his head, and they left the building. They hurried to a parked car, got in, and she drove them away.

The man they called Tom got up slowly and went into the kitchen to eat his dinner. The food was hot and quite good. Roast beef, mashed potatoes, more soup. . . . He ate everything, drank the carton of milk, and got up to make coffee before he remembered that Tom didn't drink coffee. There was a jar of instant decaf in the cabinet. He looked at it, then put it back.

All right, he said under his breath. Tom wasn't a prisoner; he had a little money. He even went shopping alone now and then. He found forty-three dollars in the chest of drawers in the bedroom, and several singles and some change in the pockets of the dirty jeans he had worn earlier. No wallet, no car keys, no identification. A key to the apartment that made little difference since *they* all had keys also. He got his poncho from the closet, put it on with the hood down nearly to his eyes, and walked out into the spring storm. That way was the cafeteria, and over there the maintenance office, and opposite both a path through the trees to the sidewalk that led to the nearest grocery store, a convenience store where Tom was a familiar figure. In the other direction, farther away, was another store, a mini market that he had been in only once. He turned in that direction.

He hadn't known what he expected to happen after reading the newspapers and magazine articles. Nothing did. He made strong coffee and drank it, then a second cup. The caffeine made him dizzy and he couldn't sit still. March 1989. It was not a surprise; after all, Tom had watched television every night, through the weekends. He had seen the changing seasons, had been aware of time in a dim way. At last he went to bed, more frustrated than before, and exhausted. He wondered for the first time if perhaps he really had had the flu.

7

When he woke up he realized he had to hide the things he had bought. Someone would come with his medicine and breakfast and he couldn't let them know anything had changed, even if he didn't know yet what the change meant. It was Friday, he thought then. He was still too sick to work, and he would have the weekend to himself. Maybe things would come clearer if he had a few days to think.

He got up and hurried to the kitchen where he regarded the table with dismay and fear. What if they had come in while he slept? The doctor would know. Another shot, many more shots, and when he went to work again it might be winter, or summer. He went to the window and pulled the shade away enough to see that it was snowing hard. Then he turned back to the table.

He had bought notebooks and pens and pencils. He had coffee and recent magazines and newspapers. He had a paperback book or two. He flushed the decaf coffee granules down the toilet and filled the jar with regular, put it back in the cabinet. He started to throw the empty jar into the trash, then drew back; they might notice. Instead he put it in his jacket pocket to toss later. He hid the other things between the mattress and box spring of his bed. When the young woman with the long braid came, he was sitting in front of the television, wrapped in the blanket.

On Monday when he went back to work, nothing was clearer. The snow was already melting. Every day he took the red capsule and spat it out later. He learned how to hold it in his mouth for longer periods, even to mumble something or other with it under his tongue. Tom never had talked very much and he didn't now. A mumbled yes or no was all he said most days.

"Any more episodes, any more dreams?"

"No."

He always knew when Dr. Brandywine was in the lobby of her building, or in the office where he reported in every morning. If he had to, he stopped to examine a flower, or to tie his bootlace, or just to gaze vacantly into the distance in order to wait until she walked into the lab or a classroom; then he went inside and got his capsule. There were three people in there usually, none of them interested in him. They were easy. Dr. Brandywine was never easy.

On those days when he knew he could not avoid her, he pulled his shell so tightly around him he felt suffocated by it, constrained so that he moved awkwardly, and he knew that was all right, in character for Tom. He tried not to look at her directly ever. Sometimes she ordered him, "Look up here, Tom. Tell me the truth. Any dreams?"

He looked at her chin, or her iron-gray hair that was thin enough that her scalp showed through like a wad of pink chewing gum. He looked at her earlobe, or the gold chain that tethered her reading glasses.

He now knew where he was, on a college campus. Tom had simply been *here*. The campus was not very large. The school was private, very prestigious, a few miles north of Denver. The student body hovered around five hundred. Dr. Brandywine's department of psychology was housed in a red brick building. Dr. Margolis's department of computer science was in the large building where the cafeteria was located; one wing was student dormitories. Dr. Schumaker was in the department of mathematics in the science building on the far side of the campus. He was there only one day a week. Those were the only three people he was interested in, and afraid of.

Every Friday afternoon he checked in at Dr. Brandywine's office and was handed an envelope with forty dollars in it. He never said anything, and usually neither did the person on the other side of the desk. When it was the young woman who wore glasses as large as saucers, and had a braid that went down to her waist, she spoke pleasantly, called him Tom, said something like have a nice weekend. He didn't know her name.

He was beginning to remember other places: a desert ringed by buttes and mountains; a semicircular volcanic caldera; a pine forest with sunlight streaking in horizontally; a misty, dripping forest of fir trees.

One night he came wide awake with the name *Nell* in his head, on his tongue. "Nell," he said. "Nell." No picture came with it. Just the name. He got up and prowled around the dark apartment. Nell. Nell.

Tom never woke up at night, never turned on lights after going to bed, and he didn't this night, but neither could he go back to sleep. He pulled the notebook from under his mattress, groped for the pen, and took them to the kitchen table in the dark. A sliver of light came in around the edges of the shade, not enough for him to read by, but enough to see the blank white paper. He had written nothing in the notebook yet. Now he did: *Nell*, and in a second he added another name: *Travis*. He couldn't make out the letters, but he knew what he had written.

He beat his hand against the table top, then grasped the pen again and stared at his fingers. The hand had written before, unbidden: It had told him not to take the medicine. That other one who was not Tom had communicated with him. *Do it again!* He tried to relax his fingers, to ease the tightness in his arm and shoulder, and finally he wrote *forbidden name* and then let the pen drop to the table.

He got up and went to the living room window to look out at the parking lot, at the looming building beyond it. A lighted stairwell, a few lights in windows up there, no one in sight. And he thought, forbidden. Not forgotten, but forbidden.

April passed. May was hot and the drought returned, threatening to scorch the grass. He mulched, and mowed, and pruned. He waxed the floors and carried out trash.

He could walk away. No one really paid any attention to him. *Take your medicine. Any more episodes? Any dreams?* He knew they would come after him and bring him back if he left, but more than that, he had to stay because he had to find that forbidden name. It was here.

The grounds were ready for commencement exercises; a platform had been erected and draped with blue and orange, the school colors. Canopies were in place; long tables were decorated with flowers for the reception. The graduates and their families and guests had not yet arrived but would within the next half hour or so.

He was rising from pulling out a stray weed from the bed of cannas in front of the administration building when he came face to face with Dr. Schumaker. He turned and fled. He did not stop running until he was around the corner of the building, and then he walked very fast to the back where deliveries were made. He sank to the ground behind a dumpster, breathing hard. Stupid, he thought, stupid to bolt like that, give himself away through something like that. Stupid. He stared ahead, but he was watching Dr. Schumaker. Without thought he had extended his shell in order to watch and listen, to see if he had given himself away through such a stupid act as running like that.

Dr. Schumaker continued to walk. At the door, he looked back, frowning.

"Morning, Walter," Dr. Brandywine said, joining him. "What a long face."

"I just ran into him, Tom. Why on earth do you keep him around?"

"Tom? Why not? He's harmless, and a good worker. Cheap, too." She laughed softly.

"Listen, Ruth. I said this before, and I'm saying it now. He's a danger to you, to all of us. Get rid of him."

"Now, Walter, if I didn't know better I'd say that's a guilty conscience talking. Besides, where could he go? At least I can keep an eye on him here. Forget it. Ready to give a rousing send-off speech?"

His voice dropped to a near-whisper as other people began to draw near. "He knows, Ruth. That look on his face . . . he knows."

"Nothing, Walter. He knows nothing. He's good for us. A little Lucas-prod keeps us all a bit more honest."

Lucas! The world changed. Everywhere lines and bands stretched taut, a web of shining lines encased him, choking him, smothering him. He flung up his hand over his eyes and screamed and pitched forward to the ground.

TWO

HE LAY IN the dirt in a fetal position, his eyes tightly closed. Voices were everywhere.

Dr. Schumaker: ". . . idealists all, striving toward the highest ideals . . ."

Dr. Brandywine: "You know I'm the only one who can help you. As long as you're Tom, you're safe . . ."

Schumaker: ". . . met by temptation at every step, and you have the inner resources to resist . . ."

Brandywine: "He did terrible things. You know that. They will give you shock treatments, a lobotomy even. Criminally insane . . ."

". . . inherit a world that appears all evil, but that is an illusion. It appears that the strong force their will upon the weak at every turn, but that is an illusion, also. You are the strong ones. Your youth, your courage, these are the strengths . . ."

"Listen to me, Tom. Listen. He must never be allowed out again. Never! Do you understand me?"

Dr. Margolis: "Good Christ! All that blood!"

"We have to get him out of here! Don't move, Lucas. Just don't move. Find a blanket . . ."

"All that blood! It won't work."

"They can't have him! Get a blanket."

All that blood! All that blood! All that blood! All tha—

"I can save you. I'll protect you. You have to do exactly what I say. Do you understand?"

"What you have learned in this academy of the utmost importance, is that you can make a difference, each one of you, in the little things you do every day, and in the big things you do that bring you acclaim . . ."

"Tom, if you ever have another episode like this, you must tell me instantly. Instantly. Do you understand? Answer me!"

"Yes."

Dr. Margolis: "We have to turn him in. My God, we can't do something like that. Look at him!"

". . . grateful for your birthright, this beautiful land, this beautiful country that is yours, and make the deepest, most heartfelt resolution that that which you find beautiful you will leave even more beautiful . . ."

"Wrap him up in it. Pick up your foot, Tom. We've got you; you won't fall. Get the blanket around his shoes. All right. Clean up the computer, get it all out. And I'll take the disks. Give me ten minutes before you call the police."

"My God, Ruth, the computer's destroyed! Everything's gone! The tape's wiped, everything's gone!"

"Get the backup disks, you idiot! We have to move!"

"That's what I'm trying to tell you. They aren't here."

"They have to be here! Let's get him out to the car and I'll help you look."

". . . only possible expression of gratitude is through service to your fellow man. The smallest act of generosity is magnified a thousandfold . . ."

"That name is forbidden. You will never again think of it. You won't hear it if anyone addresses you by it. You won't see it. The name and everything associated with it are forbidden. You are Tom."

Good morning Tom. Any more episodes? Any dreams? Take your medicine.

A strange voice, a laughing voice: "You're tangled up in the web? Take the next step, it's easy."

". . . not fame or money, but the realization of the hopes and dreams . . ."

"No!" he moaned, his eyes hurting from being closed so hard. "No!" He pulled in the shell until he felt suffocated, until the voices were stilled; he could hear his own heart beat. He had to find Dr. Brandywine, tell her it had happened again. She could help him. No one else could save him but Dr. Brandywine. He didn't move.

He was afraid to open his eyes. He was afraid to move. *They will find you here,* he thought, with words spoken in his head in the voice so like Tom's voice, but different. *They'll pick you up and carry you to bed and she will come and give you a shot, and tomorrow another one, and then another one. You won't have to tell her. When she sees you, she'll know. And when you go outside again, there will be snow on the ground.*

Or, he thought with terror, maybe this time he would not be allowed outside again. Maybe this time they would send him away, as Dr. Schumaker wanted them to do. Hospital for the criminally insane, that was where she had said they would send him.

He heard footsteps, and then voices. "What a windbag!"

"You got that right." A can popped open. "You going fishing this weekend?"

"Nope. Taking the kids up to Estes for a picnic."

Now there was applause that went on and on, swelling and ebbing. The two men approached the dumpster and tossed something in.

"It'll take a couple of hours to tear down everything. We'll leave the picking up for tomorrow, just get the tables and chairs and stuff inside . . ." They were moving away.

He had drawn up even tighter with their arrival, and now he stretched, every muscle aching. Suddenly he realized that he had opened his eyes, was watching their departing figures.

"Pomp and Circumstance" started in the distance. He began to push himself to a kneeling position, then he pulled one leg up to get his foot on the ground, and finally, keeping his gaze on his feet, afraid to look up again, he stood upright.

He had to find Dr. Brandywine, had to. He clenched his

14

hands, his eyes downcast. She would be at the ceremony, he thought then, and was able to open his fists. He remembered seeing the word *don't* scratched on his palm. This time when he looked, both palms were scarlet with imprints of his nails clearly visible. *Don't.* He was dirty from his fall; his face was dirty, both hands. He would go change, shower, and then find her. He nodded at his feet and started to walk home to his apartment, watching first one foot, then the other all the way.

Although his apartment was stifling, he closed the door and pulled down all the shades before he showered. He stayed under the spray for a long time and then barely dried himself before he went to the bedroom closet for clean clothes. He stopped with his hand outstretched and slowly he raised his face and looked at the closet ceiling. *Something else,* he thought. There was a panel in the ceiling, held in place with four screws.

Moving like a man in a dream, he turned to survey the bedroom. Barren, stripped, nothing personal in view. But there should be posters, and Nell's picture, and one of Travis. Nell! He closed his eyes and shook his head. Nell. His wife. Travis, his son. He went clammy with shock and held on to the closet door for a moment. Then, almost frenzied, he ran to the kitchen and grabbed one of the chairs, yanked a drawer open, snatched up a table knife, and hurried back to the closet.

What if someone had opened the panel? Found the tapes? This had been his apartment before . . . before. . . . He had lived here, had a stereo, a tape recorder, tapes. . . . And he had put the tapes up there. He had lived here when the workmen came to put in insulation and had cut the hole in this ceiling to gain access to the crawl space up there.

He was so frantic in his haste that he couldn't manage the screws. He wiped sweat from his eyes and took a deep breath, another, and tackled the screw again; this time it dropped into his hand. Another one, a third. He loosened the fourth one but did not take it out; instead, he pivoted the panel away from the hole exactly the way he had done the night he had hidden the tapes. Then, standing on tiptoe on the chair, he groped in the dark space and found the plastic bag where he had left it.

He started to pull it out, but stopped, considering. There was no place to hide it except up here where it had been safe for. . . . He did not know how many years. He brought the bag close enough to the hole so that he could look at it, and then pushed it back again. Sixteen two-hour tapes. Later, he said under his breath. Soon, though.

He dressed methodically and made a cup of coffee, strong and black, and suddenly found himself wishing he had a beer. Tom was not allowed alcohol. Or caffeine, he added, sipping the coffee. When he left here, first a beer, two beers, icy cold. Then a coffee shop, espresso or capuccino, maybe both. He nodded. Both.

Soon the ceremonies would be over, the punch and cookies gone, and then he could find her in her office.

He nearly fell into a chair, shaken by the fully formed thought. "No," he said aloud. Never again. And for the first time he knew he didn't dare get close enough for her to touch him. With a touch she could control him, even if he didn't know how. He knew this with certainty. He had to get out of here now, tonight. Even as he recognized his need to run, he also knew there was something else he had to do first.

More than anything, he had to sit still and think, let the snatches of memories coalesce and make sense. And he had to avoid Dr. Brandywine altogether. He knew he could not stay in his apartment; he was one of the clean-up crew this evening and again in the morning. If he didn't show up, they would send someone for him. No suspicions. No suspicious behavior, not now. He heard cars starting in the parking lot; the ceremonies had ended, people were leaving.

With his hand on the doorknob, he paused with his eyes closed. "My name is Lucas Kendricks." There, he thought, quietly jubilant, he had it back. She had tried to kill Lucas Kendricks, replace him with Tom, and she had failed. Lucas Kendricks.

THREE

He walked to the mini market that evening and bought a tiny flashlight. At two in the morning he left his apartment, ducked around the back of the complex, and made his way to the psychology building, her building. He needed money if he was going to run away. He knew they kept money in a box in the office; they gave him his weekly stipend out of the cash box. He had watched the young woman with the braid draw it out of a drawer, take his envelope from it, to pay him early this day because everything would be closed for the graduation ceremonies.

The student would be leaving during the next few days; this weekend was traditionally party weekend. Music blared all over campus, lights were on in every dormitory, students were out on the lawn, walking everywhere, dancing in the parking lot, smoking openly, laughing, screaming. . . . The academic buildings were dark and quiet, however.

He knew which window he could force; he had puttied and washed every window in the building. He eased the window open and entered. Inside, he walked silently down the corridor to the outer office, around behind the desk. No cash box was in the drawer of the desk. He was shaking with fear at being this close to her office. Somewhere on campus a string of firecrackers went off, and he nearly collapsed. He held on to the desk and waited for his shakiness to subside,

17

and then went to her office door and opened it. He felt he could not breathe; he waited until that sensation also passed, then went inside and pulled the door closed behind him.

He had been in this office many times, far too many times, he thought, now accepting the dread that filled him. Dim light filtered in from an outside street lamp; the venetian blinds were not all the way closed. For a moment he felt that anyone passing would look in, see him standing there. He swallowed hard, then forced himself to cross the pale beige carpet, to pass the comfortable wooden chair that he had sat in frequently, to go around her desk. He used his tiny flashlight sparingly; cupping the end in his hand, restricting the light, he examined the drawers, swept the beam of light across the desk top. He became paralyzed at the sight of a paperweight, a melon-sized globe with a little cottage, two small figures.

With his paralysis the flashlight dropped from his fingers; he sagged against the desk, catching his breath. *It isn't snowing,* he said under his breath. *It's all right. It isn't snowing.*

"Look at the paperweight, Tom. Watch the snow falling. Keep your eyes on the snow, Tom, falling, falling. . . ."

Now he knew that was one of the cues she used to hypnotize him. "It's snowing, Tom." That was enough to put him in a trance. Looking at the paperweight with the snow falling was enough. What else? He was sure there was a touch, also, but he could not bring it to mind.

He felt that he had been standing hunched over, his head bowed, for a long time, but at last he was able to reach down and pick up his flashlight again. The desk drawers were locked. "It isn't snowing," he whispered, and turned the light on the desk top again, looking for something he could use to pry open the drawers. Instead, he stopped sweeping the light back and forth and let it shine on a travel agent's folder, under the paperweight. He reached for it, but yanked his hand back just short of touching the paperweight. A film of sweat broke out on his face, down his spine. He wiped his lips with the back of his hand, closed his eyes, and groped for

18

the travel folder and pulled it free. He turned his back on the desk to examine the travel arrangements.

She was leaving Sunday for England! Sunday morning at six-thirty out of Stapleton. Return ticketed for July 1. He didn't look at the paperweight when he replaced the folder. He forgot about opening the desk drawers but hurried out of the office, back through the window, and to his own apartment. The campus revelry was continuing; units up and down the apartment complex were lighted, people were out on the walk in front of many of the doors. No one paid any attention to him when he approached and entered his own unit.

He dropped into bed exhausted, thinking over and over: Sunday. On Saturday she would call him into her office. She always did before leaving on a trip. His fists clenched at the thought of receiving instructions now.

Saturday morning he walked through wet peat moss around the plantings near her building. He knelt in it, smeared fertilizer and lime dust on his legs, covered his sneakers with fertilizer, coated his hands with mud, and then went in for his medicine, wiping his hand ineffectually on his jeans, paying no attention to the muddy prints he left from the door to the desk. When she came out and started to speak, he paid no attention to her, either. He could feel those black eyes drilling, drilling, and inside he was so tight he thought he couldn't move. She turned and reentered her office; he went back outside wordlessly.

Done! Now he could vanish the rest of the day, and tomorrow she would be gone. He often spent the day in the nearby woods. When she questioned him, "Where do you go? What do you do?" he mumbled, "Woods. I don't know." At least she hadn't forbidden that.

He was still nagged by the *something else* that kept just out of recoverable range. Something else. But he knew he would not wait for the nebulous thought to take shape. No more waiting. Tomorrow he would go to her house and search for the possessions of Lucas Kendricks. She must have them hidden away, up in the attic, or in the basement, somewhere,

19

just in case she ever had to produce Lucas Kendricks, or his body. He remembered her house up on the mountain side, although he thought Tom probably never had been there after those first few weeks. Weeks? He tried to recover that period and failed. Weeks? He was certain of that. Weeks. He was getting more and more snatches of memory, but in no real order, no first this, then that, no cause and effect. She had taken away his memories of Lucas Kendricks, of Nell and Travis; she had taken his identity, had taken him and replaced him with a madman, Tom.

He shuddered at the thought of the years he had been Tom, a madman who heard voices and had no past, no future, only the immediate moment. Shuddering, he wanted to strangle Dr. Brandywine. Not shoot her, or stick a knife into her heart, but strangle her with his hands, watch those black eyes bulge and then go blank.

It was a long walk. He had started immediately after reporting in and getting his medicine, and now it was at least noon. Tom had never needed a watch, but Lucas knew it must have been about two hours so far. He was drenched with sweat. The curvy mountain road was narrow, deceptively deserted-looking. The many driveways belied the wilderness appearance. Twice he had ducked behind thick underbrush to hide when he heard a car coming, and now he was nearing her driveway.

The thought, something else, beat like a drum in his head, with his pulse. Something else. He paused at her driveway: something else. Not here, farther up the road. Something else.

Another car was coming. He ran up her driveway to where it curved, was lost to sight from the road, and paused again, but this time out of caution. She might have left someone house sitting, a caretaker, housekeeper, or someone. Keeping in the cover of the woods he drew closer until he could see the house and garage; he stopped again. A dusty old Ford was in the driveway.

The house was two stories, with a cathedral ceiling in the

living room, a balcony overlooking the living room, bed-rooms off that. Kitchen, dining room, study, laundry room completed the downstairs. He could visualize every room as it had been the last time he had been here. And the Ford. Her housekeeper, he thought. Miranda. But she would not be staying, not all the time, he felt certain. He sank down behind a tree to wait.

Within an hour the front door opened and a heavyset Chicano woman emerged, carrying two plants. She put them in her car and went back inside, returned with two more. She carried out several more, locked the door, checked it, and got in the Ford and drove down the driveway.

He waited a few more minutes, but he was certain no one else was around. He trotted toward the house, detoured to glance in through the garage window, and came to a dead stop. Her Corvette was parked inside, and beyond it, par-tially covered with a blue plastic tarp, was a gray Honda Civic. His car.

He felt that he had entered a dream. All his movements were dreamlike, and as in a dream, images, words, voices floated freely before him. In the dream he broke the window and entered the garage; he opened his car door, sat behind the wheel, all the while listening to the various voices:

"Hey, who're you? You're in the web, too? Wow!"

"Lucas, get up here. I need you." Emil's voice. But Emil was dead.

He found his wallet, his watch, and car keys in the glove compartment. He slipped on the watch. It was still running. There was almost a hundred dollars in the wallet. He reached inside the compartment again, this time to bring out a bulging envelope that held forty-two hundred dollars. He knew how much was in it. The car would not start. The battery, he thought. He got out and opened the hood of the Corvette and then searched the garage for tools.

"Look, man, it's just us. Watch, damn it! He's smashed the computer, and the memory tapes, but I got the disks. You hear me?"

21

He was driving too fast up the curved mountain road, and that young voice was there: "Hey, just watch, okay?"

"I can't. I can't." Everywhere the web stretched, bands and lines, taut, shimmering, stretching, smothering him. He jammed on the brakes, pressed his head against the steering wheel, his eyes closed.

"Hey, it's okay. Don't look. You'll know when it's time to come get them. You'll know."

He found gloves and pulled them on and then lifted the battery out of the Honda, put the Corvette battery in its place, attached cables. He siphoned gas from the Corvette and put it in the Honda, put some in the carburetor, found oil for a lawn mower or something. It would have to do, long enough to get to a garage. The next time he turned the key in the ignition, the engine coughed, made gasping noises, and turned over.

He was behind the wheel, and also he remembered being bundled in a blanket, shoved into the car on the passenger side. She drove. So much blood, so much blood. He looked at the passenger headrest, dusty, gray, no trace of blood. His head had been covered by the blanket. He touched his forehead, felt a scar. She had stitched it.

"Lucas, I need you!"

"I'm coming, Emil. I'm coming."

"You'll know when it's okay to get them. You'll know."

Still in the dream, he got out of the Honda and examined the garage door, found a button that opened it, and then drove out into the driveway, heading out. If the car wouldn't start later, he could push it, get it rolling, and coast down the mountain road. Then he turned off the ignition and pocketed the keys. The license plates, he thought suddenly. He would be stopped. He went back inside the garage and removed the license plates from the Corvette and put them on the Honda, and now he was done.

Something else, he thought. Something else. He looked around, as if looking for the something else. He saw the open garage door and closed it, hoping Miranda would not notice anything amiss before Dr. Brandywine returned.

"Tom, listen to me. Did you touch the disks? Did you move them? Answer me, Tom."

"No."

He didn't search for a direction when he started to walk again, around the back of the house, into the woods on a path that had not become overgrown even if Dr. Brandywine no longer used it, not since Emil's death. Emil, he thought as if from a great distance. Dead. Emil was dead. His vision blurred and he wiped tears away. Emil Frobisher was dead.

"Tom, listen carefully. He can't ever come out again. He did terrible, terrible things. It isn't your fault. You are innocent, but you have to keep him buried. That name is forbidden. Everything associated with that name is forbidden. You will never think of him. . . ."

He came to a stop; almost directly ahead was a small barn. Emil Frobisher's property had once housed a stable; the barn was still standing. He did not look beyond the barn at the house, did not consider who might be living there now, if they were home. He looked only at the barn. There was a loft with miscellaneous lumber and some old casement windows piled up in it. Behind all the stuff, back in a dark corner where the side wall and roof joined in a sharp angle, there was a plastic box of computer disks. He moistened his lips and moved toward the barn.

He cut his hand on a broken window pane when he scrambled over the piles of stuff in the loft. The box was there. He pulled it out, tucked it under his arm, and went back down the ladder and outside. A little boy was standing there, watching Lucas soberly.

"Hi. You got hurt."

Lucas looked down at his hand. *All that blood. Good Christ, all that blood!*

He hurried past the child, back into the woods; on the path there he began to run.

FOUR

SOME SUMMER DAYS the river resembled a sleeping exotic snake, hardly moving, hardly breathing; those days it shone green with silver scales. Some times it was liquid silver flowing around quiet patches as blue as cornflowers; or, mirrorlike, it became luminous and as dazzling as fallen sky. Earlier in the season it was pale gray, its spring-fed, lake-fed water mixed with ice water fresh from the glaciers in the Cascades, racing, running deep and swift as if its mission then was to cool the ocean, and it was an overly conscientious servant intent on carrying out its duty. In winter it often turned black and looked deceptively sluggish. Now and again a raft of snow escaped from the banks, bobbed, spun in a delirious pirouette, rose and fell, dwindling, always dwindling, finally to drown in a frenzy of tumultuous death throes.

Logs twisted and twirled their way downstream; they often got caught on rocks and thrashed like living creatures trying to shake a trap. The river toyed with the logs; it sometimes held one end fast and let the other rise higher and higher only to crash it down eventually like a thunderclap.

Other objects tumbled their way downstream: a canoe paddle, a float from fishing gear, an elk, a coyote, a black bear once, Styrofoam remains from picnic packaging, cups. . . .

The river laughed, it whispered, it roared. It had songs

24

of its own. And secrets. It knew silence and sighs. The dawn sun cast silver on the water; at evening it spun gold.

Here at Turner's Point was the last stretch of untamed water in the river. Ten miles downstream was a dam; around the point the river widened and became ever calmer until it turned into a brilliant blue lake that was so cold whole trees had been preserved upright in its water.

Trees and water. Water and trees. Fir trees with shadows so dense that only creatures and plants that thrived in near darkness lived there. The ground was a mat of needles, deep and resilient; weathered lava rocks erupted through it here and there. After the fall rains, and again in the spring, mushrooms appeared in exuberant abundance.

On the far side of the river, opposite Turner's Point, a cliff rose thirty feet. Downstream, the cliff became one of the boundaries of the lake, and upstream, a hundred feet high, or even higher, it was a sheer vertical barrier to the river. On this side of the river the land rose less steeply; there was room for the highway, for Turner's Point with its several dozen buildings, the general store and gas station, and fishing camps with cabins so close together that, unless seen straight on, they looked like one long structure. Behind the store, fifteen feet above the river, was a gravel parking lot with a paved drive to a boat ramp. The cabins stopped at a boulder forty feet high, double that at the base, moss-covered, encrusted with pale green and red lichen, with two straggly fir trees sticking out awkwardly over the river.

If the boulder had not come to rest right there, Nell Kendricks could have walked the half mile from her river-front yard to the store at Turner's Point, but the boulder had tumbled and rolled and finally lodged at that point, and she had to drive, first on a private road, then almost a mile on a county road, and finally half a mile on the state highway. At Turner's Point the highway veered away from the river to start its tortuous climb to the mountain pass, and on to the eastern slopes of the Cascades.

Today Nell was one of a dozen regulars who gathered every Thursday when the bookmobile chugged into the parking lot, throwing gritty dust, grinding the gravel down in the summer, churning up a slurry in the winter. Nell had collected books for herself, a few for her daughter and son, although now in the first week of summer vacation, neither child had expressed any interest at all in reading. Travis had regarded her with unfeigned astonishment at the suggestion. Nell also had picked up some books for her neighbor Jessica Burchard. Mikey, the driver for the mobile library, walked to Nell's car with her, both of them carrying armloads of books.

"Like I said," Mikey was saying, "one more budget cut and we go belly up. That damned bus can hardly climb even this high anymore, and they're wanting us to go on up to the scout camp. Can you imagine! That's some twisty little road, and steep!" Mikey was a tall, gangly woman not yet forty, with unmanageable red hair that constantly escaped the various berets and clips and hair pins and scarves she wore. She towered over Nell, who always said she was five two and lied a bit about it, giving herself nearly an inch that nature had not.

"Why don't they let the scouts hike down here, if they want books? It's only a couple of miles, good trails," Nell said as they dumped the books on the passenger seat of her pickup.

"And be sensible about it? Why start now? Come on, buy you a Coke or something." She waved to Lonnie Rowan, a short, broad woman in red pants who had just driven into the parking area. "Hi, Lonnie! Got that new mystery you wanted."

"Go on," Nell said. "I'll bring drinks out to the back."

Mikey nodded and walked toward Lonnie, as Nell headed for the general store. She nodded to people, spoke to several, but did not pause. She knew everyone here, met them all regularly shopping, or at the library, or somewhere in the area. They held meetings at the grange, talked endlessly about how to slow down the logging trucks before they reached town, how to attract tourists, who was marrying or divorcing whom. . . .

There had been a Turner at Turner's Point at one time;

he had built the general store that had café seating attached. Chuck Gilmore owned the establishment now, the store, the gas station, most of the cabins. The store featured cold sandwiches in a case, fruit priced scandalously high, fishing tackle, worms and salmon eggs in a cooler, beer, soft drinks, bread that always seemed to be day-old. Strange, how the bread never was fresh; you couldn't get to the store early enough.

Nell made her way through the clump of people inside the door. Thursday was social hour, time for the locals to catch up, time to gossip a little. As she passed people in twos and threes, she heard snatches of ongoing conversations:

"Don't know why they always have to have the roads torn up soon's the weather gets nice. Took Maud more than two hours to drive out."

"Way I see it, if they spend all their time and money on the highway that don't need fixing they can keep right on claiming they just can't get to Old Halleck Hill Road."

"And it'll get so bad they'll barricade both ends and that'll be the end of it."

Nell reached the cooler and pulled out two Cokes, then held them up for Louise Gilmore to see. They exchanged smiles, nods; if Chuck had been there, Nell would have walked over and plunked down cash without a word, but Louise was okay. She nodded and made a note in the book. Nell edged past Dolores Lutz and Sarah Sedgewick, out the back door to the deck. A few tables were out here, rough-hewn and full of splinters, with attached benches. No one from the area ever used them, only tourists who realized too late that their clothes would be snagged and made gummy with oozing sap. Nell went to the wide rail at the end of the deck and put down the Coke for Mikey on it, then opened her own, facing the river.

Below, some men had set up a table and were playing cards; someone had started a smoky fire on one of the grills; a few boys were turning over rocks and staring intently at the exposed ground. The smoke from the grill drifted into Nell's eyes; she turned away as Mikey and Stu Hermann drew

27

close. Stu had a beer in one hand and a string bag filled with books in the other. He was seventy or more, walked like a young man, and read a book a day and had for years.

"'Lo, Nellie. How's things?" He grinned at her and eased the bag to the deck floor. "They just get heavier," he said. "Have to cut back one of these days."

Before Nell could speak, Mikey caught her breath in and expelled it again in a scream.

Farther down on the deck someone yelled, "Someone's in the river!"

Nell twisted around and saw her. For a second or two the river held up the body of a naked woman, head bowed, arms dangling, long hair like seaweed wrapped around the upper torso. Then the figure was drawn back under the water.

The pickup threw gravel as Nell took the curves too fast, but she did not slow down until she suddenly braked hard at her own drive, a continuation of the gravel road that finally dead-ended at her house. She slammed on the brakes and even skidded a little.

Pulled off the road was a truck with a chipper; two men were standing by it, regarding her now, but they had been looking at the tall noble fir tree that marked the beginning of her property.

"What are you doing?" she demanded, her head stuck out the side window.

One of the men grinned at her. It was an insolent smile, the kind of smile some very large men reserve for small women, children, or cute animals.

The other one said, "Going to take out that fir. Any minute now." He looked like a college boy, cheerful and happy.

"What are you talking about? That tree's on private property. My property. You can't touch it!"

"Honey, we got orders to take it down. Reckon that's what we aim to do."

"Wait here," she said, after drawing in a deep breath.

"You're from . . ." She peered at the truck. Clovis Woods Products. "There's been a mistake. Just wait a minute."

The one with a grin shrugged, reached inside the truck, and pulled out an open can of beer. He finished the beer and set the can on the hood of the truck, then glanced at his watch. "Five minutes, honey, then we go to work again."

Again? She looked up at the fir tree and saw that one of them already had been up there. A line dangled from the first branch, fifty feet up. It hadn't been secured yet. She nodded, engaged the gears, threw more gravel, and raced to her house at the end of the driveway, a quarter mile away.

At the house she tore through the living room, upstairs to her bedroom where she unlocked the gun cabinet and yanked out her old Remington. She was loading it as she ran through the house, back to the truck. Then she sped to the end of the drive where the two men were still lounging, gazing up at the fir tree. It was old growth, six feet in diameter, two hundred feet tall, so regular in form it could have served as a model for all other aspiring firs.

When she jumped from the truck, one of the men, the college boy, took several steps toward her. "Look, lady, here's our work orders, all signed, all in good shape. Mrs. Kendricks said take that tree down, and we're the guys who do the work. Don't give us a hard time, okay?"

Paying no attention, she walked around the truck and opened the passenger side door, pulled out the rifle. She kept it pointed at the ground. "Back off," she said to the man approaching her. "Just back off."

The other one laughed and started to move toward her. "Honey, you're a sight! That damn gun's bigger than you are."

She raised the rifle, and they could all hear the click as she took off the safety. "I said back off. Just get in that truck and clear out. I'm Mrs. Kendricks and that tree doesn't get touched. You hear me?"

The one with the paper in his hand froze; the other one threw one arm up in mock fear, but he kept moving, kept grinning. Deliberately she aimed toward the truck, and the

29

crack of the rifle was startling in its loudness. The beer can flew, spinning off the hood.

"Shit!" the one with the paper said, and turned from her.

The other stopped where he was; a dark, mean look spread over his face. "You crazy or something? Put that damn rifle down!"

"The left front tire next," she said, aiming again. When the man started to move toward her, she swung the rifle to cover him. "Or maybe a guy on my land threatening me." He stopped.

"Come on! Let's get the hell out of here!" the other one called. He paused at the tree long enough to jerk down the line; he heaved it inside the truck, then yanked open the door on the driver's side and climbed in.

Slowly, with obvious reluctance, the second man took a step backward, then wheeled and strode to the truck and got in the other side.

"And tell Chuck Gilmore that if he tries something like this again, I'll come after him. And next time I'll shoot anyone who puts a foot on my property, not just a can. Tell him!"

She did not start to shake until the truck was gone, until the trees stopped sending the echoes of the truck wheels and engine back and forth, as if examining them, until silence had returned, more palpable than she could remember.

When her shaking eased, when it was no more than a slight tremor that raced through her, making her heart pump harder for a second, relaxing again, she walked slowly to the ancient fir tree and touched the trunk, as if to reassure it. In her head her grandfather's voice murmured, "Feel it, girl. You can feel the life blood racing up if you try." She never had felt that, but she felt something that had no name. She knew better than to stand at the foot of a mammoth tree and look straight up; that invited vertigo. But she looked up now, up past the patterned bark, so deeply cut, cleanly cut that surfaces reflected light plains separated by deep valleys and chasms, up higher to where the bark became a continuous gleaming wall, and finally into the darkness of the

30

canopy that was so dense little light could penetrate, and nowhere was there a glimpse of sky beyond. It was as if the world ended in the top of the tree.

She became lightheaded and had to turn away from the tree, this time to gaze at her land, her private forest. Her enchanted forest, she had called it many years ago as a small child; her grandfather had agreed soberly that that was exactly right. From here it was downhill all the way to the houses, neither of them visible. On this side of the road her grandfather had helped his father clear out the deep woods to make room for the remaining trees to stretch out and grow up. He had kept it cleared until old age and fragility had stopped him, and then she had taken over the chore. This side was clean, no undergrowth of whips and saplings, no brambles, not even huckleberries, although brambles and huckleberries crowded the road on the other side. Here the trees were spaced parklike, and they were all giants: firs, spruces, some alders and cedars, a few vine maples because Grampa had liked their color in the fall. Down farther was the grove of black walnut trees that her great-grandfather had planted.

Gradually the noises and movements of the open forest had resumed. Small rustlings in the high grasses; two thrashers revealed their red underwings as they flew by; a jay called, another answered. Nell nodded. All was well again.

She returned to the truck, deposited the rifle on the passenger seat, and drove slowly back to the little house that she occupied with her two children. The big house was screened from view by lilacs as big as trees themselves, and blooming rhododendrons from palest pink to scarlet, yellow, orange, white. She parked in the drive outside the garage because she would have to go out again to pick up her daughter, Carol. She took the rifle out and walked into the house. It had been built by her great-grandfather of half-split cedar logs, and no one had ever seen any need to do anything in the way of maintenance beyond keeping the windows and doors in good repair. The cedar shake roof was the original roof. The garage was a recent addition, from thirty years ago, and inside the house insulation had been added. Other than those changes, it was the way her great-grandfather had planned it, the way he had left it finally.

"Travis?" she called at the living room door. "Hey, Travis, where are you?"

She went to the foot of the stairs and called again, but she knew he was down by the river. She had known that from the time she had raced away from Turner's Point. At first, all she had been able to think was, Dear God, let him not have seen that body! Halfway home she had kept a watch for him on his bike. If he had seen, he would be tearing off for another look; she would have passed him on the gravel road. But even so, she had to make certain. Her pace quickened as she left the house by the back door. There was a lawn, twenty feet wide, and then a steep descent to the river. The river made a sharp turn here, leaving her side with a stretch of gravelly sand and slow-moving water, while on the far side it was very deep and swift against the cliff.

At the top of the bank she saw Travis out in the drift boat, fifteen feet from shore. He was lying back, one arm over his eyes against the late afternoon sun, one leg dangling over the boat rail.

"Travis! Get in here!" She scrambled down the bank to the beach.

He sat up, pulled in his foot, and grinned at her. "It's tied, Mom."

"You get in here right now! Right this minute!"

"I want to stay out. You know, I might be able to get in the *Guinness Book* if I stay out here a few days. Bet no one's ever done that before."

"Travis, I'm warning you." She shook the rifle and saw his eyes widen.

"You fire that shot?" he asked. "Why?"

"You don't start hauling in by the time I count to three, you'd better hunker down in one end of that boat or the other, because I'm going to shoot it full of holes." She didn't wait for him to acknowledge the threat. "One." Travis began to pull hand over hand on the rope that tethered him to a great rock on shore.

He was muttering as he came in. "You do it all the time. We all do it. Why not me? Even if I fell in, the water's only up to my knees. What's the big deal?"

She knew all this. And they did it all the time; it was the only way fishing was possible. They had to get out close to the end of the shallow water or their hooks snagged when they reeled in their lines.

"You never said I couldn't do it alone," Travis continued as he climbed out of the boat and finished pulling it in halfway up the beach where he tied the line.

"I'm saying it now," Nell said. "You don't go out alone. Never. You don't go out there unless a grownup is here. Is that plain?"

He shrugged. It was a lifting of one shoulder, a slight movement with his left hand, exactly the way his father always shrugged. More and more often Nell saw Lucas in her son. Right now he was studying her surreptitiously, the way Lucas used to do, to gauge her mood, to test her anger. Dark curly hair, brown eyes, dexterity, these were the products of her genes; his lithe and long body, the expressions that crossed his face, his gestures, those were his legacy from his father.

He finished his evaluation of her mood and grinned widely at her. "What did you shoot, anyway?"

"A beer can. Come on, let's get up to the house." As they walked, she slipped her arm across his shoulders and told him about the men who had come to cut down the fir tree. No way would she tell him about the body in the river; he would learn about that all too soon. It occurred to her quite abruptly that she was under siege. Strangers coming to cut down her trees. Bodies appearing in her river, and thank God Travis hadn't seen that. She knew now that he had not. He would have been unable to conceal his excitement, maybe even a touch of fear. And Lucas was in the state again. Just two days ago his parents had called to tell her: Lucas was back. She realized she was holding the rifle stock so hard her hand was aching.

FIVE

WHEN NELL AND Travis entered the house, the phone was
ringing. She answered, and Travis went out the front door to
get the library books. Nell's daughter, Carol, was on the line,
pleading to be allowed to stay at her friend's house for a
cookout. Michele's mother would bring her home by ten.
After speaking with Michele's mother, Nell said sure. She
hung up as Travis came tearing in to announce that he was
going to go with James Gresham to look at a sick pig; he
needed his sweatshirt for later. Standing behind him was
James, who was a veterinarian, and Nell's tenant. James was
a tall black man, very dark, soft-spoken, and at the moment
he was smiling broadly as he listened to Travis inform his
mother about his plans.

"I asked him," James said, standing at the open door.
"We'll stop on the way home for a burger, if that's okay.
Tawna has a class tonight. A guy's gotta eat, all that."

After a moment she nodded. "But you keep out of the
way, Travis. You do exactly what James tells you. Where is
the patient?" she asked James then. Travis was already
pounding up the stairs for his sweatshirt.

James told her, nearly all the way in to Eugene, thirty
miles.

"I'm going over to Doc's to take Jessica her books," Nell
said. "If I'm not here when you get back, will you keep Travis
at your house for a while?"

"You bet. No problem."

Travis returned, panting, sweating, dragging a sweat-shirt on the floor behind him. "Will you have to cut the pig open? Can I see the guts?" He waved to Nell casually and walked out with James to the station wagon, listening intently to what James was telling him.

Now, at five-thirty, Nell walked through the woods, around the monolithic rock, on a trail that was hardly even perceptible, to the Burchard house. Nell and Doc were the only two who used the trail regularly, except for Travis, who managed to cover all the woods around here. But Travis cared little if there was a trail. Nell picked her way among exposed roots, over a mossy trunk, skirted a vigorous, newly sprouted poison oak vine, and then paused when Doc's house came into view. If houses were cars, she thought, hers would be a Model-T, and Doc's a Ferrari. It was boomerang-shaped, with the leading edge facing the river so that every room had a river view either due south or to the west.

From now until the sun went down was the best time of day at Doc's house. He and Jessica would be out front on the deck, where they spent much of their time together. They would be facing south, and later, very gradually, they would shift until they were facing west, paying homage to the sunset, completing a slow dance. Nell was in no hurry to join them. Jessica would be avid for details of what she had seen at Turner's Point, who had done what, who had been there. Nell shifted the books from one arm to the other, and leaned against an alder. Her gaze had not lingered on the house but on the river, which had been hidden by the thick woods until this point. No boats were in sight, but they wouldn't be, not upstream. Had they found that girl's body yet? She shuddered at the thought of dragging a body through the water to shore, over the rocks, over submerged logs. . . . She bit her lip and shook her head, trying to clear away the image.

Finally she gave the alder a pat and started to walk again. It seemed very strange to her that alders peeled the way they did, exposing a polished red, hard core under the pale bark. Like blood, she thought, and began to walk faster.

Doc must have been watching for her. He hurried out as she emerged from the woods, and there behind the house, he drew her to him and kissed her.

"You were down there today? It must have been awful for you. Are you all right?"

"Okay," she said, her voice muffled against his chest. She breathed in the good, sharp smell that always clung to him. After a moment she pulled back, stood on her toes, and kissed him swiftly. "We'd better go on. I can't stay very long."

He stroked her hair, then reluctantly let her go. They began to walk side by side.

He was a slender man of forty-three, with narrow shoulders and long, narrow fingers. His hair was thinning, touched with gray at the temples; his face was very angular. He would be one of those cadaverous old men you sometimes see, she had said once, laughing, running her finger over a sharp rib. He walked with a quick, restless energy— everything he did was with the same swift motions that became almost jerky, except when he was with a patient; then it was as if he shifted into a different gear altogether: His movements became fluid, his manner contemplative, even leisurely. She had met him as a patient and later had been very surprised to discover this second man coiled tightly behind that serene mask.

"I have to talk to you," she said in a low voice as they approached the deck. "Lucas is coming. He was at his folks' house Monday. He's probably on his way here right now."

Doc's steps faltered, and he jerked around to take her by the shoulders. She clutched the books to keep them from falling. "Why don't you divorce him and be done with it?"

It was more a demand than a question. She shook her head. "Down on the beach, after the kids are sleeping?"

He nodded, angry, but turned his head slightly, listening, as a car squealed around the turn in the driveway. "Later, about eleven."

They separated at the house, Doc to enter by a back door

36

as she turned the corner of the deck and started down the length of the redwood flooring to where Jessica sat in her wheelchair, gazing out at the river. Near her, also gazing at the river, was Frank Holloway, another neighbor.

Of course, Nell thought in resignation. Everyone in town would be buzzing with the story of the dead woman in the river. There would be groups all over, discussing it, theorizing, questioning those who had seen her. . . . The image of the body being dragged over sharp rocks to shore flashed before her mind's eye again, and once more she shook her head, shook it away. She made a swift, searching examination of the river: The cabins were visible from here, people standing around, some at tables, no boats tied up. They were all out there helping with the search. The river made its last curve here and was swallowed again by the forest. In the distance before it disappeared she could see several small boats. She shivered and then waved to Frank Holloway, who had turned to look in her direction.

He put down a drink, got to his feet, and took the few steps remaining for her to reach the seating area. He was in his late sixties, maybe even seventy; Nell could never judge ages. He probably was old, but she had seen her grandfather celebrate his eighty-sixth birthday, and old was not a word that could be used for both men. Frank was her lawyer, Doc's lawyer, everyone's lawyer around here, although he was semi-retired. He went to his law firm once or twice a week and even took a case now and then, but what he did most of the time was fish and work on a book he was writing.

He had thrown away his ties, he liked to tell people. Now he dressed in jeans and flannel shirts and, if it got warm enough, in Bermuda shorts and tank tops. Even on the days that he went to his office in Eugene, that was how he dressed. He had earned the right, he claimed.

He approached Nell with a look of commiseration. "You too. Poor Nell. What a shock." He put his arm around her shoulders, gave her a little squeeze, and then took the books from her.

"Thanks," she said, rubbing her arm where the book bindings had dug in. "Hi, Jessie. How are you?"

The answer was, as always, "Not too bad. What a terrible thing!" The words were appropriate enough, but her expression was one of avidity; she clearly wanted to hear all about it again.

Jessie was older than Doc, five years older, eight. No one ever said; she looked twenty years older at times, although at other times she looked like a girl. It depended on how active her arthritis was at the moment. This evening it appeared to be under control. She was leaning forward in her chair, studying Nell's face intently, one hand holding binoculars on her lap. It was hard to tell much about her physical appearance because she always wore long skirts that covered her from the waist down in gathers and folds and pleats all the way to her shoes. Her blouses were full, with long sleeves, almost always topped by a silk shawl in summer, a wool shawl in winter. Her fingers were misshapen, the knuckles grotesque and sore-looking.

"How perfectly awful it must have been," she said, looking at Nell, waiting.

"Least she didn't hang around," Lonnie Rowan said, suddenly appearing from the house, carrying a tray with extra glasses, wine, cheese, and crackers. She was still wearing the red pants she had worn at Turner's Point earlier. A murder mystery, Nell remembered; Lonnie had put in a request for a special mystery.

"Had to go home and shoot at a tree cutter," Lonnie went on, arranging the things she had brought out. She gave Nell a quick sidelong glance.

"Nell never shot *at* anything in her life," Doc said as he came out to the deck. "She either shoots it or doesn't shoot at all."

"*They* said she shot at them," Lonnie muttered.

"What has that to do with the body in the river?" Jessie asked, turning from Nell to Frank Holloway, who shrugged.

Immediately behind Doc was Clive Belloc. He was wearing jeans, a tan work shirt, and his boots as if he had not yet gone home from work. He was a cruiser for a logging company; people said he was one of the best around, that with just a little walk through the woods he could tell you exactly how much lumber you could realize to the last one-by-one. Except for the area around his eyes that was protected by sunglasses summer and winter, his skin was a rich red mahogany color, and his hair bleached out very blond.

"I went to your place, empty. I figured you were over here," he said to Nell, ignoring everyone else in a way that suggested he had not yet noticed anyone else on the deck. "You know what they're saying in town? Jesus! What happened out at your place?"

"Who's saying?"

"Was that girl shot? Do they already know?" Jessie asked. No one paid any attention.

"Two guys stopped off at Chuck's and said you took pot shots at them. Chuck's mad as hell. What happened?" Clive had drawn almost close enough to touch her, but he did not move those last few inches. He never did.

"Chuck's mad! Chuck? That bastard. He doesn't know what mad means! I'm the one who's mad."

"You took a shot at Chuck?" Jessie asked.

"Oh, Jessie. No. I didn't shoot at anyone. I shot a beer can."

Frank took her elbow and steered her toward a chair. "What we need is a little drink. And then you tell us just why you shot a beer can. And how in hell two guys thought you could be shooting at them. Unless one was dressed as a can."

Nell allowed herself to be seated and accepted the wine that Doc had already poured for her. Belatedly Clive spoke to the others, then helped himself to the bourbon.

"Okay," Nell said after a sip, "when I got home this afternoon, two guys were getting ready to cut down that noble fir at the end of my drive. I told them to stop, but they laughed, so I went for the rifle. That's all there is to that."

"And that made Chuck mad?" Jessie asked in wonder. "Doc, would you mix me another, please?" She held out her glass. She drank old fashioneds. Doc took it and went behind Nell to the table that held the liquor and wine.

"You think Chuck sent them?" Doc asked. "He wouldn't do a damn fool thing like that."

"Who else? He knows that usually I hang around and talk to Mikey and Gina, and whoever else shows up on bookmobile day. Normally I wouldn't even have got home until nearly five. Today . . . today was different, and I caught them just starting."

"Now, Nell," Frank said judiciously, "that's highly circumstantial. Lots of folks know you meet that library on wheels."

"But lots of folks aren't out to harass me—Chuck is, and you know it. I ran him off that trail he was trying to cut down to my beach. I won't let him or his drunken fishermen on my land, and I won't sell him a right of way. He has his reasons," she finished darkly.

"You threatened him?" Clive asked then. "Chuck claims those guys said you threatened him."

"Sure I did. I said I'd shoot anyone who set foot on my land uninvited."

"For God's sake!" Clive snapped. "Why didn't you just tell them who you are, that you own that damn tree? Did you even look at their work order? Maybe they just made a simple mistake—wrong house, wrong tree."

"I did try to tell them, and they thought it was funny. They didn't think it was funny when I said I'd shoot out the tires of their truck, and when the one guy kept coming, he didn't think it was that funny when I pointed the rifle at his midsection, south of the equator. That wiped the grin right off his stupid face."

"Well, they probably thought the owner of the property lived in the big house, like you'd expect," Lonnie said, standing near the doorway, and not likely to budge until she had heard it all. "How most people do it is the *owner* lives in the big house, and the *servants* live in the little house."

"Lonnie, don't start," Nell muttered. "Just don't start."

Lonnie sniffed, then looked at Jessie. "How many for

40

dinner is all I want to know. Time to get started on that, anyways."

There was discussion and persuasion, and in the end they all agreed to stay. Lonnie nodded in a way that said she had known it all along. She cleaned Frank Holloway's place once a week, and did for Clive every other week; she cooked for Doc and Jessie most nights and worked in their house three days a week. She was an indifferent housekeeper but an excellent cook, and for her there were no secrets in Turner's Point. Between her and Doc and Frank, Nell realized, all their medical, legal, and personal lives were tracked on an almost daily basis. Even though Lonnie did nothing for her, she knew the woman was keeping tabs on her just as if she had been hired to do so. Nell took almost malicious satisfaction in knowing that Lonnie had not ferreted out her secret, hers and Doc's.

"Nell," Clive said, after the dinner talk was finally over, "tell me about those guys, who they worked for."

She glared at him and got up to pour herself more wine. "I knew you'd take their side," she said coldly. "Or did you tell them how many board feet were there for the taking?"

Clive tightened his lips; a flush spread over his face. He was a few years older than Nell, but he was boyish-looking, especially now, blushing.

"He's right, Nell," Frank said then. "You'll have to get in touch with the company and straighten it out if there's been a mistake in the work order. And find out who put the order in if your name was on it."

"Clovis something," she said. "Clovis Wood Products."

"Never heard of them," Clive said. "You sure?"

She shrugged and returned to her chair.

"Use your phone a minute, Doc?" Clive asked. When Doc nodded, he went inside the house. The others looked at the river in silence.

How far had she got by now? Nell found herself wondering. She fought against the image of a woman being wafted among the drowned trees, pausing here, there,

41

drifting on, her hair getting entangled in a sharp limb, tethered by her long hair that had looked like seaweed. . . .

Clive returned, more puzzled than before. "It's a company out of Salem," he said. "Small company, mostly residential work, landscapers for businesses, that sort of thing, not loggers."

"Well, then it's a simple mistake, Nell," Doc said. "Wrong place, wrong tree, wrong county even." He laughed.

"Maybe," Nell said, wanting to leave it alone, not talk about it any more. They had had her name, she thought. Mrs. Kendricks.

"Look at it this way, Nell," Frank said then in his thoughtful, lawyerly way. "Chuck wants to get access to that little beach. Everyone knows that. 'Course, it's not your beach, and you know that. Anyone can pull in there by boat day or night, no problem." Nell made a rude noise, and he lowered his head and looked at her over the tops of his half glasses. "It's reasonable for you not to want a trail through your land, and not to want the beach turned into a public picnic area. Granted. Now what's unreasonable is for Chuck to make an enemy out of you. He's tried persuasion. He's tried bribery. He's tried just bulling his way through by starting a trail. Presently he'll probably think of something else to try. But it won't be a frontal attack. Honey, there's not a living person in this county thinks you can be swayed by cutting one of your trees. And Chuck's not stupid."

He regarded her steadily until at last, with reluctance, she had to nod. Chuck was not stupid, and that would have been a stupid thing for him to try. But someone had sent them, and they had her name. At the same moment she thought: *Lucas!*

She stood up. "I just remembered something," she said, her voice harsh even to her ears. "I won't stay. I have to go home."

Jessie reached out for her. "What is it? What's wrong?"

"I feel sick. Too much going on today. I have to do something. I'll call you, Jessie. Tomorrow. I'll call you." She knew she sounded insane, but nothing she could think of saying was right; she put down her glass and started to walk fast.

"Nell, I'll drive you home," Clive said, at her side, his hand on her arm.

"No!" She shrugged away from him. "No, I want to walk, something I have to think about. I'm okay, not really sick. Headache. That's all. I have a headache."

"Let me," Doc said quietly, coming up to her. "I'll go part way with you, Nell."

Silently she nodded, and they walked toward the woods together. Out of range of the others still on the deck, she said in a low voice, "Lucas must have sent those men. He tried that before. And his father said he's on his way here. I think he's already here, watching. Don't come tonight. Don't call. He's somewhere near."

"For God's sake! Has he threatened you? Get an injunction, keep him away!"

She shook her head. "It's all right, Doc. Just stay away until he's gone. Don't give him any ammunition." She tried to smile. "He'd know if he saw us together. He'd know. And it would be a weapon."

Doc stopped walking, his hand braked her in mid-stride. "Are you going to let him in your bed again?"

She touched his cheek gently. "No. Go on back. Just tell them I'm upset, too much happened today. Overwrought. Isn't that the word? Good Victorian genteel women got overwrought all the time, didn't they?"

He started to reach for her; she backed away, shaking her head. After a moment, he turned and stalked back toward his house. She watched briefly, then resumed her walk home.

Lucas, she thought again. Lucas. Until that second on the deck it had not seemed quite real, not true that he was on his way here after all those years, but now she felt certain that he was close, and she did not know yet how she would deal with him this time. She began to hurry. If she had believed it before, she never would have left Travis alone. Not even for a minute.

SIX

NELL PUT THE truck in the garage and locked the door. She locked the door to the shed where the tractor and mower were stored, and then went inside her house to hurry through the rooms to check windows, door locks, outside lights. Futile, she knew; the door locks were a joke. Besides, he wouldn't come here, expect to find her in the little house; they had lived together in the main house. She frowned. He might walk in on Tawna; she would have to warn her and James to keep their doors locked.

That was how it had been last time. She had come downstairs from putting Travis to bed; Grampa had been dozing in front of the television. She had entered the kitchen to see Lucas outlined against the evening sky. She caught her breath at the sharpness of the memory, the sexual awakening the memory jolted into being. She shook her head. Never again. He had stayed three weeks, and on September tenth, he had gone. Carol had been born the following June, six years ago this month. She shook her head again, harder. She would kill him first, she thought grimly.

The phone rang, startling her. For an instant she had that peculiar twinge in her stomach, the way she always did if the phone rang when the children were out somewhere, always for just that one instant certain something terrible had happened to one of them. She picked up the receiver. It was John Kendricks, her father-in-law.

44

"Is he there yet?" he asked with an uncharacteristic brusqueness.

"No. I haven't heard a thing from him."

"Nell, honey, me and Amy, we can't get it out of our heads that he's in bad trouble. And we're thinking it would be a good idea if the kids aren't there when he shows up. What if the police are after him, I mean?"

"Police? Why would they be?"

"That's just it, honey. We don't know. But there's bad trouble. We know that."

She shook her head and had to moisten her lips in order to speak. "Maybe he isn't even coming here."

"Oh, he will. He will. And, honey, me and Amy, we'd like to take the kids over to visit with Janet and Dan for a few days, a week."

Janet was his daughter, Dan her husband. He was a rancher in the Blue Mountains area.

"You're really worried, aren't you?" Nell asked in a low tone.

There was a pause, then he said gruffly, "Guess we're all worried. Something's wrong. He's my son, but those kids are my grandkids. Whatever he's done, well, he's a grown man, but they haven't done anything to bring them trouble. Anyway, that's what me and Amy's been talking about all evening, all day. And I wanted to call."

They talked a few more minutes, and she said she would call back later if it didn't get too late. Anytime, he said firmly. And he could pick them up by ten in the morning, if she could have things ready by then.

What kind of trouble did he expect, she asked silently when she hung up. Police bursting in with drawn guns? Lucas raving, crazy, on drugs? Did they think she and Lucas would fight, frighten the children? She started to prowl the house again, seeing nothing. They knew that if he showed up again, she intended to throw him out. She had told them. About time, Amy, his mother, had said through tight lips. John, his father, had embraced her and kissed her cheek.

When John called on Tuesday, she had gone numb;

brain, body, everything about her had gone numb. By Tuesday night she had managed to pretend that Lucas would not show up here. There had been time enough if he had intended to come here. He could have made it before dinnertime. By Wednesday she had convinced herself that he had gone back to wherever he had been for the past six and a half years. But during the night Wednesday, she had realized that her body yearned for his body, that she wanted him to show up the way he had done before, just be there, as if he had never been gone. She had jumped out of bed, furious with the betrayal of her body, and she had come to realize that she was afraid of him. Not for any physical threat he posed; he didn't pose any, but because her body knew nothing of time and abandonment and dishonor. Her body wanted his body. And she hated him for that more than for leaving her alone all those years, more than for impregnating her and running, more than for his denial of fatherhood, of responsibility, of simple decency.

She had needed him so many times, had cried in that need, but no more. Never again. The last time there had been no warning, no way to control that sexual surge. A cloud of pheromones, she thought; they had both been overwhelmed by pheromones, exactly the same way they had been when they met as students. *Control* was a word without meaning then, when they were so young. And again when he returned. But no longer. Never again. The passion was there, and also lust, but passion could be channeled into hatred and make that hatred flare more than love or lust could hope to equal. This time she had been warned. This time the passion he saw in her would scald him.

By the time Travis arrived home with James, her decision had been made to let them go with their grandparents.

John Kendricks was as lithe and loose-looking as Lucas, as Travis, with the same half grin, the same set of gestures that somehow looked as if they started and were deliberately stopped again before completion. A half shrug, an imcomplete movement with the hand. He was as brown as his toasted wheat, and deeply wrinkled with white lines like valleys in the brown ridges of his face. He was a wheat farmer, and Nell knew that he wouldn't really go away and leave everything for a week unless he was convinced that it was desperately urgent. He embraced her with self-conscious awkwardness, but he was almost childlike with the children.

"How did he look?" Nell asked in a low voice as the children ran back and forth stashing their things in John's station wagon. "What did he say?"

"Looked fine, healthy. Said damn little. He was pretty tired. Said if anyone came asking for him to say he hasn't been around in years. I said who would come, and he said anyone. You know how he can get."

She nodded. "But—"

"Car comes to turn around in the drive, you know how they do. And he was up like a shot, ducking out of sight, watching from the side of the window drape. Like a man on the run, honey."

"Mom, can I take the camera?" Travis yelled from the back of the station wagon.

"Certainly not."

John squeezed her arm slightly and said, "If there's room for me in that wagon, guess we'd best be on the way. Honey, take care of yourself."

Carol ran back inside to look for her Cabbage Patch doll, and Travis began to look for some comic books for the trip, and finally John Kendricks got into the wagon and leaned on the horn. Both children dashed back out. Nell saw to it that their seat belts were secure; there were more kisses and promises to call, to write, to be good. . . . Then she stood in the driveway and watched the station wagon vanish around the first curve.

When silence returned she walked to the main house to warn Tawna that Lucas might show up.

The year Carol turned one, Nell's grandfather had died. Nell had tried to call Lucas; she sent a registered letter; she sent a telegram. There had been no response. John and Amy Kendricks had worried about her being alone in such an isolated place. She inherited the land, but there was little real money, spending money, and she was afraid to touch the capital of her inheritance. And she couldn't start selling the walnut trees, not yet. Finally she had decided to rent out one of the houses, and with the same decision, she realized that she wanted to live in the original house with her two children. Besides, the big house could be rented for three times as much as the little one, and she needed the money.

Tawna and James had applied, along with dozens of other people. They had been having trouble finding suitable housing, Tawna had said with a clipped Boston accent. She had been hired at the university, and James could practice his veterinary medicine just about anywhere, but they also had teenage children. Their daughter played the flute. And sometimes James brought his work home— a sick animal that he nursed around the clock. She had been very proper, almost distant, as if relating someone else's problems, not her own.

"He treats big animals," she had said, finishing.

"Does he do elephants?" Nell asked.

"No," Tawna had said gravely, and just as gravely added, "But he'd swap all the gold in all his molars for the chance." She smiled then, an expansive, illuminating smile that grew and grew, and her teeth certainly had no gold to swap. They both laughed, and Nell said the house was theirs.

Now Nell knocked on the door, and Tawna called, "Come on in. Be right down."

Nell entered the kitchen. The table was covered with ceramic jewelry in brilliant colors. Tawna taught French and did ceramics as a hobby. She might have been able to make a decent living making jewelry, but the odds were against her, she said. The jewelry on the table was dazzling.

"Wow!" Nell said, moving closer, touching nothing.

"Hey, all right, no? Think Celsy would like these?" Tawna entered the kitchen. She wore tan slacks and an oversized scarlet sweatshirt, and she had on a pair of green and gold fish earrings, three inches long, with scales that flashed when she moved. She was tall and strongly built with wide shoulders, big bones. She kept her hair drawn back in a severe chignon, accentuating her bony face even more. The earrings looked wonderful on her. They would look wonderful on her daughter, Celsy, who was due home on Sunday from her first year at Juilliard.

Tawna took off the earrings, placed them on the table, and surveyed the assortment spread out before her. Speaking as if addressing the jewelry, she said, "But you didn't come to talk about earrings. You're bothered by something."

Hesitantly Nell said, "I thought I'd better tell you. My husband might show up, and I don't think he knows I'm not living here. He could walk in, I guess."

"Ah, the prodigal father. He walks in, James heaves him out. Or I do." She spread her hands palms up, as if to say, see how simple.

"Well, it might be better if he didn't actually get in. Maybe you could lock your doors?"

"Whatever you like. Now, you sit, and I'll pour coffee, and you can help me decide which pieces are best for Celsy. And, Nell, if you want him heaved out of *your* house, we'll be there."

Nell turned down the coffee; they chatted for a few minutes, and she got up to leave. At the door Tawna said, "But, baby, you have any trouble with that man, you have two very good friends, very close. Remember that."

Back home again, Nell began to sort through the stuff she had refused to let Travis take with him. His basketball. His cousins had a basketball, she had said firmly. Two frogs in a box. She took the box outside, removed the top, and left it under a rhododendron. She found Carol's newest Cabbage Patch doll under a sweater that had both elbows out. She had told Travis to forget it, even if it was his favorite. She held the doll, and suddenly clutched it hard against her breast and bowed her head, fighting tears.

It would be like this until it was over, until he had come and gone again, this time for good. Resolutely she put the doll on the couch and looked around the living room, cluttered with the children's stuff, messy. She decided she didn't give a damn about the mess and walked outside.

She did not go toward the big house this time but headed into the woods in the opposite direction. At the margin of woods, huckleberries thrived, and blackberries, and where the sun reached the ground unimpeded, a carpet of alpine strawberries grew luxuriantly. But within a few steps, the trees took over, and now it was fir trees, and deeper and deeper silence as the voice of the river faded and vanished. The river was like her own heartbeat, a sound she was so accustomed to that she rarely heard it; she was always startled at the silence when the river noise failed.

The trees were mossy. Fallen branches, fallen trunks, rocks—all were moss-covered; the effect was like being underwater where even the light was tinted by the ubiquitous green. She kept to a trail that climbed steadily, with many twists and turns, sometimes around boulders, around fallen trees too massive to step over, too mossy and slippery to climb over. And always upward. Chunks of lava poked up from the ground here and there, irregular brown shapes, sharp and pitted, or gleaming black and rounded. Orange lichen thrived on the lava; ferns edged close to some of the bigger pieces. At a fork in the trail she kept to the right; this section became steeper and rockier, and then the land flattened in a clearing one hundred fifty feet across, forty feet deep, strewn with rocks, boulders, and lava upthrusts. The clearing had been bisected by a waterway. Century after century the tumbling water had carved out the rocky ledge here until now there was this clearing on one side of a ravine and, twenty feet away, another somewhat smaller similar clearing. The waterfall was two hundred feet back from this point now, neatly slicing the mountain into sections. The other fork of the trail led upward, to the head of the waterfall, but she rarely went up there. This was her destination. There was too little soil here to support more than a few straggly vine maples. The southern exposure heated the rocks, and the mountain rising behind the space sealed off all noise; even the wind was denied.

For several minutes she stood surveying the clearing, checking the fallen tree trunks that had rolled down the mountain to come to rest here, checking the boulders that she knew so well, checking the vine maples, checking for intruders, for candy wrappers, beer cans, any sign of outsiders. There were none. No one else ever came here. Finally she squinted and looked at the nearly perfect globe of a rock that rested against the face of the cliff that made up the northern side of the clearing. It was exactly where it should be. Behind the round boulder was a deep cave, cut into the rock by water action in centuries long past. She used to bring her lunch this far and stash it in the cave where it would stay cool, dry, and safe. The rock was untouched. She nodded in satisfaction and only then approached her own place.

Her seat was a smooth gray boulder with streaks of blue agate running through it, and a shallow declivity that she had never outgrown. She sank down onto it now, tilted her head with her eyes closed, and felt the sunlight on her face. Her grandfather's seat was a log backed by another pale boulder. Best two seats in the house, Grampa always said.

He had brought her up here when she was a child, and later, after he could no longer make the climb, she had come alone. Her private place, alone in the world, with a view of forest and sky that included nothing of humankind. The river was not visible, no building, no wires, no roads. There were only treetops below, falling away like plains of hummocky green, sun-drenched today, often misted with rain, or in frozen silence, and the sky without limit. Now and then a hawk or an eagle appeared, magical creatures sailing the sea of sky effortlessly.

A place of magic. Up here she could say anything. The year she had found this out, she had been twelve; she had come up here with Grampa, only to rail and complain about some injustice. "God damn it," she had said, and then had stopped breathing, waiting for his reprimand.

Instead, his quiet voice had said reflectively, "Seems to me like everyone ought to have a place where they can say

51

what they're thinking. Seems only right for this to be a place like that."

She had not turned to look at him; his seat was well behind hers, but she had known he was smiling. His voice had been smiling.

When the sun became too warm on her face, she turned away, facing west, away from the falls, away from Grampa's seat. In a low voice, almost a whisper, she said, "The world's turning shitty again."

"Well, it does, you know, from time to time," he said in that reflective way he always had up here. "Why don't you tell me about it?"

She didn't turn to look at him any more now than she had done at the age of twelve. Looking would destroy something. She began to talk, almost in a whisper, saying things up here that she couldn't say anywhere else. About the body in the river and her horror at its having been dragged over rocks. About Lucas. About the men who had come to cut down the tree.

"You shot a beer can? Surprised you could hit it. How long's it been since you put in any practice?"

She shook her head, now surprised that she had hit it. He had taught her to shoot up here, shooting across the waterfall at another fallen tree trunk on the opposite side.

She would bring the rifle up and practice, she decided. Tomorrow. She hadn't done any shooting since before Carol was born, and now it appeared that she might need to keep in practice.

SEVEN

SATURDAY MORNING DOC called, and she snapped at him. "I'll call you," she said and hung up. She talked to the children, now at the ranch east of Pendleton, three hundred miles away. She felt they were as distant as the moon.

When she could not stand the house any longer she walked out to the walnut grove. The trees were tall and straight, the canopy so thick that no sunlight penetrated, the ground beneath them resilient with leaf mold. The air always smelled astringent under the walnut trees; it was always cool and damp. The squirrel population was high; jays and thrashers were everywhere, chickadees and warblers darted. Grampa's father had planted the grove, planning for the future, now; in three years the first of the trees would be cut. But already the saplings she had planted were growing tall, reaching for the sky. Each new planting consisted of three young trees in a triangle, one to stay for the next seventy or eighty years, two nurse trees to be thinned out at twenty-year intervals. They grew better, faster, and stronger if they had company. She touched a tree trunk here, walked on, touched another. The squirrels chattered at her, flicked their tails in warning, raced madly along branches overhead watching her every motion.

When Lucas came home the last time, they had walked hand in hand among the trees, and then a few days later he had brought Clive Belloc out.

"Talk to the old man," Lucas had said. "Just talk to him. Clive says it won't matter that much if you start cutting now or wait a few more years. You're both sitting on a couple of million, just waiting for the saw. They were planted to be cut, damn it!"

While they fought over the trees, Clive had stood in the driveway looking mortified. Clive had never mentioned the grove again. She never had learned the exact number he had quoted to Lucas, but it was a lot, she knew. An awful lot.

That night, after Grampa had gone to bed and Travis was sleeping, they had sat down on the little beach. "You never used to want money like this," she had said slowly. "Why now? What for?"

"Not for me. No fancy cars, no boats. It's the project. Emil's grant is running out, and he doubts he can get another one. He just can't show the kind of progress they expect."

Emil, she thought with icy fury. Emil Frobisher had taken Lucas away, had changed him, made him a stranger, and now sent him begging.

"I thought he was all set up with the famous Dr. Schumaker. I thought someone like that could get all the money in the world."

"He could, if Emil could just produce some real results. Emil is bringing in another scientist, a psychiatrist, a specialist in perceptions, something like that. She'll swing some weight, too, but they still need something concrete to show."

Nell had thrown rocks into the river as hard as she could. "And your degree? How much closer are you to it now?"

He had muttered something.

"Nowhere near it. Isn't that what you mean?" Her arm ached with a fiery pain, and she dropped the rock she was holding. Not looking at him, watching the play of moonlight on the flowing water, she had said, "They're using you. Don't you understand that yet? Have you even got the bachelor's degree yet?"

He was silent.

"I thought not. And now a psychiatrist. Maybe they'll

give you a degree in psychology and you can become a shrink. Or is it still mathematics? Or computer science? Why don't you wake up?"

"You never had any faith in me, in anything I did," he had said sullenly. "Nothing changes, does it?"

"That's not true," she said in a low voice, still keeping her gaze on the water. "We were happy. I had faith enough to move mountains. And then Emil Frobisher came along and pretended you were something you know you're not. You have something he can use, a way of seeing that he needs, and that's all he wants you for. That's what I saw three years ago, and that's what I see now. You don't know any more about mathematics than I do. If I had more money than you could count I wouldn't help you buy a degree with it, not for Emil Frobisher's work."

"You don't know anything!" he had snapped. "If we can bring this off it'll change the world. That's how big it is. And I'm part of it. I'm the one who said we need to work with younger subjects. The psychiatrist Emil's talking to just wrote a book about the perceptions of children before puberty, and the effects of the changes of puberty, the way they solidify perceptions. If she comes in, we'll be able to persuade Schumaker to stick with it a few more years. By the time Travis reaches puberty, five or six years, the whole thing will be ready. His generation will be the first to benefit. What good will it do me? We'll all get Nobel Prizes! Every one of us!"

She had stopped breathing. Travis! "If it's all so cut and dried, why are you here now? Why are you trying to raise money?"

"If we can show matching funds, it's easier to get grants and backing. And if I can come up with it, they can't ease me out. Don't you see, even if they never give me the degree, they can't ease me out!"

"Don't you hear what you're saying?" she had cried then. "You know they'll kick you out as soon as they decide they don't need you any longer." Before he could say anything, she added, more quietly, "Explain to me what the project is,

Lucas. I asked you before and you said you couldn't. I'm asking you again."

"I know I couldn't. It's too . . . complicated."

"Do you mean I wouldn't understand? Is that it?"

"Yes. Exactly. You wouldn't understand astrophysics without a lot of background, you accept that. Why can't you accept that I'm involved with something just as complex?"

"I'm having trouble with the idea that there's anything you could explain that I would fail to grasp," she said coldly. "You can't explain it, can you? You don't understand what they're doing. Can't you admit that?"

He was silent for a long time, and the voice of the river was the only sound. When the wind blew a certain way from the west, going against the grain, Grampa said, it sometimes created a new river voice, like a half-heard lullaby. She listened to the murmurous, soothing rhythm without words, and waited for Lucas to speak again.

He put his arm around her shoulders and drew her close. "Let's drop it for now," he said. "We're both beat. Let's go to bed. I've missed you so much."

She shook him away and stood up. "You know what they'd call me if I did what you're trying now? Prostitute. Whore." She started up the path. "Harlot. Call girl. Cunt. Gold digger."

He caught up with her and grabbed her arm, pulled her to a stop. She glared at him in the brilliant, indifferent moonlight. "Isn't it funny how many names they have for women selling the only thing they have to offer? How few for men."

He had shoved her arm away from him and pushed past her, running. The next day he had left again.

Nell reached the edge of the grove; from here she could see both houses through the trees. James was tinkering with his station wagon. Restlessly she started back down toward her house.

A little after noon a UPS delivery van pulled up to the door of the big house. James spoke to the driver, who drove down to Nell's house. She met him at the door.

"Mrs. Kendricks?"

"What is it? I'm not expecting anything."

He looked at his clipboard and shrugged. "It's for Mrs. Nell Kendricks and Travis Kendricks. Either one of you can sign for it."

He went back to the van and brought out a large box, set it down, and brought out another one. When he came back with it, she pointed to the living room floor. He put both boxes before the couch and she signed his sheet, then stared at the boxes without touching them. A computer and monitor. She knew they were from Lucas.

After Carol was born, after she was certain Lucas was not coming back, she had gone to the university library and looked up every reference she could find concerning the effects of puberty on cognition, perceptions, belief systems. The literature had been scant; evidently this was not a heavily researched area. But she had found the book written by a woman psychiatrist, Dr. Ruth Brandywine, and she had recognized it from what little Lucas had said about it.

The text had been difficult, not very well written, full of jargon and statistics, and the text interrupted so often by references to other works that it had been nearly impossible to follow the thesis. What Brandywine had said, or at least what Nell had got from it, was that the periods immediately before puberty and during puberty were the most efficient times to instill in children systems of belief and behavior that seemed to have effects lasting well into adulthood, possibly for the rest of their lives. She had cited rites of passage, baptisms, circumcisions, initiations into many different kinds of groups.

And now a computer, for her and for Travis, who would be twelve in August. She remembered when she and Lucas had read the ad in the school newspaper. Dr. Frobisher was hiring students to participate in a study of perceptions. Ten dollars each, they had said. With that money they could take off a day or two and head for the coast, eat clam chowder, camp out on a beach. They had gone to Dr. Frobisher's classroom and signed up. The test required them to sit before a computer; they were to watch computer images and pick out from an assortment of images which one should follow one that was given. She thought of the first image as blob (possibly a bear), then blob (possibly a dog), blob (possibly a horse), and many blobs that were abstract. She picked one that was blob (possibly a cow). And so the hour had gone. She had thought it silly, but when she compared notes with Lucas later, it had been apparent that either he saw things she had not seen, or he had had a different set of images altogether. He was called to come back and continue with the next sequence, and the next and next, until by the end of the term, he had quit his part-time job at Kinko's and was working for Emil Frobisher.

All computers, she was thinking. Then, later, even when he came back home six years ago, it was still all computers. And now he had sent a computer for Travis. She remembered what he had said that last night down on the beach: *By the time Travis reaches puberty, five or six years, the whole thing will be ready.*

She shook her head. *No!* She wanted to take an axe to the boxes, but she backed away and went to the door again. She had to get out, leave the house, walk, move, talk to Grampa. She looked up at the trees. Talk to Grampa.

Today she was not aware of the trail, the steepness of the last part of the climb, how hot she had become when she grasped a rock to help with the last step or two. Just before she climbed the last foot, before the level clearing, she came to a complete stop. Lucas!

He was the Lucas of her girlhood, a laughing boy, happy, with the same light in his eyes that she had loved when they were both nineteen. This was how he had looked when they sledded down the long driveway to the big house; when they dammed Halleck Creek and swam in the frigid, impounded waters; when they struggled through the

58

sand dunes at the coast stalking geese in the freshwater lakes. . . . He said, in exactly the same way he had said it a hundred times before, a thousand times, "Watch this!"

In disbelief she closed her eyes hard, paralyzed; when she opened them again, he was gone. She scrambled to the ledge and caught a movement from the corner of her eye. She jerked around to see him on the far side of the ledge, near the drop-off, still laughing. Before she could focus her gaze, there was an explosion of a rifle shot; Lucas was thrown backward and sideward into a boulder. He rolled off it, rolled over the side of the ledge, down into the gorge.

She screamed and screamed, and, screaming, began to run back down the trail she had just climbed.

EIGHT

BARBARA HOLLOWAY WATCHED the two customers without interest. They were giggling over a red sequinned dinner dress, one of them holding it up to her body. She was too fat for the skinny sheath from the thirties. Both women were too fat, Barbara decided, for anything in the shop to please them. She hated fat women who blamed the clothes. She was holding her finger in her book, waiting for them to wander outside again. A teenage girl darted in and pulled the door shut after her; Winnie's voice rang out from the back room: "Don't close the door, please."

The girl looked at Barbara suspiciously. "Swamp cooler," Barbara explained. "It works with fresh air."

"I don't think it works at all," one of the women said. "This place is stifling."

"So beat it," Barbara said under her breath. She raised an eyebrow at the woman and looked down at her book.

The one holding the dress tossed it over a rack, and the trio left, closing the door on the way out.

"Bitch," Barbara said, going to the door. It was late afternoon, Friday, August, Phoenix. She had finally arrived in hell, she thought, gazing out at the strip mall and the half dozen or so shoppers. The women who had just left were being steered into the Navajo jewelry shop by the girl. She shrugged. It would be just as stifling in there; they used the swamp cooling system, too.

"How's this look?" Winnie asked, coming out from the back room. She was wearing a skin-tight black satin evening dress, slit up to her thigh. A rope of fake pearls hung down below her waist.

Barbara whistled. "Gangster's moll. Terrific." Winnie certainly was not too fat for the garment she had spent the afternoon altering. She looked wonderful. Barbara didn't actually envy Winnie's slender figure; she was too philosophical about herself for that, but there was little in the shop that she would have been willing to try on. Hippy, she thought of herself. Muscular. Practical body, serviceable. Ms. Mid-America herself, average in every way. Even her dark brown hair and blue eyes, right down the middle of the norm—in most places, that was. Here in Phoenix she felt sometimes that she was an alien among all the dark-skinned people with their lovely shiny black eyes. Winnie had black hair and black eyes, long straight black hair; she was the perfect model for the slinky gown from the early thirties.

The shop was called Play It Again, Sam, with nothing more modern than from the fifties. Barbara had been here for nearly nine months now, but it was time to head north, away from the sun, away from the heat. The shop made so little money, it was ridiculous to pretend it could support two women as a real business. Winnie's ex made it possible for the shop to exist at all; Winnie was possibly the world's worst

60

businesswoman, and Barbara would have found it impossible to care less if the shop made money or not. Out of gratitude for Barbara's help in getting the divorce that had turned out to be financially successful, Winnie had said, "Honey, you've got a job as long as you want it, and the apartment upstairs, if you want that." She had added, mystified, "But why you don't hang up your shingle and make a killing as a lawyer is more than I can see."

Because, Barbara would have said if pressed. But Winnie never pressed anything. She had gone back to peel off the gown; then it would be closing time, and Barbara would go upstairs to the apartment, shed most of her clothes, and sit before a fan, near the air conditioner, with a tall, frosty drink. And finish her book.

Her apartment was a sauna day and night. The air conditioner blew hot air and a fan pushed it around some more, but the air never cooled. Moving hot air was better than dead hot air. She turned on both the fan and the air conditioner as soon as she entered, then began to strip. In passing, on her way to get ice, she also turned on her answering machine, which was blinking. Why an answering machine, Winnie had asked—a legitimate question, since Barbara had known no one but her in Phoenix at the time. Because, she would have answered, if she had bothered at all. Some things traveled with her, that was all. The answering machine, a laptop computer, a hair dryer, a very good radio with a shortwave band, a complete set of Sherlock Holmes. . . .

She stopped banging ice cubes from the tray when she heard her father's voice. "Call me." That was all.

Damn him, she muttered, and finished making her drink—a glass filled with ice, a dash of vodka, and a lot of bitter lemon. Why couldn't he be like other people? Winnie's mother talked to the machine until the tape ran out. Winnie claimed her mother preferred the machine; it never talked dirty, never contradicted her, never sassed or hung up on her. Another friend, Marla, once played back a tape from her mother that she said was typical: "You tell her to call me when she gets in, you hear me? And tell her not to wait until the price goes down, either. I want to talk to that girl this afternoon. Now you just tell her I said this afternoon." They both had laughed.

And *her* father simply said, "Call me." No identification, no number, no time of day. He expected her to recognize his voice, no matter what was going on. Yet, it wasn't really an order, she understood. It was the way he might say, "Put some gas in the car," or "Hand me that book."

Then, sprawled in front of the fan, holding the drink that was dripping ice water on her stomach, she began to think of that cool, green river out in front of his house, and the cool, dim woods all around, and nights with a blanket on the bed throughout the summer.

She never had lived in the house in the woods, but she had been there enough to remember how cool it was, how quiet. He had bought the house before his semi-retirement, a place where he and her mother had gone weekends; after her death, after he decided he didn't have to work so hard, he had given up the house in town and moved out all the way.

She rubbed the cold water off the glass and pressed her fingers to her forehead, her cheeks. Finally she put the drink down and reached for the phone.

"Hi," she said cheerfully when he answered on the second ring. "How are you, Dad?"

"Can you come stay with me a while?"

She shook her head at the suddenness of his request. She had expected him to ask, but not like this, not cutting through the niceties.

"I don't know. Are you ill? What—"

"Bobby, I need you."

A second shock hit her. Her father never had needed anyone in his life. "What's wrong?" she asked.

His voice dropped lower. "Honey, I'm afraid I've bitten off more than I can chew. But I don't want to talk about it over the phone. Can you come?"

She hesitated, the silence broken by noises from her clanking machines, line noise, a faint humming, a fainter burst of static, a click. All the reasons for saying no surged through her mind—he was trying to manipulate her; she was through with everything he represented; she needed to get a job somewhere that wasn't Phoenix, that wasn't a hundred degrees by seven in the morning, but that wasn't Oregon. He would hate what she was becoming. . . . A sharper thought emerged: Just what the hell difference did it make where she was? And it would be cooler. At least it would be cooler.

"As it happens," she said then, "I was going to leave here in the next day or two, head up to Minneapolis. Guess I could detour a bit, go by way of Oregon."

"Good! Good. And honey, you'll be on payroll from this minute on, as a consultant. I'll be watching for you. Drive carefully." The line went dead.

Damn him, she breathed as she banged down her receiver. Damn him. She had responded to his simple statement of need; he had turned it into something else.

She got up and made another drink, contemplated the telephone, reached for it, drew back, reached again, and shook her head. Then, the silent struggle resolved, she sat down before the fan again and let ice water drip on her midsection.

She would drive the desert part by night, she decided. That night. Hit Las Vegas before twelve, stay holed up with the slots tomorrow, and make Reno the second night. After that, in northern California, on up through Oregon, it would be cooler. She would decide later how to continue. She was thinking at the same time about her last lover, Craig, who had said she had something she had to settle in herself before she could settle anything with him. Then he had walked out. He had been right. There was something, there were always things. "You don't trust me worth a damn," he had shouted the last night they were together. That was right, too. His actions had proven her point, she added: He had walked out. But there were things to be settled, and she might as well get on with them. Not because of Craig; it was understood that

63

she never would see him again. Not because of anything she could put a name to; things should be settled. Because.

She packed quickly; she had very little. The computer, the hair dryer, the box of books, radio. . . . Two suitcases of clothing, everything she owned in the world, all got stowed in the car without crowding the trunk or the back seat even a little. She scribbled a note for Winnie, opened the shop, left the note on the cash register, and took a final look around. It had been fun for a time, she thought. The fun had ended. Time to vamoose.

She pulled into the driveway of Frank Holloway's house on Tuesday afternoon. It was eighty degrees, deliciously cool; the light was dim, filtered by old growth fir trees that crowded the house. Exactly right, she thought with approval, exactly what she had been imagining. Her father hurried out to meet her. He was wearing ridiculous shorts that came down to his knees, a sport shirt not tucked in, and sandals. She smiled at the incongruous figure, nothing like the man she had been imagining; in her mind he always wore a gray suit and a maroon tie.

He embraced her, then held her tightly, pushed her back a fraction to look at her, and clasped her hard against his chest again.

"I can't tell you how happy I am to see you," he said. "You look marvelous, brown as a nut, pretty as I recall, prettier even. Come in, come in. We'll get your stuff out later. Too hot now. Let me look at you."

He studied her again as she laughed. Too hot!

"You've got some gray hairs," he said in wonder.

"Way it goes, Dad. Getting old, just like everyone else." Thirty-seven, she thought. For God's sake! Thirty-seven!

He shook his head. "No. But you finally are starting to look grown up. A little grown up. Come on inside."

It was good to be here, she realized as they walked into the house. She liked this house with the cedar paneling, the cedar fragrance, the wide windows overlooking the river. And even the clutter. It pleased her that he had cluttered up the living room. Books, magazines, papers on all the end tables, notebooks here and there. For a time, after his move out here from the city, she had been afraid he would vegetate, but evidently he was as busy as ever.

She moved through the living room, examining things she remembered from her childhood—Indian pottery, Indian throws on the furniture, a copper kettle with fireplace tools. On a leather-topped coffee table, nearly hidden by stacks of old *Law Journals*, was an exquisite cut glass bowl with a cover, filled with mints. Her mother had got the bowl out only for Christmas, she remembered. Beyond the windows was the river, trees, sky. Very nice rock samples were lined up on the window sills: picture jasper, quartz crystals, thunder eggs. . . .

She looked up to see him watching her with a faint smile. She smiled back at him. "It's good to be back," she said. "Got any coffee?"

He laughed, and they walked through the house to the kitchen where she sat down as he prepared a pot of coffee. No one made coffee as good as his. He started with whole beans, dark roast Colombian, mixed with dark French, with a few pale mocha beans—to mellow it, he said. The noise of the grinder filled the room. The same table, she realized, looking at it closely. He had brought it out from the other house. She found the nick she had made with an ice skate and rubbed it gently.

"What were you up to in Phoenix?" he asked from across the room, spooning the ground coffee into the basket.

She told him about the shop, about Winnie, and made it all sound funnier than it had been; she made the drive up sound more interesting than it had been. She went on to tell him about her plans for Minneapolis, where she had a school friend who was starting a co-op health food store. Her voice trailed off when he came to the table with a tray.

"Let's sit on the terrace," he said. "Nice time of day."

There were houses on both sides of his, she knew, but from his terrace they were invisible. The cabins at Turner's Point were down there, thirty feet below, and some boats tied

65

up at wooden docks, kids fooling around, far enough away so that their voices did not carry here. There was the river, and endless trees. A breeze blew in from the west, carrying the scent of river and forest, healing scents, she felt certain. She had not realized until this moment how tired she had become from the long drive, how tense she had been over the meeting after five years.

"It is lovely," she said after they were settled in lounge chairs.

He nodded. He never had talked very much, never said the obvious, but let the self-evident be its own witness. He now took his coffee black; he used to make it almost white with heavy cream. Cholesterol? There was time, she thought, to learn about his health, his diet, his work. She would not rush things any more than he would.

Then he surprised her again. "Let me tell you about it," he said, keeping his gaze on the flowing water. He didn't wait for her to protest, to point out that she no longer practiced law, that she was on her way to work in a food co-op. "First, there's Lucas Kendricks," he said. "He came from over in Deschutes County, married a girl here, Nell Dorcas. She's thirty-two now. He left six years ago and was not heard from since until he showed up again in June. On a Monday afternoon he turned up at his father's house. He said someone was after him, not who, just someone. On Tuesday he left his parents' house and next place he was seen, same day, was in Sisters. He bought food for camping and picked up a couple of girls. He took them to the Eagleton ranch where one of the girls stayed to take pictures of the llamas; the other girl went on with him. On Thursday of that week a girl's body floated down the river and was seen by a number of people. They didn't find her immediately, however. Saturday, Lucas Kendricks arrived at a ridge overlooking his wife's property, and he was shot through the head, killed instantly. The girl's body was recovered on Sunday. She had been beaten, tied, raped, mutilated, murdered. She was identified as one of the girls Kendricks picked up in Sisters.

And last week Nell Kendricks was indicted for the murder of her husband."

"Your client?"

"Yes."

"Did she do it?"

"She says no."

"Murder one, probably life. Manslaughter, ten to twenty," Barbara said coldly. "I assume they indicted on the highest count, aggravated murder. If they bring in guilty, possible death penalty." She had not looked once at him while he spoke, and she did not look now. She poured herself more coffee. "Let me know how it all comes out."

He grunted, shifted in his chair. "I can't do it, Bobby. And there isn't anyone else." He began to list the others in his law firm, and the reasons why none of them could or would take on Nell Kendricks.

She stopped listening. A joke at Reed College had been that if you shake a tree in Oregon three lawyers and a logger would fall out.

He stopped talking. "You haven't heard a word, have you?"

"Enough. It's no good, Dad. Even if I became interested, and I won't, I can't practice in Oregon. It's pointless to talk about it to me."

"You can practice," he said. "You've been on extended leave without pay while you were doing research. That can be taken care of."

She felt so tight that she was certain if she moved, she would appear spastic. She looked at the mug in her hands. He had a set of them, each with a comic judge, a comic scene. This one had the judge leaning across the bench, asking the defendant, "You say your neighbor hit himself over the head with your pool stick just to make you look bad?"

When she was certain she could control her voice, she said, "You can't take care of it, Dad. You can't fix it. I'm sorry if you have a client who has a losing case, but that's life. Possibly mandatory life," she added bitterly. "What did you mean, you can't do it? You win a few, lose a few. Isn't that

67

what you told me? So she gets twenty years, isn't that how the game is played?"

"It's rotten, Bobby. I don't know how or why, but there's something truly rotten about this affair. And I don't know where to start."

He wasn't playing fair, she wanted to cry out. He was supposed to pick up on the cues she was throwing, revive the argument that had sent her away five years ago, that had kept them apart since then. He sounded more troubled than she could remember; he never had become *involved* with his clients. Interested, willing to fight for them, suspicious of them, but never really involved. He had always treated his clients like specimens that fascinated him for a time, exactly the way a boy would become fascinated with a frog under the dissecting knife.

"You say Kendricks left his wife six years ago and just turned up again. "Why didn't she divorce him?"

Her father looked startled, then thoughtful. "I don't know why not."

"Well, find out. And while you're at it, find out who she's been sleeping with. Or is she celibate at thirty-two?" She stood up. "I'll bring in some of my stuff. Most of it can stay in the trunk for the next few days until I take off." She left him on the terrace.

NINE

SHE CARRIED HER suitcases upstairs to the guest room she had used in the past. It had a western view, a better view of the river, actually, than the terrace. The water had taken on a golden sheen that looked like a shiny satin fabric in just enough motion to keep the highlights moving, to keep new patterns appearing, vanishing. She watched it for several minutes, her head empty, content to watch the infinite changes.

When her father's words began to overtake the peace that she could almost feel seeping into her, she began to move briskly around the room, first to examine the drawers of the chest, empty, and then to open her suitcases and begin unpacking a few things. The closet had a down jacket and two sweaters, apparently left here on her last visit. She had forgotten them. In the bathroom there was a jar of soap roses with the spicy fragrance of wild roses.

A sharp memory came to mind. Her mother, slender, white-haired, lovely, saying in her soft voice, "Dear, leave it open. If the soap air dries, it lasts longer. That's why I always unwrap them all." Barbara caught her breath at the clarity of the fleeting moment. Her mother had been talking to her father, who always closed the jar. It was open now.

She went back to the bedroom to stand in the center indecisively. There was a comfortable chair, a reading lamp, some books, magazines. Newspapers. The bed was the three-quarters brass bed from her old room, with the same quilted spread in pink and green leaves and flowers. She wanted to lie down on the bed and cry, as she had done in that distant past over this heartbreak or that.

She finished putting away the few things she had decided to unpack. Then she set her shoulders and went back downstairs.

At the foot of the stairs, her father called her from the kitchen. "In here, honey. Doing things with food."

She went through the hallway, glancing into his study on her way, and on to the kitchen. His study was more muddled than the living room, more books, many of them open, a computer setup that was new, a pair of slippers near his favorite leather chair.

"What I thought was grilled trout. You're not on a diet or anything, are you?" He looked across the room at her over the top of his glasses. She had stopped at the dinette table and chairs. When she shook her head, he went on. "Good. Good. Stuffed tomatoes. Lonnie grew them, and sweet corn. You remember Lonnie Rowan, don't you?"

"I don't think I met her."

"Maybe not. She was probably still in the hardware store last time you were around. Her father owned it since the Flood, I guess, and then a few years ago he upped and died on her. She was fifty-five. It seemed that all the promises he made about providing for her were fairy dust. He died in debt, store with a mortgage, house mortgaged, more bills than you could imagine."

As he talked he moved around the other side of the kitchen, to a cutting board where he cut the tomatoes, salted them, turned them over to drain. To a short step ladder he always had used as a stool, where he sat to shuck corn. Back to the sink. . . . She didn't offer to help. He was a much better cook than she was, and he couldn't stand another person in the kitchen when he was cooking.

"So there she was, fifty-five, broke, in debt, no experience at anything but selling hardware now and again, and taking care of her mother first, until she died, and then her

70

father." He went to the refrigerator and brought out a bottle of white wine. "Thought I was forgetting something." He brought it and glasses to the table and poured for them both. "That's better. So Lonnie started to work for different people around here. Over at Doc's—" He peered at her again, and she nodded. She remembered Doc and his crippled wife. "Over there most days, over here once a week, here and there. But what she's really planning is murder."

Barbara sputtered on her wine. "Come on! What do you mean?"

"Well, way she figures it, no matter how much she works from now on, the day's coming when she won't be able to any more, and she'll be a pauper, out in the street more than likely. A little bit of Social Security, if she holds out for enough work quarters. Some of us managed to save her house for her, not much of a house, sixty years old, sort of decrepit, but still it was home. But she won't even be able to manage the taxes, way she figures. So, if she kills someone, the right someone, she'll get sent up and live out her life comfortably."

"Loony bins aren't all that comfortable," Barbara said gravely.

"Nope. Told her that. But she doesn't intend to be taken as a loony. A political statement. Get rid of someone who deserves to be off the face of the map anyway, do the world a favor, get the maximum sentence and relax. She wouldn't even think of parole, would do whatever it might take to avoid it. Start a riot or something, I guess."

Barbara laughed then. "You're her attorney, advising her, I suppose."

"I am not colluding with her, not in a conspiracy of any sort, not advising her in methods of murder. Certainly not an accessory before the fact. Even tried to talk her out of it, but she's got her head set. Every once in a while she'll ask me what I think of so and so. A senator, or justice maybe, head of state. Once it was a talk show host. Now, let's see, hot black bean sauce, garlic. . . ."

She sipped her wine, watching him prepare their dinner.

71

She wondered, as she had so often, how aware he was of his own machinations. At one time, as a teenager, she had been certain everything he did, everything he said, was planned, calculated for effect, but she had discarded that assessment eventually. For a longer time she had understood that he worked on an intuitive level that even he was unaware of, but she had come to question that, too. He was aware, but not that calculating. His intuition seldom led him astray; he had come to trust it to the point where he could now charm her, be the amusing father she loved, lull her into passivity, and then he would press a new attack more vigorously than before. She recognized his maneuver: the way he had switched from his murder client to this other woman, letting the other matter hang unattended until he was ready to return to it, and not a second before he was ready. She sipped the wine, waiting, amused now, but waiting.

"This Lonnie Rowan, does she have a game plan? Money to travel to wherever her victim might be? A way to get through whatever security there might be?"

He nodded. "Better than that. She knows if she sits tight, he'll come to her. But she's getting frustrated. Seems every time she chooses someone, he gets the axe before she can gather her forces and actually do anything. She had a televangelist picked out, and he got the can, in prison now. And a governor kicked the bucket as soon as she began to research him. Somebody else got cancer. It's been frustrating for her, I tell you. She's starting to think she's putting the jinx on them just by thinking of them, and she knows they won't send her up for thinking people to death. Plain frustrating." He had made a sauce that he was smearing all over two large trout. "You want some peanuts, chips, cheese? Anything?"

"I'm fine. Speaking of research, what are you up to with the open books in every room? And the computer. My God, you've entered the twentieth century!"

"Ah," he said in satisfaction. "My life's work. Finally. Been waiting twenty years, collecting material all that time, and now I'm at it. A collection of great cross-examinations in two volumes. Historical stuff in one, modern in a second.

Problem is too much material. But great stuff. Great!" He wiped his hands. "Wait a minute. I'll show you some print-outs."

He hurried from the kitchen and returned swiftly with pages of fanfold paper not trimmed yet, not torn apart. "This one's a beauty. Geiger, Stan Geiger, back in Ohio, before your time. In the fifties and sixties. Very fine. Just read that."

"Wouldn't it help if I knew something about who did what to whom?"

"No. No. Just read it. You'll catch on quick enough." He was chuckling as he returned to his fish.

She read the page he had indicated:

Q. Weren't you afraid, knowing a burglar was in the room, knowing there was a chance that he was armed?

A. Yes, of course.

Q. So you hid in the closet. Wise course. You didn't have a gun, did you? No weapon of any sort?

A. No, nothing. If I had, then I would have faced him.

Q. I see. Please, just tell us once more exactly what happened.

A. As I said already—several times, in fact—I fell asleep in the armchair, and it grew dark. I woke up when I heard the window opening, and I slipped into the closet because I knew I couldn't get to the door without being seen.

Q. Thank you. Very concise.

In her father's scrawling writing was a note to reproduce the layout of the room.

Q. And there was a light at that end of the room, although the side you were in was in deep shadows, is that right?

A. As I have said several times, I was in virtual darkness at that end of the room. There was a dim light on the chest of drawers on the other side. In order to leave, I would have had to pass it. I could see him plainly in that light.

Q. Yes. I can see that it is a straight line from the closet to the safe. A good view of anyone opening the safe. Yes. But

73

I wonder why he didn't notice the light in the closet. Did he seem aware of the closet light, react to it in any way?

A. There wasn't any closet light. He never got a glimpse of me.

Q. Then you must have had the door closed all the way. Is that how it was?

A. No. As I have said, I left the door open an inch or so. I wanted to get a look at him if I could.

In her father's writing was another note: summarize the house ad, the builder's name, etc., etc. Reproduce the ad.

Q. So, you admit you bought the house only a few months before the robbery, that you bought it from Smithson and Son, Builders, and that this advertisement is a fair representation of the house.

A. Yes, but what possible difference—

Q. Please, sir. Let me continue. You see, in this ad it states quite clearly that every closet has an automatic light that comes on when the door is open. You can see the source of my bewilderment, I trust.

Her father was watching her closely as she finished the cross-examination. "Neat," she said. "Good job."

"Oh, I think so. Of course, he stole his own jewelry for the insurance. But Geiger noticed that ad and made follow-up inquiries. He called the builder, the servants, the wife. The closet lights worked fine. But he didn't really need any of that. That schmuck was tripping over his own dong from then on. Good job."

She nodded.

"Read the next one. The working title for this section is *Now You See It, Now You Don't,* but I'll find something more clever than that when the time comes."

"I doubt it," she said, grinning. She turned the page and started to read:

Q. How long have you lived at your present address, Mr. Steinmann?

A. Forty-two years.

Q. A very long time. I suppose you're familiar with every sound there is up on the hill, aren't you? The mail delivery truck, neighbors' cars, everything that moves on the gravel road?

A. Yes, ma'am.

Carefully Barbara closed the fanfold papers, restored them to order, and then pushed the stack away from her.

"That's one of the most brilliant of them all," her father murmured. "I go on to say so. She noticed that too much time elapsed from when Steinmann said he heard the car make the curve until he saw it go into the Wilson driveway, and she just got to wondering why it took so long. One thing led to another, and she found out that fog set in so thick that old man Steinmann couldn't have seen what he claimed he saw, and was too plain, dumb stubborn to change his story. Said he saw exactly what he expected to see, simple as that." He glanced at her, then turned his attention back to his meal preparations. "Little thing like that probably saved a man's life, though."

The police had claimed that Mr. Wilson arrived home, killed his wife, and left again, to return several hours later and pretend to discover her dead body. She had proven that a stranger must have been driving very slowly on an unfamiliar road shrouded in fog, and that Steinmann's identification of the car and the man leaving it was false. He could not have seen Mr. Wilson. The fog had not descended to the valley floor until after ten, but by five it was already blanketing the surrounding hills. Slowly, inch by inch, she had paved the way and finally forced him to admit that he had not actually seen anyone. But who else could it have been? he had asked.

Barbara sipped her wine without comment; her father began to whistle tunelessly. Presently he said, "You want to set the table on the terrace? Ten minutes and it's dinner."

His dinner was superlative, as she had known it would be; when she said so, he nodded. No false modesty there. The sun was gone by the time they finished and he had

75

brought out coffee. Deep, shadowless twilight lay over the river; it had brought a stillness that quieted the air, quieted the trees. Later a wind would start to blow, but not yet.

"Let me tell you a story," she said in a low voice. "It's about a girl from around here somewhere. She grew up with adoring parents who, no doubt, spoiled her, but more than that they expected her to have ideals, even talked about idealistic goals and futures and the fights worth fighting for the sake of ideals. What did the girl know? She believed her parents, trusted them to be as truthful as they insisted she must be. She nourished her ideals the way other girls nourished their dreams of Mr. Right and a glamorous career with two beautiful children who appeared when it was seemly. So, our girl went to the right schools and got the right sort of grades, clerked for the right sort of judge, but as time went by she began to notice that the grades were granted grudgingly, that she was last in line when honors were awarded, and that politics of various forms was more important than doing good work in many places. Okay, she thought to herself, that was one of the things she intended to fix. And she began to make notes of where the fixing was most needed."

Barbara paid no attention to a slight sound her father made. She was staring as if catatonic at the smooth river below; it had turned black and looked like obsidian. Her voice was as smooth as the water, as implacable. "Somewhere along the line she realized that she was not sleeping very well, that she frequently had nightmares about being run over by machines that were inhumanly oversized and out of control. She saw a shrink or two and learned that she had to come to terms with the system she had entered of her own free will, that she was always trying to force others to adopt her own idealism, that she made people uncomfortable with her own nonconformity. Her nightmares were all her own fault."

She felt his hand on her arm and knew she had become chilled only because his hand was so warm. She did not draw away or acknowledge the touch but continued to speak, continued to face the river. He removed his hand after a moment.

"So, if she wanted the good life, the full, meaningful life, she probably needed several years of therapy, or a mild tranquilizer until she was on course again, or maybe a group, an encounter group, a support group, something. Meanwhile, the world was noticing her, admiring her rise in her field, and suddenly all the things that had been hindrances became assets. It was good that she was female, young, good-looking, all good for business, good for the image of her company. She began to notice that she was assigned appearances before certain judges who had an eye for women. She was included when a bevy of attorneys met with important corporate clients. She was warned that a certain CEO might call her 'girlie' and even touch her, but what the hell, he was harmless. She had no business at all at those meetings, she didn't know shit about corporate law, but it helped the image. And she was doing good work in her own area. Very good work. And then. . . ."

"Finish it," her father said harshly when her pause stretched out too long.

"Yes. Finish it." She had realized quite suddenly that there were still parts of it she could not say, could not think through clearly. Her voice was flat when she went on. "Then she lost a client when a senior member of her firm and a crooked assistant to the DA made a deal behind her back, and all at once she knew she couldn't fix anything, there never had been a chance to fix anything. It was unfixable, all the way. She had lived in a dream world, just as the psychiatrist had told her."

"And you tucked in your tail and ran like a coward!"

She shrugged. When had it become so dark? she wondered then. She had not noticed the change as it happened. Lights flickered in the cabins below; a grill flared, subsided, flared again. She turned toward her father, his face a pale blur, his arms pale. They had not turned on lights in the house, which was very dark behind them. Finally, a breeze was starting, raising goose bumps on her arms.

"I went to Vermont," she said quietly. "They thought I was crazy. The tourists were all leaving when I arrived for the winter, not even in a ski area. I watched the snow pile up around the cottage I rented, until it covered the windows on one whole side. And I thought. But no matter where I started, it always came back to the same place. Everywhere, in all ways people are so busy consuming each other, it's a miracle anyone's left. Even your Lonnie What's-her-name. Her father consumed her and left an aging husk who will die on welfare, in an institution somewhere eventually. Behind that amusing little anecdote is real tragedy, and it's played out over and over, every day, everywhere, by everyone, it seems. I realized in the cottage that winter that you have only three choices: You can climb onto the machine and ride it wherever it's going, mindless, blind, destroying everything in its path, or you can try to stop it and be mowed down when it finally turns in your direction, and it will. It will. Or you can walk away."

"All that's bullshit, and you know it. So you've set yourself up to walk in the wilderness with a lantern."

She laughed. "You don't get it, do you? I'm not looking for anyone, or anything, nothing at all, and I haven't looked for five years."

"What's more, you didn't lose a client. He lost you. He called me because he wanted a deal, and he knew you were off on your own fight, not his. I got him the best deal going. It happens, and you know damn well that it happens. It's built into the system."

"Yes, of course, I know. He got eight years, three other guys got to stay out of trouble and count their money, the prosecutor got another gold star, and you? You just did your job. That's what keeps the machine running, isn't it? Some with real reasons for what they do, and others just going along for the ride, doing their jobs."

"Exactly. It's always been that way. And always will be."

"And that's why I'm on the outside."

"Selling damn fool doodads to damn fool silly women!

You've got a brain, the sharpest mind I know. I'm proud of you, Bobby, and you know that. You can't toss it all."

"Yes, I can! You chose to stay in, do the job. I chose out. It's that simple. I can visit you as your loving daughter, in to check up on your health, to reminisce, to look over your books when they're done, go for a ride with you. You know, the visiting daughter bit. But nothing else. Now, let's go in. I'm freezing. I'll clean up your kitchen."

"I hear you, Barbara. Now you listen." His voice was hard, his words clipped and furious. "I don't want a damn silly girl around. I want a colleague, a peer, someone I can talk to, someone who can spot what I'm missing, whose opinion I trust as no one else's. If you can't be that, I don't want you around at all. And I'll clean up my own damn kitchen."

It was fair, she told herself sharply in her room a few minutes later. She had stated her position; he had done the same. Tit for tat. Fair. But she was furious with him, and she realized that her fury was caused by his refusing to fight it out the way they had done so often in the past, yelling at each other, stamping around the living room, around his office, each accusing the other of willful blindness, of playing dumb. She had expected that, and he had not taken his part.

She never had stayed all the way out of touch; she had written postcards, sometimes even a short letter; she had called from time to time. He had responded in the same way. All without meaning. Estrangement? Alienation? She rejected both words. They simply had grown apart over the years; meaningful exchanges were impossible. And tonight didn't really count. Stating a position wasn't a meaningful exchange. She had missed him, she knew; no one else ever made her explain every step to a conclusion the way he could do. He had been the best sounding board she'd ever had and at times had reduced her arguments to babble with a question or two. His ability to spot the weakness of a defense she was preparing had been uncanny at times, and he always said the same was true of her reactions to his arguments. They had worked well together.

Then he had betrayed her. She knew that the client had called for him, not her. But her father had not told her it was happening until it was over and done with. He had been willing to make the deal in spite of her, in spite of knowing very well that her client was ready to name three others in a construction scam that had made millions in deals with the state government.

This had come too soon after her mother's death; the hurt was still too raw. What Barbara had not been able to say earlier now came back to mind; it had been her mother's fault. She had been his Jiminy Cricket, his conscience, and with her gone, he had become as corrupt as the general public assumed criminal lawyers had to be. She bit her lip hard.

It was over, she told herself wearily. Although she was very tired, she was too restless to attempt sleep yet. The drive had been too hot until she crossed over the pass of the Cascades, when the air had magically cooled. But the heat had been hard to take, had worn her out more than the driving. The thought of starting the drive to Minneapolis in the morning made her feel her fatigue even more. No matter how she decided to go, by what route, she had to cross the plains that would be an inferno. Now she was shivering; she went to the closet and took out one of the sweaters she had left years ago. It was bulky and very warm.

She sat in the chair with the reading lamp and only then realized that the newspapers had been selected very deliberately; they featured the stories about the murder of Lucas Kendricks. Sighing in resignation, she started to read, curious for the first time about why her father had taken on this case if he didn't think he could handle it, or didn't want to handle it.

As she read, she put the papers on the floor; absently she pulled a legal pad onto her lap and made a note. Her father had highlighted, or annotated, remarks, statements here and there; she paid close attention to those sections.

When she came to a statement made by John Kendricks, the father of the victim, she stopped. Lucas hadn't known about the birth of his daughter? And she was now six! She wrote: *Where was he? Prison? Institution? Out of the country?*

Abruptly she stopped writing to examine the pencil she had found on the table, a mechanical pencil with very fine lead, the kind she had always used. She had bought them by the carton and routinely lost them. For a second or two her vision blurred with tears; then she threw the pencil as hard as she could across the room. She got up, dumping the note pad and rest of the newspapers onto the floor, went to the bathroom, and began to run hot water for a bath. And then bed, she told herself. Damn him!

TEN

HER FATHER WAS on the terrace having coffee the next morning when she joined him. He peered at her over his glasses, nodded, and motioned toward the thermos carafe. "Help yourself. I'll rustle up some breakfast pretty soon." As she poured, he said, "You know, after your mother died, I couldn't sleep worth a damn in that house in town. I began coming out here on Friday afternoon, stayed 'til Sunday, and slept like a baby. Soon's I could manage it, I just came out, period. Remember the first afternoon, though. Dog tired, just plain dog tired, and I stretched out here on this chair, dozed off, and woke up to morning. Cold, stiff, sore. But it felt good, really felt fine."

"You never mentioned having trouble," she said. "Why didn't you tell me?" Even as she asked, she wondered when he could have confided. That had been a bad year, no time for confidences. At the end of the year she had fled in body, although she had fled in spirit months before the actual deed.

"For what purpose?" Frank asked reasonably. "You couldn't have put me to sleep. Pills helped for a time, but I didn't like having wool, steel wool, in my head all day afterward. Nope, I got to thinking about it after I moved on out, and I have a theory. There's a soporific in air that's filtered through trees. Maybe just fir trees. It's going to need a lot of research to narrow it down and find out if it's specific to firs, or if all trees do it. Tried to interest a chemist down at the university, but he laughed at me. Figure when I have time, I'll have to bone up on chemistry, physiology, what else? When I have time I'll do the research myself."

"Biochemistry," she said after a moment and was surprised to hear a huskiness in her voice that was strange to her ears. "Psychology, just in case the effect is psychosomatic, not physical."

He looked thoughtful, then nodded slowly. "Never even thought of that. You suppose it could all be in my head?"

"No, Dad, I don't. Tell me what you like for breakfast these days. I'm pretty good with anything to do with eggs."

She made their breakfast, and as they ate they watched small boats leaving the dock area at Turner's Point, watched two teenage boys return with a string of fish, laughing. This morning the river was clear, light blue.

"What I usually do after breakfast is walk down to the point and pick up newspapers, chat a bit, walk home. Want to take a walk?"

"How far?"

"Mile each way, or thereabouts."

She thought of the long drive she was starting that day, thought of a motel at the end of the day's drive, the heat as soon as she left the mountains again. And, she thought, she had no schedule, no appointments, no one expecting her, no reason to be anywhere at any particular time. "Sure. Let's shove this stuff in the sink. I'll deal with it later."

They walked on the gravel road that was private, maintained by the half dozen property owners who fronted it. He pointed out the houses they passed, although from the road not a single one of them was visible.

"Chuck Gilmore," he said at the one next to his. "Owns most of the point, I guess. Soon as this property came on the market, he snapped it up and built the most handsome staircase you're likely to find anywhere, from the cabin area down there, up to the road here. Then the damn fool tried to cut a trail through Nell's property and she ran him off." He chuckled. "He thought if he got it in place, got some underbrush cleared, a few people using it, he could claim squatter's rights, I guess. Wrong."

"Stupid thing to attempt. Why did he do it?"

"For access to the beach down at Nell's place. Only beach around here, and it's a nice little protected sandy strip. Shallow water, good wading, good place for the kids to play while the fathers are out fishing."

"But she doesn't buy that?"

"She's seen the dump trucks full of junk they have to haul out of the point week after week."

Barbara nodded. The next house was Stan and Lucille Bowman's place. They came out for weekends when they could manage the time. And then the Terry house. . . .

The woods pressed so close to the narrow road and were so thick that with just a few steps a person would vanish, she was thinking. There was a fringe of wild flowers and bushes, berries, and ferns, all growing in what looked like piles and heaps of greenery, with flowers poking up here and there, a branch waving now and again, as if to celebrate its escape, its freedom.

The gravel road ended at a dirt road; they turned left. This section was fairly smooth, but the right turn had led to a gutted, rock-strewn road that looked undriveable. Old Halleck Hill Road, she remembered from the newspaper articles she had read the night before. Fifty miles down that road, apparently, Lucas Kendricks had killed a girl and thrown her mutilated body into a creek that had brought her to the river. Resolutely she put that out of mind and listened to yet another of her father's stories, this time about a neighbor whose name she already had forgotten.

The walk was closer to a mile and a half, she decided when they entered Chuck Gilmore's store. But it had been a pleasant mile and a half, and she did not object. Her father introduced her to Chuck, a big, very muscular man with a tremendous chest and iron-gray hair. Two boys were trying to pick a comic book, and Chuck was keeping his eye on them. A car stopped, spilling out a family with two small children, one whining, "Is *this* where we're going?"

Barbara and her father went out back to the rail overlooking the cabins, and from here she looked up to spot his house. It was very handsome up on the ridge, and the next one beyond it was even more handsome, expensive-looking. That was Doc's house, she remembered from her last visit. The houses on the ridge were so close that only now did she understand why Chuck Gilmore wanted access to the beach. His staircase was clearly visible, wide, sturdy, also expensive-looking. A short walk from here, through his property, along the gravel road a bit, then through Nell's property. She didn't blame him for wanting it, and she didn't blame Nell for refusing. Down at the docks there were cans lying around, bits of paper. Trash, she thought. Just the normal human trash.

"Want to stroll through town?" her father asked. "I admit there's not much to see, but while we're here. . . ."

A pickup truck pulled into the parking lot; a small woman and two children got out. The boy was exactly the same height as the woman, and both had curly brown hair. Barbara steeled herself. That was Nell Kendricks, she knew. She looked hardly old enough to be a mother, much less the mother of the boy at her side. The other child was a small girl with long, straight blond hair and a serious expression.

"I didn't plan this," her father said in a low voice. "But you've got to meet them, now that it's happened. Come on."

Nell had spotted him and hesitated, then came in their direction, the two children with her. "Good morning, Frank," she said, and the boy said good morning. Carol smiled.

"Honey, this is Nell Kendricks, Travis, and Carol. My daughter Barbara."

Nell was obviously surprised when Barbara held out her hand. Belatedly she reached out and they shook hands. Barbara had been instructed to shake hands at law school at the insistence of a professor who had said *professional* people always shake hands when they meet. Remember that. Travis extended his hand, and she took it. Then Carol started to put her hand out, drew it back, and put it out again. Gravely Barbara shook hands with her also.

"Showing Barbara some of the local attractions," Frank said. "View from Turner's Point. Next, the Grange Hall."

Nell grinned. "I thought I'd find you here, since I missed you on the road. We're having a cookout, Tawna, James, us. And you're invited. You too," she added quickly to Barbara.

"Love to come," Frank said. "When? And who's cooking?"

"Tawna is, and six-thirty is when. We're off for shopping. School clothes. Travis can't wear a single thing from last year."

Travis rolled his eyes and made a face. Carol was looking serious again, staring fixedly at Barbara.

"Don't let us keep you," Frank said. "It sounds as if you've got yourself a real day lined up. What can I bring?"

"Not a thing. I'm stopping at the Metropole for bread. I'm getting some for Jessie, too. You want some?"

"Yep. One of everything they've got."

"Okay. Nice meeting you, Ms. Holloway. That sounds rather silly, doesn't it, since we'll be seeing you again in just a few hours. Come on, Travis, Carol, let's go."

Frank and Barbara watched her fasten seat belts, climb up into the driver's seat, start the engine, and drive off with a final wave. Carol waved, too.

Barbara started to walk out of the parking lot, back to the road where she turned in the direction from which they had come. After a moment's hesitation, Frank followed her.

"What happened to her parents?" Barbara asked.

"Nell's? Rumor is all I know. Stories, gossip. Her mother was from here, married a man from San Francisco. He couldn't stand it in the woods, I guess. They were back and forth a lot, anyway. He was a performer, musician, comic, something of the sort, and not very good, they say. Broke most of the time, like that. Anyway, he died, overdose, when Nell was just a little kid, about Carol's age, and her mother came back home with her. Then two years later, she died, pneumonia, and the grandfather raised Nell."

"The papers said she's a crack shot, sharpshooter deluxe class, something like that. Is she?"

"So they say. I've never seen her shoot, so I don't know. Did you read about the tree cutters and the beer can?"

"Yes. And that story didn't make any more sense than Chuck Gilmore's trying to cut a trail through her property."

"That's what I thought. I saw her the day it happened, though, and I guess she shot the can, all right." He told her about the day people had seen the body in the river, and Nell had found two men preparing to cut down her tree.

Barbara listened, concentrating on his words, comparing his account with what she had read. It made a little more sense the way he told it, but not much, not enough. She breathed deeply when he stopped talking, and began to examine the woods again.

"Anything?" Frank asked after several seconds.

"No. Just curious about why a woman like her is a crack shot."

"Her grandfather taught her, according to the gossip mill. They said he boasted that she was a natural, the best shot in the county."

Barbara nodded absently. "But that doesn't answer the question about why he taught her in the first place, how he found out that she had a talent for it. I suspect he realized early on that she was not going to be very big, that she was vulnerable in many ways, and shooting was a way to give her self-confidence. I mean, she was a child who had just lost both parents, she probably was diminutive, like Carol, and

86

probably nervous as hell. He sounds like a pretty wise old man to me. You never taught me to shoot."

Frank snorted. "Never saw any sign that you needed a boost in self-confidence, either."

There was a touch of bitterness in her laugh. "The key words are you never saw any sign. But, back to Nell. It worked. She's self-assured, self-confident, evidently doing a damn good job with those two kids. And under it all, she's scared to death."

Frank put his arm around her shoulders and squeezed slightly, then released her. "Glad you saw that, too. She's good and scared. And has a right to be."

Watching her expensive running shoes get scuff after scuff in the gravel of the road, she asked, "Why did you say you can't handle this case?"

"Because I don't think I can get her off."

"Can anyone?"

There was a long silence during which the only sounds were the clicking of gravel, the soft *swish* of his jeans as he walked, and one leg brushed the other rhythmically.

"The situation," he said finally, "as accepted around here is that she was married to a son of a bitch who deserted her and the children, who didn't even know he had a daughter, and who tortured and killed a nineteen-year-old girl on his way home. When he showed up, he must have threatened Nell, threatened the children, and she plugged him. Justifiable. Everyone agrees that he deserved exactly what he got, that she should have done it years ago, the last time he was around. Manslaughter, or even self-defense."

"But?"

"But she says she didn't do it."

"You said Lucas didn't know he had a daughter. How did anyone find that out? She didn't have a chance to talk to him, according to the papers."

"His parents did." He told her what little he knew about Lucas and his movements from the time he arrived at his parents' house south of Bend until he vanished around noon

87

on Tuesday, with the girl who was murdered sometime the afternoon of the same day.

"You'll have to have an investigator do some digging," Barbara said after a lengthy pause. "Where was Lucas all those years? Why didn't he know about his daughter if both Nell and his parents wrote to him, tried to call, and so on? Was he in an institution? Jail? Overseas? Down dope lane? Where? Doing what? Did the autopsy show drugs?"

"Nothing."

"Have the police turned up anything about his recent past?"

"I really doubt they've looked much. Doesn't seem to matter. He's tied to the dead girl, and he's dead. Nell's rifle was out and had been fired recently. Doesn't seem to be any doubt that it was the gun that killed him. She was the only one around. Her father-in-law could have tipped her off that he was coming that day, and, in fact, he even picked up the kids and took them away for an extended visit the day before the murder, clearing the field of action. The police don't seem to feel they need much more than that."

"Well, you sure as hell will need a lot more than that. But I've told you where I'd start asking questions."

"About Lucas and his past?"

She looked at him sharply and said with irritation. "Of course not. About her. Why didn't she divorce him? And who is she sleeping with?"

The walk home seemed shorter than it had in the other direction, but even so, by the time they reached the house her legs were aching, and her thighs felt on fire. How long since she had done any real walking, she asked herself, and had to think back to the previous winter. No one walked in Phoenix when the weather got hot, as it did by April, or even March. Now she found that she just wanted to sprawl, have more coffee, read the newspapers her father had picked up.

"What's next on your schedule usually?" she asked as they entered the house. It was very cool inside.

"Generally I work a couple of hours on the book, then lunch and read the papers, and then nap. More work in the late afternoon some days. Sometimes I take a little walk. Sometimes a little fishing after nap time. Some days along about five or so, mosey on around to visit with Doc and Jessie, cadge a drink or two. Busy days, as you can see."

She nodded. "If I were your doctor, I'd probably tell you to slow down. Well, leave the papers, please. After I do the dishes I'll have a go at them. Get on about your business."

He grinned and handed over the newspapers, one an *Oregonian*, one a local weekly, and the *New York Times*. She suspected that he paid a fortune to have that brought in daily, and she could not imagine his doing without it.

After Barbara tidied up in the kitchen, she made a fresh pot of coffee, not quite as strong as her father made it; when she went out to the terrace to read the papers, she found that she had no interest in them at all. She sipped the coffee, gazing out at the river, now a deep forest green, and suddenly she was visualizing Nell on the river, on a bobbing ice floe that she leaped from just as it upended. The next was no less dangerous. And that was where little Nell was, she thought then, in the middle of the river without a chance of reaching either shore. If she agreed to plea bargain, admit to a manslaughter charge, with self-defense, she would serve time, four to six. If she refused and was found guilty of murder one, she would serve even more time, ten to twenty, or even life, depending on the state's case. All this was assuming that they didn't have cause to go for aggravated murder, with a death sentence. That was reason enough for the look of terror that had lurked behind her pleasant expression, that had clouded her pretty brown eyes.

What would happen to those two kids then? Grandparents probably would get custody, but a court could decide to put them in foster homes. Nothing was certain where kids were concerned any longer. And who would guard her trees?

This was exactly why she had dropped out, Barbara thought with great bitterness. The machine was in motion, and Nell was not aboard. She had not sidestepped in time, and it was too late now; she was directly in front of the behemoth. And just what the hell was she, Barbara, doing here brooding about a strange woman and her probable fate? It was going on noon, too late to start driving, especially since her legs had failed her on such a short walk.

But it was more than simple brooding, she realized. She was seething over the bastard Lucas who had done this to Nell and her two beautiful children. The devourers and the devoured, she muttered under her breath. If he had killed that girl and thrown her into the river, he had just as surely destroyed his wife and his children. If Nell was found guilty of manslaughter, of killing him in self-defense, or premeditated murder, she was destroyed, and so was the family. No one recovered from such a history, not really. The torture wouldn't leave visible scars and physical mutilations, but there was torture and torment aplenty in store for them. Predators and prey. Always it came back to that. Pick a role, there are only two. Victimizer or victim. Toss a coin.

Angrily she stood up and gathered the unread papers, arranged them neatly for her father. She had turned her back on the machine, she told herself; she refused the coin, the roles, both of them. She had refused the machine, walked away from it. Even if she agreed to help her father on this case, nothing would be changed. Tomorrow another young woman would be devoured, or a young man, and then another and another endlessly, faster and faster. Nothing changed.

Her father would say, just as angrily, she knew, that it was the only game in town and you play by the rules. "No more," she said. "No more."

Lunch was a sandwich and an apple. Afterward, her father disappeared for his nap, just as he had said he would. She wandered around the house, then went to her room and lay down, for a minute, she told herself. She slept nearly an hour, to her great surprise. All that walking, all that soporific air, she thought, chagrined. She had not taken a nap in so many years she could not even remember the last time.

Then her gaze landed on the newspapers, the ones filled

with the stories of the two murders. Presently she sat in the easy chair and resumed reading where she had left off.

Later her father asked if she was up for walking over to Nell's house.

"How far?"

"Maybe half a mile."

"You're talking about another country mile altogether, aren't you? Let's drive."

He chuckled, and they went out to his car. He pointed out where Doc's property stopped and Nell's began; the difference was startling. Doc's place had been left wild; thick forest, the same fringe of undergrowth along the road, but then the trees became more spaced out, with great clear areas, and the regularity of an orchard. Barbara didn't recognize the trees until he told her they were the walnut trees that would make Nell a very rich woman one day soon. The road made a sharp right turn onto Nell's property. Barbara gazed at the giant fir tree that had been threatened by the tree cutters. And what had that been all about? she wondered, but did not comment.

She was surprised to find that Tawna and James were black. They greeted her father as a friend and extended that friendship to her without hesitation. Celsy, their teenage daughter, was just as friendly. Barbara was surprised again to learn that the Gresham family was living in the big house, Nell and her children in the smaller one. Topsy-turvy, she found herself saying under her breath.

Travis began to tell Frank about the horse James had treated that week. "We had to give him a shot," Travis said.

Nell spread her hands in a helpless gesture. "I keep telling James not to let him be a nuisance, but he loves to tag along."

"The day comes that he's a nuisance, that's the day I send him packing," James said. "Frank, Barbara, we're having wine and beer, but there's bourbon, some gin, maybe something else. Name it."

While he was inside getting wine for them both, Frank pulled a chair closer to the grill where Tawna was turning chicken. She looked at her daughter and said softly, "Maybe you could play something?"

Celsy glanced at the company, then said with some resignation, "Okay."

"Can I watch?" Carol asked. She said sure, and they both went inside the house.

"And *she's* a pest with Celsy," Nell said.

Frank questioned Tawna about the sauce she had made for the chicken; it smelled spicy and alien. Palm oil, chili peppers, a little this, a little that, she said. Nell began to tell Barbara about the ceramic jewelry that Tawna made. Then James came out with a tray and handed out wine; it seemed to Barbara that she had known these people for a long time and was very comfortable with them.

The sound of Celsy's flute drifted out; Tawna glanced at James and they both smiled faintly, very proud of their talented daughter. For a moment Barbara felt her eyes burn. When she looked at Nell, she knew she was seeing another side of her, relaxed, at ease, the terror deeply buried for the time being.

The chicken was delicious, the bakery bread that Nell had supplied was crisp and very good, the salad was superb. Frank praised everything extravagantly, and soon he began telling one of his funny court stories, and then James topped it with a funnier animal story. When Carol began to yawn, Nell sighed.

"Guess it's that time," she said with regret. It had become very dark.

"I'll take them," Celsy said. "You want to stay and talk a while, I'll go down with them." She was already on her feet; it was obvious that she had had quite enough of the adult evening. "Okay, bums, say goodnight and then march!" Carol giggled and said it nicely; Travis saluted and said goodnight in a computerlike voice. He began to march like a wooden soldier. By the time they were out of the light from the house, they were all giggling.

"It's been a grand party," Frank said.

"Those are great kids," Barbara added. "All three."

"Sometimes you wish you could put a bell jar over them, keep them exactly the way they are forever and ever," Tawna said in a low voice. "You know, capture them at this exact moment."

"What happens is that kids turn into people all too soon," Barbara said, and to her dismay the light tone she had intended was not there.

"People are okay," James said reflectively. "Not as nice as animals, but okay."

Tawna laughed. "If animals wanted anything more than regular meals and shelter, they'd be just like people. You better believe."

"Maybe if all people had regular meals and shelter, they'd be as nice as animals," Nell said.

"They wouldn't," Barbara said. "People don't want only what they really need. They want more, always more, and the only way to get it is by taking what they want from others. Human nature."

"Oh, no!" Tawna protested. "It's learned behavior. People aren't selfish because of their genes. Everyone can quote the golden rule, but who actually practices it? There are too many ways to learn things, and by rote, the way we teach the golden rule, is probably the worst of all."

"Nurture/nature," Frank said. "One of those problems without an answer. One of the reasons philosophers are now up to their eyeballs talking about language, and forgetting the basic questions. Because they have recognized finally that there can't be any definitive answers, just faith. Suppose, for a minute, you were granted the power to change people. What would you do, Tawna, for openers?"

"Teach them, really teach them to do unto others as you would have them do unto you. That would be quite enough."

"No," Barbara said. "It isn't. It implies reciprocation. You want something in return for doing good, you expect it. That's the basis for what passes as altruism most of the time. You'll be rewarded, if not in the here and now, then in heaven. But always there must be a reward."

"Well, maybe that's one way of interpreting it," Tawna said, but her tone said she did not believe it.

"What would you do, Barbara?" James asked.

"Maybe grant the veil of ignorance to every living being. A true veil of ignorance. Every action of every person would be just, because you would never know the recipient. Male, female, young, elderly, black, white, American, Brazilian, none of that would enter into any decisions. If the action was just, it would be just for anyone alive, not just a select few."

"That's frightening," Nell said, nearly in a whisper. "Justice without mercy is more frightening than anything I can think of."

"In my world justice and mercy would never be linked. Mercy implies one with power having pity on one without power. In my world that dichotomy would no longer exist."

"Utopia," James said, sounding relieved. "Suddenly, although we banished the philosophers, we are in the philosophical utopia."

Frank laughed. "Well, my thoughts of utopia include the idea of a warm bed and pleasant dreams. Bobby, ready to make tracks?"

"I'll get your bread," Nell said. Then she turned to Barbara. "Want to walk over to my house with me?"

Nell gave Tawna and James a hug and a kiss, and then kissed Frank's cheek, and she and Barbara left the group. They walked in silence for half the distance.

"You're a lawyer, too, aren't you?" she asked. "Your father mentioned it a couple of times."

"Was, maybe I still am. It's hard to say."

"Can I come talk to you tomorrow? Something you said. . . . You reminded me of something Lucas said a long time ago. And then I forgot again. I want to think it through, try to remember it all, and then talk to you. Would you mind?"

Barbara recognized the feeling that enveloped her not as resignation, but as despair. "All right," she said slowly.

ELEVEN

NELL ARRIVED SHORTLY after one the next day. Barbara and Frank had already finished lunch and were having coffee when she walked from the woods between Frank's house and Doc's. She was in jeans and sneakers and a T-shirt, carrying an armload of books; she looked like a schoolgirl.

Today she appeared shyer than she had yesterday when she had the children with her, and again at the cookout, as if then she had been playing the role of mother and had found security with it; now she was alone and vulnerable.

Barbara had not had a good night; fir trees filtering the air had not helped. Now she regarded this young woman with a careful neutrality. "Hello. Another beautiful day, isn't it?"

Nell nodded and said hello. She put the books on the table and sat in the chair Frank motioned to.

"Coffee? We're just finishing lunch. Still some fruit salad." Frank looked at her, questioning. She accepted coffee and turned down food. It soon became apparent that she needed the coffee simply to keep her hands busy with something. She fiddled with the spoon and stirred and stirred the coffee.

As they waited for her to start, Barbara realized with irritation how much she had picked up from her father over the years. His motto was to let the one who wanted to talk be the one to start, to point the direction.

Finally Nell put down the spoon and looked at Barbara, addressed her. "Last night when you were talking about the veil of ignorance, I began to think of a different phrase, a veil of innocence. Oh, we can't restore it, I know that, but the kind of innocence that children have kept coming to mind. And I began to think of Lucas, when I saw him that time up on the ridge. He had it restored." She looked puzzled, almost pleading with Barbara in some unfathomable way.

Now she turned to Frank, including him, where a moment ago she had excluded him. She drew in a deep breath and said, "He didn't kill that girl. I know he didn't."

Frank looked at her over his glasses, then poured himself more coffee. "Just tell us what you're getting at. We'll go on from there."

"Yes. I thought it through last night after the party. At first, it was just this flash of denial, something I knew as well as I know I didn't shoot him, but I realized that isn't enough. And I don't know if I can say enough to convince anyone else." She began to stir the coffee again; this time Barbara reached over and removed the spoon from her fingers. Nell looked embarrassed, but she set her shoulders and began.

"I met him the first year we were in college. We were freshmen together, in several of the same classes, and we liked each other from the first." She clasped her hands in her lap and looked down at them. "We were living together six months after we met. I brought him home with me, and Grampa liked him, and he was excited about the forest here, and the river. We made a little dam on Halleck Creek and swam in the water, and we went mushrooming together, and hiked. Everything was new to him. You know, he grew up on the desert, with junipers and some pine forests in the mountains but nothing like over here. You saw how Travis was last night talking about going out with James to watch him take care of animals? Excited, everything new and wonderful. No value judgments, no reservations, just accepting everything. That's how Lucas was. We were both so happy. Everything was beautiful and funny and exciting. And that's how he looked that last day. His eyes were

96

laughing, he was laughing all over, filled with the same kind of excitement and happiness. He couldn't have been like that if he had done something so horrible."

Barbara regarded her thoughtfully. "You say that quality was restored, and that means that after the early years it was gone. What happened?"

Nell got up and walked to the low railing on the terrace, then turned to face them, outlined against the distant tree, with the gleaming water vanishing among them. "Frobisher happened," she said in a low voice. "Emil Frobisher killed something in him, and it came back to life for that instant, and then. . . ."

Frank had not moved, hardly seemed awake he was so still, and Barbara waited also. She had seen people tell astonishing things that they had not intended to bring up at all, simply because someone had to fill in the silence.

"Emil Frobisher was a professor at the university," Nell said finally, and she returned to her chair, picked up the coffee that had become cold, and put it down without tasting it. "Lucas and I had married that summer, and I was pregnant, and it was still wonderful. Then Frobisher put an ad in the paper. He wanted volunteer subjects for an experiment in perception. He was willing to pay, and we decided to go for it. We wanted a last weekend at the coast before I got too big. Anyway, I didn't work out for the experiment, but Lucas did, and he was more or less hired as a regular for Frobisher. And for a long time that was all right, nothing changed. Travis was born and Lucas was crazy about him, about being a father. He was so proud and still so happy. But he was putting in more and more time in Frobisher's lab, and he began to talk about a time when he would be a real assistant, and maybe something even more important, a co-worker on some project. Frobisher was encouraging him to think this, and he was changing, week by week, month by month he was changing."

"You objected? Didn't you see this as an opportunity for him?" Barbara asked when Nell stopped talking. Now that the direction had been indicated, she was free to keep things moving.

"I objected," Nell said bitterly. "Lucas simply wasn't like that—a researcher, I mean. He didn't really like school, didn't like having to study, do papers, any of that. I did most of his papers for him, or they wouldn't have been finished. He was smart enough, but not interested. Not a scholar, or a brain, as we used to say. Anything abstract bored him, math bored him, science bored him." She looked helplessly from Frank to Barbara. "I'm not trying to make him out to be an idiot, or dumb, not subnormal, just not like that. And yet there he was talking about being a colleague of Emil Frobisher, a co-worker on his project." She shook her head. "It just didn't make sense, unless they were using him in some way, feeding his vanity to keep him interested. When I said something like that, he exploded and said I was jealous. That was our first argument."

"How long did that go on?"

"For two years. Then Frobisher got an offer from Walter Schumaker." She looked at them uncertainly. "He got the Nobel Prize for some work in mathematics fifteen years ago, I guess. Anyway, he was the big time. He had read a paper by Frobisher and got in touch with him; he said they were working on the same material and should work together. Frobisher talked Lucas into going with him. He promised that Lucas would get advanced degrees out of the work, a doctorate, even, if he stayed with it. I tried to see Frobisher myself, but he was always busy, or somewhere else, and it never worked out. I tried to call him and never got through, and he never returned a call. In the end, Lucas went with him to Colorado."

"Travis was what? Two?"

Nell nodded and got up again, this time to pace back and forth with restless energy.

"Nell," Barbara said slowly, as if testing each word, "is it possible that Lucas was simply not ready to be a husband and father? That he was still growing up and not ready to settle into married life?"

98

"No. I could have understood that. Before he left he said they were going to change the world, that he was going to be part of the biggest change in all human history, that what they were doing would make people like gods. He believed that. He was excited about it, and scared, too."

"Okay. He left. Was there any possibility that you could have gone with him?"

"No. That was one of the things I wanted to talk to Frobisher about, but Lucas said that the work would intensify to the point where we'd never be together, and it would be too hard on Travis, and on me. What he was really saying," she added dully, "was that we'd be in his way, hinder him."

"Did you keep in touch when he was away?"

"Oh, yes. I wrote every day or at least twice a week, and he called pretty often. And then he came home, when Travis was five. And he was like a stranger. At first, it was the old Lucas, but within a day or two, he was a stranger. He wanted to cut down the walnut trees to raise money for the project. They had run into financial trouble, and Schumaker was talking about leaving. We fought again that time, and he took off again." She shrugged slightly and sat down once more.

"This time when he was gone, you didn't hear from him? Is that right?"

She nodded. "Nothing. I wrote like before, but in just a few weeks my letters started coming back. He had moved, no forwarding address. When I knew I was pregnant, I sent registered letters, and his father did, and we both tried to call him through the university. No number for him." She looked at her hands, again tightly clasped in her lap. "I could have hired a detective to find him, I guess, but . . . I thought he just wanted out of our lives, that he had made that decision, and what would be the point of tracking him down? I wouldn't have asked him back if he wanted out."

"He abandoned you and your children," Barbara said. "Why didn't you divorce him and get on with your life?"

Nell seemed to hunch her shoulders and draw herself into a tighter little mass. "I don't know."

"I think you do. And it's something we'll have to know."

Nell glanced quickly at Frank, away again. "I . . . I thought that if I just waited, after enough years, he could be declared dead. Legally dead, I guess I mean."

Barbara studied her and finally shook her head. "Were you afraid of him?"

"No! He wouldn't have hurt me! It was. . . ." She looked at Frank again. "One time, over at Doc's, we were all talking about a custody fight that was in the news. You probably don't remember, but I asked you if a parent could ever deny the other one visitation rights, and you said in some cases, of proven molestation, or criminal offenses, or if a morals case could be made. There might have been others, I don't remember. But I knew that I didn't dare raise the issue with Lucas. I didn't want him to claim visitation rights. I thought that if I started divorce proceedings, he would have to know, and he would demand visitation."

"You were afraid for Travis?" Barbara asked in surprise.

Miserably, Nell nodded. "The last time he was home, he said a new person was joining the research team, a psychiatrist who had written a book about how children's belief systems became frozen during adolescence. He said that when the project was done, Travis would be exactly the right age, that his age group would be the first to use whatever it was. And I knew he would try it on Travis if ever he could. Then, he came home again, and Travis is at that age, an adolescent, twelve." She moistened her lips. "Anything I say just makes it look as if I'm adding motive on top of motive for wanting him dead."

Barbara agreed with her. She thought for a moment, then asked, "How was he different when he came home, when Travis was five?"

Nell lifted her shoulders in a helpless gesture and looked from Barbara to Frank. "I can't describe it. He . . . he would be looking at me, and it was as if I wasn't there, as if he was looking through me to something else. For hours he would be quiet, not saying a word, and then he would start to talk so fast I couldn't even follow what he was saying. And his talk about the project sounded crazy. I think he had lost faith

100

in it, in his part, anyway. That's why he wanted money. He said if he could provide matching funds for a grant, something like that, they wouldn't be able to phase him out." Her misery seemed to deepen as she spoke. "He was so unhappy that time, so worried, and distracted. Distracted," she said again as if she had made a discovery. "I don't think he was ever really here after the first day or two, not until we had another fight the day before he left again."

Abruptly Barbara stood up. "I'm going to make some fresh coffee. And then, if you can stand to tell it once more, I'd like to hear about that last day, the day he was killed." She didn't wait for Nell to respond but picked up the carafe and entered the house. No decisions yet, she told herself firmly. Keep an open mind. Something good might still come up, not just piling more and more damning statements on top of one another. Nell thought her child had been threatened, she found herself arguing, as if for the prosecution, and she shook her head. Stop. In any event Nell could not be put on the witness stand. She would tell her father that much. But even as she thought about telling him how to conduct this case, she accepted that she was kidding herself. He was right that he couldn't manage it. He was too close to Nell. "And never practice law for your spouse, your family, or your friends." She heard the words in her head in the voice of the professor who had repeated them so often that it had been almost a joke.

The kitchen was positioned so that the working area was in the front of the house, the road side, and the dining space overlooked the river. As Barbara stood at the sink waiting for the coffee to finish dripping through the automatic machine, she caught a glimpse of motion in the driveway. She went to the kitchen door to look out. A man was leaning against the hood of a Land Rover.

She stepped out. "Hi, did you want something?"

He was tall and broad in the shoulders, with blond hair that was bleached out by the sun to nearly white in the front, and he was dressed in work clothes, tan trousers, a tan work shirt, boots. He snatched off his sunglasses; he had bright

101

blue eyes surrounded by pale skin. Suddenly he seemed many years younger than he had with the glasses on.

"Oh, sorry. Didn't mean to interrupt or anything. I'm waiting for Nell. She thought she might be done here around two. I'm Clive Belloc, a friend of hers."

Barbara glanced at her watch and was surprised to see that it was two-thirty. "Sorry to keep her so long," she said. I'm Barbara Holloway. I'm afraid we'll be another half hour or so. Is there anything I can get you? Do you want to come inside?"

"No," he said hastily. "I'm fine. You're Frank's daughter? Glad to meet you. And please don't mention I'm out here, will you? I wouldn't want her to feel rushed or anything."

Barbara nodded and went back inside; the coffee was done. When she returned to the terrace, Nell appeared poised and steeled. Barbara poured the hot coffee for them all. Someone had dumped Nell's cold coffee, but this time she didn't bother with the spoon; she ignored the coffee altogether and started to talk as soon as Barbara was seated again.

She recounted the morning concisely through the time of the UPS delivery of the computer and her climb up the mountain to the sheltered clearing. Then her voice faltered, and she sipped her coffee for the first time.

"I saw him just before I got to the top, and I froze. I guess I was more shocked than anything. I shut my eyes for a second before I went up. Then I took the last step and looked around and saw him at the edge of the clearing. He was laughing. And there was the shot."

"Why did you say before that he was happy? It seems you hardly had time to notice."

"But he was! He was laughing. He said, 'Watch this!' just like a child might say it, pleased, delighted even. Just happy."

"What did he mean, 'Watch this'? What was he doing?"

"Nothing. Just standing there, laughing."

Barbara frowned at her. "Did he have anything in his hands? Anything he might have wanted to show you?"

Nell shook her head. "I'm sure not. I didn't see anything.

102

When he. . . . The shot threw him backward, and he jerked up both hands. I'm sure they were empty. I didn't see anything."

Her voice had become more and more strained, and now broke entirely. She drank some coffee and drew in one deep breath after another. Barbara waited, dissatisfied and deeply troubled.

"Okay, then what?" she asked finally.

"I ran back down the trail to my house and called Doc. I knew he would be home on Saturday. I said I was going to go look for Lucas and he told me to wait, not to do anything until he got there. That's what I did. He called the sheriff, and we went together to look for Lucas. We hadn't found him yet when the sheriff's deputies arrived. They found him."

"And they found your rifle in the living room later," Barbara said slowly. "Why was it out?"

Wearily Nell told her about the men who had started to cut the tree down, and about the beer can. "I should have cleaned the rifle Friday night, but I thought I'd do some target practice on Saturday, and then I forgot all about it."

Barbara knew there were many more questions she should ask, but, she thought wryly, she didn't know yet what they were. And Nell was looking pinched and pale, her hands trembling when she raised her coffee cup. Barbara leaned back in her chair. "This has been hard, I know. But you've been fine, just fine. There's something I'll ask you to do over the next few days. Don't rush it, and don't try to make sense out of it, but jot down everything you can remember that Lucas ever said about the people he was working with, the project they were involved in. And what that first test you tried was all about, the perception experiment. Will you do that?"

Nell looked bewildered. "Sure," she said. "But they're in Colorado, you know. That's where they were working."

Barbara shrugged. "It might not help, but at this minute I'm thinking we need all the information we can gather, and that's part of it." She glanced at her watch and saw that it was after three. "I'm afraid we've kept a friend of yours waiting a rather long time. Clive Belloc is out front."

Nell looked surprised, then mildly guilty. "I forgot he was coming," she said. "He's going down to Turner's Point to the bookmobile with me, and then out for a sandwich or something. I forgot all about it." She stood up and began to stack the books; there were a lot of them, ten or twelve. "We'll drop in to leave Jessie's books after while," she said. "Will you be over there?"

Frank said probably, then explained to Barbara, "Thursday, library-on-wheels day. Nell is Jessie's private librarian, pick-up-and-delivery service. And then we usually get together and gossip. Where are the kids?" he asked Nell.

"Out swimming with Tawna and Celsy, up at McKenzie Bridge Park. They won't be back until six-thirty." She had the books in her arms, ready to leave, but hesitated. "Everyone's been so good. Tawna and James, Celsy, Clive, Doc and Jessie, people in town. . . . They've been so good."

She appeared ready to weep, and Barbara said briskly, "Well, let's go relieve Clive. Now there's a patient man." Actually, she thought cynically, she just wanted to see Nell and Clive together. Was he the one? She was thinking not when she returned to the terrace a few minutes later. Clive was perfectly aware of the invisible line Nell had drawn between them, and he had not violated it by as much as an inch.

"Well?" her father said, watching her over the tops of his glasses.

Why didn't he get contacts, or regular glasses, she thought irritably. "It's a bitch, and you damn well know it. She can't testify."

"I know."

"Did anyone else around here even know him?"

He shrugged. "I never met him. Doc and Jessie might have. And he brought Clive around to give an estimate on the walnut trees seven years ago."

She made an impatient gesture. "Accident? Someone out with a rifle let go a random shot, got him."

104

He shrugged. "Could be, but wrong season. And target practice on private land? Not very likely. But it's possible."

"She doesn't believe Lucas killed that girl. The papers say he left the car on the other side of the mountains and hiked over here. My God! Why? What do you have about all that?"

"Damn little. That was over in Deschutes County. We can find out what they have." He looked thoughtful, then said, "Be better for her to believe he killed that girl, though."

"If she's going for self-defense," Barbara agreed. "But she says she didn't do it, remember?"

"Yep. I remember. Just commenting."

"What about that professor who preyed on Lucas? Emil Frobisher? Anything?"

"Something. But not good. He's dead. Killed by a boy, a prostitute."

"Shit!"

Frank grinned. "I missed my nap. See you later, honey."

"Don't be so damned smug. I haven't made any decisions yet."

She could hear his chuckle as he walked into the house behind her.

TWELVE

FRANK AND BARBARA strolled through the woods to Doc's at five-forty-five. He led on a narrow path, and, watching his easy gait, she thought she had never seen him so healthy, so vigorous. Country living had been good for him. All that walking every day, she added ruefully. Her own legs were aching from the second trip to town that morning. Maybe in a month or so she would be able to keep up with her elderly father.

The woods were wild and completely natural here; no one had trimmed anything except for the trail. This was old-growth forest, the trees massive, the light dim under them; nowhere did visibility extend more than ten or twelve feet as the trail wound and snaked its way in and out of obstacles.

They entered Doc's property on the garage side and walked around the front of the house, which was very nice, she thought again. Wide redwood planks, and floor-to-ceiling glass, the broad deck, partially covered. The land-scaping appeared to be professionally maintained; it had that precision look with broad plantings of azaleas and rhododendrons, and a velvety lawn that looked as if no human foot had ever trod upon it. The view was magnificent, forest and river and sky.

"Hello," Jessie called out. "Now I remember you. Of course, I do. Doc kept telling me we met you a few years ago, but I couldn't bring a face to mind. Now I remember. How nice to see you again."

Doc said hello and what did they want to drink, and Jessie said come sit by me, please. A martini would be good, Barbara said, and when her father said wine she realized suddenly that he was completely off hard liquor. She hadn't thought of it until that minute. He used to drink martinis at lunch, again before dinner. And all that walking, she thought; a thrill of fear coursed through her as she thought of the other changes—no cream, low-fat diet, good healthy food, naps. Unaccountably her fear was replaced by anger.

As if aware that she had not yet engaged Barbara's attention, Jessie reached out and placed her hand on Barbara's arm, and if she hadn't Barbara would not have realized that Doc was the man in Nell's life. At the same moment that Jessie touched her, Nell and Clive appeared on the deck, and for an instant, almost too quickly to be certain about it, Jessie's hand clutched spasmodically. The instant passed, but, because she had been cued, Barbara saw the swift glance Nell and Doc exchanged. Then he was the charming host at the bar again. But there it was, she thought. There it was.

They were all saying hello and how are you and such and Nell came to Jessie and kissed her cheek, and then put several books on a table near her. Jessie moved binoculars to make room for the books.

Doc brought Barbara's drink, and wine for Nell. He took Jessie's glass for a refill. Clive and Frank were chatting about low water in the lake for this time of year. The good life, Barbara thought, happy hour among the nice people. Why Doc? To her eyes he was a tired, middle-aged man who could use a tranquilizer. And he was married to a woman who spent her days in a wheelchair. Jessie was fumbling in a large bag attached to her wheelchair. She brought out a Polaroid camera and asked Barbara if she minded; she liked to keep a photo album of events, Jessie said.

Nell kept glancing at her watch, and after no more than five minutes, she finished her wine and stood up. "I have to go. I promised the kids dinner would be ready the minute they walked in."

Clive was already on his feet. She waved him down. "You stay and talk. Our dinner will be hot dogs and hamburgers." At the disappointed look on his face, she said, "You would hate it. And the kids will be cranky and worn out. You know how it is when you've been swimming all afternoon. Early dinner, early baths, early bed. Why don't you come over tomorrow night? I'll cook something real."

"Let me drive you home," he said.

She shook her head. "That would be supremely silly, now, wouldn't it? It's five minutes. And I like the walk." She picked up the books she had separated out, waved to them all, and left.

There was silence until she was out of sight around the end of the deck. As soon as she was gone, Clive looked at Frank. "I'd like to talk to you sometime," he said.

107

"All right. Nothing wrong with now."

"Alone."

Doc sat down in the chair Nell had left and regarded Clive. "If it's about what you were telling me earlier, you might as well go ahead. I already told Jessie about it."

Clive's quick glance at Barbara was involuntary, she felt certain, and only a tinge of bitterness damped her amusement when he tried to pretend it had not happened, that he had been adjusting his shoulders or something. She had seen that kind of quick rejection too many times to miss it. What he had said with that reflexive look was that she should find something to do elsewhere and let him and her father get on with it. She settled back more comfortably to watch him with a steadiness that she knew he would find disconcerting.

"Well," Frank said meditatively, "you can make an appointment and I'll charge regular office-hour fees, or you can unload here and now and keep it on a neighborly basis. Your choice." He finished drinking his wine and looked at Clive over his glasses, his lawyerly look. "You should know that anything that concerns the law, I'll probably pass on to Barbara, unless it's too boring to bother her with. After all, she is a partner."

Barbara did not turn to glare at him over that last comment but continued to watch Clive, who was startled, and that meant, she added to herself, that Nell had not told him much about the long interrogation that afternoon.

Clive hesitated a moment, then said carefully, "Frank, I think you know how highly we all value you around here. We trust you, and we come to you for legal help without reservation. You've done good things for many of us. But I think Nell needs to bring in someone else to defend her." He walked to the table outfitted as a bar and helped himself to bourbon.

"All right," Frank said.

"What do you mean? You agree?"

"No. I mean you stated your opinion, and it's all right for you to have that opinion. Couldn't prevent it in any case."

Clive's face darkened, and abruptly he sat down. "Frank,

108

damn it, I'm scared out of my wits for her! She needs someone with great trial experience, someone younger, someone who can stand up to Tony DeAngelo. I asked around about him. He's a son of a bitch, and he's out to win!"

Barbara had fused right into the chair. She did not look at Frank because she could not move. She should have known. Maybe she had known from the start and simply had not let herself think about it, had not let herself even breathe the name.

". . . no more than most prosecutors . . . faced him before. . . ."

Her father's mild rejoinder seemed disconnected, words free-floating all around her, and then Clive was saying something else just as disjointed. Gradually she felt that she was separating from the chair, felt that her blood was circulating again, that her skin felt clammy from the breeze coming in from the river, not from any internal system that had gone haywire. She lifted her glass and saw that her hand was not trembling, and although she did not look at him to confirm it, she knew her father was watching her, that she had passed a test of some kind.

"Barbara is young, and she's faced Tony down, too. Several times, in fact."

"But for something like this, a murder charge. . . ." Clive stopped helplessly and turned to Doc, who shrugged.

Barbara set her glass down and said in a good, crisp voice, her court voice, "Mr. Belloc, when a client hires an attorney, that relationship cannot be put aside by a third person. If Nell decides she wants different counsel, that desire will be sacrosanct, but unless she decides that, no outside influence will be tolerated by our firm. I am fully qualified to defend a client against a charge of murder. Actually, Mr. Belloc, the phrase is death qualified. I am fully death qualified. Dad, shall we be on our way now?"

Jessie protested. They had to stay for dinner, she said, but her insistence was feeble. She had blanched at the phrase *death qualified*. Doc shook hands with Barbara and studied her face for several seconds before he released her. She

109

could tell nothing from his expression. Clive stood up and said nothing at all as she and her father left them. Clive, she thought with satisfaction, was mad as hell. Tough, she also thought; so was she. Madder maybe.

As soon as they were out of range, Frank said, "He'll ask around about you now."

"Let him. Just who does he know to ask, by the way? Who'd he want, Clarence Darrow?"

Frank took her arm, laughing. "Let's go out somewhere and eat, somewhere fancy with good wine."

She nodded. If she asked him why he hadn't brought up Tony's name, she knew he would say something like, why expect anything to change around here? And why indeed?"

In the middle of a dinner that Frank said was excellent and she had hardly tasted, she put down her fork, put her elbows on the table and her chin on her clenched fists, and said, "Okay. On one condition."

"Which is?"

"My way, from start to finish. I'm not an assistant; it's my case."

He put his own fork down and reached across the table. "Deal."

They shook hands, and then she began to eat her lamb brochette, which really was excellent. Before he resumed his meal, Frank said, "Honey, I wouldn't have brought up his name before you were already committed. I want you because I think you can do that girl some good. Understood?"

She nodded. No vendetta, no revenge, no lingering hatred to cloud her judgment. Like hell, she thought.

It was after ten when they arrived back at the house. She started to pace, but that was too strenuous, her legs reacted with alarm signals of pain, and she had to settle for a chair in the living room. Frank watched her for a short time; when she didn't offer to talk, to ask anything, he yawned and said he was ready to pack it in.

110

"Tell me something about Clive first," she said, as if only then remembering him. "How long has he been sniffling around Nell like that?"

Frank laughed. "My God, you haven't learned to tone it down a bit, have you? Couple of years, probably. Got divorced about four or five years ago. I filed for him. No big deal, they just decided the grass was greener, that kind of thing. They probably get together over a beer now and then. But it turned him loose, and a few months later, I noticed how the hairs on his arms reacted when Nell came anywhere near him. You also saw that she's not interested, not really. He tells people which trees to cut, you see."

"He appraised her walnut trees for Lucas. So he knows the value of them."

"Honey, everyone in this county who knows anything knows that."

"I guess so. Lucas is the key. Where was he all those years? And where was he from Tuesday until he turned up around here on Saturday? Who are you using for investigations these days?"

"Bailey Novell, like always."

"Okay. He's slow, but he can do it. Someone has to find out who ordered that fir tree cut down."

Frank shook his head. "You're jumpier than a flea tonight. Why that? Why now?"

"Because Tony will find out, and if it was Lucas, it's another nail in her coffin. If he can build up a strong enough motive, he may force us to put her on the stand. He'd like that."

Frank remembered that evening on Doc's terrace. Slowly he said, "At first she was sure it was Chuck Gilmore." Barbara made an impatient gesture, and he went on. "I know. I know. Real stupid, too stupid for him. I think we convinced her of that, and suddenly she jumped up and had to rush home. I think she must have thought at that moment that it might have been Lucas. She just might have had that thought pop into her head."

"Probably. I sure thought of it. I want Bailey to get on it

111

as soon as he can. And I want the names of everyone connected with whatever that project was that Emil Frobisher was working on. And I want to know if Lucas was gay. What else?" She frowned, staring ahead at nothing, thinking. "I want to talk to John Kendricks myself. And the sheriff over in Deschutes County."

Frank came to her chair and kissed her forehead. "And I want to go to bed. Call Bailey in the morning. Your case. Give him marching orders."

"I will. What's the limit, Dad? Do I have to check in for expenses?"

"No limit. Whatever it takes, and you sure as hell never checked in for expenses in the past. Why start a precedent now?"

Still staring off at nothing, she didn't really acknowledge his answer, and she didn't hear his "Good night" a second later.

A bit later, she started, "Do we have a tame . . . ?" Belatedly she realized she was alone. The rest of the question had been "renaissance scientist," someone who could understand a project that involved a world-class mathematician, a computer nut, a psychiatrist, and God alone knew who else. She stood up, but instead of going to her room she went out to the terrace and sat down again.

She watched the lights go off in a few cabins, the rest of them were already dark, and then there were only the dim flickering lights from the parking lot and store. They looked lonesome. The river was invisible; the woods had vanished into solid darkness. And now, alone, almost as if she had waited until the rest of the world was sleeping, she permitted herself to consider Tony DeAngelo.

She had not been prepared for a man like Tony— intense, passionate, ambitious. His first big case after being hired at the district attorney's office had been her last case, and he had won. She could admit that. He had won. He had left her in bed, left her drowsy, languid with love, and had gone to her client to make a deal. She could admit that now.

At the time she had accused her father of initiating the deal, but that had been wrong. It was Tony. And he had used ammunition furnished by her. Now she could even admit that she had been stupid, a blind fool, a romantic who thought that love came wrapped in trust, beribboned with absolute confidence. She had been too stupid not to give trust and confidences, and she had thought she was receiving them in turn. She had defeated the state's cases three times out, with Tony prosecuting each one, and she had believed him when he avowed respect and even awe at her skill.

"You're good," he had said, taking her by the shoulders, gazing intently into her eyes. "My God, but you're good!" Soon after that they had become lovers.

There had been a recklessness about him that she had taken for courage, a ruthless drive that she had taken for strength. Her mother was dying; her father's strength carefully marshaled hour by hour, to be spent daily on his dying wife. Nothing had been left over for her, Barbara, who had felt thrust out, abandoned, and terrified. She had turned her back on them, left them to each other, all either ever needed, and immersed herself in work, in Tony, until much later.

"What are you talking about?" Tony had yelled at the end. "This has nothing to do with us, nothing personal. I didn't get sore when you beat me."

"It has everything to do with us. Why didn't you tell me you were assigned to my case?"

"Because it didn't make any difference. You work to save them. I work to prosecute. What's the difference? We both know he's guilty as hell. Don't try to ride that unicorn around me."

"You could have got all four!"

"Could have, maybe. But I fucking well know I got one. And that's what counts, not could haves or maybes. And I got my one without a trial."

"And next week, next month, tomorrow, are you going to sneak around behind my back again? Is that the only way you can see to get even? Do we need to even the score and then start fresh?"

"You think I give a shit about those penny-ante cases? Get real! This was the big one, the one that got me noticed."

"Get out! Just get out."

"Come on, Barbara, calm down. We've got a neat thing going. We make a good bed pair. Let's keep our professional life and personal life in two categories and get on with things."

"Just get the hell out of my house!"

"Okay. Okay. I'll look for an apartment. Now calm down, for Christ sake!"

"Now! Right now!"

He shook his head and started to walk toward the kitchen. She grabbed his briefcase, a tooled leather case with brass fittings, much more expensive than anything she owned, and she swung it as hard as she could and heaved it through the living room window.

"Now!"

His face turned a deep red, a narrow-eyed mean look added sharpness to his already sharp features, his fists clenched. She picked up a bottle of wine he had brought in—to celebrate with, she supposed—and heaved it out after the briefcase. He opened his hands and stared at them, then at her, and he left.

Until that second she had not fully realized how hard he was working to control his anger, and in that second when he had gazed at his own hands, he had appeared afraid. She also realized when the door slammed that she had wanted him to hit her, to fight with her, because she had wanted so desperately to hit him and hurt him.

She had sent him a note: I'm taking off for a week. Get your stuff out of my apartment before I get back. And she had gone to the coast to think things through only to find that she was unable to think. She walked, she watched waves roll in, watched sea gulls in flight, ate seafood, and had not a single coherent thought.

When she told her father goodbye, he had been incredulous. "Over one lousy case? Your client turned chicken, and you know it. It had nothing to do with you."

114

He had said often that the law was a game and the state had the high cards, had the power; it was their job, his and hers, to bring a little balance to the world. She had believed that. That night she had interrupted him to ask, "Did you ever box? Do any violent sport?"

He had looked bewildered. "You know better than that."

"Yes, I do. But those games, Christians and lions, two boxers out to destroy each other's brain, war games, nuclear armaments games, they're games only as long as people are willing to play them, other people are willing to watch and finance them. I don't want to play any longer."

For five years she had not played. And now, sitting thoroughly chilled on the terrace in the dark forest, she did not know why she was in again. Her token was on the board; she was committed. In her head she heard the voice of a judge who had come to lecture her senior class: "The one thing an attorney must not do is use his clients to satisfy his own needs, whether those needs are noble or base, whether they are cloaked in the purest, most pristine robes of justice or wrapped in gutter rags, whether they are the true revelation from the Almighty or issue from the lips of Satan. An attorney's role demands that he put aside his own needs and serve only the needs of his client."

She had fumed at all the *he*'s and *his*'s, but she had remembered. She had remembered most clearly when Tony had yelled, "You think I did it just to feather my own nest? Is that what you think? Well, honey, I've got news for you. That's what we're all in it for. You, me, your father, every one of us. You think you can twist your own clients into helping you reform the world, and it ain't gonna happen, doll. It doesn't mean a fucking thing to them if you put another little chink in the dam. You want to do good, join the Salvation Army, put on a nun's habit and save souls, go dish out wheat in Ethiopia, set up a storefront counseling service in a slum. Just keep out of the way of those who have a job to do and intend to do it."

In Vermont that winter, watching the snow pile up, she had come to accept that he had nailed her. She had used

115

people in trouble for her own ends. Victim or victimizer, or bystander, no other roles were available. Yet here she was in again, and she didn't know why.

It would be comforting, she thought, to believe she was doing it for Nell's sake, to believe that she alone could save her. Nell was like a forest creature, tough and self-sufficient in her own world, and doomed to a merciless death outside it. She tried to imagine Nell under the kind of examination Tony would subject her to, and shook her head. But even thinking this, she had to admit to herself that she was not in it for Nell's sake. Nor for her father's. He was right in saying he couldn't handle it, but she was not the only one who could. Not because she feared for his health suddenly, certain now that he must have had a warning sign that made him change his habits completely. But not for that. Not for revenge. She had really decided before Tony's name had surfaced, and unless at an unconscious level she had already determined that she had to face him in court, he had not influenced her decision. But something had, and she could not name what it was. She felt that from the moment she had heard her father's voice on her answering machine, she had been committed, exactly as if a line had been cast, and she had been hooked; in spite of her denials and twisting and struggling, she had been reeled in inexorably.

A deep shudder passed through her, and abruptly she stood up. It was too cold, she thought, entering the house, denying to herself that the shudder had started from within.

THIRTEEN

ON FRIDAY BARBARA talked to Bailey Novell and told him what she wanted—no one, two, three, she said, but all at once, immediately. He grinned. He was a wiry man, five feet six or seven, with prominent sinews and long, snaky muscles—a runner. She was remembering: Everyone in Oregon ran, or hiked, or skied, or cycled, or most likely, did all.

That afternoon she set up a makeshift office in the dining room. She put a leaf in the table and brought in a gooseneck lamp, arranged her computer and paper, and was ready to start work.

On the way home from their walk to town on Saturday, Barbara paused at the entrance to the private road to eye the dirt road that looked impassable for a wheeled vehicle.

"How far up is it to the trail to the waterfall?" she asked Frank.

"Not half a mile, I'd say."

"You always say that. Think I'll have a look. Want to come?"

"Part of the way, then I'll sit and read my paper."

The road was as bad as it looked, with great rocks strewn about, and deep ruts with cracked dirt in them; they would become mud traps after a rain. The road twisted and turned so much that during the half mile or more they walked upon it at no place was there visibility for more than a hundred

117

feet in either direction. The forest was very dense on both sides, with brambles and huckleberries crowding the road- way.

"Can anyone really drive it?" she muttered after a few minutes.

"Sure. Four-wheel drive and off you go. Used to be able to go clear over the mountain all the way to Bachelor Butte, but last year or so, it's been getting a bit rough, and last spring there was a washout just about on the county line. On this side they say Deschutes County should fix it, and over there they say we should. Or the state. Or someone. Hikers say leave it be, let it be an east/west foot trail."

They crossed a narrow one-way bridge and immediately came upon a hairpin turn. She eyed the road with distrust. A killer road, she thought. Then Frank stopped and pointed.

"There's your trail. Down there it branches at the head of the waterfall; left fork's a dead end at the ledge, right fork down to Nell's side of the ledge, and on down to her place. As for me, I'll be around here somewhere." He glanced about, spotted a fallen tree whose diameter was nearly as high as he was, with a great branch that formed a natural seat with backrest. He grinned. "Right there. See you later."

"That bad, huh?" she said morosely, gazing at the trail. It didn't look so terrible—narrow, but no harder going than the road, it seemed.

"Getting down's no trouble," Frank said, settling himself comfortably.

She started. Within a dozen paces, her father was lost from view, and there was no sound, no wind, no scurrying of small creatures, and practically no sunlight. Forest primeval, black forest, impenetrable woods—she remembered descrip- tions she had read by early explorers of the northwest, remembered how the Europeans had feared the black forests of northern Europe up to modern times almost. She could sympathize; people did not belong in the dense, dark forests that seemed to hold their breath at human intrusion. The trail started to descend, and she knew what her father had meant by saying going down was no trouble. The way

118

became steeper; she found herself holding onto tree trunks, testing for safe footing step by step. Never in wet weather, she muttered under her breath; go in on your butt when the trail was mud-slicked.

For some time she had been hearing the music of the little stream, Halleck Creek, but it was invisible off to her right until she came to a level area, and the stream was there. Although it was not very deep, inches only, and six feet wide, it had cut a gorge, three feet at least and twice as wide as the water. In the spring, with snow melt, the gorge would be filled; even now at the end of summer the stream raced furiously, tumbling, falling, swirling around rocks with white-water sprays. Up ahead there was a rail fence. On the other side of it the trees parted; massive rocks had been uncovered and now sheltered luxuriant ferns. The waterfall.

Nearer the waterfall a tree had fallen across the creek, a natural bridge. She did not cross it but went to the fence and looked down. The water fell two hundred feet here, straight down into a boiling pot. The trail she had followed continued downward through the woods; on the other side of the bridge she could make out a second trail.

She frowned. She would have to cover each trail, she knew, and this side was as good a place as the other to start. Doggedly she continued downward. She already knew what she faced in climbing back up, and she might as well finish.

The trail got no better, but neither did it get worse, she added quickly, almost as if trying to convince herself that getting back up to the road would be possible. Then she reached the wide level area of the rock ledge.

She looked around it carefully; the trail she had used was the only access from above, and apparently there was no trail down from this side. Dead end. She repeated the words and walked to the edge where she looked down at the creek far below. Then she studied the other side, twenty-five feet away, across the chasm. It appeared to be identical to this side, except for size—barren, rocky, a couple of tree trunks, boulders, some straggly vines that looked dead. She backed up to a boulder and sat down, gazing at the opposite side.

119

She had hoped to find a possible alternative to where the killer had been, she realized. Or, if not that, a route the killer could have taken to the ledge. She discarded both hopes. Not from over here. Nell would have seen anyone on this side; there was no place to hide, no way to cross the gorge.

She could not see the trail Nell had used to climb up to the clearing, or the one that came down from the waterfall, but from where she sat in deep gloom, it didn't seem plausible that someone could have come down that trail at exactly the right time to catch Lucas in a gunsight. And at exactly the same moment that Nell had taken the last step up.

"Ah, Tony," she breathed at last, "is it going to be your game again?"

She would have to go over to the other side, but not today, and not from the top down. She would go up from Nell's. From where she sat brooding there really did not seem much point in it. She did not see how she could convince a jury that coincidentally three different people had appeared at this one isolated place at the same moment: victim, killer, and innocent bystander. Always the same division, she thought then. It always came back to the same division.

She heaved herself upright and took a deep breath, then started back up the trail.

By the time she reached the top again, she was drenched, her legs throbbed and burned, and she felt that every breath was too difficult to complete. She stopped in the woods for several minutes to rest before she emerged to see Frank leaning against the tree trunk where she had left him.

"Wasn't going to call out the rescue team for another ten minutes or so," he said cheerfully.

"It wasn't so bad."

"You always sweat right through your jeans like that?"

Her shirt was clinging to her back; her legs were sticking to the wet jeans; her hair was wet through.

They started to walk slowly, and she was thinking that it was better to move, because once she stopped she might never want to move again.

"Couple of questions," Frank said. "If someone was

following Lucas aiming to shoot him, why didn't he do it before? Why wait until he got to that ledge? And he must have been following pretty close, or how did he know Lucas went down that way? So he must have been visible. And the next question is why did Lucas stop for sightseeing on his way home? He knew that ledge, nothing there to hold his interest."

They walked in silence for several minutes until she asked, "When did you go down there?"

"June. Wanted to see for myself, same as you."

"Anyone go with you?"

"Now, Bobby, no nagging, no checking up. Okay?"

Alone, she thought with a tight feeling in her throat. She said nothing; no nagging for now. But soon they had to talk. Soon. She began to think of the coming days, a trip into Eugene to the library, to the newspaper morgue, to the university maybe. On Monday a trek over the mountain to meet Lucas Kendricks's parents, to quiz his father in particular. And to meet and quiz the sheriff. Busy day. But for now, she wanted to stretch out and not move. By afternoon, no doubt, she would feel like death, and on into tomorrow, but by Monday back to work, if she had to rent a wheelchair, or borrow one from Jessie. She made a slight face. She and Frank were going to Jessie and Doc's for dinner that evening.

The drive over the mountains was pleasant early Monday morning, but the day was going to be hot. Barbara had thought she had been overheated from the strenuous climb on Friday, and that had been partly the reason, but also, a heat wave had rolled in from eastern Oregon, and Saturday and Sunday it intensified until the thermometer had climbed to ninety-five on Frank's terrace. Today was going to be even hotter.

Frank drove slowly through the village of Sisters on the eastern slope of the mountain. The village had been done over in modern Americana tourist, he said drily, and didn't comment further except to point out the café where the two girls had met Lucas Kendricks, the grocery store where he had picked up camping food, and a sporting goods store

121

where he had bought other camping gear, a propane stove, a water bottle, things like that. He sped up as soon as they left the village behind. Now the forests were open, airy pine forests with an occasional juniper tree, and undergrowth that became sparse as they traveled toward the high desert country. It was very dry; dust swirled in gusts created by traffic. Widely spaced sage brush plants were dusty and listless-looking.

In the town of Bend, Frank drove straight to the county building where the sheriff's office was located. It seemed that minute by minute the air was becoming hotter and drier. Few people were on the streets, few in the building when they entered. A uniformed officer directed them to the office where the sheriff was waiting for them.

"Ms. Holloway, Mr. Holloway? Timothy LeMans. Come in. Come on in," he said in a kindly way. "Too hot out here for anything." He was a tall, rectangular block of a man, as solid-looking as the mountains, with scant gray hair and a deeply sunburned complexion. He was dressed in cowboy clothes: embroidered shirt, dungarees, high boots, even a silver buckle on a wide, heavy belt. He held the door and they entered an air-conditioned suite of rooms where a couple of people were working at computers, others at typewriters.

"In here," the sheriff said, holding another door open. This room was comfortably outfitted with upholstered furniture in tan slipcovers; the sheriff's desk was bare.

Barbara glanced around, then stopped to look closer. On the walls were many pictures of the sheriff in a tuxedo, holding a viol; one was a group picture of a symphony orchestra. One of the pictures was of him and three others, two of them women, all in formal wear. It was labeled: Bach Festival, Eugene, Oregon, 1987.

Although his eyes were twinkling when she turned to face him, he said nothing about the pictures but shook her hand in a firm, no-way-competitive grip. "Hate meeting people in the hall," he said, repeating his name. "There now,

122

that makes it official." She could feel her tension oozing away before she was seated.

Barbara glanced at her father, who was simply waiting. Her game. She said, "Sheriff, as I mentioned on the phone, we represent Nell Kendricks, and there are a lot of questions about what happened during the days before her husband turned up on her land."

He was nodding. "First thing," he said, "guess it's only right to tell you I've known John and Amy Kendricks all my life, known their family, and their family's families, too. Doesn't make me altogether unbiased, you see. John and I have been friends for a long, long time."

"I think that can only help," Barbara said. "Nell doesn't believe Lucas killed that girl."

"Anything to go on besides that? Just what she thinks?"

"I'm afraid not much. She said when she saw him he was too happy to have something like that on his mind. He was laughing."

Sheriff LeMans had seated himself on the edge of his desk, one leg swinging; now he stood up and went to one of the walls with a roll-up map. He pulled it down.

"I'll give you what we know," he said. "Lucas showed up at his dad's place Monday night, June fifth. Left Tuesday morning about eight-thirty." He pointed to a spot on the map south of Bend. His fingers were broad; they looked too thick to play an instrument of any sort. "He stopped for gas here in Bend, paid cash, and next thing he shows up in Sisters." He traced the road. "At twenty before ten he was buying camping gear including topo maps of the Sisters Wilderness, then the supermarket for food, and then he went to the café where he got coffee and a Danish."

He took his hand away from the map and studied the floor for a second or two. "The girls were in the café before he showed up, laughing, giggling, being silly. There's pictures of the llamas on the café walls, and they were going on about them, didn't believe anyone out here had llamas, like that. Three, four people in the café were kidding around with them. The girls were from Austin, Texas, on their way to Alaska, hiking, hitching rides, going by bus, camping out, having themselves a real ball. That day they were going to go on into Eugene by bus, but it wasn't due in Sisters until late afternoon, so they had plenty of time. Anyway, in comes this guy that no one knows, and he says he's going to pass right by the Eagleton place if they want a ride out there. It's early enough to ride out there, look around, and then walk back to town, a couple of miles, in time to make their bus, and that's what they decide to do. No one gives much thought to it. He seems nice enough, and two girls, with one guy driving, all that. Besides Tyler Drury made a point of taking down the license number, and the guy just grins, like it's a big joke." He turned back to the map and pointed again.

"That's the Eagleton place, and on the way there they got to talking and the guy told them he was going over the mountain, be on the other side by early afternoon, and one of the girls decides she'd rather do that than hang out in Sisters most of the day. The other one, Candy, wants to take pictures of the llamas. So they split. Candy was going to walk back to Sisters after she got the pictures, catch the bus later on, and be at a friend's house in Eugene that evening. The other one, Janet Moseley, left with the guy."

The car, he went on, pointing as he traced its route, headed out one of the forest service roads, over a crushed red lava roadway, and made it all the way to the lava beds, probably went in a bit beyond the county line, and then had to come back out because the road had washed out. When they found the car it was headed back the way it had gone in, so Lucas must have turned around and at least started out that way.

His voice went altogether flat then. "Whatever happened, happened at the car. We found some of her clothes on the ground by it, a boot under the car, blood on the ground. She had a broken jaw, two teeth broken all the way out. Her neck was broken, and she had a deep gash on the side of her head. She got hit real hard, and fell real hard. Raped, sodomized, torn up pretty bad inside."

124

He stopped and didn't continue this time until Frank said, "The news stories said she was mutilated."

"I know what they said. I'll tell you the rest, but it's not for the papers. Agreed?" They both nodded. "Right. He, whoever it was, tied her hands together and dragged her by the rope over the lava bed to the other side where the mountain starts going down and tossed her in the creek over there."

"Oh, dear God," Barbara whispered. "Was she still alive?"

"Yes. Probably unconscious, maybe paralyzed from the broken neck. But she was alive and bleeding bad much of the way. Bleeding stopped finally, when she died, the medical examiner said, but she was cut up, lacerated, damn near skinned before she ever reached the creek."

Suddenly the air-conditioned room was like a freezer. Barbara hugged her arms about herself.

"I'll get us some coffee," Sheriff LeMans said, and strode from the room.

Neither spoke again until he returned. The coffee was terrible, but it was hot. The sheriff watched Barbara shrewdly, and after she had swallowed a bit of the steaming coffee he said, "We know she was still alive at about one o'clock. She was taking pictures. Photographer here said the shadows were one o'clock shadows. Of course, *he* could have taken them, but her prints were on the camera, no one else's."

"But how did she end up in the McKenzie River?" Barbara asked.

"That part's easy enough. In June all those creeks were high with runoff. And they all end up draining into the McKenzie on that side of the pass. Took a couple of days, but it was bound to happen sooner or later."

"And Lucas? What next on him?"

"Nothing definite. We put trackers to work on it and found where he probably camped each night. I say probably because all we can be sure of is that someone camped in those places during that time. Here's the first one." Again his thick, competent finger landed on the map, this time across the county line in Lane County.

"How far is that?" Frank asked in surprise. "Too far to get in an afternoon?"

Sheriff LeMans shrugged. "Depends on who you are and how much hiking you've done and how recently, and how well you know the country, and how much a rush you're in. Funny thing, though. When Lucas turned up dead, I called the medical examiner and asked a few questions, and I don't think Lucas was in that good shape. Hard-worked hands, calluses, but not muscular like a hiker. And he was wearing work boots, not hiking boots. No traction, no support. His feet were badly blistered and infected. But there's not a sign of a camp before that one, and believe me, we looked."

He pointed out the campsites for the next three nights, and then he went around his desk and sat down regarding them both with a sober expression.

"Now, that's what I know, like I said. But there are some funny things, real funny things, going on. And I don't know what to make of them. First off, a guy comes in here and hires the same tracker we use to retrace the route Lucas must have taken. Pays good money, too much money. Just goes in and looks, takes pictures for a book he says he intends to write about the crime. So our guy thinks okay, nothing wrong with making a buck. But I got curious and I went back a week, two weeks after that, and every single campsite has been torn apart. Looks to us as if three or four guys went in there searching for something, and they hit every spot where he landed."

"What about the car?" Barbara asked after a moment.

Sheriff LeMans nodded. "Same thing. We kept it for the lab boys to go over and then released it to John. Nell, she said she didn't want it, to let him do whatever he wanted. So he and Amy came over and he drove it home. That night someone ripped it apart, took off upholstery, ripped up the floor boards, made a real mess. They did it very quietly, didn't make a sound. And," he said more slowly, "after that happened John told me that when he and Amy came home, after Lucas was killed, and they were up near Pendleton at the time, but when they got home the house had been ransacked. He hadn't mentioned it before because what was the point? They thought vandals, kids, dopeheads, something like that. Now he doesn't think so."

Barbara felt there was too much to think about. She didn't even know what questions she wanted to ask yet. It didn't make any sense. None of it made any sense. "Who could have known the body would end up in the river, in the lake? He must have intended to hide it. But that's crazy because he knew someone had taken down his license number."

"Not as crazy as it sounds," the sheriff said. "The license was stolen, and the battery. Both from a Corvette down in Colorado, a psychiatrists's car. She was in England at the time."

Barbara shook her head. Battery? She let that go for the moment. "Of course, that water would have washed away a lot of evidence, semen, for example. But from what you say, rape was clearly evident?"

"No mistake about that. But you're right, no semen, no blood."

"What else then? The time of death? When was the time of death?"

"The cold water makes that almost impossible. All we've got for sure are the pictures taken at one, and the fact that he made camp before dark and took at least eight hours to reach it. Ten's more like it, if you ask me, but that's opinion, not fact."

She looked at him sharply, studied his broad face. "You don't think he did it?"

"That's opinion, too," he said without hesitation. "Not the Lucas I used to know. Not dragging a girl over that lava like that. Not the sock in the jaw hard enough to break her neck, her jaw, and two teeth. He didn't have any marks on his hands, by the way, but he could have used a rock, or a branch, something. River washed away that kind of evidence, too."

127

Barbara remembered all the accounts she had read of the murder and asked, "You haven't closed the case, have you?"

"Nope."

Unhappily she gazed at the map. The contour lines revealed the steepness of the terrain out there, and again she thought of Halleck Hill Road with no visibility more than a hundred feet. "How did anyone happen to find the car? Seems it could have stayed hidden for months."

"Ranger spotted it." He put his long, square finger on the map again. "See here, Route 242, they call it the Scenic Route these days. Crookeder than a coon dog's hind leg. Anyway, here on the pass there's an observatory built out of lava, in the middle of the lava fields. From the building you can see Mt. Jefferson, Black Butte, the North Sister, Three Finger Jack. . . . There are slits in the walls with names so you know what you're looking at, but for folks from these parts, it's just a good place to stop for a bite to eat, coffee, and to have a look around. We mostly all do it, no matter how many times we've been up that way. So this ranger is going to stop up there and eat his lunch, have his coffee, and naturally he has his binoculars. He's taking a look around, and he spots something that's out of place. Right about here." He pointed south of the pass. "It's ten miles downhill, but a trick of the sun made it possible, I guess. Sun flashing off the chrome of a car in a place where a car shouldn't be. And by then, of course, everyone was on the lookout for the girl and the car. At first he thought the car was in trouble where the road washed last spring. So anyway he called in, and other guys closer to the spot went in and found it." He nodded at the map. "Used to be that road wound in and out of the lava beds and joined up with forest service roads or logging roads and you could make it all the way in to Eugene eventually. Guess you still can, but on foot these days."

"Sheriff," Barbara said then, "thanks. You've been more than generous. I appreciate it."

"I'd guess you won't want to call me as a witness," he said, and again a shrewd glint was in his eyes.

"You'd guess right. At least at this point."

"Well, when you called, I figured you'd want some of the stuff we've got together. Autopsy report on the girl, times, a map, things of that sort. I got it together in case." He pulled a large manila envelope from his desk and slid it across to her.

"Is the name of the tracker in here?"

He nodded.

"And the psychiatrist in Colorado, the one whose plates he stole?"

For the first time he was surprised. "Afraid not. But it's an easy name to remember. Brandywine. Dr. Ruth Brandywine."

FOURTEEN

THE KENDRICKS FARM was nearly twenty miles out of Bend. As they drove, Barbara remembered spending a week out on the high desert in her elementary school days. A field trip to Malheur Preserve where shallow, salty lakes had been swarming with birds, egrets, whooping cranes, even pelicans; she could no longer remember all the different species, but at the time it had seemed miraculous to travel over the desert and find waterfowl by the thousands. Today there was no sign of birds; the desert was dun-colored as far as she could see, dead-looking as far as she could see, and always ringed with the never-ending buttes and mountains. Wherever you are out here, she thought suddenly, you're in the middle of a ring of mountains.

The roads were like systems of veins, the main trunk, a U.S. highway, then a state road, now a smaller one still, and from there they turned again onto a gravel driveway. And now the nerve center, she thought, when they came to a stop before the farm house. It was painted white, neatly maintained, and shaded with tired cottonwood trees that drooped in the heat.

Amy Kendricks met them on the porch. She said hello to Frank and took Barbara's hand in both of hers and held it while she studied Barbara's face. She was a capable woman, Barbara thought, not fat, but strong with muscular arms and strong, firm hands. She was deeply sunburned; her hair was streaked with gray, cut short. As soon as her husband appeared, her suntan looked almost like pallor compared with his. He was like a tree trunk, brown, hard, deeply carved. He shook hands with Frank, said hello to Barbara, but did not offer her his hand.

"Come in," Amy said then. "I made up some iced tea. It's cooler inside, but not very much."

It felt a lot cooler at first. The house was dim; the blinds and drapes were closed against the glare and heat, and a large fan hummed on the floor. The overstuffed furniture was covered with pale green and tan cotton covers; it was a very comfortable room with books on tables, flowers in a vase, and everywhere pictures of the children, of Nell, of another couple with children, no doubt her daughter and family. . . . There was one of Nell and a man who must have been Lucas; Barbara looked at that picture with interest; he looked as bland and innocent as a schoolboy.

A pitcher of iced tea and glasses were on a tray on a coffee table. Amy began to pour; she looked at Frank. "Sugar, lemon?" Then, while she was adding a slice of lemon to his glass, she said, as if addressing the tea tray, "You should know, Ms. Holloway, Nell is relieved that you'll be helping out. And we think of Nell as our daughter. We love her like a daughter. Both of us."

John Kendricks looked somewhat embarrassed, but he nodded.

"We just want you to know," Amy went on, forgetting now to busy her hands with the tea things, "she has our complete support and confidence. We'll do anything at all that we can to help her and the children. Anything." She went back to pouring tea for them all, and apparently it demanded her complete concentration. She let her husband recount what happened the night that Lucas showed up.

As it turned out, they were able to add little if anything to what Barbara and Frank already had heard from others. He had shown up exhausted, road dirty, unshaved. They already had had their dinner, but Amy fixed dinner for him while he showered and shaved. He kept his backpack with him and didn't seem to have anything except that. He had acted like a man on the run, spooked by a car in the driveway, jumpy as a jackrabbit.

"About the pack," Barbara said, interrupting John. "What kind was it? Big, on a frame? What?"

"Not one like hikers carry all their gear in for a week or two in the mountains, but bigger than a day pack." He held up his hands indicating midway between the two types.

"Did you pick it up?"

He shook his head. "Amy started to reach for it, and he was there quick as a flash, got it first. It wasn't filled to the top, not bulging like some you see. Can't say much more than that about it because I wasn't paying that much attention then. And we didn't pressure him to talk because we took it for granted that he'd be here for a couple of days, time enough to catch up the next day. He was too tired to talk Monday night. Nearly fell asleep before he was done eating. And Tuesday morning he took off again." He finished with a dull voice and looked at the water running dizzily down the side of the pitcher on the table.

"And he didn't know about Carol?" Barbara asked. "How did you tell him?"

Amy touched her husband's hand, and she said, "He went to the mantel, the pictures. And he said, who's the little girl. I thought he'd pass out when I told him it was his daughter."

131

"Was that Monday night?"

"Tuesday morning. I don't think he saw anything Monday night. I thought, the way he acted, that he meant to go straight over there and see Nell, see his children. He said he had to leave right now, this minute, and not to say he'd been here if anyone asked. And I just assumed he meant to go home and see the daughter he never even knew he had." For the first time the hurt that Amy was carrying surfaced; she looked down swiftly, her eyes filling with tears.

There was very little more. As they got up to leave, Barbara asked, "What about his car when he got here? Did he put it in the garage, seem concerned about it?"

"Nope," John Kendricks answered. "Didn't even lock it." He drew in a breath and said, "Whatever those people were looking for had to be in the pack. And it didn't weigh much; he carried it over his arm real easy like."

Frank cleared his throat; when Barbara glanced at him, he said, "Nothing about searching the house or the car came out at the grand jury hearing. Nothing about the backpack. Just when he showed up here and when he left. And the fact that no one told Nell when to expect him. Tony got a bit testy about that, in fact."

"He tried to make me say I warned her he'd be there on Saturday, that's why I wanted the kids out on Friday. But I never said that. I didn't know where he was, why he hadn't already showed up."

"They'll pound on that nail again," Barbara said in warning. They left then, after Barbara told them she would be back before the trial started. And would they help or hinder the trial, she wondered, settling herself in the Buick once more. Help, she decided; it would be too unnatural for parents to maintain loyalty to a daughter-in-law who they believed had killed their son. And Tony would say, for the sake of the innocent grandchildren, they would try to protect her. She leaned back and closed her eyes as the car raised a cloud of dust.

"You want some lunch?" Frank asked when they were back on the highway. It was over a hundred degrees. She shook her head. "Me too. Let's head for the mountains, Sisters."

Dust devils danced across the drab wheat fields, water mirages teased on the blacktop road, and the heat mounted. Barbara's lips were so dry they felt as if they were cracking. It would be cooler in the mountains, she told herself; it had to be cooler in the mountains. She closed her eyes against the glare.

In her mind's eye the image of a hunched figure in black appeared, dragging a rope with a bound girl, over lava that was cruelly sharp, razor sharp, leaving a bloody, gory trail. . . .

She jerked awake, free of the beginnings of a nightmare. They had started to climb the mountain now, but it was not yet any cooler. They had lunch in the café with llama pictures on the walls; afterward, Frank drove past the Eagleton ranch turnoff, then made a right turn, heading west, back home. On the summit of the pass he stopped, and they got out to look at the observatory made from lava rock, an imposing, ugly, black and brown building. Neither had the energy to climb the stairs to enter it. Instead, they stood at the guard rail at the parking area and looked out at the forest, down there where Lucas had stopped his car, where the girl had been killed. Today the air was hazy with smoke—a forest fire was out of control in the wilderness area south of here—and visibility was too bad to see much of anything. Barbara was not convinced that anyone could have seen ten miles even if the air had been crystal clear that day. To her eyes it was all forest, wave after wave of rolling tree tops dropping ever lower, in a pattern that repeated endlessly, intersected by rivers of stilled black lava, and then all was fuzzed by haze, like a Japanese landscape.

"Let's go home," she said abruptly, too hot and too discouraged to want to see anything else, to want to talk.

Frank gave her a swift, appraising look, then wordlessly got back into the car and started the engine. The road deteriorated immediately after they left the lookout spot.

The switchbacks came closer together, and curves were posted fifteen miles an hour, ten miles, and it seemed impossible that two cars could pass each other.

"Deadman's Grade," Frank said, but he was holding the steering wheel tightly, concentrating on the road, not at all trying to make a joke.

The heat continued for the next four days. The air cooled when the sun went down, but it was relative; cooler now meant eighty degrees at night. On Friday Bailey Novell came back with some preliminary reports. He was driving a battered Ford sedan, and trailing along behind him was a flatbed truck with wooden sides. A tall young man climbed down and stood at the hood of the truck grinning. He had long, curly brown hair, deep dimples, and very blue eyes. He was so muscular he made Bailey look frail in comparison, and he was so young he made Bailey and Barbara look old in comparison, she thought. It was fine for Bailey, sixty and showing every year of it, but she was not happy with the idea that this young man made her feel more tired than the heat warranted.

Barbara looked from Bailey to the young man and back with raised eyebrows.

"This is Lucky Rosner," Bailey said. "He works for Clovis Woods Products. Thought you might want a word with him." Bailey's eyes were twinkling, and he was grinning almost as widely as Lucky Rosner.

He was altogether too pleased with himself, Barbara thought suspiciously. It was as unnatural for anyone to be grinning in such heat as it was unnatural for that young man to be so pretty.

"Hi," she said. "I'm Barbara Holloway. Come on in. Dad's around back. He'll want to hear it too, whatever it is."

Bailey looked past her and said hello to her father, who walked out at that moment, and they all stood in the driveway while the young man told them about last June.

"You see, me and Pete Malinski were going out on a job and these two guys came up and stopped us. They said they

134

wanted to play a joke on a lady friend of a friend of theirs, and they wanted to hire us to go along with it. What they said first was they wanted to rent our truck and gear for a day. That's all. And Pete and me, we knew it'd be our necks if they did that. I mean old man Clovis would have had our skins for something like that. We said no way. Then they said how about hiring one of us to drive, let one of them go out and play this trick, and the other guy would stay up there in Salem with whoever didn't go. Me. Pete drove and the guy told him where to go and all. Me and the other guy hung out in a pool hall. They paid all expenses, gas and whatnot, and two hundred each for us. We didn't see any harm in it."

When he paused, Barbara asked, "So you don't know what they actually did? Where's Pete now?"

"Gone to his brother's wedding, down in Ashland. Be back in a couple of weeks, but I can tell you what he told me, if you want."

"Oh, we want," Barbara muttered. "Go on."

"So they come out here somewheres, and they pretend they're going to cut down a big old fir tree, that's all. The lady comes and brings out a gun and shoots at them, and they take off. End of joke. Some joke, Pete said. They could have got themselves killed."

Barbara glared at Bailey as if it were his fault that Lucky Rosner found life so enjoyable. Bailey wagged his finger at her, loving every minute of this. Her father was no help; he was leaning against the porch rail, not missing a thing, but not interfering, either. She looked back toward Lucky.

"Okay, I'll bite, what next?" she asked.

"Well, me and Pete, we kept wondering about all that stuff, how much money they paid us and all, and we got to thinking that pretending to cut the tree down wasn't what they really wanted to begin with. That was like a cover, know what I mean?"

She nodded. "Cover for what?"

"See, Pete says when they got out to the place, this guy said he wanted to climb the tree and attach a rope, make it look legit. Like I said, they had the company truck, all the gear, and so what the hell, Pete thinks. Why not? The guy gets on the harness and up he goes. He can climb, but he's not a pro, Pete says, and he's pretty shaky when he gets down again. He just sort of slung the rope over the branch, but it was enough to fool the lady when she got home."

Barbara's eyes were narrowed now as she frowned at Lucky. "You think he wanted to put something else up there? Was that it?"

Lucky nodded. "What we decided. Then we figured those guys must be detectives, and the lady maybe was playing around a little, and her old man's out to get the goods on her, and so they wanted a bug. That's what we figured."

A few minutes later Barbara, Frank, and Bailey stood on Nell's gravel driveway beside Frank's Buick and watched Lucky Rosner climb the tree. He was very fast, very agile, and although it looked easy the way he did it, Barbara's stomach twisted in reaction as he got higher and higher. He leaned back against his harness, grinning down at them, when he stopped at the first branch, where he reached out and picked up something and held it up; it gleamed in his hand. He tucked it into his shirt pocket and began to come down, even faster than he had gone up.

Bailey whistled when he saw the object. "That's some fancy piece of equipment," he said in admiration.

Back at the house, Frank made out a check for Lucky Rosner, who never stopped grinning. After he was gone, they took the bug to the terrace, where Bailey opened it.

"Still working?" Frank asked. He looked more troubled than before, older than before.

"Not any more," Bailey said.

"Damn idiots," Frank growled. "Stupid way to go about it. Who'd do such a thing, and who'd pay for it? Just plain stupid to call attention to themselves like that to hide a bug."

"I'm not so sure," Barbara said slowly. "You really can't get near either house without being seen. The kids were home from school, Nell in and out, James and Tawna in and out. That must have seemed as good a way as any. And it's been up there for months without anyone suspecting a thing." She looked at Bailey. "Can you find out where the receiver is? What the range of that thing is? Who those men were working for?"

"Was," Bailey said, touching the bug. "Where the receiver was. Even if they've been hanging around, they sure would be packing it in by now."

"Try," she said. "What else do you have?"

It was not much. He had the names of the scientists, Herbert Margolis, Walter Schumaker, Ruth Brandywine. And Emil Frobisher, who had died nearly six years ago. If he had been gay, Bailey added, he had kept it a secret. Nothing on Lucas Kendricks before the Sunday he had turned up in a computer store and bought a computer outfit.

"How much was it? How did he pay?" Barbara asked.

"Thirty-eight hundred, cash. He bought a tape recorder, too. It was in his pack. No tapes."

"Wow! And on a Sunday! Okay, let's think. Do you have someone in Denver you can use? Or go yourself?"

"Denver? Jesus! You think it's hot here, try Denver. To do what?" He looked at Frank. "You got any beer?"

"Oh, sure. Sorry." Frank ambled off in no particular hurry, and while he was gone Barbara began to fill Bailey in on what they had learned from the sheriff and from Lucas Kendricks's parents.

She was summing it up when Frank came back out with the beer, a pitcher of lemonade, and a bottle of vodka. "So, someone hired them to find whatever it was that he had, and I don't think it's turned up yet. What is it? And where was his car for all those years? He probably didn't drive it very far to collect a battery and license plate, maybe not at all. Where was it? Where was he for the last seven years? And I want an inventory of his possessions that were on the body, and in the car. And everything he bought in Denver and Sisters. What all was included with the computer? Anything else?" she asked her father.

He shook his head and handed her a frosted glass filled to the brim. Bailey opened his beer and they drank in silence for several seconds while he thought.

He had looked to her for instructions, she realized, when he turned now to her father. "This is all going to add up to a bundle, you know."

Frank shrugged. "Our client can afford it, and she's up for murder." His voice was so neutral, so noncommittal, that Barbara looked at him sharply. He seemed withdrawn, deep in his own world of thought now.

"Right. Okay. I'll go, but I'll put on a guy when I get there. And I'll get that inventory before I take off, if they haven't put a tight lid on things. You could do that part," he added to Barbara.

"I want to keep out of sight as long as possible. Let them think Dad sent you, if it comes up."

He made no comment but drank his beer, frowning. Then he said, "They, whoever they are, spent a mint, looks like. I'll need someone, Hank Littleton, maybe, to go over to see the sheriff, talk to the tracker. You got his name?" Barbara nodded. "And Hank can start the hunt here for where the listeners holed up. Probably the fishing camp," he said, nodding toward the cabins below. "Or one of the summer vacation cottages. Okay, can do." He stretched out his legs and regarded the river that ended in haze today. "And I thought this was just a simple case of a mad wife blowing away a jerk of a husband."

"Let's keep it that way for now," Barbara said. "Not a word that we're after anything except proof that Lucas was a jerk."

He gave her a look of deep hurt.

Bailey had been gone only minutes before Clive Belloc arrived at the front door. Clive was more dressed up than Barbara had ever seen him, nicely pressed trousers, a handsome sport shirt, shined shoes. He looked at her with a sheepish expression. "Can I come in for a minute? I should have called first, but I thought if I found you home, I'd say something, and if not, then another time, but not like a formal appointment." That sounded as if he had rehearsed it word for word.

"Sure," she said. "We're back on the terrace wondering if it's worth thinking about doing something about dinner. Come have a drink with us."

He followed her through the house to the terrace and nodded awkwardly at Frank. If he had a hat, he'd be twisting it, Barbara thought. "I'm having lemonade with vodka, Dad's sticking to straight lemonade, and we have beer and wine."

"Lemonade," he said. "Sounds good."

"Right back." She went inside for another glass, not a large one, because he clearly had not come here for a long drink.

"A new fire up near Black Butte," he was saying when she returned and poured the drink for him. "Could be a bad autumn."

He thanked her for the lemonade and even drank some of it, and then put it on the table.

"I really wanted to see both of you," he said then. "I made a fool of myself over at Doc's the other day. I'm sorry." He said it in a rush, but it didn't sound at all rehearsed, and she thought probably the speech he had intended would have been long and involved and not quite as sincere as the little one he actually gave.

"No big deal," she said.

"I talked to Nell, and to a couple of people I know in Eugene, and they tell me you're as good as she's going to find, and she's happy with the arrangement, so I am too. And if there's anything I can do to help out, let me, please. Being helpless is maybe the worst part of this for me." His broad face was a study in pain and frustration. "But that's one thing I can't get out of my mind. You said you were death qualified. What does that mean?"

She looked at the glass she was holding; water ran off it crookedly. Her fingers were white-tipped with the chill. And she thought the chill was somewhere deep within her, and it had nothing to do with the glass or the miserably hot afternoon. "It means," she said slowly, "that only an attorney who has done criminal law, who has had a client accused of a crime that could invoke the death sentence, is qualified to

139

represent such a client in the future. The first case must always be as a junior attorney to another attorney who is death qualified, and then the junior is qualified."

He blanched at her words. "Oh, my God!"

"Right." Briskly she went on. "I'll remember what you said, and if anything comes up that you can help with, believe me, you'll hear from us. In fact, something already did. Dad said you found out that Clovis Woods Products was in Salem. Did you follow up with that?"

He shook his head. "As much as I could. I called up there on Friday, the day after those guys came around, and the secretary swore they never sent anyone out this far. If they had, she would have known about it. Then Lucas was killed, and this hell began for Nell, and I didn't give it any more thought. She must have made a mistake with the name on the truck."

"I guess," Barbara said. "Did she think she could have been mistaken?"

"I didn't bring it up," he said swiftly. "I'm not a real dope. She sure didn't need anyone asking more questions, casting doubt on what she said, least of all for me to be the one."

Barbara smiled at him with understanding. "But it must be tough for you, in your job, I mean. Or is that something else you don't bring up with her?"

His deep sunburn seemed to darken a shade, and he looked sheepish again. "Actually, I haven't done any cruising since the week after Lucas was killed, not for sales, that is. I started applying for a new job, and next week I start work on a new job. Cruising, still, but for different reasons, to settle estates, tax appraisals, things like that, not for timber sales."

"New job?" Frank exclaimed. "And I haven't heard about it? Now that's strange."

"No one's heard yet, except Nell, not until I actually start," he said. "I sure haven't mentioned it to Lonnie."

Frank laughed. "That explains why I haven't heard."

Clive looked at his watch and stood up. "I'm glad I found you both like this. Thanks for hearing me out. And I mean it, if there's anything I can do. I've got to get along now. I'm taking Nell and the kids to an air-conditioned restaurant. One that doesn't smell like woods on fire."

Frank walked to the car with him, and Barbara leaned back and watched the river move away without end. She found herself thinking of the sheriff playing Bach with those big broad fingers. Bach fugues, she thought, remembering a description she had read: ever-rising fugues, repeating a theme without end, varying it slightly each time, but always the same theme. Always the same river even if it did flow away forever, and was forever changing; it was the same river.

"Well," Frank said on returning. "Just that. Well."

"Yes, indeed. Poor Clive, what a burden to think that he met her through Lucas, on a job to estimate the value of her beloved trees. I bet he thinks Lucas had that stunt pulled, just as much as Nell thinks it."

"If he does, you'll never hear him say so. He's not likely to furnish any ammunition for the prosecution. And that's a fine motive, added to all the other motives she already had."

"I know. But I bet he thinks so. What's on your mind, Dad? You've been glummer than a constipated judge."

He grinned fleetingly at the words, one of his favorite phrases. Then he said in a slow, thoughtful way, "I don't like how this is all shaping up. I don't like having a troop of operatives ransacking houses and cars, trekking through the woods, placing bugs in trees. Too much money involved. Too much we don't know anything about. They could be feds, for all we know. We don't have an idea where Lucas was, what he was involved in. Could be drugs—real bad news. I just don't like any of it, and I don't think any of it is relevant to your case."

"Maybe it's too soon to know that," she said, equally mildly, equally thoughtful, even though she was seething inside, because, she had to admit to herself, he was probably right. But if it wasn't relevant, there was no hope for Nell.

"Let me finish," he said, staring ahead at the river. "What I'm afraid of is that you're going to find out things that will make you want to bring down justice on the heads of half a

141

dozen other people, and I don't give a damn about any of them. I want to save Nell as much grief as possible, keep her out of the state penitentiary if we can, or see that she gets the least possible amount of time if it goes that way."

Moving very carefully, Barbara stood up. Again, she thought. Like the fugues, like the river, like everything, it was always the same.

"Before you stalk off, consider what I'm telling you, Bobby. You know as well as I do that Tony will fight to keep anything to do with Lucas and the last seven years all the way out, and probably he'll have a judge go along with that. Because it isn't relevant. What is relevant is that Lucas turned up in an isolated spot, and Nell turned up there, and he ended up shot through the head. That's what's relevant, and not a damned thing beyond that. If anyone bugged that ledge and a tape turns up and proves that he didn't even threaten her, that kills any self-defense plea. And that's what's relevant."

He didn't say it, he didn't have to; it played through her head without audible words: If Tony had the tape and Nell's story was verified that Lucas had said nothing more than "Watch this," Tony could even go for murder one.

"You think she did it, don't you?"

"I've been to that ledge, and so have you."

She did not want to continue playing this scene, she thought distantly. She had even got up in order to run away from it, but her feet were one with the deck; she could not move, had to let it run itself all the way through even if she dreaded the outcome.

"Why did you call me?" she whispered.

"I told you. I can't manage this one alone."

"You mean you can't get her off. And you don't think I can either, do you? You don't think anyone can. Finally it will be a plea bargain, won't it? Self-defense, manslaughter."

"She says she won't confess, no matter what."

"Because she didn't do it. Isn't that why? And you think when the time comes, when I have pushed and poked and probed and got nowhere, I'll help you persuade her that it's the only way out for her, the only way to be able to have any time with her children before they're both grown up."

"I didn't say that!" His voice was harsh; he was flushed, with a line of sweat on his lip, and he looked like an old man who was very tired. "I didn't say that," he repeated quietly this time. "But the day might come when she'll think two years in the pen sounds better than twenty. And God help me, I don't want either."

The wheel turns, she thought, and we're all on it. It turns, goes this way and that with a curious wobble, and sometimes you think it's taking you to someplace brand new and wonderful, everything looks fresh and interesting, and then with the next turn, you're back at the same place. Everything different, everything the same. Different details, different cast of characters, and the same. Ever-rising music, ever-flowing river, ever-changing people; all the same forever and ever.

"I'm going to see if I can find something cold for dinner," she said.

She walked away from him. As she entered the house, he said, "Bobby" in a weary voice. She kept walking, as if she had not heard him. Even dinner, she thought almost wildly, even dinner would be the same. Leftovers thrown together in a big salad, the same as last night, but different. She wanted to laugh, but even more she wanted to weep.

FIFTEEN

DOC HAD TAKEN a wing of the house for a study where he could go and be assured of quiet and no interruptions. Separated from the rest of the house by a pantry, the kitchen, and a guest room, it was the closest point to the end of the trail that led from Nell's house to here. The room was paneled with glowing, golden oak, carpeted with a forest-green plush carpet, with gold drapes at the windows. There was a black-lacquered wet bar and a coffee maker, a tiny refrigerator, a desk, a chest of drawers, several comfortable chairs, a music system that was very good, and a twin-size bed. He had a telescope at a window overlooking the river; often there was a chess problem set up with handsome gold and silver pieces. He kept his medical journals here, and always a current biography that he was reading. It was his retreat, as private as if it were on another continent, on another planet. Lonnie never cleaned in here. No one but Doc was supposed to enter; he ran the vacuum now and then, dusted now and then, sometimes slept all night in here, or worked on a patient's intractable problem for hours.

Nell loved the retreat. Because she would never leave the children alone, and she could not hire a sitter while she was keeping a tryst, her visits were infrequent during the summer, and almost always during the afternoon when the children were at friends' houses. Doc had two afternoons a week free, but because of the investigation, so many people coming and

144

going, they had not met often this summer; they had been afraid to. Now that school had started again, things would be better, Nell thought. They would, they would. They never mentioned Jessie in here, and, until his death, they had never talked about Lucas in here.

There was an outside door for which she had a key. Sometimes she came to the retreat even when she knew Doc would not be here because it was theirs, his and hers, a place where she was safe. Sometimes, more often, she simply waited for him, knowing almost to the minute when he would arrive. Today she had to wait only ten minutes before she heard his footsteps on the deck.

At first she had been afraid someone would find out and cause him serious trouble, and she still was scrupulous about never leaving anything of hers behind. But anyone who entered the room would know, she thought. There was an indefinable something of hers, of theirs, that made the room different, that would betray them.

He entered then and caught her up in a hard, fierce embrace. Their kiss was just as hard and fierce. "It's been so long," he said over and over. "My God, I've missed you!" His hands were trembling as he began to undress her.

Their lovemaking had a quality of desperation that never had been there before. Afterward, Nell wept against his chest as he stroked her hair, her back. She had not realized until then exactly how tense she had become, that she had turned into one long raw nerve.

"You've lost weight," he said softly. "Poor little Nell, you have to eat more. Are you sleeping?"

"I'm fine," she said, and sniffed. He handed her a tissue. "You're the one who's all bones. Hie thee to the closet, skeleton-man."

He held her closer, and for minutes neither spoke. Finally she went to the bathroom. When she came back, wearing one of his dressing gowns, barefoot, she sat on the side of the bed. He was making coffee, naked.

"You'll get a chill," she said. His shoulders were hunched as if he already was cold. She went to the closet and took out

145

a robe, returned and draped it over his shoulders. He kept watching the coffee as if it needed his help. "Doc, what's wrong?"

"Us. You. Me. This." His voice was strange, as if he were talking about an incident from his childhood that he was recalling with regret—the loss of a pet, the death of a distant grandparent. . . .

"Doc? Look at me, will you? What are you talking about? Why now?"

"If they find out, the prosecutors, they'll smear you." He did not look at her but drew on the robe and tied the cord.

"Doc, I love you."

"And that's no good, either!" he cried, finally facing her. "I'm too old for you, and I've got a wife who probably will outlive both of us. And I told you I can't leave her."

"I never asked you to. Or expected you to."

He looked haggard. "I'm tired of it," he said faintly. "The sneaking around. Fooling everyone. Being starved for you and having you only a few minutes at a time. I'm just tired of it all."

Nell hugged her arms about herself, chilled all the way through. "You never said anything like that before. You said a few minutes were a blessing, like drops of water to a man thirsting to death."

"I said a lot of things. We both did. But, Nell, it's no good. You're young and you need a husband, a full-time husband."

"You said I should go out with Clive, to prove something or other. I forget why. Tell me again, Doc. Why did you tell me I should go out with Clive? To prove what?"

"Nothing," he said with a touch of irritation. "I don't know why I told you that. It doesn't look natural for someone so young and good-looking not to go out, I guess. I don't want any questions about you, speculation about us. I don't know."

"I see," she said slowly, and for a moment she thought she did, but she could not have said what it was she saw; whatever it had been during that flash of insight was inexpressible in any words she knew. That desperation, she thought then, had not been the desperation of a man thirsting for a few drops of water, but the desperation of a parting, a goodbye. She picked up her clothes and walked to the bathroom, trailing her jeans on the floor. When she came out, dressed, neither of them spoke as she drew the key from her pocket and put it on the bedside table, and then left the room.

There was no one she could talk to now, she was thinking as she walked the trail through the woods. She had not been back to the ledge since. . . . Even now she could not finish the thought, but the ledge had become forbidden territory; she would never go there again. There were so many things she had wanted to tell Doc, all the things Barbara was doing—taking people up to the ledge, trudging all over the property, asking question after question. Preparing her defense. And none of that had seemed important suddenly. Her life, her trial, her possible imprisonment, none of it had seemed relevant somehow.

At lunch in one of the most exclusive restaurants in Denver, Herbert Margolis blinked his big cow eyes at Ruth Brandywine and said, "I don't have any reason to lie to them if they ask me anything."

"And I have far too much at stake to risk getting involved in any investigation," Walter Schumaker said. The restaurant had been his choice; he maintained a table there for four days a week, to be readied instantly if he called or simply showed up with guests.

He was cultivating the leonine look, Ruth thought bitterly. He had thick, dark gold hair that he wore long and full; it made his head seem even larger than it was. He looked very handsome, very impressive on the covers of magazines where he appeared with some regularity, always accompanied by the beautiful fractals, the incredibly colored Mandelbrot sets that seemed to have become his icons.

She said softly, "I don't swing alone, boys. Believe me, I don't. Herbie, my love, your signature is on every single disk

Lucas stole, and you know it. And Walter, your name is on the work, and your name is on a check for the detectives. Stupid thing to do, pay with a check. But there it is."

"All I did was help Emil set up a program. I had no idea what he planned to do with it. I never asked," Herbert Margolis said, nearly tripping over the rushing words. "That's what I do all the time, help others set up programs, make sure they run. I can prove it."

"That might even work," she said icily, "but not if the disks turn up and anyone bothers to run them all."

"They won't turn up. If they were still in existence, the detectives would have found them. If the police had them, they would have been around before now. Lucas either destroyed them, or Emil did before the end, or Lucas hid them somewhere and they'll stay there until the Second Coming." Herbert Margolis leaned back in his chair; although he was breathing fast, like a runner crossing a finish line, he looked smug, self-satisfied. "I examined every possible scenario with the new expert system I'm developing, and that's how it works out."

"I don't swing alone. That's *my* scenario," Ruth Brandywine said.

"We're each approaching this from unique perspectives," Walter Schumaker said thoughtfully. "From mine, it seems that some work I was involved in many years ago was placed on disks without my knowledge. The originator of the work died in a sordid manner, and I put all thoughts of the work and his demise out of mind and continued with my own projects. If this person who has recently been murdered was involved in that old work, I had forgotten it entirely. He was an aide, a student, a hireling of no more consequence than the person who cleaned the lavatories. When I learned that someone had broken into your garage and vandalized your automobile during your trip abroad, out of personal friendship I hired an agency to try to find him, to bring him to justice because the police were doing nothing." He nodded as he finished, as if he had mentally ticked off one point after another and found them all satisfactory.

"You're both assuming that the disks will never be found and played," Ruth said. She noticed a waiter hovering and waved him away. It was after three; the restaurant was nearly empty now.

"No, Ruth," Walter Schumaker said, "I make no such assumption. But I do assume that if those disks turned up tomorrow, no one except one of us could possibly make any sense from them. A lot of pretty pictures, Julia sets, Mandelbrot sets, fractals, abstract images, and the ravings of a madman, that's all those disks would reveal to an outsider. No one questioned that Emil was quite mad at the end, no one. And the disks would simply confirm that opinion. That's our insurance, Ruth, and I am comfortable with it. Old work, history, of no significance to anyone."

After several seconds she nodded. "And you'll both say you had no idea that Tom the maintenance man was Lucas Kendricks, Emil's assistant?"

"Come now, Ruth. Who notices maintenance people? I was only on campus one day a week and I certainly did not inspect the workers."

Herbert Margolis was nodding like a drinking bird. "Same for me. Exactly like that. Who would have noticed him?"

"Ruth," Walter Schumaker said, "who can say differently? He's dead, isn't he? I told you to get rid of him. I told you he knew, but that's history, too. The salient point is that he is dead and he can't deny anything you say. Now, can we drop this, put it behind us, and get on with other things?" He did not wait for her response but signaled to the waiter to bring the check.

"Yes," she said very softly, "by all means, let us put it behind us, but pray, Walter. Pray that the investigation doesn't get real."

In her mind a disk appeared, cut into four wedges, four pieces of a tempting pie; then Emil had gone, and it had crumbled to dust. They had withdrawn into their separate orbits again, the three who remained, but there were after-effects of the perturbation of a wild player who hadn't known

149

his orbit, his rightful place, who had swung erratically back and forth, first into this orbit, then that, and even though he was gone, his tracks remained, distorting the hard lines of separation everywhere he had been, and there were no clean boundaries, no sharp divisions. Where he had been there was chaos.

Barbara walked along the lava trail on McKenzie Pass; here the lava had run like a river, scouring everything before it, creating rough river banks for the river of molten rock. In another section the lava had been more sluggish; it had piled up higher and higher, then tumbled down, creating a mini-mountain of razor-sharp edges that still retained lethal cutting power. Lava gargoyles hung over the lava river bed, eternally on guard. The lava was black, brown, encrusted here and there with lichen, pale gray-green like something out of a witch's trade catalog. A pocket of soil held a miniature fir tree, nature's bonsai. Another such pocket held a single daisy whipping in the wind, tenaciously defiant.

She looked at her watch for the fourth time; finally it was approaching two o'clock. She retraced her steps, around the lava-rock observatory where teenagers were shrieking at one another about the various volcanic mountains they were viewing. On all sides the peaks rose, each named, each one a volcano that was not dead, just resting. The thought made her uneasy as she crossed the road and went to the guard rail near her car. She was carrying her father's binoculars. At a minute before two she began to study the scene below, trees and more trees, lava flows and more lava flows. The day was clear, a tingle of cold in the air, the sun hot. Good ozone, good air, good vibes, good something, a perfect day in the mountains. Visibility was fine; more lava flows, more trees. She glanced at her watch, thirty seconds past two, and concentrated again on the view. At last she saw a red flag snap back and forth. The flag waved and snapped for another minute, then started to inch westward and was lost in the trees. In a few seconds it reappeared, flapping, moving the other way, and this time she could make out a human figure, and then a glint of sunlight on metal—his truck. In the wrong place at the wrong time, it would attract attention if a knowledgeable person happened to be looking and knew it did not belong there. Then flag, figure, and truck all vanished among the trees.

She drove back the tortuous road so preoccupied with her thoughts that she had none left to frighten her as she negotiated Deadman's Grade. But it was better to be the driver than the passenger, she decided, when she realized that she was down, turning onto the private road, nearly home again.

Lonnie's old Dodge was in the driveway; it was her day to clean Frank's house. When Barbara went inside, her father came from his study to meet her.

"How's it going?"

"Fine. Beautiful day again."

"You had a call. A Mike Dinesen."

"Oh, good. Did he leave a number?"

"I took it down. Here."

"I'll call him from upstairs. Thanks, Dad. Oh, before I forget again, I won't be here for dinner."

"Oh. Dinesen?"

Before she could answer, Lonnie said from the kitchen, "Clive and Nell. I'm baby-sitting for her."

Barbara shrugged and started up the stairs. And that's how home life was going, she thought, as if she were not aware of the hurt on Frank's face and the stubbornness that made him set his mouth in a way that would not allow him to express that hurt, or to back up and say he had been wrong. Or even to admit that he had called for her to come to do his dirty work. She stopped midway up the stairs, however, when Lonnie came from the kitchen talking.

"That Clive, he's like a boy these days. Such a cut in pay that he took and he's grinning like a baboon. His heart wasn't in it any more. Money doesn't mean a thing if your heart's not in it. Best thing that ever happened for Travis, having him around. Get his nose away from that computer, out in the open air, in the woods."

151

Barbara continued up the stairs. Trust Lonnie to know who was going to dinner with whom, and how Travis was doing, what he was doing most of the time. And Travis, even Nell had admitted, had become a computer hacker practically overnight.

She called Mike Dinesen in her bedroom and made an appointment to talk to him on Friday at two. On her table were stacks of books that had to be returned to the university library; she would do that Friday, also. Frank had reminded her that the bookmobile would get anything she might want; she had thanked him politely, but had not said what any of the books were about. Chaos, fractals, Mandelbrot sets, fractal geometry, strange attractors, turbulence. . . .

She dialed Bailey Novell's number then. "Hi, want some lunch on Friday?"

He made a growly sound that she took to be assent.

"Where's the most likely place that Tony DeAngelo eats these days?" she asked, and loosened her grasp on the phone consciously; her hand had tightened unconsciously.

He named the restaurant and she said how about there, would they need a reservation, and would he get it. When she hung up, she felt as if she could not get quite enough air, the same way she had felt as a child afraid to get out of bed in the dark because she did not know what was under the bed, only that something evil was there.

By the time she went downstairs again, Lonnie was gone, fresh coffee was made, and Frank was waiting for her at the kitchen table.

"You going to tell me who this Dinesen is? Old school buddy, something like that?"

"Never met him. He's a mathematician. How's the book coming?"

He gave her a cold look and pushed his cup back. "I never thought the day would come that you wouldn't trust me."

"Neither did I," she snapped.

He glared at her. "You're acting just like your mother when she got in one of her ice-cold rages!"

"No, I'm not! I'm acting just like you, before you traded in your conscience. Mother always yielded and you never gave an inch. Not a goddamn inch!"

He stood up and stalked from the room.

At dinner with Nell and Clive that night she said, "We'll talk about anything and everything you both want except the case. Agreed?" She already had extracted a promise from Clive that he would not reveal what they had been up to that day. Although they agreed to her terms for dinner, it soon became obvious that Nell had nothing to say. Finally Barbara turned to Clive. "Tell me about your job, the one you left, the one you have now, how you trained for it, everything. Okay?"

He looked unhappy and at a loss until she prodded him, and then he began. Nell was polite, excessively polite, and very distant. She began to glance at her watch within the first hour, and all in all the dinner was not a happy affair.

Dinner at Doc's house was not a happy affair, either. Lonnie had made a casserole with instructions about how to finish it in the oven, and Doc made a salad and grilled salmon steaks that Lonnie had left in a marinade. Jessie ate with better appetite than Doc. They ate most of the meal in silence until she had her decaf coffee.

"Someone from the district attorney's office was out talking to Chuck," she said then.

"Don't see what for. He doesn't know anything about what happened."

"Oh, you never know. Lonnie said they spent nearly an hour together. They must have found something to talk about." She finished the coffee and nodded when he held up the pot. He poured more for her. "They called me, you know. They want to come talk to me next week."

"What on earth for? Tell them you can't do it, your health won't allow such nonsense."

"But I should do my duty, don't you think?" She stirred her coffee, but when she started to put the spoon down, it slipped from her fingers and clattered against the saucer.

She snatched her hand away, put it in her lap out of sight. "I'm surprised that they haven't got hold of you yet," she said.

"They've had my statement for months," he said. "You know that. I told you I went down there and signed a statement. I have nothing to add to it. And I don't know what you can possibly say."

"There's always something," she said, and her chair began to roll back away from the table. "Lonnie says that Clive is over at Nell's three, four times a week these days. That's nice, isn't it? Poor Clive. He's waited a long time." She was halfway across the room; she turned to look at him over her shoulder. "Good night, dear," she said, and smiled slightly.

"Jessie, hold on a minute," Doc said then. He pushed his chair back roughly and strode toward her. "What are you up to? What do you have to tell the DA's man?"

"How can I know until I hear what questions he has?" she murmured. "But what could I possibly know, stuck here in the house all day every day?" She started to roll again. "Will you come help me undress in half an hour, dear?"

He watched her roll down the broad hall toward her room at the far end. Then he returned to the table and started to stack the dishes. He left them abruptly, went to the kitchen and poured himself a tumbler half full of bourbon. After the first large swallow, he added a touch of water, and then sat down at the kitchen table to finish it off before he helped her undress and get into bed where she would watch television for hours. He planned his evening. Another drink, maybe two, as many as it took. Then sleeping pills. They would not talk again that evening.

154

SIXTEEN

SUMMER WAS BACK, more summery than it had been in high
season. Barbara carried her jacket as she walked through a
small park in downtown Eugene, past the large fountain that
never erupted but oozed water silently in a never-ending
flow over a concrete lip, down to a catch basin, back up a
center pipe to start all over again, forever. Every bench was
taken by people eating sandwiches, eating yogurt, drinking
juice. She had forgotten all this. She used to come out here,
too, for lunch.

The Park Bar and Grill was new. She couldn't remember
what used to be in the space, another restaurant, the name
gone, replaced; the new one had been decorated to look old,
older than the one it had shouldered out of the way. There
were booths with high backs, dark tables with softly polished
wood, nothing flashy, nothing to suggest newness. Small
lamps with Tiffany-type shades, a long bar with brass and
leather stools, a dimness that was inviting, all new, but very
familiar, as if the decorator had copied the same pictures that
Barbara had seen off and on for most of her life.

Bailey Novell waved from a booth. Few people were in
the restaurant; it was half an hour before the real luncheon
crowd would gather. She had suggested the early time. She
wanted to be seated, to have their orders in before Tony
showed up, if he showed up. There were no familiar faces
among the half dozen other patrons, but, she thought, that
might change as soon as the regulars arrived.

155

"Hi. How's it going?" Bailey asked; it was the same sort of question as "Hot enough for you?" No answer was required.

"Hi, Bailey; let's trade places," she said. Bailey was in the seat facing the door.

Without comment he got up and they switched. She motioned to a waiter, who came over instantly to take their orders. Bailey was watching her with more interest than he had shown a minute ago.

"Stage setting," he said when the waiter left.

She gave him a quick grin and leaned forward to speak in a low voice. "Working lunch," she said. "On our bill?" He nodded and she went on. "Sooner or later, today, two weeks from now, some time, Tony will find a way to get you alone and ask a few questions. He'll probably do it himself. I'm betting on it. First, say it sure was easier working for the father than for the daughter. Words to that effect, however you want to put it, whatever reasons you want to add, if any." She paused to wait for him to stop laughing. "All right already," she said. "Don't overdo it. He's too smart for that. The next thing is harder. Somehow you get in the fact that I sent you chasing off to Denver and then told you to forget the whole thing. Something like it can't do Lucas any harm now to let it out that he was crazy. Again, your words, that meaning."

Bailey's eyes narrowed. "According to that bitch doctor, he *was* crazy. You think Tony doesn't already know that?"

"I don't know what he knows. I just know what I want you to get across to him, and then clam up. Good, here's our food."

When they were alone again, Bailey said, "You know, honey chile, you're making the first part of this a cinch. It was easier to work for the old man than the kid." He drank some of his beer and then said, "That spy gizmo covered an area of half a mile, straight line. I need a topo map to see if it could pick up what happened on the ledge. Nothing yet on the organization. They hide good."

"And how many pointers do you leave lying around when you're out working?"

"Damn few." He looked thoughtful, then added, "You know, I could do my reputation a lot of harm, letting things slip to the enemy in a careless sort of way." Although he seemed genuinely concerned, he soon shrugged and began to eat his sandwich.

Barbara had eaten only a few bites of her salad when Tony and two other men entered the restaurant. He looked exactly as he had the last time she saw him. She didn't know why that surprised her so much. He was still as lean and hungry-looking as a shark. Was there such a thing as a fat, complacent shark? She did not let her gaze linger on him even a second but looked straight at Bailey, across from her, his mouth full.

"And I'm telling you, it's my way right down the line. Just send me your bill and get lost. Okay? You understand what I'm saying?"

Her voice was not loud, but she knew it carried. In her peripheral vision she could see the half turn that brought Tony around to face her directly. She could not see the expression on his face, but she thought there was an electric jolt effect, a swift full-body ripple, followed by an unnatural stillness. She did not look at him to check the impression.

"Jeez," Bailey said, and took a quick drink of his beer. "Jeez, Barbara, just calm down, will you? I said I'm sorry. A mistake, that's all."

She began to gather her things, her jacket, her purse; she checked inside it for keys, and then a shadow fell across her. She glanced up, and blinked rapidly to refocus her eyes.

"Hello, Barbara. You look wonderful. How are you?"

"Hello, Tony." Her voice was hollow-sounding, as if it had to travel a very long way.

"I heard you were in town," he said. "I've been meaning to call. Are you staying at your dad's place? Buy you a drink?"

"Another time, Tony. I'm in a hurry, an appointment." She clutched her purse and jacket and stood up; she side-stepped him and nearly ran from the restaurant. She did not look at Bailey again.

She hurried to her car in a parking structure a block

away, no longer pretending nervousness, confusion, if ever she had been. Her mind had become detached, as if she could watch from afar as her hands fumbled with the car keys and shook when she tried to put the right key in the ignition. Show's over, she told her trembling fingers, the audience is gone, curtain down. The fingers paid no attention.

Whoever said a liar could not look you straight in the eyes? she wondered then. Tony's deep-set eyes could look straight at her, had always been able to look straight at her, through her eyes to whatever lay behind them, and never waver, never blink. She wanted to find the books where the lie was written and correct it. Margin notes, end notes, footnotes. Red pencil.

Gradually that detached part of her was drifting back into place, reporting in, she thought; her performance had been good, convincing, maybe too real. How much act, how much reality? And what difference did it make? Her fingers responded to that calm and somewhat sardonic other part and turned the key with a steadiness that seemed unreal after the violence of the tremor only moments earlier.

She had returned her library books, checked out three new ones and a magazine, and was now on the steps of the library, undecided what to do next. It was fifteen minutes before two, too early to expect Mike Dinesen, but if she moved her car she probably would not be able to find another parking space and get back here on time. Although registration had not even begun yet, the campus was filled with students who looked like children to her, many of them with parents. Indoctrination week, she realized, remembering it from her past as a freshman on this same campus. She had not taken into account that the campus would be overflowing with children, parking lots jammed full, and no place for her car except a tow-away zone posted for twenty minutes. She had been here twenty-five minutes already.

She moved aside as a young man led a group of freshmen up the stairs to the library, with several parents trailing along. The students didn't look old enough to go away to college. From the unhappy look on some of the parents' faces, it was clear that they thought the same thing.

Then she heard someone say, "Barbara Holloway?"

He was younger than she had thought from his telephone voice, low thirties probably. He was dressed in sky-blue running pants, sweat shirt, running shoes. Give him a tennis racket and plop him down into a Fitzgerald novel, she thought with misgivings; she had wanted a staid, responsible mathematician. His hair was medium brown, straight, his eyes light blue; he was deeply tanned, and muscled like a jock.

"Hi," she said. "Mike Dinesen?"

They shook hands.

"You're disappointed," he said.

"Don't be ridiculous. You're just not what I expected."

"Exactly what my mother said, they tell me."

She laughed. "I have to move my car before they tow it away. Is there someplace close by where we can talk for a few minutes?"

"Sure. You're running early, I'm running late. Let's compromise. You drive me home, five blocks, and we'll talk there after I shower and change. Or, we can meet somewhere in half an hour."

"Your place," she said without hesitation and set a brisk pace back to her car. A campus-security woman was ticketing a car just three spaces down.

"Nick of time," Mike said. "First a warning ticket, then, fifteen minutes later, the towing company. Eighty-five bucks before you're through with them. You'll want to head out that way." He pointed. "Before I moved in close enough to walk back and forth, I paid out two hundred eighty dollars in parking tickets in one year. Actually, I never paid a cent; they took it out of my paychecks."

He sounded serious, but when she glanced at him, his eyes were sparkling with amusement. "And I had a parking permit," he added.

He directed her to his house, six blocks, not five. It was

a two-story duplex; he had the lower floor. There was a flower box with dead geraniums and petunias and a sleeping orange cat. The cat got up, flowed out of the planter, stretched, and sniffed her with interest, then began to tangle itself around his legs.

"Saber Dance," he said, motioning toward the animal. "Come on in. Come on, Saber, you too."

The room they entered had two rattan sofas with garish covers in lime green and purple. There were rattan tables here and there in what appeared to be no order whatever, and a dozen or more large plush pillows. Two walls were floor-to-ceiling bookshelves. Three lower shelves held hundreds of record albums; a stereo at the end of one of the sofas was impressive, expensive, she was certain. And two computers were on a long table made from a door, supported by sawhorses. The wall behind the computers was covered with pictures—Mandelbrot sets blown up to large size, each one dazzling and beautiful. There were fractals, Julia sets, other computer art, little of it framed, some overlapping.

"Kitchen that way," he said, moving past her, pointing. "Help yourself. Make coffee, tea, see if there's anything in the fridge that you want. Back in a second."

She wandered slowly through the house, a tidy kitchen with flour and sugar, an assortment of dried beans, all in mason jars on a counter. There was a small table and two chairs. On the table another mason jar contained several withered daisies. What appeared to be at least a week's supply of newspapers was stacked on the floor, apparently never opened. Beyond the kitchen door was a large back porch and another orange cat regarding her. A second door led to a dining room that had been converted to an office, with yet another computer system, file cabinets, and an army-issue metal desk covered with stacks of books and unruly piles of papers.

She returned to the living room and sat down, strangely pleased with this house and its absolute disregard for the Joneses. Mike returned a few minutes later, toweling his hair.

160

He was wearing jeans, a tee shirt with fish swimming across it, and sandals. Just right, she thought approvingly. He was of a piece with his house.

"Didn't you want coffee or anything?" he asked.

"I'm fine," she said. "Please, don't bother. I promised I wouldn't take up much of your time, and I suspect you have classes to prepare, things to do."

"Yep. And first on the list is coffee. You said Wiley Aronsen gave you my name. Friend of yours?" He was walking from the room as he talked; she followed him to the kitchen.

"Friend of a friend," she said, and for the next few minutes, as he made coffee, they checked each other's circle of friends and acquaintances.

He cut it off by sitting at the table and saying, "So what do you want to know, and why?"

"As I told you on the phone, I'm an attorney—"

"You don't look like a lawyer."

"What are they supposed to look like?"

"Men in four-hundred-dollar suits pretending they're not wearing corsets that pinch."

She laughed. "I have a three-hundred-dollar suit, actually. And I have a girdle, or used to. Somewhere."

"Still not right. No corset pinching you twenty-four hours a day every day. That shows every time."

"Well, a lawyer is what I am, and my client is Nell Kendricks." She raised her eyebrow questioningly, and he shook his head. She already had decided to tell him no more than what had appeared in print, and she did so succinctly, and then said, "So I'm left wondering what they were working on. A mathematician, a computer expert, a psychiatrist, and Frobisher, who was a mathematician also."

He nodded thoughtfully. "And you're sure they were concerned with chaos? Mathematicians, sure. But computer people don't like it. They like things to be on or off, no indecision, and they hate the almost-intransitive. And a psychiatrist? Behavior maybe, but psychiatry? I don't see how

161

that fits in." His coffee maker was making rattling noises, done. He got up to pour coffee for both of them.

"What's almost-intransitive?"

His thoughts apparently had galloped far beyond that already. He shook his head slightly, came back to the table with two mugs of coffee, and wandered away again for cream and sugar. He took both, she took neither. "Okay," he said, "let's use weather, or more precisely, climate. Say for millennia the weather is balmy, moist, subtropical; that's the Earth climate. Then, for no reason that anyone knows, it changes and we're in an ice age, and everything gets stuck there for years and years. Then it changes again. And so on. But the point is that during the period of ice age, or subtropical, that's the Earth climate, and it continues long enough to take it for granted that that's the stable condition and always will be that way with minor fluctuations that we call weather, and then it changes. The change can be awfully fast."

"Damn," she muttered, "and I thought I was getting a glimmer of understanding. What about the butterfly effect; you know, the butterfly in Brazil changes the weather in New York?"

He shook his head. "That's something else again, the Lorenz Effect, talking short term now, not eons. That says that a minute change in a system can have very large effects. And since you can't predict the minute variation, you can't predict the large system. Meteorology is deep into chaos these days."

She sipped the coffee, frowning. "According to the books I've already read, the chaos theory is being applied up and down the line in every field you can name."

"Hardly a theory," he said. "We like to say the laws of chaos." He was grinning at her. "Look, do you have a couple of hours? Let me give you the introductory lecture I'll be using this term, complete with slides. Like I said, I can't make a connection between the shrink and the mathematician, but maybe something will occur to me. Game?"

"With equations?"

He laughed. "Two or three, no more than that, I

162

promise, and they're pretty elementary. Come on. You can always stop me."

But it would have been impossible to stop once they began to view the slides, and he began to point out strange attractors, the fractal qualities of coasts and trees and clouds, and turbulence, and phase space. The slides he had arranged for the lecture were astonishingly beautiful, compelling.

"Start with the whole tree," he said, "and then the single leaf, and now the veins in the leaf, and the root system, all similar. Not identical, mind you, but self-similar. And in this slide, see how the attractor seemed to fly out of control and create islands? Then it got back on the main course, but if we zoom in on one of those islands, magnify it, see? Similar to the whole. And zoom in again, focus on details that are smaller and smaller, and you can see that the island's not isolated at all, but attached by that filament. Nothing's isolated, nothing. It's all connected."

He changed the image again. "Now, about scaling. It's very simple really. We usually use the island of Great Britain because we have such good satellite pictures of it. How long is the coastline? The answer must be infinite. At this distance, from space, the coastline would be a few inches." The NASA photograph showed the whole of the Earth, and then the whole of the island of Great Britain in sharp detail. Mike traced the island with his finger. "You could print out a picture and measure it with a tape measure. But get in closer, change the scale, you see, and the measurement increases. As the distance narrows, the measurement increases." He zoomed in on a section of the coast, then again on a bay, again to a miniature bay, and again and again. Each time the similarity was there; each time with more and more detail, the measurement changed. "Until finally," he said, "you are down to measuring grains of sand, and you could go to the molecular level, the atomic, the subatomic. The same land, the same island, always similar, always using a different scale. Where does it stop? Only when we get beyond where our instruments can follow."

The screen cleared and a magnificent Mandelbrot set

appeared with golden seahorse figures, and pale green dragons, flaring bands of fluorescent blue, and silver filigree. He zoomed in on a tiny section of the border to reveal the self-similarity again, and again. "It's infinite," he said softly, "limited only by the number of decimal points the computer can handle. Fourteen in this instance. You fall right into it and through it forever, and it's all one thing, all connected, whole. Science has done a complete flip-flop. Reductionism is dead, holism lives. It's a brand-new game we're into."

Suddenly the show ended with a constant, unhurried zoom after zoom into a new Mandelbrot set, this one silver and blue. The illusion of falling forever was so strong that when the screen went blank, Barbara felt vertiginous. She was holding the edge of the computer table as tightly as she could.

Mike laughed and moved away. Until then she had not realized that his hand had been resting on her shoulder. "So how do you think it will play in Peoria?"

"A sellout," she said weakly.

"Good. Let's have some more coffee and then in a while go out for Mexican food. You do like Mexican, don't you?"

"Yes, but. . . . I have to make a call first. And use your bathroom."

And just what do you think you're doing? she demanded of herself, standing at the bathroom sink holding a bar of soap. But she knew, and so did Mike. They would have coffee, go out to dinner, come back here, and go to bed together. It had been inevitable from the moment he had laid his hand on her shoulder because it was a natural thing to do, and she had accepted the naturalness of the act, from the moment he said her name on the library stairs, from the moment she dialed his number, from the moment she heard her father's voice on her answering machine in Phoenix, from the moment of her birth. It had been inevitable. They had stepped on the edge of one of his infinite images, and they would fall forever, bound together by an invisible filament that had been drawing them together all their lives.

164

SEVENTEEN

"DO YOU UNDERSTAND any of this?" Frank Holloway asked Barbara on Sunday afternoon. She was on the terrace, surrounded by newspapers, but had paid no attention to any of them for a long time, had gazed at the river, at the trees, the clouds, everywhere but at the paper. She looked up at her father, who was holding two of the latest books she had borrowed from the library. One had an article by Ruth Brandywine; the other was yet another book on chaos.

"Not enough," she admitted. "The Brandywine article is all about the transition from one belief system to another in the adolescent. She's a lousy writer." She motioned toward the other book, with another of the lovely Mandelbrot sets on the cover. "That has some pretty neat pictures. Have you looked at it?"

"Some. Pretty pictures. So?"

"Look." She took the book from him and opened it to the first of a series of magnifications. "This is the original set, then this little area is enlarged a thousandfold, and here it is in detail. Enlarged again, and again. See that little black speck? The author chose it for the next magnification, and look, it's another Mandelbrot, like the original one. Zoom and there's a new border, not exactly the same, they never are, but similar. And again and again you find those same black specks, each one containing universes of new sets that never end."

Frank shook his head and sat down opposite her, studied her over his eyeglasses. "Again, so?"

"So why did Brandywine and a computer expert write an article together linking chaos to child behavior? Reference is made to it in that book. Tomorrow I'll start tracking it down. And why did Brandywine and a Nobel laureate in math work on joint papers on the same subject? How on earth does it tie into Lucas Kendricks and his murder?"

"Maybe it doesn't," Frank said. "What's happened to you? Mind, I'm not asking where you were for two days. None of my business, and all that. But something's happened."

"Yes," she said, looking again at the river. Fractal river, she rephrased it in her mind. Everything was fractal. Everything. "I don't know yet what happened. Maybe nothing. Too soon to tell."

He continued to study her for another minute, then got up heavily and started to reenter the house. "Honey, you've got a bitch of a case on your hands, and you know it. It's not the time to be distracted. Not now."

She looked at him in surprise. She had never felt more concentrated in her life. "Gotcha," she said. "And, Dad, I rather think that Tony will call and say he's going to be in the neighborhood in the next week or so, and can he drop in. Tell him sure, will you? And let me know when?"

"Good God," he said. "You're not starting that again, are you?"

For a moment she could not think what he was talking about; it was almost as if a long period of her life had been folded over and was now out of sight, out of mind. She shook her head. "This is business, all the way."

Still Frank hesitated. "Bobby, just be careful. Tony won't be manipulated, you know, any more than a card shark will be cheated at his own game."

"We'll see," she said slowly. "We'll see." She thought it interesting that Frank used *shark* in connection with Tony, exactly as she had done. Even more slowly she said, "Dad,

166

sooner or later I'm going to need some legal help, citing help, things like that."

"There's a lot of help available at the office."

"I'm going to need someone who knows where to tell help to start searching," she said, still speaking very slowly, carefully, keeping her voice as neutral as possible.

They did not look at each other, but she knew exactly when he breathed in, breathed out; knew how his fingers held the doorknob, how his gaze remained fixed straight ahead; and she knew he was equally aware of her every nuance. They were like two gunfighters, one in gray, one in blue, fingers on hair triggers, not wanting to do battle again, avoiding the direct look, the confrontational challenge, caught up in a dance whose motion had been frozen, a dance that neither could easily end.

Finally he spoke, his voice as flat as she had kept her own. "A long time ago, before you were born, a very good judge, Harry Bromleigh, gave me some good advice. He said never walk into the arena blindfolded. He said a lot of different things could act as blindfold—money, love, loyalty, ambition, hatred, religion, politics. You go in with the blind-fold on, they carry you out."

She nodded slightly.

"When the time comes you want help, that's the time to talk about it."

She nodded again, a nearly imperceptible motion, but enough. He opened the door and went inside the house.

Almost lazily she began to reconstruct the last two days, but the edges were blurred already. They ate, they went to bed, they got hungry and ate again, and went back to bed again. She smiled at the river. And they talked. With their mouths full, sitting on cushions on his floor, propped up with pillows in his bed, walking from a restaurant to his place or along the river, always talking. His past, hers, his parents, hers, his work, hers. He talked hard, but he listened just as hard, and he asked questions, made comments.

At one point she had said, "I'm not cut out to practice

167

law. What a thing to find out after passing the bar exam, after all those years in school."

"What are you cut out for?"

"Nothing. I had no business taking this case, but here I am, and every time I try to rationalize it, I trip and fall flat."

"You took it so we would meet. It's so simple. I never would have come to see you at work in court, you know. And you would have been just another good-looking woman passing by if we happened to be in the library at the same time, or on a sidewalk."

He had been smiling. She remembered suddenly how big his smiles were, how total. That was his quality, she decided then; he was involved totally every minute, every second, and there was no way the absent-minded-professor image could ever be linked to him. And, she reminded herself, he was very naïve, very innocent and ignorant. His life had been in academia from the time he was a child, academia and the abstractions of his work in mathematics.

"I can't make any commitments," she had said sometime during those two days. "I just don't know what I'll be doing after this case is over."

"So we have now, and then another now, and another one." He held her hand. "Do you expect to win the case? Will that influence your decision about afterward?"

"I'm going to give it my best shot," she said. "Win? I don't know. What's win in this instance? Nell can't win; she's been hurt too desperately. Her kids can't win. Lucas can't. *Win* has lost all meaning. But Nell can lose more than she already has, and that's what I'll try to prevent. Accept that there are no winners, and limit the losses. And that's why I'm dropping out. It's a rotten system."

"What kind of system would you have instead?"

"One in which no one ever kills anyone else, except in accidents. In which the system isn't rigged like a game, an adversarial system where scores are kept. In which the government's investigation doesn't stop with an accusation, as if the case has already ended. In which the deck isn't stacked against the helpless, the powerless. In which no one has to lie

168

and if anyone says I didn't do it, the statement is accepted as truthful because it is the truth." She stopped abruptly when she heard a stridency giving her words a harshness she had not intended. Not now, not with him.

"Utopia," he said softly. "I'll go there with you if you find it."

Was that when she had wept? She believed so, but the edges were blurred; one moment melted and became a different moment in a different time, a different place, and yet it was all one. She had wept. If not then, then another moment in that magical *now* that had lasted from Friday afternoon until Sunday.

On Wednesday Bailey checked in to say the fish was hooked. Tony had cornered him in a bar and interrogated him severely. Barbara let out a long breath. Bailey chuckled and said he'd drop in with more stuff tomorrow. He had a line on the detectives who had planted the listening device. Barbara could have kissed him, and in fact when he showed up on Thursday, she did kiss him. He was terribly embarrassed.

Barbara listened to his report intently. She did not ask anything stupid, like "Are you sure?" when he said that Walter Schumaker had paid the agency five hundred dollars with a check. Just a retainer, Bailey said; their fee would have ended up in the thousands. And they left Turner's Point the afternoon that Lucas had been killed. Upped and left, he said, without any attempt to retrieve the bug. Too many investigators swarming by then. Just another item on a very large bill.

"That other guy, Emil Frobisher. I got all there's to be got on his death."

She nodded. "It's been a while, I know. Tell us."

Frank looked removed, as if he were not even listening, but she knew better than that. Bailey scanned notes that from Barbara's perspective looked like hieroglyphs.

"Okay," he said then. "It's not pretty. Frobisher picked up a street kid in Denver, a fourteen-year-old male hustler,

169

and took him home to play with. Leads to a lot of speculation about what he was up to with Lucas, nothing specific, but he was one of a series of guys Frobisher took home and kept, sometimes for months at a time. Anyway, after a couple of weeks the kid freaked out, maybe withdrawal, maybe something else. A lot of blanks in the police reports, and the newspapers didn't have much more than what they were spoon-fed, but since the autopsy didn't show drugs, the speculation was psychosis. Brandywine's diagnosis. Anyway, the kid flips and there's real carnage at Frobisher's place, things wrecked, the computer system trashed, records destroyed, furniture torn up, the works. That evening a colleague, Herbert Margolis, paid a call and found Frobisher dead, shot, and the kid dead, shot. Frobisher was cut up pretty bad before the shot, and the kid was cut up. Blood everywhere. Hard to tell who did what to whom apparently, but the final report was that the kid went for Frobisher, who defended himself, accounting for the knife cuts they both had, and then the kid shot him and turned the gun on himself. At least, the gun was in his hand when Margolis found the bodies."

"My God," Barbara muttered after a moment. "This whole affair is like being caught up in a food processor. Where was Lucas Kendricks when all that was going on?"

"At Brandywine's house. She says he was her patient by then, in her care at home. She was trying a new treatment with him that demanded that kind of personal care. She says."

"So what's wrong with that?" Barbara asked. Bailey's face was so expressionless he looked asleep, except for his eyes, which gleamed the way they did when he had something he called "interesting."

"Interesting thing," he said then, "is that Brandywine's house is just a short walk through the woods to the Frobisher place. And it seems that the day Lucas Kendricks took her battery, he paid a visit to the Frobisher place. At least, he went to a barn on the property and carried something away with him. Different people there now, of course, but a kid

170

saw him, a little kid, and his father was the one who called the police to investigate a stranger prowling about. No description of what he took away with him. The kid just said a big bag."

That finished what he had found to date, and they talked about it for a few more minutes. Barbara asked him to find out what he could about the ranger who had spotted Lucas's car from McKenzie Pass, and he left soon afterward.

She sat frowning at the river for a long time, not willing to look at her father, who was still imitating a carved Buddha. There was too much, she had to admit. Too many loose ends, too many directions to pursue. It made her most unhappy that adolescents kept popping up. Lucas had been twenty when he went to work with Frobisher, Nell said a very young twenty; the boy involved with Frobisher's death; other boys; Nell's twelve-year-old son; even the teenage girl Lucas was accused of murdering. Too many young people. Things tended to get too messy when young people were involved; emotions flared, tempers erupted, judges got either testy or sentimental, both death to a case. And maybe none of it had a thing to do with Lucas's murder. She could say that to herself, but she didn't want to hear it from her father. It was all connected, she told herself firmly; it had to be.

That same afternoon Tony DeAngelo called Frank. He would be in the area the next afternoon, and would like to drop in if Frank and Barbara were both going to be home. As soon as Barbara heard this she called Mike Dinesen and invited him to dinner on Friday. Frank did not comment. When they took their daily walk to town they talked of many things that did not include Nell Kendricks and the murder case against her. But Barbara had talked a bit about the mathematician she had met and his gallery of art and slide show. Frank had looked at her in disbelief. A mathematician?

The weather had changed; it was too cool now to remain on the deck in the evenings. As soon as the sun went down the chill in the air drove them inside, where Frank lighted the fire in the fireplace. But in the afternoon with the

171

lowering sun softening the light, erasing hard edges everywhere, and the river turning golden and motionless, the deck was still first choice for any gathering.

Barbara waited in her chair while Frank went to answer the doorbell and admit Tony that Friday afternoon. She did not rise or offer to shake hands when he appeared. She nodded. "Hello, Tony. Sorry I was so rushed the other day."

"Not just rushed," he said, examining her face with the same kind of intensity she remembered, as if he had to rememorize her features time and again.

"Not just rushed," she repeated lightly. "Mad as hell, was what. Sit down, help yourself to the booze, coffee, whatever. We're very informal out here in the boonies."

He was dressed in a gray suit with a red tie that he now loosened. He hated ties, always had. Frank took his usual chair and tasted his coffee to see if it was still hot.

"How are things, Tony?" Frank asked. "It's been a long time."

"Very long time," Tony said. He pulled another chair closer to Barbara's and shook his head as if in wonder. "I can't get over how marvelous you look. You went off and found the Fountain of Youth or something."

"Or something. Do help yourself to a drink."

He poured coffee but kept his gaze on her. "Have dinner with me later?"

"Can't. We have a guest coming. Sorry, but thanks."

"Another time, then. I'll give you a call."

She sipped her coffee and looked at the molten river. "I think I'm going to be pretty busy."

There was a silence of several seconds. When she glanced at him again, his eyes were narrowed, and a watchful expression had chased his openness and friendliness of moments before.

She regarded him candidly, waiting for whatever he intended to say, making not the slightest pretense at real interest. She knew his expressions so well, she realized, when it changed again, and subdued anger made his sharp face look even sharper; his cheekbones, his nose, his chin all

172

seemed more prominent, as if the skin had stretched tighter over them. She found herself thinking he looked like a man whose corset pinched unmercifully. She knew this controlled anger had been one of the things about him that had attracted her in the beginning. It was dangerous, she had suspected; such anger so close to the surface, too tightly suppressed, would erupt and ignite everything in its way. That had been exciting.

"We'll be sending you an official notification," he said then, very cool, the anger still there, still stretching his skin too tight. "I thought I might as well bring it up while I'm in the neighborhood, give you time to object if you want to. We're planning to obtain perpetuation of testimony from the psychiatrist, Ruth Brandywine, probably on video, as soon as we can arrange a time with her."

Barbara turned away and raised her cup to her lips. After a few seconds, she said, "Shaky case, Tony? Need more ammunition? I'll fit it in somehow, of course."

"So glad you can find the time," he said coldly. "Well, it's been interesting, seeing you again after so many years. Thought you'd have found yourself an accountant or something by now."

"And you? Find a glamorous heiress yet?"

"As a matter of fact, there is someone, and she is quite well off." He stood up. "Good to see you, Frank. Beautiful place you have here."

Frank got up to walk out with him. Barbara murmured, "So long, Tony. See you in court." He nodded. As soon as they were gone and she heard the car crunching gravel in the driveway, she stood up and poured herself a shot of bourbon and drank it down neat.

"Nerves?" Frank asked, returning to the terrace. "My God, you didn't show a sign of nerves."

She grinned. "Celebration."

Once or twice a week Barbara cooked dinner, and they went out to a restaurant at least once a week, but Frank made dinner the other nights. Her suspicion that he merely

173

tolerated her cooking was confirmed when he said incredulously, "You're going to make dinner for the young man? Must be easier ways than that to get rid of him."

"It seemed fair; he's my guest, after all."

"And it's our reputations. I'll cook."

She kissed his cheek. "You're really not bad as a parental figure, you know? I wonder if I can do anything about the dining room table." She went to the doorway to look at it, then shook her head. The table was covered with her papers, books, maps, her little computer. . . . "Okay, kitchen it is."

When Mike arrived, Frank was putting the finishing touches on a duck in pumpkin seed sauce, and the kitchen table was perfect since she could sit there with Mike and they could all talk. She was ridiculously glad that Mike did not bring a bottle of wine, or a token flower, or anything else. And she was glad that he was in jeans and a sweater. Himself. Within five minutes he and Frank were arguing about whether children should be forced to study math.

"I never would have got out," Frank said. "The law would have lost a brilliant attorney, and for what? So I can get the right change in the supermarket?"

"I can't always do that," Mike said. "But you would have got out. If you had known without a doubt that math was required, you would have mastered it exactly as you mastered whatever it is that lawyers have to study."

Frank laughed. "Law. The Constitution. Civics. History."

"Give me a quadratic equation any day."

Frank came to the table and poured himself a glass of wine. "What's so great about chaos? Barbara showed me the pictures, and I said, 'So what?' She didn't really know so what."

"We're finding out so what at a pretty good clip," Mike said. "We have tools we never had before to measure and predict aspects of nature that were out of bounds for centuries." Barbara had put candles on the table; he picked up the matches she had put down and lighted one. "Watch the smoke," he said. A column of silvery smoke rose straight up, then started to swirl around and disappeared. "Turbu-

174

lence," Mike said and blew out the candle. "We've always known it was there, in smoke, in the flow of water, in the heart, the brain, but we couldn't do anything with it. We didn't have the tools. Now we do. We know now that it's not incremental, but catastrophic in nature. Turbulence arrives all at once, the way a pot of water boils all at once. Or the smoke breaks out of the smooth column."

Frank sipped his wine, listening with a careful expression. "You say predictions, but I read that no one can predict the weather any more than my grandfather could."

"That's right," Mike said cheerfully. "But that's an important thing to know, you see. What we know now is how sensitive systems are to initial conditions, and we know we can't always predict those initial conditions, therefore no guaranteed weather predictions. But do you have any idea how much money has gone into research of weather with the goal of perfect predictions?"

"No," Frank growled.

"Me neither. But gobs and gobs. Now a lot of it can go into something more productive."

"How do those pretty pictures figure in all this?" Frank took his wine back to the working half of the kitchen and began to stir something in a pot.

"Those Mandelbrot images are derived from one of the simplest algorithms ever discovered—" He stopped when Frank groaned very loudly. "Anyway, from this very simple instruction those sets are derived; they have fractal properties, that is, they are self-similar, no matter what the scale is, and they are infinite. From the simple comes the most complex. And that describes just about every natural object that exists, they all have fractal properties. The most complex dynamic systems can be described by another equation that is equally simple, and it has a universal application. That means it can be applied to all turbulent systems up and down the line. We used to think each one had to be considered independently and painstakingly worked out. Now there is a universal algorithm to use. What we're learning is that under the most chaotic-appearing systems, there is order and simplicity. And from order arises chaos. And the world is not what it seemed to be just a few years ago."

Frank put the lid back on the pot and looked at Mike directly. "Can you see any way any of that could pose a threat to someone? Would anyone kill for any of that?"

"No," Mike said. "I can't see anything like that. Not yet, anyway." He looked apologetically at Barbara, who shrugged. "Frobisher was a minor-league player," he said. "I looked up what he published, and it's not really much. Of course, he started before there were any clear indications where any of this would lead. He was one of the pioneers, but unfortunately he seemed to have a knack for dead ends instead of the mainstream."

"Wasn't any of his work any good?" Barbara asked. "Why did Schumaker invite him to collaborate then? And Brandywine? They seemed to think he had something."

Mike pulled out a folded paper and glanced at it. He folded it again and wrote down a few figures. "Look, you have to understand something basic or nothing else will make any sense. This is the algorithum for the Mandelbrot sets. You take one number, C, and assign it a value. Say one and a half. Z is an imaginary number with a value of zero. You simply add Z to C and feed the result back in over and over and over. It's the iteration that creates the set. You don't even need a computer—that just makes it go faster, but they can be plotted by hand on a grid. An ordinary grid with a horizontal and a vertical axis. Each time you iterate the formula you put down a dot, and eventually you have a pattern. But sometimes the formula will give you a result that flies right off the grid, out to infinity, and that's what fascinated Frobisher. Not the sets, but the ones that sent the attractor into infinity. And he believed and was attempting to prove that there were visual cues that would lead a good perceptive observer to anticipate which sets would end that way. Remember that this was in the infancy of the research, no guidelines yet, no mentors to ask questions of, damn little in print, and a half dozen people who were obsessed by the whole field. All of them were interested in the transition

176

zone, the phase space, where one thing becomes another. If Frobisher had been able to come up with an equation that would eliminate the ones that didn't work, he would have made his name. That's why Schumaker got interested in his work, I guess. He's an operator, an opportunist. He's worked with nearly everyone in the field at one time or another, just to keep his name up there, and now he's on the lecture circuit, the big bucks circuit. I think he's pretty much dropped out."

"And Brandywine? She was into juvenile schizophrenia. How could that tie in?"

Mike shook his head. "I just don't know. No way that I can see." He glanced at Frank, who was standing immobile with a wooden spoon in his hand. "Remember the time element," Mike said. "You're talking about seven or eight years ago, maybe ten or even twelve years ago. There just wasn't any money for chaos research. Schumaker swung a lot of weight and could have got funded for just about anything he wanted to do, but Frobisher and Brandywine? I don't think so. And if they were onto something big and important, something that could have brought fame and fortune the way it's happened to a few of the early researchers, if that was the case, why didn't they publish? Why did they all stop? And apparently they did stop whatever they were doing. Brandywine is back into her juvenile studies, as far as I can tell. And Schumaker hasn't done anything real for years. The other one, Margolis, he's into artificial intelligence, in computers, nothing at all to do with chaos."

Frank had too much sense to say I told you so, but the unspoken words were in the air, and Barbara could feel only a deep frustration. She had learned that a strange attractor was not simply a point but could also be a pattern that repeated over and over, always similar, never exactly the same, and she felt that the pattern of those scientists circling around Lucas, the dead boy and the dead Frobisher, all made up a strange attractor. It was all of a piece, and without that piece she had no case for Nell Kendricks. She, Barbara, was part of the pattern, she acknowledged, although she could

177

not say how or why. But she was part of it and had to see it through to wherever it took her.

A strange butterfly in Brazil had awakened, had floated off a leaf somewhere in a jungle, and she had been set in motion. So far, she felt almost certain, she had made the right movements, but with each new choice, each new decision, each new bit of information, there was the danger that she would be flung off the grid, out to infinity. If that happened, she followed the line of thought, she would not be able to finish something she had started, something important—not only for Nell, but for her, also.

EIGHTEEN

ON FRIDAY FRANK, Barbara, and Nell had a final conference before the trial. They were in the living room of his house, before a fire muttering to itself, as, outside, a cold wind drove fir needles against the windows. Frank had insisted on the topic that headed his list of priorities for discussion.

He watched Nell closely over the rims of his glasses when he started. "You still have the option to change your plea. You know that, don't you?"

She nodded. She was wearing an oversized sweater that accentuated her diminutive body; she had lost weight in the past months, and she appeared more frail and more vulnerable than ever.

"Right," Frank said. "You can opt out right up to the time the case goes to the jury. You know what Tony's offering: manslaughter—he wouldn't fight self-defense—and a probable sentence of two to four years."

"I know," she said. "But I can't do that. I didn't do it."

"Okay. So we go all the way." He leaned back in his chair and let Barbara have the floor, but he was troubled. Every line on his face, his posture, his voice all attested to his concern.

Barbara began to outline the procedure. "First, they will establish that the cause of death was a gunshot wound to the head. There will be the sheriff's men who responded to the call, the search for the body, autopsy, all of that. And it will be ugly." She paused. "Do you ever take tranquilizers? Would they help?"

Nell shook her head. "I don't react very well to most drugs. Tranquilizers do funny things to my system and even make me hyper. Doc says I should leave them alone."

Doc. Barbara wanted to find him and give him a swift kick, but she did not comment. No one had commented about the forlorn look that had come to lodge on Nell's face. Barbara continued to prepare her client for the ordeal to begin the following week. "Next, there will be evidence about the location, who had access, things of that sort, and the weapon itself, your abilities as a marksman. I'm afraid he'll call various neighbors of yours to add to the details, and that might get hard to take."

Nell nodded, white-faced, her eyes too large.

"The next part will be motive. I doubt that they will try to do much with that, but what little they do will again rely on neighbors and your in-laws. About all they can establish is that you were an abandoned wife. The problem is that they won't need much more than that for a motive, if they can establish that you were the only one with opportunity, because most murders are within families. Tony is certain to concentrate on that fact in his summation. That and the fact that circumstantial evidence is sufficient. In your case that means opportunity, being in the place at the time; weapon, probably your rifle, or one exactly like it; and the ability to use the weapon, which I think they will more than substantiate. Now, I can't deny any of those bits, no one can. All we can hope for is to demonstrate that another person had equal opportunity and took advantage of it."

Nell looked almost wildly to Frank, who appeared even more grim than he had before. He shook his head.

Very slowly Barbara said, "Nell, if the case were confined to the points Dad made a while ago, I would tell you to pay close attention to what he advised. Tony will fight to keep the past out of it, to limit everything to what happened on that ledge that Saturday, and I'll fight just as hard to expand our playing field to the utmost. The judge will decide finally what will or won't be admitted as relevant. And right now I can't guess what that decision will be."

Now the jury was in place and Judge Kendall Lundgren was on the bench. He was an ascetic intellectual, pale-faced, with thin, sandy hair, in his early forties; he would have looked at home in a monastery. According to Frank's summary, he had no sense of humor and little patience with theatrics in court or with stupidity. He had talked very briefly to the jury about the gravity of a murder case, about reasonable doubt, and mandatory sentencing guides. It had been so brief that Barbara had begun to worry that he might have a date in Hawaii, a hanging maybe, or more likely a burning; he could be itching to get on a plane. She knew he was considered to be a fair judge, but still she worried, exactly as she always did. Tony was finishing his opening statement.

"What the state will prove is that Nell Kendricks deliberately shot to death her husband, that no one else could have done it, that no one else had cause to do it. Her rifle was the instrument of death, and no one else had access to that rifle. We will prove that no one else could have entered her house that Saturday in June, no one could have taken the rifle. And in fact no one else knew that her husband would arrive that day or any other day."

When Tony concluded and resumed his seat, he did not look at the defense table. He had not looked at Barbara a single time yet. He had nodded in her direction, but his eyes had focused on a spot just over her shoulder. She and Nell were alone at the defense table. Her father had chuckled when she said that that was how she wanted it. He was seated directly behind her, one of the law clerks from his office on one side of him, and John and Amy Kendricks on the other. Clive was in the scant audience—not directly behind the defense table, but off to one side where he could see Nell's profile. Mike planned to come by between classes; curiosity, he said. When Mike asked if she would wear her three-hundred-dollar suit, she had said no emphatically. She wore a skirt and jacket, a very simple blouse, nothing fancy, nothing expensive, just in very good taste. Nell was in a dark dress, low heels. Barbara had told her to wear low heels every day, and she had been bewildered but compliant. Barbara knew that when they stood together the jury would notice and remember how very small Nell was. Barbara was seven inches taller than Nell, wider in the shoulders; she felt gargantuan when they stood together.

She got to her feet unhurriedly and approached the jury. "Ladies and gentlemen," she said, "the defense does not have to prove anything except that there is not simply a reasonable doubt, but in this case a great doubt, that Nell Kendricks killed her husband." Tony had been declamatory; she was conversational. Go for the contrasts, one of her instructors had said, and treat the jury as if you really believe they have a brain among them. Sometimes they may even have one. "It is the duty of the state to investigate every lead, to pursue every bit of evidence, to actively search out those who have testimony concerning the crime being investigated. If the state fails to discharge that duty, there is a basis for reasonable doubt. The state has vast resources at its disposal—manpower, subpoena power to gather testimony, financial resources to carry the investigation to wherever the evidence leads—and if the state misuses those resources, or fails to use them, there is basis for a reasonable doubt. The state would have you believe a murder was committed in isolation, and that it does not matter where Lucas Kendricks was for the past seven years, and yet, you and I, ladies and gentlemen, know that human acts of such violence do not take place in isolation. The defense will demonstrate that Lucas Kendricks had powerful enemies who were actively pursuing him, that those enemies performed illegal acts in the course of that pursuit, and that Lucas Kendricks knew he was being followed, pursued, and he was fearful because of it. And that, ladies and gentlemen, is a basis for a reasonable doubt. Nell Kendricks did not shoot her husband, the father of her two children. She did not know where he was. She did not know when or if he would visit her. The defense will demonstrate that his enemies knew those things, and that provides a basis for a reasonable doubt. The state, with all its power and all its resources, has brought the wrong person to trial."

Tony was whispering to one of his assistants, who got up and left the courtroom. When Barbara took her chair, Frank's hand pressed her shoulder briefly, and he passed her a slip of paper. *You're walking a thin line. Keep an eye on KL's face.*

Judge Kendall Lundgren ignored her and said to Tony, "Let us begin, if you please." He, Barbara thought, was part of the state. She nodded slightly to let Frank know she understood.

Tony efficiently led his first witness through his testimony. Sheriff Bernard Gray established that murder had been done, when, and where.

"Sheriff Gray," Barbara said when Tony concluded, "I have a map also. Will you look at it, please, to make certain it is essentially like your own?" It was much bigger, in greater detail; it showed, as did the one already introduced, the trail from Old Halleck Hill Road to the waterfall, the bifurcation there, the dead end side, and the continuation that led down to Nell's property. The sheriff agreed that it was the same.

"Will you examine these photographs, please, to make certain they are comparable to the ones you took." Like the map, the photographs were enlarged conspicuously. When they were accepted, Barbara put one on an easel before the sheriff. "Where would you place the mark in the rocks where the bullet struck? Please, indicate it on the photograph."

He looked from his picture back to hers and finally touched a spot. Barbara marked it with a red pen. "Thank you. You said in your testimony that it is about four feet high, is that right?"

"Yes, Ma'am."

"And you testified that you did not find a spent shell casing, is that right?"

"Yes, Ma'am."

"Where did you look?"

"All over the place."

"Show us on the photograph, will you? All over where?"

Sheriff Gray looked patient and long-suffering as he pointed at the photograph. "Four of my men searched every inch of that ledge," he said, pointing to the section on Nell's side of the gorge.

"How about below the ledge?" Barbara asked.

"There, too."

"All four of them?"

"I don't think so. That trail's hardly wide enough for one grown man, but they looked below, too."

"Three men looked around there?"

"I think maybe one." Quickly he added, "Wasn't much point in looking down there. The shot couldn't have been fired from there, not and hit anyone. You couldn't have seen him from below, not until you got up to the ledge."

"All right. How about on the side of the ledge, where the main trail starts to climb?"

"We looked there, too."

"How many men looked there?"

"I don't remember."

"Could it have been just one man?"

"Objection," Tony said. "The witness has said he doesn't remember."

"Sustained."

She got him to admit that the bullet they had recovered had been so badly deformed, with just fragments remaining, that it could not be stated with absolute certainty that Nell Kendricks's rifle had fired it.

"And you went to her house where you found her rifle. Where was it?"

"On the couch in the living room."

"And shells?"

"On a table by it. A box about half full."

"I see. So you examined the rifle, looked for fingerprints?"

"Yes, Ma'am. There weren't any prints, just a few smudges."

"Did you find that strange?"

"I didn't think of it one way or the other, I guess. There was a towel on the couch. I guess I just thought she wiped it off."

"Oh? You assumed that at the time?"

He looked confused for a moment. "I just didn't think anything of it," he said then.

"What about the box of shells? Did you examine that for fingerprints?"

"Yes, Ma'am. Smudges, that's all."

"And did you think anything about that?"

"Objection, Your Honor," Tony said. He sounded bored. "What the witness thought at the time has no bearing on the facts."

"Sustained."

"You found a backpack on the ledge and a wallet in Lucas Kendrick's pocket. Was there anything about the contents of the wallet that you found strange?"

Sheriff Gray flushed slightly. "His driver's license expired in 1982. I guess that was strange."

"Yes, I think so. How about credit cards?"

"Two. They expired, too."

"In 1982?"

"Yes."

"Did you look for a car?"

"No, Ma'am."

"Why not?"

"I didn't see one at the head of the trail, and I guess we just took it for granted that he walked in."

"Did you know Lucas Kendricks?"

"No, Ma'am."

"Do you know Nell Kendricks?"

"No, Ma'am."

"Yet, you said in your direct testimony that you got the call about Lucas Kendricks and you headed straight out to the old Dorcas place. Did you know Nell Kendricks's maiden name was Dorcas?"

"Your Honor, I object! I can't see the relevance of any of this!"

"Ms. Holloway, is there any relevance here?"

"Yes, Your Honor. Did this witness know that Lucas Kendricks had been away for seven years? I think that is relevant to his investigation."

Judge Kendall Lundgren nodded slightly and said to the sheriff, "You may answer the question."

"Yes, I knew who she was. And I knew he had been gone a lot of years."

"But you guessed that he had walked in? Is that what you're telling us?"

"Yes."

She turned away from him for the first time in many minutes. The jury was following closely, and Tony no longer looked bored. "Did you know where his car was, Sheriff?" she asked, and watched a muscle move in Tony's jaw as he stood up swiftly to object.

"Your Honor, objection. Where the car was has no relevance, nor does the fact that the sheriff knew or did not know its whereabouts."

"I agree," Judge Lundgren said. "Sustained. Ms. Holloway, please confine your questions to the scope of this trial."

"No further questions," she said quietly, and resumed her seat to listen to Tony undo some of what she had done. He took the sheriff over the marks on the rocks and got him to state that bullets tumble erratically at times, especially after going through bones. She had expected Tony's line of

185

argument, and he well knew that she had her own expert witness to call to dispute what the sheriff was saying. And so it goes, she thought. Nothing unforeseen, everything in order, as predictable as movements in a stately dance in rhythm with unheard music. What no one could foretell was when the music would become discordant, when a false note would break the rhythm, or even if that false note had already been played, if the ripples already were forming, the pattern already altered irretrievably.

John and Amy Kendricks left the courtroom when Tony began questioning the medical examiner about the body of their son. Nell was the color of chalk, and after the first question she bowed her head and kept her gaze on the table before her. She did not move again. Barbara had known Dr. Emerson Riley for a long time; he was her father's age, but not yet retired. A gentle man, a beekeeper by hobby, and scrupulously fair, he treated each case in which he was called exactly like all others; for him justice was completely blind.

"So the bullet entered here," Tony said, pointing to a picture that showed a line drawing of a head with the path of the bullet in a thick black line. "And it exited here. Almost a straight line."

Dr. Emerson Riley held up his hand. "May I correct you, sir?"

"Of course."

"We cannot be certain of the exit; the damage was too intensive. As I stated, we can only estimate from the trajectory that we are certain about, how it continued."

Tony inclined his head. "Thank you, Doctor. Now if the victim had his head lowered even a little, this much—" he tilted the drawing so that the heavy black line was almost horizontal, then a bit more so that it now was slanting upward instead of down—"we could account for the trajectory, couldn't we?"

Barbara heard her father's breath and knew he would be objecting by now, but she made no motion.

Dr. Riley glanced at her before answering, then said, "Yes, you could say that."

186

"Or if he was kneeling—tying his shoelace, for example—that trajectory would fit the situation. Is that correct?"

Again there was a very slight pause; again Barbara made no movement. The doctor said that was so.

Tony was finished with him quickly. There was a glint of malice in his eyes when he passed Barbara on his way to his chair.

"Dr. Riley," she began, "it is possible that I could describe a number of positions that would account for the trajectory of that bullet, isn't it?"

"Yes. Of course."

"Tracing the trajectory of a bullet through a human body is a fairly exact science, isn't it?"

"It is."

"Yes. Exactly what you can tell about the position of the victim before the bullet strikes?"

"Nothing. If all we have is a body with a wound, we can't tell a thing about the position before the wound was inflicted."

"Thank you, Doctor. Was Lucas Kendricks in good health as far as you could ascertain from your autopsy?"

"Yes, he was. But he was dehydrated."

"Dehydrated. He had not been drinking enough fluids?"

"That's right."

"For how long? Could you tell that?"

"I would say more than one day, but not more than a week." He talked about the condition of the kidneys and the blood in terms that Barbara knew were too technical, but she did not interfere. He had said what she wanted.

"So he had been eating things like trail mix and dried fruits and had not been drinking enough water for a number of days. What else did you observe about his body?"

"His feet were badly blistered. Some of the blisters were infected."

"And can you estimate how old any of those blisters were?"

"Some about five days, maybe four, some brand new."

187

"I see. And what conclusion do you draw from your observations, Doctor?"

He shrugged slightly. "The man had been hiking for four or five days in improper clothing without enough food or water."

"Improper clothing? What do you mean?"

"Wrong kind of boots. No change of socks. Cotton socks with threadbare heels and toes. Just not dressed for a long hike."

Barbara nodded and walked toward the defense table, where she turned and asked, "Were there any traces of any drugs in the body?"

"None."

"Not just illegal drugs, but medications?"

"Nothing."

"How tall was he, Doctor?"

"Five eleven."

"So the entry wound was about five feet five inches above the ground, and angled downward?"

"Objection," Tony snapped. "The witness doesn't know the position of the victim when the shot was fired."

"Sustained," Judge Lundgren said.

Barbara turned to regard Tony for a long moment. Then she said, "I withdraw the question. I agree entirely, Mr. DeAngelo. The witness doesn't know that."

Tony jumped to his feet, but before he could object, Judge Lundgren said sharply, "Ms. Holloway, please save your commentary for your summation."

She was aware of a stir in the jury box, but she looked at Dr. Riley again. "Thank you, Doctor. No more questions."

Tony hesitated momentarily, then said that he had no further questions. It was almost four, time to adjourn for the day. Barbara stood with Nell at her side as the judge left the courtroom, and she knew every eye of the jury was on the small woman at her side.

NINETEEN

THE NEXT DAY Tony called to the stand the UPS delivery man, Ed Seligman, who testified that when he delivered the computer to Nell's house, he had seen the rifle on the couch and the box of shells nearby. He had noticed because that seemed a strange place to keep a rifle in June, out of hunting season and all. Barbara had no questions for him.

James Gresham was next, a dignified witness who was succinct and obviously unhappy about being called. He admitted that no one could have gone to Nell's house after the delivery man because both he and his wife had been in the driveway or on the porch the entire time until they heard the shot. No one had come in past them.

Tawna, equally reluctant, recounted Nell's warning to lock her door because Lucas might show up and walk in. She confirmed that no one had entered by the road after the delivery man.

Lunch that day was subdued. Nell went off with her in-laws, and Frank and Barbara went to the Park Bar and Grill a block and a half away.

"It's going to get worse this afternoon," she said gloomily.

"You bet." Frank leaned over and patted her hand. "You haven't lost your touch, honey. I'm proud of you. Tony's racking up points, but so are you, Bobby. So are you."

She took a quick breath, but did not voice the swift and

bitter retort. Points, she thought, his points were as abstract as . . . as Mike's points that he charted on his computer. Now and then one sailed off into infinity, he had said, grinning; and when that happened you just started over with new numbers. Not with people, Barbara said under her breath: no more abstractions, no pretty computer pictures. Here and now Nell's life was the only point. Yesterday the jury had stirred with interest for a brief time; today they were zombielike, settling in deeper and deeper as if the emerging pattern had spread out too far, beyond their range of comprehension, beyond their vision. A bad sign. But nothing was off the chart yet, Barbara added grimly; she would make them see the connections, make them see the whole pattern. She knew she had to.

Tony was playing it very close; he was not giving her an opening to the past, and if she tried to bring in the past, he was on his feet objecting instantly. Judge Lundgren was going along. Although her father was looking drawn and anxious, so far he had not said, *I told you so.* She was grateful for that. She was also grateful that he was not reminding her that once the jury had decided, it would be a monumental job to undecide them. She attacked her salad with some vicious-ness.

Tony's next witness was Jessica Burchard. There was a hush in the courtroom as she rolled forward in her wheel-chair. She was a striking figure with a blue-gray shawl around her shoulders, a gray skirt that hid even her feet, a blue long-sleeved blouse that left only the ends of her fingers visible. She was obviously in pain. She looked very brave.

In a reverential voice Tony asked permission for her to be allowed to remain in her own chair, not to stand to take the oath; the judge nodded solemnly.

After Tony established her identity, he said, "Mrs. Bur-chard, did you ever hear Nell Kendricks threaten to shoot anyone?"

"Yes. I heard her say that."

"Please, just tell us about it in your own words."

She twisted to look up at the judge. "I don't think she meant anything by it. You know how people say things. . . ." Her voice was faint, and she was twisting a handkerchief around in her hands.

"Please, Mrs. Burchard, speak up. That's for the jury to decide," Judge Lundgren said kindly.

"Mrs. Burchard?" Tony said, equally gentle. "When did you hear Mrs. Kendricks say that?"

She looked down at her hands and said in a low voice, "On Thursday, a few days before he, before Lucas Kendricks, was shot."

"Go on. Just tell us about it."

She appeared to be making a great effort to force herself to speak, but when she did, the words tumbled out fast. "We were on my deck, and she said that she would shoot anyone who trespassed on her property. She was a very good shot, you see. And then when he, when Lucas was shot, I remembered what she had said, and I thought that he had told her he intended to cut down the trees. He tried it once before, before he ran away the last time, and I thought he must have told her he would actually do it this time. To raise money, of course. When I heard that he had been shot up on the ledge, that made me recall what she had said." She let out her breath and looked up at Tony, then looked past him to the defense table, and whispered, "I'm sorry."

Barbara turned as if to confer with her father, but in fact she was looking at Nell, who had become as cold and pale and rigid as an alabaster statue. "Take it very, very easy," she murmured to Nell, and then said to her father, "Bitch." He nodded and pulled out his notebook and made a note, as if she had reminded him of something or had made a request.

If Tony was as smart as she remembered, he wouldn't go much beyond that, Barbara thought. He was behaving like the perfect, solicitous, tender prosecutor doing a distasteful job that he didn't want to prolong. In fact, he asked only one more question.

"To your knowledge, did anyone else overhear what Mrs. Kendricks said that day?"

191

"I don't know," Jessie said. "I can't be certain. Except for my husband, of course. He was right at my elbow."

When Barbara stood up she felt as if she were on a slippery slope to a viper pit. Tony had been the good guy, and now she would play the heavy and take terrible advantage of this poor, brave, suffering woman.

"Mrs. Burchard," she said, "how can you be so certain that was on Thursday?"

"That's the day my husband is home in the afternoon. We always have open house, neighbors drop in."

"Isn't Thursday the day the bookmobile arrives at Turner's Point?"

"Yes."

"Was that the Thursday that people at Turner's Point saw a body in the river?"

"Your Honor, I object!" Tony said sharply. "It has not been established that this witness has any direct knowledge of what was going on at Turner's Point."

"Sustained."

"Who else was at your open house that Thursday?" Barbara asked.

Jessie shook her head. "I'm sorry. I just don't remember."

"Did any of your guests appear upset, excited?"

"I don't know. I don't remember. We always have open house on Thursday, and they seem to blend together. It's hard to remember any one in particular."

"But you recall exactly what Nell Kendricks said? Is that right?"

"Yes. Because when Lucas was shot, I remembered what she had said, and I thought that he had told her he intended to cut down the trees. He tried it once before, before he ran away the last time, and I thought he must have told her he would actually do it this time. To raise money, of course. When I heard that he had been shot up on the ledge, that made me recall what she had said."

Barbara nodded gravely and walked away a few steps,

192

her hands clasped before her, her head bowed a little. "How long have you known Nell?"

"Nine years, ever since we moved out to the river property."

"And her children? You know them?"

"Well, of course."

"You've seen her during times of trouble, and during good times, then. Is that right?"

"Yes, for nine years."

"Was she troubled on that Thursday? Excited?"

"I don't remember that she was."

"What were you all talking about when she said she would shoot a trespasser?"

"I can't remember. I just remember what she said."

"Yes, I see. Do you have children, Mrs. Burchard?"

"No." For the first time her voice sharpened and was clearly audible.

"How big are your parties when you have open house?"

"I don't know. It varies."

"Six people? Ten? Just a rough estimate."

"I don't know. Five or six, probably."

"And Nell Kendricks was usually one of them?"

"Yes, she used to come regularly."

"In fact, she picked up and delivered your library books, didn't she?"

"She used to."

"Yes. Did your group discuss literature at those open houses?"

"Not usually."

"Politics? Art? Local affairs?"

Jessie looked helplessly at Tony, as if to ask if she had to submit to any more of this. Barbara waited. She was standing by the corner of the defense table. Although she had not glanced at Tony, she knew that the expression he was wearing would be one of outrage at her badgering of this ill woman. Probably the jury was sharing that outrage by now.

"I don't know what we talked about," Jessie said fretfully. "Different things, local things, logging, things like that."

"So in the middle of discussing local affairs, Nell Kendricks said. . . ." Barbara paused. "Just remind us of that afternoon, will you?"

"Yes," Jessie said clearly. "We were on my deck, and she said that she would shoot anyone who trespassed on her property. She was a very good shot, you see. And then when he, when Lucas was shot, I remembered what she had said, and I thought that he had told her he intended to cut down the trees. He tried it once before, before he ran away the last time, and I thought he must have told her he would actually do it this time. To raise money of course. When I heard that he had been shot up on the ledge, that made me recall what she had said." She finished with a defiant, steady voice.

"Yes," Barbara said slowly. "I see. Did you make a note to yourself to help remember what happened that day?"

"No. I don't think it will ever fade in my memory. It made that kind of impression on me."

"Did you confide in anyone, tell anyone how bothered you were? Your husband, perhaps?"

"No."

Barbara looked out at the spectators, more today than yesterday, but still not a great crowd. She saw Lonnie among those watching. She did not turn back to Jessie, but now looked at the jury instead. She met hostility there, and regarded them soberly as she asked her next question.

"Did you confide in your housekeeper, tell her what you felt you had to say?" From the corner of her eye she saw Lonnie sit up straighter, but she continued to gaze at the jurors.

"No. I simply worried about it by myself."

"So you thought he had told her he actually would do it this time?"

"To raise money, of course," Jessie said.

"Go on," Barbara said softly.

Jessie looked bewildered.

"When you heard that he had been shot. . . ."

"When I heard that he had been shot up on the ledge, that made me recall what she had said."

"Mrs. Burchard, do you have a tape recorder?"

"Yes."

"You stated that you did not confide in your husband regarding your testimony here, or your housekeeper, or anyone else, and you said you did not write it down to help your memory. I ask you, did you rehearse it with a tape recorder?"

Tony was on his feet instantly, but Jessie cried, "No, I didn't have to rehearse it!" and his objection was drowned by her words.

Judge Lundgren said dryly, "Since the witness has chosen to answer the question, I overrule the objection."

Barbara looked at Jessie for a second, then shook her head; she glanced at the jury, and this time the hostility was gone.

"No further questions," she said, and sat down.

Chuck Gilmore testified next. Although a very large man, over six feet, and broad through the shoulders, with a deep chest, he always had appeared comfortable with himself, at ease in flannel shirts and jeans. Now in a suit and tie, he squirmed in the witness chair. To Barbara's surprise he was as reluctant as James and Tawna Gresham had been. Tony had to work at it, but in the end, Chuck Gilmore said that Nell was a natural with a rifle; he had seen her shoot at different times, and she had threatened him a few years ago when she found him on her land.

"Mr. Gilmore," Barbara said in her cross-examination, "when were you on Nell Kendrick's land when she threatened you?"

He shrugged. "Five, six years ago."

"Was it in the winter, spring, when?"

"Spring, maybe February."

"Wasn't that the spring following the death of Nell Kendricks's grandfather, Benjamin Dorcas?"

He squirmed and shrugged his shoulders, ran a finger under his shirt collar, and finally said maybe it was.

"Yes, you know it was, don't you, Mr. Gilmore? Please, just yes or no."

"Yes."

"Mrs. Kendricks found you on her land, cutting down brush one day. Is that right?"

"Yes."

"Was she alone when she came upon you?"

"Well, she had the baby, but no one else."

"I see. Her baby was with her." Barbara faced Nell. "You knew her grandfather, didn't you, Mr. Gilmore? Was he a friend?"

"Yes. More than twenty years he was a good friend."

"And yet, within months of his death you started to cut a trail through the property he bequeathed to his grand-daughter."

"Objection, Your Honor. Counsel is jumping to conclusions. There is no preparation for such a question."

"Sustained. Ms. Holloway, perhaps you should lead up gradually to such a conclusion."

"Thank you, Your Honor. Mr. Gilmore, why were you on Nell Kendricks's property cutting brush?"

"I wanted to make a trail down to the beach," he said without hesitation.

Barbara very carefully did not turn to look at Tony. "Mr. Gilmore, if you found someone on your land cutting down brush, what would you do?"

"Objection," Tony snapped. "That's pure conjecture."

"Sustained."

"Did Mrs. Kendricks have a gun that day?"

"No. She said she'd get it and come back and if I was still there, she'd perforate me until I'd work like a sieve." He sounded proud of Nell. Someone on the jury chuckled, and someone else echoed it.

Barbara smiled also but become sober once more as she asked, "Did she ever threaten you again, after that day?"

"No. I never set foot on her land again, neither."

"Were you told that she had threatened you indirectly?"

"Objection," Tony said. "Counsel knows better than to introduce hearsay and rumors."

"Your Honor," Barbara said swiftly, "if this witness received a message that included a threat, that is not hearsay, but direct testimony."

Judge Lundgren nodded to Chuck Gilmore. "Overruled. You may answer the question."

"No," he said after a slight pause. "There were rumors, like he said." He looked at Tony. "But no one told me anything to my face."

"You heard such rumors when, Mr. Gilmore?"

Tony objected and was sustained.

Suddenly Barbara realized that she was doing exactly what Tony expected. She walked to the defense table thinking, remembering what Nell had said about that afternoon at Turner's Point. Chuck had not been in the store, and now she believed he had not been in Turner's Point at all. No matter how she approached the matter of the two men who had claimed to be tree cutters, Tony would object and be sustained, because this witness knew nothing about it except what he had been told after the fact. Abruptly she turned and said, "No more questions, Mr. Gilmore. Thank you."

And that surprised Tony enough that he was not instantly prepared to have his witness repeat his most damning statements. Barbara took little satisfaction in knowing she had judged correctly this time. She felt like a quarry being run in tighter and tighter circles; no matter how clever her maneuvers, they were delaying tactics only.

"I'll have to testify!" Nell cried that evening. "I have to tell my side."

They were in a dim restaurant; it was not yet dinner time, and they were the only customers. They had agreed on meeting here at the Swiss Chalet for a drink, for a conference, for relaxation before Nell and John and Amy Kendricks returned to her place, and Frank to his. Barbara was staying in town, she had announced, things she had to look up.

197

Now she regarded Nell soberly. She shook her head and nudged her father with an elbow. "You do it." He looked as tired as she was feeling, as discouraged.

"Right," he said, and cleared his throat. "Why did you get the rifle out of the gun cabinet a second time? Why did you leave it on the couch that day? Why did you send your children packing the day before their father was due? Did you ever let them go away without you before? In fact, didn't your father-in-law warn you that Lucas was coming by noon Saturday? Why did you call the doctor who lived a few minutes away instead of James Gresham, who was already at hand? Did you need a few minutes in order to try to wipe the gun clean? Didn't you take the gun up to the ledge and, when your husband appeared, shoot him? Weren't you afraid that you would not be able to resist him if he said he was moving in again? Why didn't you divorce your husband after he abandoned you and your children? Did he tell you that this time he fully intended to harvest the trees, claim his share?"

He had done this so rapidly that no one had reacted, but abruptly John Kendricks reached out and put his arm around Nell's shoulders. "My God," he said. "My God!"

Amy Kendricks picked up her glass and drank most of the bourbon and water in it. Nell was wooden.

"That's for openers," Barbara murmured. "It would get worse. Are you prepared to say exactly what happened on the ledge?"

"I told you," Nell said faintly.

"You told us something, but there's something else, isn't there?"

"I don't know," Nell said. "I've tried and tried to make myself remember every second, but. . . . I don't know."

"Exactly," Barbara said. "Tomorrow, Mr. Kendricks, it will be your turn, and then, if Tony thinks he's made enough of a case, if he blocks my every move to get that girl's murder included, he'll probably rest."

"But you can bring up things like that when you do the defense, can't you?" Amy asked. "They can't keep the whole story out like that, can they?"

Barbara glanced at her father. He had been brusque, his questions so fast they had been staccato, but now he said very gently, "Mrs. Kendricks, the problem is that the prosecutor may convince the judge, and the jury, that it doesn't matter where your son was all those years, what he was involved in, where he was that last week of his life even. They may take the position that since Nell didn't know any of those things, they are immaterial to the state's case. All they need do is prove to the satisfaction of the jury that she was the only one who could have shot him."

"There has to be a way to get at the truth!" Amy Kendricks cried. "They can't just pretend nothing else happened to Lucas. Nell didn't shoot him, but someone did! They have to let you find whoever was chasing him, who it was who wrecked his car, and our house! They can't pretend it didn't happen."

Nell glanced at her watch and said they had to go; the kids would be anxious if she was late. "All this is pretty upsetting for them," she added. She sounded defeated, her voice was dull, and her eyes were filled with tears that she kept blinking back. What will happen to them, if . . . if . . . ? she had asked early on. She had not brought it up again, but the question hung around her like an aura.

They all stood up. "Mr. Kendricks, tomorrow will be an ordeal for you," Barbara said. "Tony will try to keep you on a very short leash, and I'll try to stretch it out. Try to get some sleep tonight. You, too, Nell," she added, and she put her arms around Nell, and then kissed her cheek. "It's not over yet," she said. "I have every intention of blowing this whole damn thing right out of the water."

At eleven-thirty she stirred in Mike Dinesen's arms. His breathing had changed; he was falling asleep, and she was afraid if she did not get up this minute, she would fall asleep also. A hard rain beat against the windows; she was warm and content—dangerously warm and content, she realized as she caught herself drifting. This time she eased Mike's arm off her and tried to roll away without waking him up.

199

"You really meant it?" he asked sleepily.

"'fraid so," she said. "Go back to sleep. Don't wait up. I'll be late."

He pulled her to him and kissed her, and then rolled over onto his stomach. She swatted his bare bottom and got up.

Earlier, she had made coffee and put it in a thermos, and now she dressed quickly, collected her various things, the briefcase, purse, umbrella, and the thermos, and opened the door. The rain was businesslike, purposeful, a hard November Oregon rain that had gone on for hours and had not even started to show its stuff yet. Taking a deep breath, she went out into it, heading for Frank's law office, the law library. Two hours, she muttered to herself, but it was four in the morning when she returned to Mike's bed; he did not wake up.

The fragrance of coffee brought her struggling up from a very deep pit. By the time she reached the kitchen the coffee was done; Mike was at the table gathering sheets of computer paper. Often when she stayed overnight she found the table covered with pages of arcane symbols that she could not decipher any more than if they had been Martian recipes. Those times she realized that not only did she not know what he actually did, she did not even know the language he used for his work. Those times she regarded him with a touch of awe, mixed with a touch of skepticism in about equal proportions.

He finished clearing a corner of the table and jumped up to take her by the shoulders and guide her to a chair. He brought her coffee.

"You look like hell," he said cheerfully.

"Thank you."

"Did you sleep at all?"

"Sure."

He sat down opposite her and waited until she had sipped the hot coffee. "It all comes down today, doesn't it?"

"I don't know."

"I'll be there. I'm giving my graduate class a problem I can't solve. That's how they used me as a graduate student. Now I can see the point. I'll be there."

She finished the first cup of coffee and thought vaguely that after three or four more she might start feeling human again.

"Barbara," Mike said then, "what if she did it?"

She got up and walked past him to the counter and the coffee pot. "She didn't."

"You can't really know that. No one can except her. But what if she did? Won't it be worse for her to keep denying it and then be found guilty than to admit it and express remorse? I read somewhere that the expression of remorse is worth five years."

"With tears, more like seven," she said darkly.

"I was in court yesterday," Mike went on. "She's taking a real beating, isn't she? I began thinking, though, that no matter what Lucas was involved in, what that group was up to, what he took that they want back, it could still come down to the simplest motive in the world. Man, woman, fear, revenge, betrayal, all those understandable, natural forces that drive people. And none of that other stuff makes any difference at all."

"Dear God," she breathed. She returned to the table, shaken more than she wanted to admit. That was exactly the line Tony would take in his summation for the jury, exactly the line her father had expressed from the start. She knew very well that ninety-nine out of a hundred murders were committed for one of those basic, human reasons: jealousy, hatred, money, revenge. . . . A deep shudder passed through her. And we call them understandable, natural forces; Mike's words echoed in her head.

She looked at the messy papers with their scribbles and said, "It must be comforting, being a mathematician. You work with your problems and find a solution—I know, an elegant solution—and send it off to your peers, all seventeen of them, who follow your steps and say right or wrong. And you know. That must be comforting. How do you know the

201

truth about people, Mike? How? She says she didn't do it and I believe her. She could be punished more for denying it, for telling the truth, than for lying and confessing. And we call it playing the game. The law game. The game of justice. The only game in town. What we need is a reliable truth sniffer, a grace sniffer. Everything that's been invented so far has proven indecisive, unreliable. Invent me a truth sniffer that can't be denied, Mike. That day the whole game ends, no more courts, no more trials, no more guessing did she or didn't she, or making book on which lawyer is more persuasive, which knows better how to manipulate a jury of twelve good and honest citizens."

"Hey," Mike said softly. "Hey."

"Oh, God, I can't cry now. On top of not enough sleep I really will look like hell warmed over." She got up and ran from the room.

TWENTY

FRANK GAVE BARBARA'S cheek a quick peck and then looked over her shoulder at the three or four law books his clerk was depositing on the defense table. "And I thought you were out carousing all night. Sorry."

"That, too," she said. It was hard to tell which pleased him more, her carousing or her doing her homework. Then the judge entered and the real day began.

John Kendricks was a good witness, calm and attentive, and determined to tell what he knew and what he suspected.

Tony did not allow him much leeway, just as Barbara had predicted. Twice he had to ask John Kendricks to answer simply yes or no, and very quickly John Kendricks became a hostile witness, more reluctant than any of the others so far.

"You hadn't seen your son for nearly seven years and you didn't ask him his plans?"

"No. There wasn't enough—"

"You've answered the question, Mr. Kendricks. Did you ask him when he planned to visit his wife?"

"No. I'm trying to tell y—"

"Mr. Kendricks, did you call his wife to alert her that her husband was coming?"

"I called her."

"To warn her that he was coming?"

"To tell her he might come."

"Mr. Kendricks, when you picked up the children, your grandchildren, did you warn Mrs. Nell Kendricks that her husband would arrive the next day?"

"I didn't kn—"

"Why did you agree to take the children away?"

"I didn't agree. I sug—"

"Did Mrs. Nell Kendricks—"

"Your Honor, I object," Barbara said then. "The prosecuting attorney is not permitting the witness to finish an answer before pummeling him with another question!"

Tony threw up his hands as if in disgust. "Withdraw the last question. No further questions." He gave John Kendricks a look of contempt and sat down.

Barbara led John Kendricks through a description of his family, his and his wife's relationship with their two children, and then asked, "When your son returned home from Colorado nearly seven years ago, did you see any significant changes in him?"

"Objection," Tony said. "Let counsel be specific about changes, not use the word in such a loose, meaningless context."

"Sustained," Judge Lundgren said. He seemed ready to add to this, but Barbara was already nodding in agreement.

"Did you think your son was mentally disturbed when he returned home from Colorado the first time?" Her voice was very gentle.

"Objection. The witness is not qualified to make such a judgment."

"On the contrary," Barbara said swiftly, and now she went to the books on her table and opened the top one to cite her first reference. "*Rawleigh* v. *Rawleigh*. . . ." She read the decision. "And *The State of Indiana* v. *Lomax*." In both cases the judge had ruled, on advice from a panel of psychiatrists, that the immediate family was most often the first to notice behavioral changes that signified mental illness.

Judge Lundgren listened intently, then nodded to her; that was as much pleasure as he would allow himself to show, she realized. He liked case law, liked having attorneys rely on what had gone before. "Overruled," he said. "You may continue."

"Thank you, Your Honor." She walked back to stand near John Kendricks. "Did you think your son was mentally disturbed when he returned home that time?"

"No. He was preoccupied and worried and unhappy, like a man with a hard problem to solve."

Tony objected several times as she asked questions that allowed John Kendricks to describe the years that Lucas was gone the second time, his efforts to get in touch with his son, the returned mail, unanswered telephone calls.

"Your Honor," she said in response to one of his challenges, "Mr. Kendricks tried very hard to answer the questions put to him by the prosecution, and he was blocked each time. My questions were all implied by the prosecution although no answers were permitted. The prosecution brought up the matter of the seven years of absence; I am trying to clarify what happened during that period."

The judge allowed her to continue. She was beginning to appreciate the description of fairness that her father had applied to him.

"What about Christmas, birthdays?" she asked John Kendricks then. "Did he write or call on special occasions?"

"Not a word."

Bit by bit the past was filled in. She did not rush him, and she met each one of Tony's objections head on now as she moved in a triangular pattern from the witness chair, to the jury box, to the defense table, making certain that those twelve good and true peers kept their attention focused on this witness and this defendant. She stopped moving back and forth at one of the answers. Seven years ago Lucas had driven off in a pretty new Honda, the same car that he had driven back last June.

"Mr. Kendricks, you have told us that your son was preoccupied and worried on his visit seven years ago. How did he appear last June?"

She was turned so that she could see Tony and the slight flush that spread over his face. He had got the point. That was the question she had prepared the ground for, had cited references to cover more than forty-five minutes earlier. Tony did not move.

"He was scared to death," John Kendricks said in his deliberate way. "People were hunting him down, and he was scared."

He finished describing the visit and finally came to the last time he had seen his son.

"So he drove away without saying what he planned?"

"Yes. He was pretty upset, and really scared. He said he'd be in touch and left."

"In his Honda?"

"Yes."

"You never saw him again, or spoke to him again?"

"No. Never."

"What about the car, Mr. Kendricks? When did you see his car again?"

"Objection! Defense counsel is trying to introduce matters that are irrelevant to this case, and she knows it."

"Your Honor, Lucas Kendricks left his father's house in his car on Tuesday and four days later turned up on foot, having hiked for days in unsuitable clothing. I maintain that it is relevant to determine where he had been and what happened to his car." She walked to the defense table and moved aside one of the books she already had read from in order to open a different one. "I refer you to. . . ."

Judge Lundgren was smiling faintly; it would have been easy to miss the expression as a smile. He held up his hand. "No need, Ms. Holloway. I agree that this is a relevant issue. Please proceed. Overruled."

That was just as well, because the only case she had been able to find was so weak that she would not have dared cite it without first calling up two very strong cases.

John Kendricks described the ransacking of his house and the car. There still was not a word allowed about the rape/murder of the young woman in the woods, or about how the sheriff had come to have the car, but Barbara was satisfied. None of that was within the scope of John Kendrick's knowledge. She took him back over his testimony about Lucas's careful handling of his backpack, which she introduced as evidence, and his fear that he was being pursued. That was where she had intended to lead him all along, where she had intended to end her cross-examination.

When she sat down, she wrote a hurried note. *Have B find out when L bought the car, how and when it was paid for, and how many miles on it.* She passed it to her father without giving a thought to the fact that she was asking for his active help and that without hesitation he was giving it. He glanced at the note, nodded, and left his seat, left the courtroom. She listened to Tony make the same points he had made in his direct examination; he ignored all the new information as if he had not even heard it. But he had a dilemma, she knew. He had to open the case, admit the past, or she would have a good argument that the district attorney's office had not done its job in investigating the murder. By now the jury had been teased so much about the car that not to tell them about it would simply irritate them to the point where they could take their frustration out on Tony and his case. He knew that as well as she.

But he also knew that once opened, the case could blossom like a field of daisies, making it hard, even impossible, to control what else would be introduced. He liked his cases simple: Prodigal husband returns home and is shot by abandoned wife. Simple. Easy to comprehend. Understandable. Natural. That basic simplicity now threatened to turn into chaos. She was pleased with the analogy. *That* seemed natural to her. From elementary simplicity to chaos.

Tony was badgering John Kendricks; although tempted to start objecting, she resisted. John was a strong witness, not flustered, not visibly angry; he was calm and quiet, and he was making Tony look more boorish with every midsentence interruption.

Instead of calling his next witness, Tony approached the bench after John Kendricks was dismissed. Judge Lundgren motioned to Barbara to come forward also.

"Mr. DeAngelo has asked for a recess until three this afternoon in order to present his next witness. If you have no objections, that is what we shall do."

"None, Your Honor."

"Very well. You may summon Sheriff LeMans." He nodded to Tony.

That afternoon the courtroom was packed. "Someone leaked that the murder of that girl will be introduced," Barbara muttered glumly to her father.

"Way it goes," he muttered back.

Sheriff LeMans liked cowboy outfits and apparently saw no reason to dress differently for a court appearance. His boots had a mirror finish, and his silver belt buckle gleamed. His shirt was embroidered in rainbow colors. Barbara had trouble trying to picture him playing Bach in a chamber music group.

Tony had come on like a sophisticate trying to get a simple answer from a slow man when he questioned John Kendricks. With Sheriff LeMans that image yielded to a different one; he was detached and coolly professional as he led the sheriff through the events that led to discovery of the Honda.

When Sheriff LeMans described the injuries suffered by the young woman, there was a collective gasp in the courtroom, as if many people simultaneously breathed, "Finally!"

Tony made him repeat the list: She had been brutally raped. She had been sodomized with a foreign object, probably a stick. She had been badly beaten, her neck broken, her jaw broken, two teeth broken out. Her wrists had been tied with a rope, tight enough to lacerate them severely, and she had been dragged over the lava for hundreds of feet, resulting in further mutilation of her naked body. Cause of death was internal injuries and exsanguination: She had bled to death. Finally she had been dumped in the creek.

Barbara heard Nell's choking gasp at the mention of dragging that girl over the lava, but she did not turn toward her at the moment. When she did, Nell's face was ghastly in its pallor.

"Hang in there," Barbara murmured. "Do you need a recess?" Nell shook her head, but she looked as if she might vomit any second. Barbara patted her arm and turned her attention back to the sheriff.

He told about taking the car in and, after the laboratory had finished with it, turning it over to John Kendricks. Tony had him point out on a map the location of the car, of the landslide that had closed the dirt road, and had him trace how the road used to meander around the mountain until it eventually connected to Old Halleck Hill Road, the same road that Lucas had used to reach the trail down to the ledge.

"Why isn't this case marked closed?" Tony asked sharply toward the end of his direct examination.

"I never close a case until I'm satisfied—"

"How long have you known John and Amy Kendricks?"

"—that all the questions have been answered—"

"Just answer the question, Sheriff, please."

"I'm trying to do that, Mr. DeAngelo, but one at a time, like you asked them."

208

"Your Honor, please instruct the witness to respond to the direct questions."

"I believe he is doing so, Mr. DeAngelo," Judge Lundgren said.

Tony turned back to Sheriff LeMans, who said in his deliberate way, "I've known John and Amy Kendricks all my life, and theirs."

"Thank you," Tony said with heavy sarcasm. "When did they tell you their house had been broken into?"

"In July, the eleventh."

"Ah. Was that when they claimed the car had been torn apart?"

"Yes, it was. And the car *was* torn apart. I saw it."

"You went out to their house on the eleventh of July to inspect the car? Is that right?"

"Yes, it is."

"And was the house torn up, too, Sheriff?"

He shook his head. "No. They had cleaned up the mess long before that."

"In fact, you don't know that there was a mess to clean up, do you, Sheriff?"

"Yes, I do. They told me."

"They told you. Did you check the car for fingerprints?"

"Yes, we did."

"And what were the results?"

"Nothing."

"Nothing? No prints at all?"

"No, I mean no outsiders' prints. John had driven the car home. We found his fingerprints, his son's, Janet Moseley's, and some of our own people's."

Tony stopped soon after that; he was satisfied, the expression on his face indicated. None of this would damage his case, he implied by that expression. So Lucas had done a heinous crime on his way home—that didn't change the events once he got there. He sat down, propped his chin in his hand, and watched Barbara approach the sheriff.

"I'd like to start back when you first learned that Janet Moseley was missing. When was that?"

"Wednesday, June seventh. Eleven in the morning."

"And you immediately went to the town of Sisters to start tracing the movements of Lucas Kendricks and Janet Moseley?"

"Sent a deputy, Bob Silverman."

"Tell us what you learned in Sisters, Sheriff."

Tony objected, and Judge Lundgren stood up. "The hour is getting late, and I'm afraid we're all fatigued. We will have a fifteen-minute recess and resume. Ms. Holloway, Mr. DeAngelo, in my chambers, if you please."

When they arrived at his room, he was standing at a wide window with his hands clasped behind his back. Heavy mist seemed to press inward against the window pane. The room was furnished in delicate-looking French-empire antiques; there were two skylights, each decorated with a mobile of hanging plants in silver filigree pots. Beyond the skylights the gray sky seemed too close.

"I've sent for coffee," Judge Lundgren said. "Sit down, sit down." He continued to stand at the window until a second or two later there was a tap on the door; it opened to admit a gray-haired woman with a tray that contained a silver pot and very fine Haviland coffee service.

After she left, Judge Lundgren went to the desk to pour the coffee for them, and then took his own around the desk and sat down.

"Mr. DeAngelo," he said, then paused and shook his head. "Tony, I am very well aware of what you are attempting. I appreciate your efforts to keep your case confined to the vicinity and the time of the murder. And, Ms. Holloway, I am equally aware of your efforts to broaden the scope of the trial. Now, Sheriff LeMans is a qualified officer of the law, well regarded, and highly skilled. He is a competent witness, as competent as the sheriff of this county. I will not permit you to hobble your own witness, Tony. And I intend to keep the court in session until the sheriff is finished with his testimony today, however long that takes. I have no intention of either keeping him in town overnight, or return-

210

ing him tomorrow from his own county." He lifted his cup and peered at Tony over the rim before he sipped. "Do I make myself clear?"

"Yes, sir," Tony said without hesitation. "But this is all a delaying tactic on her part. It has nothing to do with what happened on that ledge."

Judge Lundgren inclined his head slightly. "At some future time I may concur with that determination, but for now, this aspect of the case has been introduced, and I shall let Ms. Holloway pursue it." He turned his gaze toward Barbara; his pale blue eyes were cool and very remote. "Are you prepared to make a connection between these events and the death of Lucas Kendricks?"

"Yes, I am, Your Honor," she said steadily.

"Because if I decide that you are introducing conspiracies and muddying the water in order to obfuscate the facts, I shall instruct the jury that they cannot consider in any way any incident that occurred before Lucas Kendricks and his wife confronted each other on that ledge. Do you understand?"

"Yes, of course. They are connected."

"Very well. One other matter." Looking at Tony again, his voice very formal and proper, he asked, "Mr. DeAngelo, you are not required to answer at this time, but I should like to know if you intend to introduce the perpetuation of testimony of Dr. Ruth Brandywine. If you choose not to make that decision yet, very well, but if you have already decided, I should like to know. Also, will that be your last witness, as you have previously indicated?"

Barbara's hands were moist, but she made no motion to wipe them; she did not move as she waited for Tony to answer. He had not expected that, she thought with satisfaction. He had thought he would have until tomorrow to mull it over, and, of course, he still could. Judge Lundgren would not insist on knowing now, as he had made clear, but not to answer was probably out of Tony's range of possibilities. He was a firm believer in the power of authority, and the judge was on a higher step of the power ladder than he was.

211

"Yes, Your Honor," he said finally. "I was hesitating because I didn't see any point in smearing the memory of Lucas Kendricks, but now that this whole other aspect has been brought up, I will introduce the video. And at this time I have no further witnesses to call."

Judge Lundgren nodded thoughtfully. "Ms. Holloway has filed a formal request for a short recess in order for Dr. Brandywine to be subpoenaed as a hostile witness who was evasive and not forthcoming in her testimony." He drank his coffee and put the cup down. "I shall make my decision and tell you when court adjourns today. You are both ordered not to divulge this development to the public, or the press, or to allow it to leak." He looked at Tony with a frown. "I am very unhappy at the direction this case has taken toward becoming a circus. Now, there is very little time remaining of our recess. Thank you both for coming." He stood up, dismissing them.

In the hall outside his door Tony swung around to say harshly, "You really think you can get Brandywine up here to accept a subpoena? You're whistling in the dark. I intend to get your client. In the end she'll be on that stand crying, pleading, saying she's sorry she did it."

"Who do you really want to see crying and pleading, her or me?" she said just as harshly. He stalked away.

There was no time to confer with her father when she returned to the courtroom. She nodded, and he left his seat and the room, and she began to guide Sheriff LeMans through the events starting with the call about the missing girl, on through the ranger's spotting the car, and finding it and the evidence of a crime.

"Exactly what did the ranger report seeing, Sheriff LeMans?"

"Just that he spotted a gray Honda Civic on the forest service road. We had an APB out on the car, a description of the man and the young lady, and her name."

"When did he report this?"

"Late Friday evening, six, seven."

"And then what did you do?"

"I sent two deputies in a jeep to check it out. They took a camera, and their instructions were to interview anyone they found, or take pictures if no one was there, not to touch anything, and then hightail it to a telephone and let me know. That's what they did. I went out with a crew first thing Saturday morning.

"And the pictures? Will you identify this packet of pictures, please, Sheriff LeMans?"

"They're the ones," he said, after looking them over. "They handed in the camera and the department had the film developed and marked each picture."

"Which way is the car headed here?"

He took the picture and looked at it, then handed it back. "East. Someone worked real hard to get it turned around. My boys found red lava dirt in the rocks where the car dropped it in getting turned around."

"Heading back the way it had come?"

"Yes, Ma'am."

She started to walk toward the jury box with the pictures. "It's very muddy, isn't it? The car, I mean. Could you tell where it had been by the dirt on it?"

"Pretty much. That's mostly red lava dust and mud. There was a lot of melting snow around there back in June, and a lot of mud everywhere. It was a mess."

"So that was Saturday afternoon. When did you trace that car to Lucas Kendricks?"

"Not definitely until the next week." He explained about the stolen license plates, and the missing registration. "By late Saturday, we knew that Lucas Kendricks had been shot, and that's when I suspected he must have walked across the mountains, and I got the tracker to find out how, to find out where he camped, look around his campsites, things like that. We still didn't know what happened to the young lady. Me and the sheriff from Lane County put together a crew to try to trace her down that creek."

"Some days later did your tracker report that he had been hired to show a stranger where the campsites were?"

"Yes. It's in my report. Seemed a curious thing, so I included it in the report."

"And then what did you do?"

"I went over the campsites myself, each one. They'd all been torn up, like someone had been searching for something. Ground disturbed, logs rolled over, rocks moved, even a little digging."

Barbara went to the big map and pointed. "This is where the car was found, and here is the first campsite. How far apart are they?"

"About ten miles, depending on how you go. Could be longer, twelve or thirteen miles, if you stick to the Forest Service roads."

"Your report shows that the pictures you developed from Janet Moseley's camera were made at about one in the afternoon. Is that right?"

"Yes, it is."

She pointed to the map again. "This is the stream where her body was thrown in. How far is this from the car?"

"Nine hundred yards."

"Did you find the rope?"

"No, we didn't."

"Was there any rope in the car, or around it?"

"No, there wasn't."

She thanked him then and had no more questions. Tony was on his feet quickly, and he made the sheriff admit that there was no way to know with certainty who had made the various campsites they had located. And, in fact, they had no way of knowing for certain anything about the trail Lucas had taken, where he had slept, where he had rested.

"Isn't it true that whenever there is a grotesque murder, curiosity seekers gather, Sheriff?"

"Yes, it is."

"And don't these ghouls sometimes hamper an investigation, even destroy evidence in their eagerness to participate in some sick way?"

"I object, Your Honor. These questions are both leading and improper in their generality."

"Sustained."

"No more questions," Tony said.

Judge Lundgren called Barbara and Tony to the bench to inform them that if Tony had no witnesses to call after Ruth Brandywine's statement was presented in court, he would recess the trial on Friday, the next day, until Tuesday at nine.

That meant the jury would have all weekend to ponder the very damning testimony that Ruth Brandywine had voiced, a bad break, and from the expression on Tony's face she knew he was thinking exactly the same. He was not quite smirking. But it also meant that there were four days in which to dangle the bait for Brandywine to snap.

TWENTY-ONE

THAT EVENING THE reporters swarmed around the halls of the courthouse. Frank maneuvered Nell, John, and Amy out through them with aplomb; he had done this many times, and while he never actually shoved anyone, neither did he allow anyone to impede the forward momentum of the group he was herding. Barbara, waiting until they were out of sight, the hordes of news people dragged along like a wake, was surprised when Clive Belloc appeared at her side.

"Can I drive you around the block, or to a bar for a drink or something?" he asked. "I can get my car and meet you at the door in five minutes."

"Fine with me," she said. A car waiting in the rain, a quick dash through the reporters, a getaway, fine. He hurried off and she began to time him. As long as she remained in the courtroom, the reporters would leave her alone, and she knew she did not have the finesse her father always showed with them. She was not above shoving.

After exactly five minutes she pulled her raincoat tighter around her, put her hood up, and made her run; the cameramen were there, the television crews, the newspaper reporters, all of them poised since she was the only one remaining now. She got through them to Clive's car without uttering a single word, not even "No comment." She did not push anyone. She felt pleased with herself.

The rain was little more than a drizzle, an ever-descending cloud. It was ten minutes after six.

"A bar?" Clive asked. "I thought maybe you had a date, a dinner date, or something, and it's been a tough day, but is there time for a drink?"

Actually it was not a date. She and Mike had an understanding, and how had that come about so soon? If she showed up by seven, they had dinner together, always at a restaurant; he did not cook, ever, except breakfast.

"There's time," she said, "if it's someplace near and the service is pretty fast."

"Know just the place." He drove to the valet parking garage at the Hilton, where he turned the car over to a youth who looked no more than fourteen; they stepped into an elevator that whisked them to the top floor, all in under five minutes. From their table in the lounge they could see the lights of Eugene, haloed with mist.

The drinks were less prompt than he had been, but even so, the timing was loose enough to let her start to relax. But Clive was looking awkward and embarrassed, as if he was not quite sure how to launch into what was on his mind. The pale area around his eyes was hardly noticeable now that his deep, rich tan was fading.

"I've been in the court every day," he said, just as the cocktail waitress brought their drinks and arranged them.

He waited until she left. "Anyway, I've really admired the way you're handling everything. What I said back in the beginning, that's more idiotic than ever. I'm really sorry about that."

Barbara shrugged. This wasn't what he had brought her up here to say. She sipped her wine.

He looked out at the city below, cleared his throat, sipped his drink, cleared his throat again, and finally said, "If Nell is seen out with someone, me, would that go against her now? I mean, all those reporters, if they found out that she's going out or anything, would that matter?" His fingers were pressed so hard against his glass they had whitened; a tic played in his jaw. He put his fingers on it, then, even more self-conscious, jerked his hand away again. He was like a college boy facing his orals.

"Depends," Barbara said judiciously. "If she's spotted getting rowdy in a topless bar, for instance, that could be an item for comment. Or snorting up in a dim discotheque. Not that the jury should be influenced by it, of course. No way could it be introduced as evidence, but still they do read papers and watch television news even if they aren't supposed to."

He looked sheepish and more embarrassed. "I didn't mean anything like that. I mean dinner, a drive to the coast. You know. With just her, not the kids. We've all done things like that together, family friend sort of things, but I'm thinking of just the two of us."

Barbara smiled at him. "She's a free woman, free to do what she pleases, with anyone who pleases her. Forget it. If Tony had been able to cast any suspicions on her character, he would have done it long ago. He couldn't, and now it's too late to worry about it."

He took a long drink and set his glass down firmly. "Thanks. That's really what I thought. The other thing I wanted to ask is would you and your friend come to dinner Sunday night at my place? I'm asking Nell, of course."

"I'll have to let you know. I've got your number. I'll give

you a call tomorrow." She glanced at her watch and finished her wine. "And now, it's time again."

He left a ten-dollar bill on the table; they retraced their steps, got into his car when it was delivered, and he drove her to the garage where she had parked. When she got out, he said, "Barbara, just thanks. For everything. Thanks."

They went to Mazzi's, where Mike had calzone and she had Adriatic snapper and vegetable salad. Months ago when he said he never cooked, she had responded, "Neither do I!" thinking he had been suggesting that she should. Instead, he had nodded in complete agreement.

"Good. So, Mexican, Chinese, Italian, what?"

"I pay my way whatever we decide," she had said.

"Fine. So name it."

It was not that he was stingy, mean with money; it was rather that he did not care. She paid, he paid, it simply did not matter. And he relished whatever he ate; Italian was his favorite when they were in an Italian restaurant. Then Chinese was the world's finest cuisine, or Mexican was. . . . One night, she would actually cook dinner, see if he thought that was the best thing since sliced bread. Don't you eat vegetables, she had asked early, and he had become enthusiastic over a vegetarian restaurant that he knew.

"What were you writing in court today?" she asked at dinner that night.

"You saw? That's really surprising. You seemed to be concentrated to an inhuman degree."

"Is that how it looks?" she asked. She never had considered how she appeared to others in court.

"Don't you know that? I thought it must be one of the things they drill into you in school. You look absolutely *there*, with what is being said, what the jury is doing, what your client is doing, just *there*. One day I might decide you're someone to be afraid of, you can get so concentrated."

"What on earth are you talking about? Afraid? Of what?"

"I think you must be analyzing every word all the time.

At least in court you seem to be doing that. If you decide I'm lying, all is lost."

"When's the last time you lied to anyone?"

"It happens." He looked thoughtful. "I'm sure it happens to everyone, maybe on a daily basis, but we're all so used to it that we don't even notice any more."

"Yes, I agree. But when's the last time *you* lied?"

"See what I mean?" he said, leaning forward, grinning. "You've got that concentrated look."

"You can't answer because you can't remember lying." She took a quick breath and found herself saying swiftly, "You don't need to lie about anything because nothing's in your way; you have what you want; you don't envy anyone; and the world's just another interesting problem that you may or may not be able to solve. Either way, it's all right. If you can't, maybe someone else will, or maybe not. You would never be afraid of me or anyone else because you are totally self-sufficient. If I left tomorrow, you'd regret it for a time, but not too much, not enough to interfere with your life. You might be tempted to try to reduce our relationship to a formula that you can work with, try to simplify the complexities so they can be expressed with your magical symbols and so dealt with." She was out of breath, and appalled at her own words. She had not planned that, had not thought through any of that, would never have brought any of it up this way, in a restaurant, on purpose. It had happened, had taken them both by surprise. She reached for her wine, kept her gaze on her hand, the glass. "You're keeping score at the trial, aren't you?"

He sat back in his chair. "See why I could be afraid of you? Yes."

"You can't even lie about that, can you?" Now she felt she was no longer out of control; her voice was measured, reflective. "You knew it might make me furious, that I might create a scene here in a public place and you would feel like dying of embarrassment, but even so, you won't lie about it. Do you have a formula worked out yet?"

219

"It's harder than I thought it would be," he admitted. "But I'll get it."

She shook her head. "You won't. I don't want to know how your score is shaping up, by the way. Don't stop, but don't tell me. Okay?"

Her own outburst, she wondered, how could something like that be factored into an equation? How could mathematics formulate the moment of unendurable jealousy, inexpressible yearning, the moment when anger found expression in an act of violence, the wrenching fear of a parent with a desperately ill child? No equations, she told herself, not with people.

They had walked to the restaurant, just five blocks from his house; they walked back holding hands in the drizzle. He never cared if it was raining, or if it was warm, cold, what the weather. At his house, where her car was parked at the curb, she said she wouldn't come in, too tired.

"I need sleep, lots and lots of sleep," she said.

He held her hand and studied her face in the unsteady, flickering glow from a distant streetlight. "You're not mad at me? Really not?"

"Really not," she said.

"I thought you would be."

"I know, but you see, I'm not one of your funny little squiggles with a plus or minus sign, or an equal sign before or after me. Or, God forbid, x times the square root of minus one anywhere in my equation."

He laughed and pulled her hard against his chest and then kissed her. "I'm learning more about people these days than I knew there was to know. When will I see you again?"

That was new. Neither of them ever asked the other that particular question. Just as neither ever said I love you. He had to go first there, too, she had decided. She told him about Clive's invitation to dinner on Sunday.

"And later? Your place or mine?"

She definitely was not ready to keep him overnight in her father's house. The decision was instantaneous. "Yours," she said, laughing. They kissed again, and she got into her car and left him standing in the drizzle as she drove away.

The drizzle became rain briefly, then drizzle again, then the moon was sailing through streaky clouds, and the drizzle came back. She even saw some stars for a short time when the city lights were well behind her and the countryside closed in dark and mysterious, as if the world ended where the light from her high beams got lost in the trees on both sides of the road.

For long stretches she was alone on the road. An occasional car passed her, a truck, another car or a cluster of traffic, some came opposite her, vanished with twinkling red taillights.

"Okay," she muttered at one time, to herself, the rain, the oncoming lights, or nothing. "Okay." She was thinking of Mike Dinesen, and their noncommitment to each other, their denial of the future, not through words, but the lack of words. Neither of them wanted the future wrapped in plain brown paper; neither was willing to be the trailing spouse while the other achieved fame and fortune. He would be in Oregon through this year, and then where? He had no idea, was unconcerned. For three summers he had been in Austin, Texas, working with people he spoke of with a touch of awe. Gods, she had decided. She could not imagine anything short of a god inspiring him with awe. All over the country people were willing to kill for tenure, but he had shrugged it off, not caring that the university here had given it to him in spite of his lack of enthusiasm. There were other offers pending; she knew so little of his field that she could not tell if they were important, and he seemed to treat them all the same way— interesting, but not compelling.

Up ahead she could see the lights of a covered bridge, the last landmark before the road twisted and turned as it followed the shoreline of the reservoir. Ten, twelve more miles, then a hot bath, a boring book, and sleep. Her eyes burned with fatigue.

221

The road made a Y at the bridge, the right lane aimed at the bridge; she made the left turn, went under an overpass, and suddenly her car was out of control as the windshield seemed to explode, not throwing glass—it was tempered and didn't do that—but cracks ran through it, glass shattered and dropped out, and the car careened dizzily from the right lane to the left, grazed a rocky formation, was flung back to the right lane and sideways into a tree, then another. She was jerked from one side to the other, thrown against the steering wheel, then snapped back sharply as she fought to control the car. And then it scraped a tree again, and this time both right wheels were off the road, dragging. The car turned halfway around and finally came to a stop. She had a cramp in her foot from pressing on the brake.

After that her memory played games with her. She was sitting in the car, dazed, afraid to move, twenty feet above the reservoir, and then she was driving again, with rain in her face, but there was no memory connecting one event to the other. She was parked on the shoulder, blinded by a red film in her eye, then driving again, just as before, without memory of stopping or starting. Driving, stopping, driving again, she continued through Turner's Point where there were a few lights still on; she did not even consider stopping. She found herself on the private road without any recollection of arriving there.

Now she found herself leaning against the front door of her father's house, as if a giant hand had plucked her from the car and propped her there. When the door opened, she fell.

Frank took her to the hospital, where they kept her overnight for observation but they did not let her sleep. Every time she closed her eyes, someone came along and made her open them again, to do this or that, submit to this or that new procedure or test. By Friday afternoon she was so tired she wanted to cry; when Frank came to take her home, she warned him that she intended to sleep for twenty-four hours and not to be alarmed, and if he valued his head, not to try to wake her up because she would have the head of anyone who did.

"Did you watch the video in court?" she asked as a nurse's aide wheeled her down the corridor toward the elevator.

"Yes. Just what you expected."

She groaned.

He left her to get his car, and took her home. She went to bed and slept.

When she woke up, the light beyond her windows was twilight; she did not know if it was morning or evening light. She dressed, moving very cautiously, every muscle aching. She felt her head gingerly; there was still a lump, not as bad as it had been, she could actually touch it without flinching. Progress, she muttered, and started downstairs. Then she heard voices from the kitchen. Frank had company.

At the door she paused again, but they all jumped up, and her father hurried to her side. "How are you? How do you feel?"

"Like someone who got in the way of stampeding elephants. Not too bad."

Mike was there, on the other side of the table; she remembered that he had been in her hospital room most of the day, whenever that day was. He grinned at her and sat down again. And the sheriff, Tony's sheriff was how she thought of him, Bernard Gray, had been at the table having coffee; he was on his feet now.

"Ah, Ms. Holloway, good to see you up and about."

She nodded at him and regretted moving her head that way. She took the fourth chair, and Frank put coffee down in front of her.

"Hungry?"

"Ravenous," she said, surprised. "What day is it?"

"Saturday," her father said. "Four in the afternoon."

Already? Two days of the mini-vacation gone. "Damn," she muttered.

Sheriff Gray had come to report that there was nothing

to report and to see if she had anything to add to what she had said in the hospital. She didn't, and he left again after a few minutes.

"So," she said after the sheriff was gone, "tell me what they're thinking. And about my car. And what happened in court."

"Car's a real mess. Two new doors, front end, right and left needs replacing, windshield. It'll take some bickering with the insurance company. I say call it totaled and get a new one." He had gone into the other part of the kitchen and was stirring eggs as he talked. He looked at the eggs in the bowl, not at her. "Miracle that you could walk away from it."

"I'm tougher than a heap of metal and glass. Just goes to show," she said, but she remembered the careening car, and she had to agree that it was something of a miracle that she had not ended up in the reservoir. Mike covered her hand with his and squeezed it slightly. The bastard had not even sent flowers, she thought. But he had spent most of the day in the hospital, and now here he was again. "How long have you been hanging around?" she asked softly.

"Not too long," he said.

From the stove Frank said, "He got here at noon. I sent him packing twice, but he does a good yo-yo act." He dumped the eggs into a hot skillet and stirred them. "The Brandywine video was a good show. Real dragon lady with a brain, the worst kind."

About the accident, he went on, nothing had been found on the overpass where someone had tossed a twelve-pound rock down at her car. Could have been a kid, a transient, an enemy. Only thing it could not be was an accident, although it was less certain if she had been a particular target, or just any automobile that happened by at the right time. No way of knowing that.

Frank brought the scrambled eggs and toast, poured more coffee, and sat down.

"What have you been doing out here all day?" she asked Mike then.

He told her that he had met Nell and her children and

224

had gone home with them to show Travis a couple of neat programs he could play with. She ate as if food were going out of style, she realized, but that didn't deter her; she buttered another slice of toast and listened. This evening there was a meeting going on at the grange, and probably a fight would start in town. They were debating the spotted owl issue again.

"Bet Nell and Clive will pass on this one," Frank said. He explained to Mike: "He used to cruise, estimate timber, for one of the big companies in the valley, and part of his job, I guess, was to report on the owls if he came across any. Some folks say the company fudged the reports, and Nell accused him of doctoring the numbers. It's like the Civil War, dividing families, friends, making just about everyone sore, no matter which side they come down on."

"She told me she'd see us at his house tomorrow, if you're up and able to go," Mike said to Barbara. "So at least they're speaking. She said the kids were going home with their grandparents this afternoon, coming back tomorrow night. Give them all a little break, and let the parents check on the farm. It's been tough on all of them. She's really scared." He seemed to regret that remark; instantly he went on to say that the problem with the spotted owl controversy was what they called it, the spotted owl controversy. "If they called it destruction of a forest ecosystem, or wildlife habitat, or something like that, they'd win over more people. But it's hard to convince people they should care more for an owl than for a human being and jobs. The environmentalists were outmaneuvered, and it's too late now to change. It'll be called the spotted owl fight, no matter what's really at risk."

"You think that's going to hold you until dinner?" Frank asked when he removed her plate a few minutes later.

"Depends. What time's dinner, and what's for dinner?"

"Good God!"

"I brought a few things out with me," Mike said. "Just in case I got invited to spend the night or something."

Frank snorted. "He asked how many bedrooms we have,

225

and if he could park in one of them for the next couple of days!"

Mike nodded. "I don't have to be in class until ten Monday morning."

And that was the extent of his manipulative ability, Barbara thought. He would come right out and ask, and then admit it. She wondered if Clive had come out and asked Nell's in-laws to go away and take the kids with them for at least one night. And if he would admit it if he had. She doubted that he would admit to anything of the sort.

The phone rang, surprising her when her own answering machine took the call. Her father had always said he refused to have such a thing in his house. "Reporters," he growled. "You made all the news." They listened as the voice floated around them, a local radio station wanting her to call back at her convenience. There were several more similar calls that afternoon, but at six it was Bailey Novell's voice on the machine, and Barbara took his call.

"Heard you got whacked, kiddo," he said. "Tough. You okay?" She assured him that she was, and he went on, "Right. Got that info you wanted about the car, and a couple of other things. You receiving callers?"

"Hang on a second," she said, and covered the mouthpiece. "Dinner?" Frank nodded, and she invited the detective to join them at six-thirty.

As much as she wanted to, she knew better than to ask for any details, or to ask the most important question until she saw him. Was Brandywine sniffing the bait yet?

TWENTY-TWO

"SHE'S INTERESTED," BAILEY said cheerfully a little later.

Frank handed him a glass filled to the brim with mostly scotch. How such a little man could drink so much with no apparent effects was a mystery to Barbara. Funny metabolism, she had decided a long time ago, but was no more satisfied with that explanation now than she had been then. And he ran marathons! A single ice cube looked lonesome in the drink; the trickle of melting water was not enough to change the color. "We're holding all conferences in the kitchen," Frank said. "Because I'm cooking. Shoot."

Bailey cast a speculative glance at Mike, whom he had just met.

"He's one of the gang," Barbara said. Mike looked so much at home in that kitchen that it was as if he always had been there, had always been part of the gang.

Bailey shrugged. "If you say so. I got the tracker, Roy Whitehorse, to call her, and he played it just fine. He heard she was looking for something and he had found something, only not papers. Then he clammed up. She wanted a number, and thirty seconds later called him back. Cagey. Wanted to make sure the call was coming from Redmond, where he lives, not from this side of the mountain. Anyway, he wouldn't say another word, and she said very little, very, very little. She'll be in touch."

Mike was looking totally bewildered. Barbara grinned at

227

him. "We need to get her in the state to serve the subpoena. And she did lose something. She'll find out that her testimony was presented and think she's in the clear by now. I hope. Go on," she said, turning back to Bailey.

He consulted his notes. "This Kendricks pulled a vanishing act back in 1982, and not a trace of him turned up again until he walked into that Denver store back in June and bought the computer with cash."

Barbara made a sound, then said, "Never mind. It'll keep."

Bailey grunted. "Whatever. Anyway. Car bought in Denver September 1980, co-signed by Nell Kendricks through the mail, four-year loan. Paid off with a cashier's check November 16, 1982. Insurance canceled about the same time. Registration expired the last of December, same year. Nineteen thousand miles on it."

Barbara narrowed her eyes in thought. "November 1982. Isn't that when Emil Frobisher was killed?"

"Yep. November fourteenth." Bailey glanced over his notes again. "Here's the whole of it. Kendricks was registered in the graduate housing unit that fall, special assistant to Dr. Emil Frobisher. In November his telephone was disconnected, his car was paid off, and he closed out his checking account. Little over four thousand in it. In January his apartment was registered as being occupied by a Tom Mann, or Manning. It's down both ways. No forwarding address was recorded for Lucas Kendricks, and Tom Mann didn't have a telephone, or anything else that I can find. He lived in the apartment until June, under the special care of Dr. Ruth Brandywine. His occupation was listed as maintenance personnel."

"Wow!" Barbara breathed. "They killed Lucas Kendricks in 1982! What kind of paperwork can you round up by Tuesday?"

Bailey looked incredulous and drank deeply of his scotch.

"Wednesday, at the very latest," Barbara said, paying no attention to his expression. "I probably can stall that long. I may have to faint in court, or something, but I'll manage that."

Bailey was saying he would do what he could, and, in fact, he already had a couple of things, when Barbara interrupted.

"When he bought the computer, it could have roused suspicions, paying cash. See if they kept a record. And if his bank kept a record when they closed his account, you know, fifties in a series, that sort of thing."

Bailey nodded and made a note. "But not by Tuesday," he grumbled.

"Don't be silly," Barbara said. "Of course you can." She stood up as she said, "Let's see what you've already rounded up." Even she could hear how strange the words sounded, and she swayed with sudden dizziness.

Mike was at her side, holding her arm almost instantly, and from across the kitchen at the same time Frank yelled, "Catch her."

"I'm all right," she said, but she let Mike push her back into her chair without resisting.

"You're pale as a ghost," Mike said.

"I've got a right, I guess," she said, "considering I was damn near murdered." And there, having said the words, she realized that that was exactly what she believed. That someone had tried to kill *her*, not just a random driver. Frank banged down a pot and she jumped at the sound. "Maybe I need something just a bit stronger than your good wine," she said to him.

Bailey finished his scotch hurriedly and held up his glass. "I second that. Fainting women give me the creeps."

Frank brought the bottle and two glasses to the table. Mike shook his head, and Frank poured for Bailey, and Barbara, and then a third glass, which he kept.

"You pull that stunt in court Tuesday and the judge will give you an extra week or more if you ask for it," Bailey said to Barbara. "I'll get the stuff for you." He patted her shoulder as he passed her chair on his way to retrieve the briefcase he had left in the living room.

229

"Can't it wait until tomorrow?" Mike asked.

"He'll be back in Denver by tomorrow," she said. "I'm okay. Really."

"Okay is not the word I'd use," he said shaking his head. "Formidable is more like it."

Bailey came back with a folder, and as they went over the papers he had collected, she told him which ones to have certified, witnessed, all the while aware of Mike's gaze on her. Reflective, alarmed, bemused, puzzled, a mixture of all those things, as if he only now was becoming aware of who she really was. She was not certain at the moment that the person he was now perceiving was the person who had attracted him in the first place, or, if he reached that same doubt, how he would settle it.

They were having dinner at the kitchen table again; Barbara's materials were still strewn all over the dining room. Tonight Frank had made a leg of lamb, with a thick crust of garlic, rosemary, coarse black pepper, served with a marsala sauce.

Mike took his first bite and said, "Can I move in?"

Frank laughed. "Maybe. Might set conditions, though." Barbara glared at both of them. "There was this time in court," Frank said grinning, "Old Judge TapToe was reigning. Called him that because if he got impatient with the way the case was going, he'd start tapping his toe. Didn't ever seem to be aware that he was doing it, and most of the time no one else could tell. Little jiggle in his robe now and again, about all you could see. Now, Old Judge TapToe was getting a bit hard of hearing and he had an amplifier set up so he never missed a word. But he couldn't hear what was going on under the bench, you see. And this time in court someone had taken away a heavy rug they always put in place for that restless foot to light on. So you could hear old TapToe when he got going. Anyway, the prosecution brought in this whole family of Doolittles. Papa Doolittle, Mama Doolittle, the kids, and their kids, and cousins and uncles and aunts and the like. A real crew of them. Said they were having a family reunion the day a neighbor house got robbed, having a feast out on the patio when this fellow showed up and entered the next house over. They described him just fine, and picked him out of a lineup, and things were going swell for the prosecution. But he overdid it by having them all testify; one after another they got up to say yes sir, that's the guy. And pretty soon old TapToe starts tapping, and that rattles the prosecution some, and there's some in court who are nodding in time to the judge's foot, and that rattles everyone some, and the judge never does catch on that he's setting the pace. He just taps harder. Now the defendant maintains that he didn't do it, that he was out with his girlfriend, probably doing things he shouldn't have been doing. And she says that's right, but there's one of her, and one of him, and there's a passel of Doolittles, eleven, twelve of them, and things are looking bad indeed."

Frank was laughing softly by now. He sipped wine and continued. "So there's the foot tap, tap, tapping, and witness after witness saying the same thing, and the defense attorney asks Uncle Doolittle what they had to eat that day. That sets up a row of objections, but the judge isn't having any more nonsense and he says let the witness answer, just to get some variety in the testimony, probably, and the uncle says fried chicken and potato salad and blackberry pies, biscuits, corn on the cob, real reunion food for a summer day. And defense asks what the feast was in celebration of since it was late July, not the Fourth or anything, and uncle says it was to celebrate Mama Doolittle's successful surgery for gallbladder. Defense keeps looking at the bench where that tapping is coming from, and the witness is looking, too, and he begins to add things on his own. He remembers they had homemade ice cream on the pie. Defense asks what time he and his wife got there, and what time others arrived, and so on, and uncle is moving his head in time to that foot, and he says four, five, a little later. And defense says you mean poor Mama Doolittle, just out of the hospital, had to fry chicken for twelve people, and make potato salad for them, and all the rest of it? She must have started cooking the day before. Wasn't she too

231

weak for all that work? And uncle says in time to the foot that mama was still too weak, Papa must have made the dinner. Now papa jumps up, back there in the middle of the crew of Doolittles, and says that's a damn lie. He never cooked a meal in his life."

They all laughed, and then Mike asked, "And what happened? How did it come out?"

"Oh, they all cooked it up, all right," Frank said happily. "Got to calling each other names and the bailiff had to clear the court, and when the dust settled the case was thrown out, the defendant was excused, and the crew of Doolittles was charged with breaking, entering, burglary, the whole works, including perjury. When court resumed the little rug was back in place and old Judge TapToe never did know that he'd hypnotized the witnesses. Uncle could have been led anywhere in time to that foot."

Later, Barbara realized that Frank must have had conversations with Mike while she slept; someone had told him that Mike didn't cook, and that someone was not she. The thought pleased her in an obscure way, even though it annoyed her also. What else had they talked about?

Bailey left immediately after dinner; Mike did the dishes, while Barbara began to read through the transcript of Ruth Brandywine's testimony, not in a serious way, but to refresh her memory. She found that she remembered very well what the woman had said.

They sat in the living room, where the fire was burning softly, chuckling to itself now and then, muttering with a show of sparks now and then. When Barbara glanced at Mike he was jotting his squiggles on a yellow legal pad, and when she caught him glancing at her, she was jotting notes on a different yellow pad.

"Could I have a look at the computer?" he asked a bit later. "Not the portable. I'll load the program I gave Travis, to create Mandelbrots."

Frank yawned and stretched. "I'll show you and then leave you to it. Bedtime for me."

Barbara watched them walk out together. Mike looked more muscular than ever next to her father, who, she realized with dismay, was looking old. At her insistence he finally had admitted that he had had a *very minor* heart attack, of absolutely no significance, with absolutely no after-effects.

She listened to the murmur of their voices coming from his study, a chuckle, a snorting sound, the murmur again. When the silence that followed stretched out too long, she got up to join them. She ached abominably, but her head was not hurting, and that was what they had told her to watch for. No more dizziness, no headache or fuzzy vision. . . . Her father and Mike were together at the computer, watching the monitor, where a rainbow of colors was forming.

"I'll just be damned," Frank said absently, peering at it. "Look, there's that same little hook."

Mike saw her in the doorway and grinned. "Nice computer. Not quite as fast as the one Travis has, but pretty good. I told Frank to leave it on overnight, with the monitor turned off, and by morning it will be finished."

"You put that same program on Travis's computer? He must love it."

"Not the same. I thought I could just load it here, but Travis's drive used the old floppy disks, and this one takes the three-and-a-half size. I keyed it in. Needs a little tinkering with to get out of it, but I'll do that after Frank goes to bed."

Another line of the emerging pattern was completed, and a new one started. Already half an inch of the pattern was visible. Frank leaned in closer, drew back, but he did not take his gaze from the monitor. Barbara watched for another few seconds before she returned to the living room, something nagging at her. Her laptop and her father's computer were compatible; she had not bothered with a printer because she could print out from his using her disks. The salesman had told her emphatically that the old floppies had become obsolete and were being phased out as fast as people upgraded. So why had Lucas bought a big expensive computer that used them? She frowned at the diminishing fire.

Because he had worked as a maintenance man for the last six years of his life, she answered herself finally. He bought a computer that was as nearly like the last one he had used as possible. That simple? Maybe, she admitted. Maybe it was.

Mike returned then and sat on the floor by her chair, leaned against her legs. "And this is what domesticity is like," he said softly.

"This is it. You like it?"

"I do for right now. But how long? That's the question, isn't it?"

She put her hand on his head. "That's the question, all right." His hair was crisp under her fingers.

"I like your old man quite a lot."

"But you think he's pushing?"

"He pushes. And he's shrewd as Solomon. He called me at home at one in the morning. I got to thinking about that later on. You weren't in danger, no skull fracture or anything like that. He didn't think of me until his anxiety was something he could handle, but then he called. Said he thought mathematicians stayed up all night playing with numbers, and that he thought I'd want to know."

She gritted her teeth and tugged his hair slightly. "Push back. I learned thirty years ago that you have to push back."

"I'll have to bone up on my pushing act." He tilted his head to look up at her. "You want to hear a thought that crossed my mind while he was playing with the Mandelbrot?"

"Tell me."

"I began to wonder why Lucas Kendricks spent nearly four thousand on a computer. Your laptop is around fifteen hundred; Frank's is about twenty-five hundred, and they're both more than adequate for what you do with them. Glorified typewriters, that's what you bought. But why did Kendricks spend that kind of money unless he intended to work with it? I mean really work with it. And that made me wonder at what."

"You think he intended to continue the work he was doing with Frobisher years ago? From what Nell says about him, I doubt that he was capable of doing it alone. She could have misjudged his abilities, I suppose."

A second later his hand pressed hers, which was still on his head; she realized that she had been patting him while her mind took the thought and played it this way and that. Slowly she said, "He bought the kind of machine he was familiar with, but you don't have to be familiar with the newer ones; they work the same way. What if he had disks that ran only in that drive? They were after disks! I'd bet anything!"

"It's too easy to get data transferred from one size to another, from one language to another."

"But was it seven years ago? His knowledge of computers could have stopped back in 1982, remember. Maybe it never even occurred to him, or maybe he didn't dare risk taking them to a shop anywhere. He knew people were after him." Her hand had started to play with his hair; he pulled it away, kissed her palm. "I have to call Bailey," she said suddenly, and started to get up.

"Hey, have a heart," he said, shaking his head. "You know what time it is? After one."

"Damn. Tomorrow. You're a genius, you know?"

"I know, but I just stated the obvious. I still don't know why you're excited about it."

"You gave me the ammunition I need to get Brandywine up here. She'll come for disks. Want to bet?"

"No way. This is your game. I don't even know the rules. For instance, I don't know why you want her if you have the paperwork from the detective."

She felt a jolt of surprise; it had seemed too obvious to mention. "I can impeach her testimony, but that won't get anything new put in the record, just remove some of the damning statements she's already made. I want her to have to say she lied. I want to back her into a corner and see what comes out if she gets mad enough."

For what seemed a long time Mike was without movement. He could do that, go utterly still without giving a hint

235

of what was happening in his head. Whatever it was then he did not mention, but said, "Let's go to bed."

She felt herself tighten at the words, and found it curious that she could react like a schoolgirl at the idea of having her father find out that she was having sex. And that was really stupid, she knew, because he was throwing them together like a paid matchmaker.

"Not together," Mike said, getting to his feet. He stretched and made creaking noises. "I as much as promised that I would stay in the guest room."

She looked at him incredulously. "He brought it up?"

Mike laughed. "I did. I think what he was doing was giving me permission to creep into your tent."

They went through the house together turning off lights, making certain the fireplace screen was in place, the stove was turned off; then they went upstairs hand in hand. He kissed her cheek at her bedroom door and continued down the hall to his room.

It was just as well, she told herself as she undressed, groaning now and then. She was one big bruise, sore from top to bottom, but more, she found that she was growing angrier and angrier. That long silence, and then no comment after she explained why she wanted Brandywine, what did that mean? She knew what she would mean with that kind of distancing silence. She was angry enough to go to him and demand . . . what? an explanation? apology? a replay? She withdrew her hand from the doorknob, went to the bathroom and began to run water for a long, soaking bath to relax her sore muscles, to relax her mind.

By the time she was prunelike the anger had changed; it was no longer hot and demanding immediate appeasement, it no longer drew her face into a furious scowl. Now it was more like a forest that had been ravaged with fire and looked benign again, but to the knowledgeable eye there would be evident a layer of hot embers under the surface of forest duff, needing only a breeze, a scuffle, a nudge to flare again hotter than before.

* * *

236

Sunday afternoon Nell leaned against a tree trunk at the small beach and watched the river moving away, always moving away. It was almost black and very swift, but quiet. The shallow water that played over the rocky beach was gray. It edged in, left, edged in again endlessly, always the same, never the same. Here it had a whispery voice, the voice of someone so ancient that words were no longer needed; the whisper, the rhythm was enough. She closed her eyes and tried to make that rising and falling voice sound out words, tried to make it become her grandfather's voice, but it remained the ageless river engaged in its ageless monologue.

Grampa was up on the ledge, not down here, and she could not go up there ever again. She stared at the river. Sometimes when she had a problem she could take both sides of a dialogue and work her way through it, but not now. Clive was a problem that eluded her. He was a good man, she felt reasonably certain, even though he had worked to fell the forests. She was unable to continue. She made herself add another sentence. A lot of good people do things that other people see as evil, there is no absolute, and people change all the time. But the second sentence was abstract, and she could not apply it to Clive.

"I've changed," he had said last night. "All my training, school, the job, everything I did, everyone I talked to, they seemed to accept that trees grow, you cut them down, and they grow back. I thought the other side, the environmentalists were crazy, selfish even. I was wrong. Can't you see that people change?"

"I know," she had said. "It's not that. Really. I just can't think now. Not about you, about anything. Let's leave it at that until. . . . Let's just leave it at that."

The problem was that she was paralyzed with fear, something he could not help. She could not think of him, of Doc, of next month and Christmas and shopping, of anything. She was caught in a great invisible net whose sides were inexorably closing in around her; she would feel them with her hands if she dared reach out to try. She felt that her breath hit the wall before her and doubled back, stifling her, and when the net drew in close enough, Tuesday, Wednesday, whenever it happened, she would die of suffocation. She caught herself drawing in air deeply now and then, as if testing that there was enough.

"It doesn't matter what Barbara brings in as evidence," she whispered to the whispering river. "It really doesn't matter, does it?" She was terrified of the prosecutor, Tony DeAngelo, with his sharp face and cruel eyes and his contempt for her, for Barbara. He would convince the jury that no one else could have done it. Maybe he already had convinced them of that, and no matter how hard Barbara tried, how many lies she uncovered, how many others she drew into the defense case, that one fact would remain. No one else could have done it.

They were making Lucas out to be a monster, an insane monster who had done monstrous things to that poor girl. If she took the stand and said how afraid she had been of him, not for herself, for the children, if she said he had threatened her children, his daughter, if he had threatened her, and suddenly he was shot and she could not remember firing the gun, if she did all that, those cold looks from the jury would turn to compassionate looks, she felt certain. They would understand that. What they didn't understand was denial when no one else could have done it.

A bit of wood swept by, in the place where Travis had been in the drift boat back in June. She had a clear image of him contented out there in the boat, that lazy grin on his face, that incomplete gesture that was so like Lucas's gestures. And over his face was juxtaposed the image of Lucas on the ledge, laughing, the college boy she had fallen in love with restored for a single moment. Swiftly there came another image, their first time in bed together. She had been a virgin, and he had confessed that there had been only one girl before her. How awkwardly they had started, and then, afterward, he had rolled to his back and laughed that same joyous laugh, and she had laughed with him.

In November when there was no sun, only low-hanging clouds, daylight yielded to darkness imperceptibly, like a light on an automatic dimmer, fading, fading. It had grown nearly dark before she shook herself and turned to climb back up the bank, back to her house, to change her muddy clothes, face dinner with people who could still talk about things that didn't matter at all. She paused at the top of the bank to look back briefly at the small beach, the only place she had left that was still wholly hers, wholly private. After a step or two, she could no longer see the beach or hear the whispers of the river.

In her house on the table was a pan of cinnamon rolls and a scrap of paper with the note: *A snack for the kids when they get home. T.* She wanted to cry. Just a few weeks ago she had come home to find a cord of firewood stacked by her garage, a gift from James. And Clive was being so good to her and the children. She folded the note carefully and took it to her room to put away.

She had asked if dinner could be early because she wanted to be home when John and Amy brought the children back, and she had said she would stop by for Barbara and Mike. Barbara had never been to Clive's house, which was hard to find in the dark. But really she had not wanted any argument when it was time to leave and had not wanted Clive to insist on picking her up and bringing her back. This seemed easier.

The house was on a dirt road at the western edge of Turner's Point, up on the side of a mountain. The road was narrow and winding, pressed hard by dense forests on both sides. Clive met them at the door.

The first few minutes were okay as Clive took their coats, asked about Barbara's injuries, and showed them to the living room. Nell had never been inside the house and looked at it with some interest, a bit surprised to find it so comfortable. The ceiling was low with exposed beams. Twin couches were covered with Indian throws, and a Navajo rug was on the floor. A wood-burning stove with a glass door was in one corner, and there were two walls of bookshelves jammed so

239

full that books had been wedged in on top of those that were upright.

Clive was mixing and passing drinks, but when that was finished it seemed that no one had anything to say. Nell found that she didn't care. She watched the fire shadows dancing on the door of the stove, but she was aware of Clive's gaze, which left her, only to return instantly.

Almost desperately Clive asked Mike where he was from; he appeared vastly relieved when Mike actually began to talk about Indiana, and then went on to talk about other schools he had attended or taught at—Texas, Louisiana. . . . "They're all running scared," he said. "Too many problems these days with communicable diseases, not just AIDS, but herpes, venereal diseases, and, of course, drugs. What kind of test do you administer to reach all the bright young people who might also be infected with something, or addicted?"

"Jesus," Clive said, "You don't *reach* them. Those shrinks, let them earn their pay, find a way to identify them all. Especially the gays, the perverts. Toss them out to sink or swim. Who gives a damn about what they do, as long as they don't involve the rest of us? Sure, we should let them choose, with the understanding that they pay the price, they don't come begging us to bail them out when things get rough. I say old Mother Nature has found a way to weed out the perverts and we should just get out of the way and let it happen."

The silence that followed this was prolonged and awkward, until a bell went off from somewhere. "Timer," Clive said, jumping up in relief. "Be right back."

Barbara got up to look over his books, many of them on forestry. He was just voicing what two out of three people believed, she said under her breath; it simply sounded shocking to hear the honest words. She pulled out an oversized book of photographs and opened it on the coffee table. Beautifully photographed trees, page after page of trees from all over the world.

A sequoia tree on facing pages stopped her. Nell had

240

come to her side, was looking at the pictures. "My grandfather used to say that the trees have hearts that pump fluids just like hearts in people pump blood. He said a sequoia tree has to pump two hundred gallons of water a minute to survive."

From the doorway Clive said, "It isn't exactly like that, but close enough. I think of the whole world as alive with a giant pump sending rivers to the ocean, water vapor back into the air to rain down on the forests and start it all over again." He looked embarrassed then as he said, "You guys want to see some of the photographs I've collected here in the state?"

He led them to his office, where two walls were covered with his photographs, not as professional, not as perfectly printed as those in the book, but an impressive display. He pointed, naming them: noble fir, spruce, alder, lodgepole pine, ponderosa pine, incense cedar. . . .

In his office were the tools of his trade, several cameras, one on a tripod; binoculars, one small, one very large; a telescope on a tripod, and a wall full of maps, some rolled in slanted bins, some mounted on the wall, some on pull-down rollers.

The timer went off again, and he glanced at his watch. "I think it must be dinner," he said. "Right back."

Nell looked at the room and felt herself shrinking. He had planned this whole evening in order to show her this room, his pictures, she thought then. She had turned down several invitations to come to his house, and he had found a way to get her in this room with the pictures that proved how much he actually cared about the forests, the trees. It was undeniable; he did care. There was a picture of a glade where vibrant, green moss covered everything, the rocks, a log, the tree branches; a single shaft of sunlight penetrated the space to land on a gleaming golden fir cone. How long had he waited for the right moment, for the sunlight to reach the cone with its Midas touch?

Clive returned and said that yes, indeed, it was dinner. He was looking at her, not the others. She said softly,

"Thanks for showing us all these. Your pictures are wonderful."

His big weather-burned face broke out into a jack o'lantern grin, and for the first time that evening he relaxed.

His dinner was very good baked salmon, and he admitted that he was a fisherman, just like everyone else up and down the river. "And let me tell you, it's a bitch getting the boat up my road, but worth it. Take it down in the spring, bring it home in the fall, cursing both ways." He said to Nell, "Sometime I'd like to take you on a white-water trip down the Owyhee." Now that he had relaxed, he talked with animation about the places in Oregon that were little known, places so far off the trails that for days and days you could wander and never see a sign of human destruction, human trash, not even a candy wrapper. Hard to get to in many cases, he admitted, and worth every second of misery to reach.

Although the evening had gone better than she had dared hope, by nine Nell was back in her own house with her children and her in-laws, just as she had planned to be. They ate the cinnamon rolls from Tawna and talked about the farm and the trip, and she watched her children, touched Carol, touched Travis; she listened to their words, and their silences, and she began to relax. The earlier part of the evening faded from memory so fast it might never have been.

In Frank's house, Barbara said to Mike, "I think you should go on home tonight. I have work to do, and you have classes in the morning. As you can see, I'm perfectly fine."

He regarded her for a moment, then nodded. "If that's what you want."

She wanted to yell at him to ask what was wrong, what had happened, so they could sit down and talk it out, let her explain her position as a lawyer for a defendant in a murder trial. At the same time, she was afraid for him to ask that, because she feared that she would sound like her father

242

defending the indefensible. So be it, she thought bitterly, as he waited for some response. He had seen this side of her; let him go away and think about it. It was his move. She nodded, and neither spoke again as he started to gather his belongings and then went to tell Frank goodbye. She stood at the door, where he hesitated; after a moment his face tightened and he said, "So long. See you around."

When she turned away from the door again, Frank was in the hall scowling fiercely. "You're both two damn fools!" He wheeled, went back inside his study, and slammed the door.

TWENTY-THREE

ON TUESDAY, WHEN the trial resumed, Tony was as angelic as his name suggested; he didn't challenge a single character witness; he looked supremely bored. "Doesn't mean a damn thing," her father had grumbled once about character witnesses. "Even the devil has pals who swear by him. But you've got to do it." Tony would agree and would not prolong anything he didn't have to, Barbara knew, not know. Time was running out for catching Ruth Brandywine, and Tony had a very good sense of timing. She had no doubt that he had timed her defense almost as carefully as she had.

Tony first objections came when she called Pete Malinski. She argued that the prosecution had introduced the subject of Nell's shooting at people and the issue had to be clarified. Pete Malinski took the stand after ten minutes of a near shouting match. He was twenty-eight with a smooth, rather babyish face, and brown eyes as pale as butterscotch. His hair was lush and curly, reddish brown. He worked full time for Clovis in the summer, he said, and part time during the school year, when he was studying engineering. He looked like the son every mother yearned for, earnest, honest, good-humored, and now very nervous.

He told how he and his partner had been hired by two men to play a joke on a lady, how he had gone to Nell Kendricks's place with one of them, who said his name was Sam. When he got to the gun part, he looked at Nell with some admiration. "What a shot!" he said. "That beer can sailed off to heaven just like that."

"And then what?"

"We got back in the truck and got out of there. I was feeling that it wasn't such a hot joke by then. I stopped at the store in town and got a Coke and told the woman there that she"—he nodded toward Nell—"said she'd shoot anyone who put a foot on her property. Thought I should warn some-one."

"What about the man who called himself Sam? Did he go inside with you?"

"No, Ma'am. As soon as we got in the truck he kind of slouched down with his hat over his face and went to sleep. Didn't say another word all the way back to Salem."

Barbara had him describe the two men, and then she was finished.

Tony looked lazy and not very interested as he got to his feet. "Mr. Malinski, did either man say who hired them?"

"No. Just a guy."

"No more questions." He sat down.

"You said he paid you in cash," Barbara said then. "Two hundred each, isn't that right?" He agreed that it was, and she went on, "And another hundred for the use of the truck. Five hundred dollars in cash. Did you see him take the money from his wallet?"

"Yes, Ma'am, and he had a stash you wouldn't believe in it."

"He paid you in fifty-dollar bills?"

"Yes, Ma'am."

She thanked him and let him go. Judge Lundgren decided that it was lunchtime, and the courtroom began emptying as soon as he left the bench and the jury was led out by the bailiff. At Barbara's side Nell said softly, "He'll just claim that Lucas hired them."

"And I'll prove otherwise. It's going okay, believe me." It was what one said, she told herself as Nell left with John and Amy Kendricks, and besides, what else could she have said?

"Where is that creep Bailey?" Barbara muttered over a lunch she did not want.

Her father was eating placidly. "He'll show this afternoon. I know him, he'll come through."

"Well, if he does, he has to get in touch with Roy Whitehorse. Tell him for me, will you? I want Whitehorse to call Brandywine tonight, if she hasn't called him back yet. He's sore. He's lost his job, or is on suspension, over showing the campsites, and it's costing him. Someone has to pay for that. He should be in an ugly mood, maybe sound a little drunk even. If she doesn't want what he has, maybe the defense lawyer will buy the disks before the defense has to rest its case tomorrow. He should say it like that, and then no more. But make it plain that tomorrow he wants to unload and get some spending money. And he won't turn them over to anyone but her or me. He knows the sheriff wouldn't give a cent for them. Think he can handle that?"

Frank was watching her with a slight frown. "You said disks. You're gambling high stakes."

"I know I am, but it's going to take some strong medicine to shake that lady. That could do it. How about Whitehorse? How good is he?"

"I don't know. Never met him. Bailey says he's a teacher, grade-school level, and Timothy LeMans says he's the best tracker in the west. What does that tell you?"

"I wish I knew," she said. She looked at her salad with distaste and drank a second cup of coffee.

"Well," her father said, "maybe he teaches drama, and he longs to do Shakespeare and is a hell of an actor."

Lucky Rosner was not grinning today. He was wearing a suit and tie and looked very uncomfortable in his clothes. And he looked even younger than Barbara remembered, no more than sixteen or seventeen. He verified Pete Malinski's story about the two men and said he had stayed in Salem with the second man, Joe, and they played pool that afternoon.

"What happened next, Mr. Rosner? Did you read or hear about the death of Lucas Kendricks?"

He shook his head, then swiftly said, "No, I mean. I never knew anything about it until a detective came around asking questions."

"And he questioned you?"

"Yes, Ma'am. The secretary didn't know anything about that day, so he hung around and asked some of the guys, and when he got to me, I told him about it."

"Was he with the police?"

"No, Ma'am. He was a private detective."

"All right. Just tell us what happened then."

At first hesitantly, then with more confidence, he described going to the tree with Barbara, her father, and Bailey and told about climbing the tree and finding the gadget. Barbara picked it up from the exhibit table and showed him.

"Is this the device you found in the tree?"

He nodded, then with a nervous glance at the judge, he said, "I mean, yes."

She thanked him, nodded to Tony, and went back to the defense table. Her father was not in his seat. She breathed a small prayer that Bailey had arrived finally.

"Mr. Rosner, did either man say who hired them?" This time Tony didn't bother to leave the prosecution table. He stood at his seat.

"No, sir. They said a guy wanted to play a joke on the lady."

"And that device was just lying up there on a limb?"

"No, sir. It was stuck to the tree with some gummy stuff."

246

"Could you tell how long it had been up there?"

"No, sir."

"You and your partner believed a man wanted to spy on his wife, isn't that why you went along with this scheme?"

"Yes, sir. That's one of the things we thought of."

Tony sat down. "That's all."

Barbara's next witness was an electronics expert, Daryl Simpson, who told them more about listening devices than they wanted to know. He held the device lovingly as he talked. He was a thin man with sunken cheeks and a greenish complexion, as if he were ill or just recovering from an illness. When he began to describe the range of this particular device, she had him demonstrate on a map.

"So it would have picked up any conversation in either house on the Kendricks property," she said then. "Not the beach, because the bank would interfere. What about the ledge here? It's higher than the device was."

"That doesn't matter," he said. "Imagine a dome, half a mile diameter, half a mile up. That's the range of that one."

"Anything that was said on the ledge would have been recorded?"

"If it was working."

"What about the receiver? Where would that have been?"

He talked about receivers at great length. But the jury was being very attentive, and she did not try to hurry him.

She referred to the map again. "So, in a straight line for up to two miles, and you said it was directional. Does that mean it would transmit in that one direction only?"

"Yes, it does. Not through rocks or cliffs, but trees wouldn't interfere."

"For example, the end cabins down here would be in line with it, but not the ones under the cliff?"

He said that was right. Whoever put it up probably had aimed it where he intended to set up his receiver. Usually there would be a van or something nearby, but the cabins would work just as well.

"How much would you say this kind of device would cost?" she asked then, taking it from his hand.

He looked saddened and kept his gaze on it, not her. "Seven or eight hundred dollars."

After she thanked him and sat down, Tony got him to admit that the listeners could have been in a number of places—in Nell's house, or the big house, on the ledge, in any of the houses along the ridge, even across the river.

"In fact, there's no way to know, is there?"

"Not really. Just within two miles in a straight line."

Tony went on quickly. "Could you tell how long that device was in the tree?"

"It wasn't rained on, I'd say, but it was dirty, dusty." He began to talk about the adhesive gum, but this time Tony cut him off.

"Thank you. You don't know how long it was up there, isn't that your answer?"

"Yes. I don't know."

Asshole, Barbara thought at Tony. Next he'd suggest that she had climbed the tree and planted the bug. She heard a rustling behind her and turned to see Frank. He nodded. Bailey was back.

Her next witness was Louise Gilmore, who had rented one of the end cabins to two men on Wednesday, June seventh, the day before the two men had gone to Nell's place to cut the tree down.

"Is this the guest register?" Barbara asked, showing her the book.

"Yes. There are their names, Sam and Jerry Johnson." Barbara let her continue. "They wanted the end cabin, out of traffic they said, and they paid in cash, double our rate because they were anxious to finish some work they had to do. I thought they were writers with a deadline—one of them said something to that effect."

She had done some juggling with the cabins, she said, because they were booked up, but they had put a couple of people in their own house, and it had worked out. She described the men; her description was of the men who had

248

hired Pete Malinski and Lucky Rosner. They had rented a boat, she said, but hadn't used it much, and not to fish. And they had been out all Wednesday and most of Thursday in their car. She had not seen them again after they checked in. They left Saturday afternoon. All their stuff was gone, and the door had been left open, the key on the chest of drawers.

"How did you know they were gone? You said you didn't see them after they checked in."

"Well, up in the store we were talking about that girl's body and how everyone who had a boat was out on the river helping with the search, or letting someone borrow their boats to do it. And one of my customers said that boat number fourteen was on shore, funny that those people weren't out. I just thought I'd tell them that someone else might use it if they didn't want to join the searchers. And I found the place empty. But the boat had been out that day, it was still muddy. Maybe they had looked earlier."

When Barbara asked her how much the men had paid for the cabin she said without hesitation, "One thousand fifty dollars in cash, one week in advance."

Tony challenged some of her statements; how did she know the men hadn't fished if she never saw them?

"You live on the river all of your life like I have, you know."

In the end her story was intact, and he sat down, shaking his head as if to say, so what?

But the jury was paying close attention. It was all that money, Barbara knew. One of them, a delicate-looking woman of seventy, tightened her mouth more every time another sum was mentioned. Her lips had vanished altogether. Social Security, fixed income, Barbara remembered from the examination of the jurors. This was very big money to her. And a youngish, bookish man was looking pained as the numbers kept mounting. Barbara wished they could leave it right now, come back tomorrow, but Judge Lundgren was showing no signs of doing that. She called her next witness, Frederick Yost, the Forest Service ranger who had spotted the Honda on the dirt road. He had been sitting with a young woman and another man, both men in spotless Forest Service uniforms, so sharply pressed they looked like paper clothes. Yost was athletic, broad through the chest and shoulders, like Smokey the Bear with a people mask on.

After the opening questions about his age (twenty-six), education, and experience, she said, "Friday afternoon, June ninth, you were on your way to Bend, Oregon. Is that correct?"

"Your Honor, I object," Tony said sharply. "This witness has nothing to add to this trial. He was not even in the area when the murder occurred. This testimony is irrelevant to this case."

"And perhaps the prosecuting attorney would like to take his place in the stand and answer other questions I have for this witness," Barbara said just as sharply.

The judge held up his hand. "Ms. Holloway, Mr. DeAngelo, please, no personalities."

"Your Honor, I must object if the prosecution is going to play both prosecutor and jury in this case," Barbara said hotly.

Judge Lundgren's face seemed to draw in on itself in a curious way, as if he were struggling to control a flash of anger. "Ms. Holloway, I admonish you, no further remarks of that nature."

Tony started to say something, but the judge silenced him, also, and then sent the jury out with the bailiff and called Tony and Barbara to the bench.

"Ms. Holloway, are you going to establish relevance with this witness, and soon?" His voice was intense, but too low to carry past the two attorneys standing before him.

"Yes, Your Honor," she said, keeping her voice as low as his.

"How?" he asked bluntly.

"This witness misspoke in the statement he made to the investigating officer. Correcting his statement is vital to the defense of my client."

"You can't impeach the testimony of your own witness," Tony said furiously.

"If the police had done their job it wouldn't be necessary!" she shot back.

"Stop this instantly," Judge Lundgren said icily. "This court will not tolerate incivility!"

Tony cleared his throat, and the judge nodded to him to speak. "She intends to confuse the jury with so much irrelevant material they won't be able to think about the sole object of this trial, the death of Lucas Kendricks and the murder charge against Nell Kendricks."

Judge Lundgren looked again at Barbara and studied her for another moment, then said, "Ms. Holloway, be advised that the admonition I gave you last week is still pertinent. If I decide that you have been introducing material that is not relevant, I will instruct the jury most forcefully that they may not consider *anything* that happened before that Saturday when Lucas Kendricks was murdered. Do you understand?"

"Yes, I do."

"Very well, you may proceed." His expression, his eyes, his tone were all of a piece, frigid and remote, and very angry.

The jury was brought back and she resumed exactly where she had left off. "Mr. Yost, please tell us what you were doing and what you saw that afternoon." The self-assurance that had enwrapped him earlier was gone; now he looked nervous and wary. She smiled reassuringly, as if to say that none of that business at the bench had anything to do with him. He swallowed hard and nodded slightly.

He had stopped at the pass to eat a sandwich and drink coffee. When he looked over the forest with his binoculars, he had seen the Honda. He said it quickly with no detail, no elaboration.

Barbara glanced at a paper on her table, as if to check his statement with his written statement. She looked up at him from the defense table. "You received a commendation the next week, didn't you? For being alert and playing a significant role in an ongoing investigation."

251

He looked down at his hands and shrugged, then said yes.

"How long had you served in the Sisters Ranger District, Mr. Yost?"

"I was just assigned it. I was on my way to my new job."

"Oh. Where had you been stationed before?"

"The Willamette District."

She picked up a paper and scanned it, then said, "When you called in about the car, exactly what did you tell them?"

"I said I spotted the Honda the bulletin was out about."

"Yes, but do you recall your words?"

He shook his head. "I don't think so. It's been a long time."

"Of course. Let me refresh your memory. You said, didn't you, that you caught a glint of sun on the chrome of the grill?"

He nodded, then said ruefully, "But I was wrong. It turned out that the car was pointed the other way. I must have seen the rear end of it."

"Oh, I see." She put the paper down as if relieved, then picked up a photograph of the Honda. She handed it to him. "Can you point out what you saw of the car?"

He looked at the picture in confusion. No chrome was visible from the rear. "It must have been the chrome strip down the side. It goes all the way to the rear, but it doesn't show in this picture."

"I have another shot," she said, and found a different photograph, handed it to him.

He nodded vigorously. "See, that strip is chrome. The sun must have hit it just right. I only saw a small section, less than a foot probably."

She took back the photographs and walked to the jury with them. "From that little section you knew it was the gray Honda?"

"Well, you know, guys are pretty up on cars from the time they're little kids."

"Of course. In your report you told the sheriff's office that it was on Forest Service road 4219, didn't you?"

"Yes. I had a good map. It had to be that road."

"A map like this one, I understand, since this is the official Forest Service map." She indicated the map they had already used several times. He nodded. "So you were up here on the highway, and ten miles away was the Honda on Forest Service road 4219. Can you point out that road for us, Mr. Yost?"

Reluctantly he left the stand and approached the map. He peered at it closely and twice started to put his finger down, then drew back. At last he pointed to the road. Barbara thanked him and studied the map as he returned to the witness chair. "There are seven Forest Service roads between that one and the highway where you were. No wonder it took you so long to find the right one."

"It's different when you're out there," he blurted.

"But you had to identify the road by using the map, didn't you? You couldn't be expected to look out over the forest and pick out an individual road and know it instantly. Especially as a newcomer to the district."

"Objection," Tony snapped. "Let counsel ask her questions without making speeches."

"Sustained."

"Do you wear glasses, Mr. Yost? Or contacts?"

"No." He was watching her with a sullen expression now, sitting so stiffly that he must have been concentrating on not betraying any nervous mannerisms. His stiffness was more revealing than fidgeting would have been.

"What power binoculars did you have?"

"Seven by fifty. But you can see a flash of light farther away than that with almost any binoculars."

"But you also saw enough gray to identify the Honda, didn't you?"

"I thought it was the car they were looking for. I saw enough to reach that conclusion. Maybe I shouldn't have, but that's what I thought I saw." He had gone the route from an abject desire to please, the perfect witness, to wariness; he had become sullen, saying with his body language that he was being picked on and didn't deserve it, and now he had reached this new phase, defiance. One more, Barbara thought. One more stage.

Barbara returned to the exhibit table and sorted through papers until she had the sheriff's report. She scanned it briefly. "What time did you see the Honda, Mr. Yost?"

"About three-thirty."

"But you didn't call in the report until six?"

"I had to go to Sisters to call. The line was busy the first time or two, so I had a cup of coffee and tried again."

Barbara looked at him in surprise and walked to the map. "But here's a government camp, less than a mile from the observatory on McKenzie Pass, less than a mile from where you were. It's clearly marked. Why didn't you go there to phone?"

"I didn't know it was there, or that it was open."

"You didn't know it was there," she murmured. "I see."

"I didn't mean that. I meant I didn't know it was open."

"Mr. Yost," she said slowly, moving back to the exhibit table, where she started to look for something, "have you ever driven on that service road, 4219?"

"No. But I've been on plenty of other service roads in the forests."

"So you understand how they are, muddy in places, bone dry in others?"

"Yes, that's how most of them are."

"Yes. I have a few more pictures for you to look at, Mr. Yost. These are pictures Sheriff LeMans's deputies took of the car they found on Forest Service road 4219. Will you examine them, please."

She handed him three pictures and watched the defiance fade from his face. He paled slightly and moistened his lips as he put the first photograph under the others to examine the second one. When he finished looking at them all, he did not raise his head but kept staring at the last picture. The pictures showed a car so spattered with mud and red lava dust that it was impossible to say more than that it was an automobile. A small area of the rear window had been wiped for visibility; no paint was discernible, not even the license plates could be seen, nor any chrome at all. If anyone had tried to guess at the color of the car under the heavy coating of mud, the first choice would have been red.

Very quietly Barbara said, "You never saw the car, did you, Mr. Yost?"

He swallowed but did not speak, did not raise his head.

"You were used very cruelly, Mr. Yost, and once you had made the statement you found it impossible to take it back, didn't you?"

The courtroom had gone so quiet that it was uncanny. Judge Kendall Lundgren drew in a breath and said, "Mr. Yost, you must answer the question."

"Yes, sir," he mumbled.

"Did you see the car?" Barbara asked.

"No."

"How did you know it was there?"

"A man called me and said he had seen it and he knew everyone was looking for it, but he didn't want to get involved." The words were choked; finally he looked up, out past Barbara, out to where the young woman he had entered with was seated, by another young man in another spanking-fresh uniform. There were tears in his eyes.

He had reached the final phase.

Barbara led him through the story quickly now. He had no more resistance. A man had called him Friday morning; he said he had read a little article about Yost in the local paper, giving his name, address, mentioning that he was being assigned to the Sisters District. The man said he had seen the car Thursday afternoon. If Yost would drive on McKenzie Highway he could see it clearly from the pass. The man told him exactly where to look, what road the car was on. Yost had looked but had seen nothing, and for the next hour or two he had wavered, then finally made the call, thinking there could have been an accident. If the car wasn't there, no harm done, but if it was, they needed to find it.

She asked a few more questions, but little new was

255

forthcoming. "Mr. Yost," she said finally, "did this stranger tell you precisely where to look?"

"Yes, he did."

"You consulted a map and looked exactly where he told you to, is that right?"

"Yes."

"And you couldn't see a thing out there, could you?"

"No. Just trees and the lava flow."

"Mr. Yost, do you think it's possible that anyone could have seen the car from that viewpoint on the pass?"

"Objection," Tony said. "Counsel knows that is pure conjecture."

"Sustained," Judge Lundgren said, but in the witness box Frederick Yost was shaking his head.

TWENTY-FOUR

THE FIRE HAD died; there were ashes left, and the end of a log faintly glowing. She should have added a log, banked it, Barbara thought moodily. Already the living room was chilled, as if the heavy fog had penetrated as soon as the flames failed to forbid entrance. She drew her arms around her closer.

"Bobby, it's getting pretty late," Frank said at the doorway.

She nodded, not really surprised that he was still up. "I told Bailey he could call as late as one in the morning."

Frank did not move from the doorway. Before he could

say anything, she said, "I was thinking of Mother." She heard his quick breath, and then he came across the room and sat opposite her. She kept her eyes on the glowing spot in the grate. "I was remembering one time when I was about twelve, thirteen at the most, and you came home one night as mean as a cat in a trap, snapping, snarling, stamping around. I wanted to ask you something, and she said, 'Leave him alone.' Just that, but in a tone of voice that she never had used with me before. I was pretty shocked, enough to send me upstairs to my room. She knew, didn't she? What it was like, I mean."

"She knew," he said quietly. "You never wanted to talk about her before. It's been a cruel barrier, not talking about her."

"I couldn't. I was too confused, I think. And jealous."

"Good God!"

"I know," she said in a very small voice, still not looking at him, aware that he was leaning forward, that he was tense, that he wanted to take her into his arms and pat her, and didn't quite dare, not yet. That was how he used to treat her when she was troubled; he would gather her up in his arms and pat her back and say, "There, there. World's not coming to an end, not just now, anyway."

"You both had each other," she said then, "and it was so clear to me that I was an outsider, not needed, loved but unnecessary, superfluous. You had each other. And she understood you in a way I couldn't. She accepted you exactly as you were, but I kept thinking you should change a little, stop doing this, start doing that, whatever this or that was at the time. Funny, I can't even remember now in what ways I wanted you to change."

"I used to practice my summations before her," Frank said. "She was the best audience I ever had, and sharp. She could find the flaw that I thought I had buried so deep it would take an archeologist to dig it out again."

"You never tried another murder case after she died, did you?"

From the corner of her eye she could see him shake his

head slowly. "Couldn't seem to do it. Something went out, something died in me, too."

"I failed you both," Barbara said in an even lower voice. "I was jealous and ran out on both of you." Her mother's death had been like an explosion, she thought, hurling everyone else into erratic orbits, while her mother had gone flying off into some infinity that was unimaginable.

"Honey, no one ever thought that." His voice was soft and very gentle. "You had your life to get on with. We both knew that. She never once reproached you for going on about your own life. She loved you very much."

"I know she did. Toward the end, she tried so hard to make me accept that she was dying, and I wouldn't. I pretended I didn't believe it. Maybe I really didn't believe it. I could have helped her, but I was afraid. Then Tony came along. He was my armor. She died before I could explain how afraid I was. I didn't even know how afraid I was. She was so *good*. And because you had her, you could borrow that goodness, but I didn't have anyone to tap into, anyone who was good enough that there was some extra, to hand out. I began to realize how evil people can be. Truly evil. Before that I just didn't believe in God, but afterward, I began to believe, and I hated him more than I can tell you." She looked up at her father finally. "I never told you any of this. I couldn't. I saw God as the cause of the evil, the injustice, the hurts, the deaths, the destruction of decent people. That boy I destroyed today, he didn't deserve what happened to him. He's just a stupid, vain boy, and he's destroyed. God and I are killing people, Dad. God set up that stupid boy, and I shot him down. Working together, in tandem, we're killing people. I ran when I realized that he was using me, as much as he used Tony, or you after Mother died, or the judges, or anyone else. I had to get out. There can't be any justice, because he stacked the deck, he stocked the Earth with us, and programmed us to go out and get each other any way we can. We were warned, the story of Job spells it out; he set up Job and he's been doing it ever since. He'll keep setting up dumb kids like that boy today, and we—you, Tony, I, all of us—we'll shoot them down, another life destroyed. I learned that I can't beat him, can't even engage him in a fair fight, and I ran away from it all. I swore I wouldn't let myself be used by him. But here I am, doing it again, being used, using anyone I can. And he's off somewhere laughing. God's will prevails."

"Barbara, stop it," Frank said sharply. "That man lied, he wanted glory and fame, a commendation. He lied. He didn't care who he hurt or how much as long as he got a little piece of glory. He doesn't deserve a grain of regret."

She shrugged. "He did exactly what he had to, given who he is. Do you think he had it in him to resist that kind of temptation?"

"A person with some decency in him would have called the sheriff and told him exactly what happened."

"You're making my point, Dad," she said wearily. "Where do we find those persons with some decency? Mother had it and she's dead. Nell is a decent person, and where is she? Face it. We live in the charnel house, and are so inured to the carnage that we don't even see it any more."

The phone rang then, and she jumped up to take the call.

"Got her," Bailey said. "She called Roy earlier tonight and he put on his act, the one you outlined. She said to sit tight, she'd call back. And she did. She's taking an early flight to Eugene, tomorrow. Arrives at nine-fifteen."

When she hung up, her father had closed the fireplace screen and was at the door leading to the hall. They both knew that the moment for intimacy had ended.

"I heard," he said. "Good job. His gaze was level and indecipherable then. "What I came in here to tell you before, and got sidetracked, was that this evening after court Mike was looking for you, to talk, he said. I'm afraid I told him to leave you alone in a pretty sharp voice. He was a bit startled. I just wanted to tell you." He walked out and at the stairs he said, "Good night, Barbara."

Ruth Brandywine was dressed in an elegant mauve cashmere suit with a mauve silk blouse. The clothes were lovely, but the color was not good for her sallow skin; it gave her a purplish cast that was reminiscent of late-night horror movies on a bad color television on which everything that wasn't a shade of green was a shade of purple. Her thin hair had been fluffed and teased in an attempt to make it appear fuller, but now it looked like a steel wool pad that had been pulled out from the center. Her eyes were like little drops of black ice.

Barbara studied her for a moment from the defense table, where she remained as she asked, "When did you first meet Lucas Kendricks?"

"I don't remember."

Barbara picked up the transcript. "From your perpetuation of testimony which the court watched on video, I see that you stated that you never met him under that name. Which is right, Dr. Brandywine? That you don't remember, or that you never met him?"

Dr. Brandywine shrugged and said, "I may have met him years ago, but I don't remember the occasion. As far as I am concerned, it's the equivalent of saying I never met him."

"And when did the man you called Tom Mann, or Tom Manning, become your patient?"

"Early November, 1982."

"Can you recall the day?"

"No."

"How did he become your patient?"

"At the request of a colleague who asked if I would be willing to help the young man. I was willing."

"You had a private practice at that time?"

"No."

"Just one patient?"

"Yes."

"Who was the colleague who made this request?"

"Dr. Emil Frobisher."

"He was a teacher at Rocky Mount College?"

"Yes."

"And you joined the staff at the college in September of that year?"

"Yes."

"When did you meet Dr. Emil Frobisher?"

"I don't remember."

"Well, did you know him before you were offered the position at Rocky Mount?"

"No."

"The position was offered to you in August, I believe you stated. So you met him between August and November?"

"I can't really say."

"But we know that Dr. Frobisher died on November fourteenth of that year, and you said you met him after you were offered a position at the college in August. Doesn't that mean that you met him during that period, between August and November fourteenth?"

"If you put it that way, I suppose so."

Barbara shook her head and moved to stand directly before the woman. "Dr. Brandywine, did you meet him during that period?"

"Yes. I believe I must have met most of my new colleagues during that period."

"Thank you. That must have been a very busy time for you, making a major career change, finding a house, moving, preparing for your classes, meeting so many new people?"

"Extremely busy," Dr. Brandywine said.

"Did you and Dr. Frobisher become close friends during those few weeks?"

"No."

"He was a mathematician, not even in your department, isn't that right?"

"Yes."

"Would you estimate that you met sixty people during that period?"

"Perhaps even more. I really don't remember."

"Of course. So we will call it sixty. And Emil Frobisher was simply one of them, in a different field from yours, with few if any similar professional interests. A virtual stranger, one might even say. Dr. Brandywine, why did you agree to accept his student as a patient?"

"I was interested in the case."

"Did Dr. Frobisher offer to pay for your services?"

"No."

"Did the young man pay for his treatment?"

"No."

"How long did you continue his treatment?"

"Until he left in June."

"June of this year?"

"Yes."

"You accepted him as a patient before Emil Frobisher was killed on November 14, 1982?"

"Yes. A week or ten days before that."

"But you didn't know he was Lucas Kendricks at the time?"

"No. If the name was mentioned, I forgot. In my files he was Tom Mann."

"How was he presented to you? How did you meet Tom Mann?"

"Dr. Frobisher brought him to my house."

"You treated him there?"

"Yes. He stayed with me for six weeks and then he had a unit in student housing on the campus. I saw him as an outpatient from that time on."

"You accepted him into your home?"

"Yes."

Barbara regarded her for a second, then turned away and walked back to the defense table. "Why, Dr. Brandywine? Isn't that highly unusual?"

"Not really."

"Had you done such a thing before?"

"No."

"Have you since then?"

"No."

"What was your diagnosis of his condition?"

"Acute paranoid schizophrenia. He was totally helpless,

catatonic, dissociated, hallucinating. I thought I could help him, and I did."

"So he was having a mental crisis? How long did that phase last?"

"A severe crisis. It was in December that he began to function, and after that his recovery proceeded normally and he was able to take a job in January and live in the student housing unit."

Barbara nodded. "What did the young man have with him when he moved into your house?"

"Nothing, just the clothes he was wearing."

"Identification, money, a car?"

"I said nothing."

"Do you know what happened to his possessions, his wallet, his car?"

"I supposed that Emil Frobisher had taken care of those things. I didn't ask."

"Who put his car in your garage?"

Dr. Brandywine shook her head. "No one did. It was not in my garage."

"Do you know Miranda Cortealta?"

"Of course. She is my housekeeper."

"When did she start working for you?"

Dr. Brandywine shook her head again and looked past Barbara toward the jury, then toward the crowded court-room. "I don't know. Sometime that fall or winter, I think."

"Dr. Brandywine, this is the report of the officers who investigated the theft of your car battery last June. Quote: 'According to Miranda Cortealta, housekeeper for Dr. Ruth Brandywine, a gray car was also missing. She did not know the make or model, only that it was a small car. It had been parked in the garage ever since she could remember.' Was a gray car missing from your garage at the same time the battery was stolen?"

"Miranda was mistaken. I never had a gray car in my garage."

"Did you tell the investigating officers that?"

"No. They never asked as far as I can remember."

263

"So when you first met Lucas Kendricks, he was incapable of communicating? Is that right?"

"I met a man called Tom Mann. That was the only name I knew him by. And acute paranoid schizophrenics seldom communicate," Dr. Brandywine said sharply. "I told you, he was in crisis."

"Yes, you did. For how long was he totally incapacitated?"

"Weeks, at least."

"He was unfit to drive, or go into town to conduct business, or to continue whatever work he was doing with Dr. Frobisher?"

Dr. Brandywine sighed. "I have said this already as clearly as I know how. He was in crisis, incapable of any business whatsoever."

"Yes, you have said that clearly. Dr. Brandywine, I have a few papers I'd like to have you identify if you can. Do you recognize the name of this bank?"

She handed a document to Ruth Brandywine, who fished in her purse to draw out glasses, and put them on deliberately, adjusted them, and then peered at the paper.

"Yes. I bank there in Boulder."

"And the manager's name? Is that familiar to you?"

"Yes."

"Dr. Brandywine, I ask you this, did you go to that bank with Lucas Kendricks on November 16, 1982?"

For the first time she hesitated, but it was a very short pause; she drew herself up and said as firmly as before, "No."

"Did you draw out a cashier's check for three thousand two hundred twenty two dollars on November the sixteenth?"

"No!"

Barbara nodded; she picked up another paper and walked to Ruth Brandywine. She kept this sheet and said, "I read the sworn statement of Lawrence Spaulding, manager of the Bank of Boulder. Quote, 'On November 16, 1982, Lucas Kendricks closed his checking account in person, taking his money in cash. The teller, Doris Huntley, as

264

instructed in such cases, made note of the serial numbers of the bills, which were hundreds. Because there had been several confidence scams in the past few months, she also alerted me, and I left my office to observe what was transpiring. Lucas Kendricks was known to me at the time, and his companion, Dr. Ruth Brandywine, was also known to me. After closing the checking account Lucas Kendricks and Dr. Brandywine left the bank together.' The starting and ending serial numbers are included," Barbara said, and handed the paper to Ruth Brandywine. She walked back to the defense table where she stood without motion until Dr. Brandywine finished reading. Barbara nodded to the clerk, who took the statement and handed it to the jury foreman.

"Dr. Brandywine, did you go to the bank with Lucas Kendricks on November 16, 1982, and stand by him while he closed his checking account?"

Ruth Brandywine took off her glasses and folded them, replaced them in a gold case that she carefully put back in her purse. Then she looked at Judge Lundgren and said, "Your Honor, I must refuse to answer any further questions without the counsel of my legal advisor."

"I object, Your Honor," Barbara cried furiously. "This witness can answer the question immediately. She has made statements that are contradicted by others in sworn affidavits. She can admit she went to that bank or deny it without any legal advice. Either she did or she didn't. It doesn't take expert advice to tell the truth of the matter."

"Objection!" Tony yelled then. "Counsel is harassing this witness. Under our system of jurisprudence witnesses are granted legal rights, as counsel knows very well."

"That doesn't include the right to lie under oath. Don't be idiotic!"

Judge Lundgren banged his gavel hard and glared at Barbara and Tony. "We will have a ten-minute recess," he snapped. He stood up, stalked from the bench.

When the recess was over, Judge Lundgren nodded to Ruth Brandywine. "You are excused until nine-thirty tomorrow morning. You may step down." He looked frostily at Barbara. "Do you have additional witnesses you wish to call before continuing with Dr. Brandywine?"

Barbara watched Ruth Brandywine leave the stand and walk in front of the defense table, pass out of sight. Brandywine looked neither right nor left; her head was high, her face expressionless.

"I have various statements I would like to enter as defense exhibits," Barbara said as neutrally as she could manage as soon as she knew Ruth Brandywine had started the walk from the court. Every eye was following her.

"Very well," the judge said. "You may proceed."

Deliberately Barbara turned to watch Ruth Brandywine, who had reached the door to the corridor. She waited until the woman left the courtroom, and attention returned to the defense table. Then she introduced the bank statement concerning the car loan Lucas Kendricks had taken out, and the official notification that the loan had been paid in full by a cashier's check in the amount of $3,222 on November 18, 1982. She read the insurance cancelation notice, and the note indicating that a refund check for $285 was attached. A newer notice was stapled to that one: the check had not been cashed or returned. Next came an accounting from the housing administrator's office at Rocky Mount College. Through December 1982, Lucas Kendricks had paid for his meals and his apartment; after January 1983 Dr. Brandywine's office had been billed for the same apartment and meal tickets for Tom Mann. Her final document was the bill of sale for the computer system, and a note about the serial numbers of the hundred-dollar bills that had been used to pay for it. The identical numbers, she pointed out, that appeared on the bank statement about the closing of Lucas Kendricks's account in 1982.

After court adjourned until the following morning, Barbara sat at the defense table for several minutes trying to identify the source of a silent alarm that was sending adrenalin throughout her system. Brandywine, she decided. Some-

266

thing about the way she had looked at the jury, at the courtroom, at Barbara in a cool appraisal. Something about the way she had walked out. Something about her that was not yet comprehensible. Finally she got to her feet, and as she turned, she saw Frank and Mike waiting.

"You want a drink?" Frank asked. "Mike's buying."

"You bet I do."

"And some dinner in a little while?" Mike asked. "I'm buying that, too."

"Don't be silly," she said. "Remember our agreement? You pay, I pay. And if Dad goes, he pays, too."

Mike shook his head. "Not this time. I owe you one."

She looked at him closer and drew in a long breath, and then nodded. "Okay." But this was insane, she thought; he was looking at her as if they had just met, and she felt as awkward as a girl trying to make a good impression. It was more like a first date than their first evening together had been. That had been like two old lovers getting together, not like strangers exploring each other's range of interests or testing for mutual compatibility.

As they started to leave the courtroom Frank took her arm and said, "Well, you're stuck with me since I have the car, unless, that is, Mike wants to drive you out later."

Mike was at her other side, but he was not touching her. She looked at him almost shyly and said, "Tomorrow's going to be a tough day. Let's have that drink and dinner, and then I'll go home with Dad." He nodded.

When they reached the street, the fog was back, thicker than the night before. "Driving home will be a bitch," Barbara said with a shiver. "I hate fog. I can't tell you how much I hate fog."

"It reminds me of the year I spent at Oxford," Mike said.

She looked at him in surprise. That hadn't come up before.

They went to a restaurant that had a large, fine lounge, where they relaxed before an oversized fireplace with a mannerly fire. Mike talked about his year at Oxford, but he kept watching her; there was a softness in his face that she had not seen before, not even when they made love, or

267

afterward. It also surprised her to find that she was reacting to this new side of him with confusion. She had assumed that she had learned this man, only now to find a layer that had not surfaced before, and that made her wonder how many more layers there were.

Frank talked about a sailing trip he had made with his wife, Barbara's mother, when they were newly wed. He told it dreamily. Then Mike told about trekking across the High-lands in the fog and mist, and no one expected Barbara to say anything, but neither did they exclude her. They went to their table and ordered, and the pleasant chatting continued as they ate.

The comfort was banished as they waited for coffee, and Mike said, "That Brandywine woman is going to be danger-ous to someone."

The shiver that had been stilled by the pleasantries returned to Barbara's spine. "What do you mean?"

"She's been set up. No way could she have had enough clout in a few months at that school to get Kendricks in that apartment with meal tickets billed to her, get him a job, the whole thing. You noticed that the statement you got said it was billed to her, not paid by her. Bet no one paid. But aside from that, someone with clout had to vouch for her, for the arrangement. I'd bet it was Schumaker."

"But you said dangerous to someone. Who?"

"I wouldn't want to be Schumaker," he said thoughtfully. "As soon as she realizes it's all in her name, she'll throw him overboard, but she'll do harm along the way to anyone in her path. You, Nell, anyone. It'll take some doing, but she's a smart lady. You see them, men and women like her, in the academic world, playing every single angle. They are politi-cal geniuses."

The waiter brought their coffee and they were silent until he left again. "Thanks," Barbara said then to Mike. Another side of him that she had not known about, this ability to come up with a very good analysis. It matched her own thoughts in an uncanny way. "Now that she'll have a lawyer at her side, it's going to take forever, but I've got forever if need be. I'll do my damnedest to make her either take the Fifth or refuse to answer. Lundgren probably will be a devil, and I know Tony will be."

"Lundgren's big on respecting authority," Frank said. "In his eyes, no doubt, she represents authority just a bit more than you do."

Barbara snorted with laughter. Lundgren had made it clear that he considered her a barbarian, as her name implied, while Tony DeAngelo's name summed him up. And now a Ph.D. as well as a medical doctor. The totem pole was getting higher and higher, and she felt it resting squarely on her own shoulders, with Ruth Brandywine so high above her she was hardly visible.

"After Brandywine, then what?" Mike asked. "Is she the last witness?"

"Afraid so. Since tomorrow's Friday, summations probably won't start until Monday, and then Lundgren will instruct the jury, and we wait it out."

Mike looked startled. "I didn't realize that Nell wouldn't speak for herself," he said carefully.

Frank grunted. "Let me tell you a story about when I was a kid," he said. "About eight. We had neighbors with two boys, one my age, and one about four. One Easter they got two little chicks, one dyed green, one blue. Fluffy little things, you know, barely big enough to walk alone. Well, that little one loved them to beat the band. He stroked them, and put them up to his cheek and kissed them, first one, then the other. Gentle, sweet, my God, he was unbelievable, considering his age. Just about four. And then, he had one in his hands and he began to squeeze, and he kept squeezing. His old man paddled him good, but his brother told me that the next day he got his hands on the other one." He lifted his coffee cup and finished drinking.

For a few seconds Mike looked blank, as if he was waiting for the story to end; then he blinked in comprehension. "Oh," he said, very softly.

Frank excused himself then, and when they were alone, Barbara said, "I'll be working on my summation over the

269

next few days. I'd like to practice on you, if you wouldn't object. You and Dad."

"I would be honored," he said seriously; then a big grin broke out on his face. "Am I allowed to make comments?"

"That's the whole point," she said. "But if you use a certain tone of voice, or laugh, or point out too many inconsistencies, or do anything else I find offensive, then I get to hit you."

He considered it. "I'll try to do it right."

He was watching her again with that look of hesitant discovery that she had found so confusing. It still was. "This has been a very nice evening, Mike. Thanks. I was wound as tight as the springs could get. This has been good. Even if I don't quite understand how it happened," she added.

"Well, that part's simple. Your old man said, hey, bud, she's a woman doing a job you find incomprehensible. And you're a man doing a job we both find incomprehensible. And the lights came on for me. It all became very simple."

"You have a formula, an equation?"

He shook his head. "Still working on it."

"Let me know if you find it," she said. "Maybe it will be one even I can understand." Then her father returned, and they got up to start for home.

TWENTY-FIVE

THE NEW ATTORNEY was Gregory Erlich, a very tall, very thin man of middle age, with tremendous energy and a booming voice. Ichabod Crane with a backbone, Barbara thought, studying him. A chair was brought forward for him and placed midway between the defense and prosecution tables. He smiled at everyone, and even his teeth looked too energetic; they were very large teeth.

Barbara had the last question read by the clerk: "Dr. Brandywine, did you go to the bank with Lucas Kendricks on November 16, 1982, and stand by him while he closed his checking account?"

Ruth Brandywine said in a thoughtful manner, "I went to the bank with Tom Mann on one of his lucid days. I have no way of knowing what the precise date was."

"What did he do with the money he withdrew?"

"I don't know."

"Did he put it in his pocket?"

"I said I don't know. I wasn't watching."

"And then what did you do that day?"

"I took him back to my house."

And resumed treatment?"

"Yes."

"He was calm, controlled, capable of conducting his own business at the bank?"

"Under supervision only."

"But you didn't feel the need to watch him closely. Dr. Brandywine, you said earlier that he was immobilized for many weeks, not capable until December. Which is right?"

"He was incapable for most of the time, but he had lucid moments."

"Did he have his checkbook with him that day?"

"I don't know."

"You can't just walk into a bank and say, 'Give me my money,' now, can you? Is that how they do it at Boulder Bank?" She let the sarcasm and disbelief come through with the words and turned her back on the witness chair.

"I wasn't watching his minute-by-minute actions," Ruth Brandywine said coldly. "I was observing his general behavior. I don't know how he withdrew money if that is what he did."

"How did you treat Lucas Kendricks?"

271

"Objection," Tony called. "The witness has stated many times that she knew her patient by the name of Tom Mann."

"Sustained," Judge Lundgren said.

Barbara bowed her head slightly and rephrased the question. "Dr. Brandywine, how did you treat the young man you call Tom Mann?"

"Your Honor," Gregory Erlich said, and he was on his feet and halfway to the witness chair before he finished the two words. "If I may. . . ."

Judge Lundgren drew in a breath and spoke to the clerk, who instructed the bailiff to take the jury to the deliberation room. The look he gave Barbara while this was happening was baleful, as if to say, now it starts. Then they all waited for Gregory Erlich and Ruth Brandywine to conclude their whispered conference.

Erlich finally withdrew from her and approached the bench. "Your Honor, may I?" he asked, but he was already there.

Judge Lundgren beckoned Tony and Barbara to come forward also. "Yes, Mr. Erlich? What is it?"

"Your Honor, I have instructed my client that she cannot be forced to betray the confidentiality of the doctor-patient relationship with Tom Mann. She will have to refuse to answer any questions pertaining to any details of his medical treatments under her care. May I suggest that it will save much time if counsel simply abandons that line of questioning."

"Your Honor," Barbara said swiftly in a furious voice, "the witness has already opened that door with her vivid descriptions of the patient, complete with diagnosis. I intend to prove that the treatment she administered was inappropriate for the condition she has described."

"Give me a break," Tony muttered. "What difference does it make? All that's irrelevant, and you know it."

Judge Lundgren held up his hand for silence, his thin, ascetic face very pale, his lips so tight they were pale. "You may not pursue that line of questions," he said to Barbara. "I rule that the doctor-patient relationship is to be respected in this court. Now, let's get on with it."

"Dr. Brandywine, are you the author of this article?" Barbara held up a copy of a journal, opened to an article titled "New Approaches to Understanding Why They Believe."

"Yes."

"In the article you describe your methods for learning the most deeply held beliefs of adolescents. Is that right?"

"The article can't be summed up like that—"

"I quoted from the box caption accompanying the article," Barbara said. "Dr. Brandywine, did you hypnotize children and ask them questions concerning their beliefs?"

Erlich was on his feet, moving like lightning to her side, and this time Barbara said in her sharpest tone, "It's published, it's public information, you gave a paper about it. Did your method involved hypnotizing children?"

"Objection. This is irrelevant," Tony said.

"Overruled," Judge Lundgren said tiredly and motioned to the bailiff.

The jury was led out again; the conference was held in whispers; the jury returned, and finally after ten minutes Barbara got an answer.

"Yes. That is standard procedure for that kind of inquiry."

"Did you coauthor this article—"

Again and again the play was enacted. She asked questions, the jury filed out, Erlich and Brandywine conferred, then the jury filed back in, Erlich resumed his seat, and some of the times Brandywine answered the question asked.

She had done a study with Herbert Margolis. They had used a hypnotized subject to investigate the ability of the human eye to compensate for incompletion of a computer image. The subject was identified only by initials: LK.

"Who was the subject?"

"I don't know."

"Did you hypnotize him yourself?"

"Yes."

"Did you recognize him?"

"I don't remember who it was."

"My question was did you recognize him?"

Deliberately Ruth Brandywine said, "I don't remember."

She admitted to doing a paper with Walter Schumaker, again using a hypnotized subject, again identified only by the initials: LK.

"Was it the same person?"

"Probably, but I don't remember. That was a long time ago."

Some of the jurors were starting to look grim and angry. Judge Lundgren looked no less grim and angry, and now his anger had begun to generalize and was no longer concentrated solely on Barbara. He was starting to regard Gregory Erlich with a frown as the lawyer hopped up and darted to his client again and again.

"Tom Mann lived in student housing facilities, is that right?"

"I believe he did."

"Yes. And he had meal tickets that provided his meals. Altogether, the college brochure indicates that the room and board comes to five thousand eight hundred dollars a year. In your perpetuation of testimony you stated that he paid for his accommodations himself. I ask you now, who paid for Tom Mann's accommodations?"

"I don't know," she said. The expression of her face never changed. Her voice became sharp now and again, and her gaze swept the courtroom now and again, but for what purpose was impossible to say; her facial muscles might have been carved from wood.

"Bills are regularly sent for room and board," Barbara said, enunciating each word as if their problem was one of understanding language. "Where were his bills sent?"

"All his bills were sent to my office," she said after a slight pause.

"Did you pay those bills?"

"No. Other arrangements were made."

"Who paid his bills, Dr. Brandywine?"

There was another conference, a lengthy one this time, and when Erlich sat down again, Ruth Brandywine looked cooler and more remote than ever.

"Who paid his bills?" Barbara repeated after the jury was seated once more.

"I sent all his bills to the office of Dr. Schumaker. Presumably his office paid them."

"Is that Dr. Walter Schumaker, the same man who did the study with you, coauthored the paper with you?"

"Yes."

"And used a hypnotized subject whose initials were LK?"

"Yes," she snapped.

"In your statement you said that Tom Mann got a job with the maintenance staff at the college. He was not listed on the payroll, no taxes were collected for him, no medical insurance issued. Who paid his salary, Dr. Brandywine?"

"The psychology department paid him a stipend."

"Oh? The department? Or your office?"

"My office."

"Your own discretionary funds?"

"Yes. That happens."

"How much did you pay him?"

"I don't know. It was insignificant, money for his personal needs. All his major needs were taken care of."

"Twenty dollars a week? Thirty?"

"I said I don't know."

"You treated him for a number of years, seven years in all. You must have learned something of his habits, his lifestyle. Did he read books?"

"No."

"Did he buy albums, listen to music?"

"Not that I know."

"Did he have any outside interests? Art, perhaps? Sports?"

"Nothing like that. He watched television."

"So this young man worked, ate his meals in the cafete-

275

ria, called at your office for treatment regularly, and that was the whole of his life. Is that what you are telling us?"

"His life was better than it would have been in an institution, and that was the alternative."

"You provided all that at your own expense? You paid him, in fact, to cut grass and weed the flower beds at the college. Why? What else was he doing for you?"

"I was basing research on his mental condition," she said grimly.

"Did your research require you to hypnotize him regularly?"

Dr. Brandywine looked at Gregory Erlich, who obligingly stopped the questioning for another conference. Afterward, he again approached the bench. Tony and Barbara joined him.

"Your Honor," Erlich said, "my client was doing very sensitive and proprietary research using the young man as her subject. The nature of her work requires complete confidentiality at all stages until she has concluded her research and published the results. We submit that further questions regarding it will be inappropriate and irrelevant to the case being heard in this court."

"Your Honor," Barbara said in a low, intense voice, "if she was hypnotizing that young man, paying a minimal stipend, turning a brilliant young intellectual into a robotized manual laborer, that is not irrelevant to this trial."

Almost before she had finished, Tony said, "I agree that there is much here that needs further investigation, but I also agree that what we are hearing today is irrelevant to the matter this court is considering."

Judge Lundgren nodded slowly. He looked as if he wished they would all go away. "The witness will answer that one question," he said finally, and then said to Barbara, "But you may not pursue her research any further than that one question."

"Yes, Your Honor," she said. She hoped that her triumph did not show, that no one guessed that she had had no intention of taking it beyond that one question.

She waited at the defense table until order was restored again, and restated her question, "Dr. Brandywine, did you hypnotize that man you called Tom Mann?"

Ruth Brandywine looked at Erlich, who simply shrugged this time, and said, "I must refuse to answer that question."

Judge Lundgren leaned forward to peer at her. "On what basis do you refuse to answer?"

"On the grounds that it would violate the confidentiality of the doctor-patient relationship. He was my patient."

Judge Lundgren glanced at Barbara, who raised both hands as if in defeat and said, "I withdraw the question, which has already been answered, however."

"Objection!" Tony yelled. "Counsel is implying an answer that was not given. I move that counsel's remarks be stricken."

Judge Lundgren agreed, and Barbara went to the defense table and picked up a paper. "Dr. Brandywine, can you identify this document?"

It was a year-end report made out by the school infirmary of the supplies and drugs it had furnished to the psychology department in general, and Dr. Brandywine's office in particular. After Dr. Brandywine identified it, Barbara took it back and summarized one part of it.

"Every month you received a month's supply of the drug glutechmiazone, billed to your office. Is that right?"

Dr. Brandywine shrugged. "I don't have any records with me. I can't say if it's right."

"I see. Presumably if it were not correct, you would have objected, and corrections would have been made. Isn't that so?"

"Presumably."

"What is the drug glutechmiazone?"

"I believe it's a mild tranquilizer, something of that sort."

"In your perpetuation of testimony you stated that you treated Tom Mann for a psychotic condition from the time he became your patient until he left. It appears from this summary that you ordered no anti-psychotic drugs, just

277

glutechmiazone in five-hundred-milligram capsules regularly. Isn't it true that this drug is never used for a psychotic condition? Isn't it, in fact, a very powerful hypnotic drug? Isn't it true that it is never used in that large a dose except to achieve a hypnotic effect?"

"Your Honor," Gregory Erlich said in his booming voice, "that's in the area of doctor-patient relationship."

"I object," Barbara said icily. "Counsel is in the court to advise his client on her rights, not to advise the court."

"The witness is not required to answer the question," Judge Lundgren said.

"Dr. Brandywine, you ordered this drug regularly in this dose. Presumably you read the reference regarding it. Did you also read the manufacturer's information sheet concerning its usage?"

"I don't remember. I am careful with medication. No doubt I did read it."

"I quote: 'Glutechmiazone in the range of three hundred milligrams to five hundred milligrams per day is a powerful hypnotic, and the patient must be monitored closely on a day-by-day basis to avoid loss of volition and self-determination.'" She looked up from the sheet and said slowly, "It goes on to say that the effect is cumulative, and the drug remains in the system with diminishing effectiveness for up to ten days after it is discontinued. Did you ponder the implications of that information sheet when you ordered and used that drug, no matter who it was used on?"

"I am a medical doctor," Ruth Brandywine said stiffly. "I do not prescribe any drugs without careful consideration."

Barbara nodded and walked back and forth a time or two. She came to pause at the defense table. Her voice did not rise, but it was sharp and clear and carried without effort now when she said, "Dr. Brandywine, I ask you, did you prescribe that drug for the young man you call Tom Mann? Was he not a psychological prisoner, rendered helpless by it, his will destroyed, reduced to manual labor, an obedient—"

The uproar on her left drowned out the rest. Tony was on his feet shouting, and Gregory Erlich's loud voice shook the room. On the bench Judge Lundgren banged his gavel furiously.

"Ms. Holloway," Judge Lundgren said in a loud voice that silenced both Tony and Erlich, "this court finds you in contempt for deliberately pursuing an area that has already been ruled improper. The last question will be stricken. Court is adjourned until two o'clock." A bright flush tinged his patrician face; even his eyes looked red. He threw down the gavel, which skittered on the bench before coming to rest, as he rose and walked very stiffly from the room.

The moment he was out of range, the courtroom erupted into a cacophony of voices behind her. She did not yet turn, did not move at all. At her side, Nell reached out and put her hand on Barbara's arm. "Are you all right?"

Barbara looked at her and nodded. "Fine. I'm fine. You go on and have lunch. I want to sit just a minute or two."

Nell squeezed her arm lightly, then got up and left. Barbara waited until the noise level had faded to nearly normal before she stirred. Outside the courtroom, she stopped when she saw her father and Mike waiting for her. Not a replay of last night, she thought almost wildly, no polite and meaningless chit-chat, Mike's look of wonderment about who was under her skin. "You two, you go on," she said. "I have to walk a bit."

Mike opened his mouth, but her father said, "Sounds okay to me. Be sure to get a bite before you come back." He winked at her; there was a glint in his eyes that could have been joy, or understanding, or even recognition and appreciation of her timing. Another time it would have been enough to make her go hug him, but not at the moment. "Come on, Mike," he went on genially, "tell you about the time I was hit with contempt five times in one case." He took Mike by the arm and steered him away.

She walked the few blocks to the foot and bicycle path that followed the winding river. It flashed green and silver, twirled white water around submerged rocks, flowed as slick as glass, and erupted again into a frenzy. Bicycle riders sped by her, boys and girls, two women with white hair, a woman with a child in a carrier seat. . . . The traffic sounds were distant down here by the river, the city was distant, the courtroom most distant of all. The air was cold and wet, while overhead the fog hovered, ready to settle to earth again at a moment's notice. No wind blew. She stopped to watch a gray heron at the edge of the river, stilt-legged in the shallow water, one with the flowing water; it became even more beautiful when it lofted itself into the air with the ungainly legs stretched out behind it, like a Japanese impressionistic heron, now one with the gray lowering sky that enclosed it rapidly. Leaning against a tree, she watched until the bird was lost to sight, and only then did she let herself voice the thought that had come over her: She wanted to destroy Ruth Brandywine, Walter Schumaker, and Herbert Margolis. She wanted them utterly destroyed. And she wanted to be the one to do it.

The thought made her stomach feel weighted, made her throat constrict, made her hands ball up into fists. Ruth Brandywine was the Snow Queen, she thought, and experienced a surge of the terror the story had stirred in her as a child. A touch that chilled even unto death, a kiss that froze one's tears, froze one's heart. . . . Abruptly she turned to retrace her steps, find a place where she could get a cup of coffee, think about the afternoon. But the image of the young man they called Tom came to mind, frozen by the Snow Queen, kept in place for seven years, and even that was appropriate; seven years was the magic number from the Bible, from fairy tales. Lucas serving the Snow Queen for seven years, turned to ice by her touch, her look, her words. She remembered what Nell had said: On the ledge he had been happy, laughing and happy. Freed of the spell, happy, dead. She walked faster.

"Dr. Brandywine, you stated that you were on your way to England when you were called about the theft of your battery and license plates, and you flew home. Who called you?"

"The police."

280

"According to the police report, you were already home when they were called about the theft. You flew out of Denver on an early flight Sunday, June fourth. Is that right?"

"Yes."

"You spent the day with friends in New York, waiting for an overnight flight to London, is that right?"

"Yes. There was a call waiting for me at the airport, and that's when I learned that someone had broken into my garage."

"Who called you in New York? It wasn't the police department; they had not yet been notified."

"Objection," Tony snapped. "This is irrelevant."

"Overruled," Judge Lundgren, said, just as snappish.

"I believe it must have been a colleague, then. I had forgotten who it was."

"Which colleague?"

"Herbert Margolis called me, I think."

"And told you your garage had been broken into?"

"Yes."

"How did he know that?"

"I don't know."

"Dr. Brandywine, do you recognize the name Florence Steinmen?"

"I believe she works at the college."

"She does, in the administration building. I have her certified statement, which I would like to read at this time."

There were objections, but in the end Barbara read the statement. "'I work in reception. Someone is on duty every day, and I was on that Sunday. We had orders that if Tom Mann didn't show up for his medicine, we were to call Dr. Brandywine. But if she wasn't available, then we were supposed to call either Dr. Schumaker or Dr. Margolis. Well, she was gone to England. We all knew that, and Dr. Schumaker was in Canada, I think, so that afternoon when I realized that Tom hadn't come in I finally called Dr. Margolis. It was about four when I remembered to call him.'"

Barbara looked at Dr. Brandywine for a long time, then said, "So it wasn't about the garage, but about Tom Mann. He had not taken his medicine. He had escaped. Is that the message Dr. Margolis had for you?"

"Objection," Tony said. "Counsel is making implications that are improper, as well as asking and answering her own questions.

"Sustained," Judge Lundgren said.

"On Monday, after you arrived home again, did you hire a private detective agency to find Tom Mann?"

Gregory Erlich was already on his way to consult with his client. The jury was herded out, and Barbara sat down to wait. The conference lasted a long time.

When Dr. Brandywine finally answered the question, she said carefully, "I did not hire a detective agency."

"Do you know who did?" Barbara asked softly.

"Yes. Dr. Schumaker hired them. He realized—"

"You've answered the question," Barbara said sharply. "Was the agency hired to track down Tom Mann?"

"To find my papers," Dr. Brandywine said. "Tom stole some very important papers, my research, his files."

"And this concerned Dr. Walter Schumaker, a mathematician, to the extent that he hired an agency to find them for you? Why, Dr. Brandywine?"

"He knew their importance, I suppose."

"On Sunday he was in Toronto, and on Monday he flew back to hire detectives to find your work. Is that what you're saying?"

"I. . . . Yes."

"What name were they provided, Dr. Brandywine? Tom Mann or Lucas Kendricks?"

"It would have been Tom Mann. That was the name he was using."

"Then why did they go to Lucas Kendricks's parents' house? Why did they track his trail through the forest? Why did they plant a listening device on the property of the wife of Lucas Kendricks? Didn't you tell them exactly where his wife lived, where he might be heading?"

"Objection!" Tony yelled.

At the same moment, Gregory Erlich leaped to his feet;

his great voice filled the courtroom. "Your Honor, this is improper, this is harassment of the vilest—"

Judge Lundgren banged his gavel and glared at them all. "Mr. DeAngelo."

"I object. It has not been established who did the things counsel is talking about. The questions are improper."

"Sustained," he snapped. He turned his furious eyes to Gregory Erlich. "Sir?"

"I concur with the prosecuting attorney, Your Honor. No basis exists for those questions. My client has already said she did not hire the agency. She has been trying to cooperate in a very difficult—"

Judge Lundgren tapped the gavel, softly this time, but enough to cut him off. He looked at Barbara. "I will tolerate no browbeating, no harassment of a witness in my court. I believe you know your questions were improper. If you persist with such improper methods, I have no recourse but to find you in contempt of court a second time. You may proceed."

Barbara nodded very slightly and turned back to Ruth Brandywine. "Did you ever consult with the detectives that Dr. Schumaker hired?"

There was only a hint of hesitation before she said no.

"Did you ever sit in on any such consultation?"

"I . . . yes. They talked in my presence."

"And who else was there?"

"Dr. Schumaker and Dr. Margolis."

"So the three of you, the three people who had done papers together that all used a hypnotized subject with the initials LK, were together while Dr. Schumaker talked to the detectives. Is that right?"

"Yes."

"Did you see any of the reports the detectives made?"

"No. Never."

"Did you discuss them?"

"I don't remember doing so."

"Did they make tape recordings of conversations at Nell Kendricks's property?"

"I don't know."

"So who was given the information the detectives were gathering?"

Ruth Brandywine's face did show a change then, a minute tightening, a firming of her mouth, a gleam in her piercing black eyes. It vanished almost instantly. "Dr. Schumaker," she said then. "He handled all of that. And I know nothing about it."

Barbara kept at it all afternoon, sometimes getting an admission, often getting objections, or sitting and waiting for the private consultations to end. She felt as if she were trying to chip granite with a feather duster.

It was late in the day when she said, "Someone paid for his room and board, roughly six thousand dollars a year for seven years. You paid him a stipened for manual work, and some research that you won't talk about. Someone carefully kept his car for seven years, his wallet with all the money he withdrew from his account. You believe you might have helped pay for the detectives who were hired by Dr. Schumaker. You cut short your trip to England, and Dr. Schumaker flew to Toronto one day and home the next day because he was gone. Why, Dr. Brandywine? We are talking about many, many thousands of dollars. Why was Lucas Kendricks, or Tom Mann, worth that kind of money?"

There were objections, and in the end Ruth Brandywine said, "The research was important, not the man. I just wanted my research to be completed."

It was nearly five when Barbara was finished. She felt finished in every bone, every muscle, every nerve. Ruth Brandywine looked as impervious as she had early that morning.

The courtroom was crowded; big names had been introduced, and the case had exploded into a whole new pattern. Judge Lundgren was bitter when he said he would sequester the jury over the weekend. When the judge left, and the jury was led out, Tony was in a head-to-head conference with the district attorney. Big names, Barbara thought, had brought out the top man. There would be more conferences while they decided how to handle the perjury of Dr. Ruth Brandywine, how involved they would get, who else would be brought in for questioning. She made a bet with herself that the DA would handle that part of it, not Tony; the names suddenly had become big enough to guarantee a lot of publicity. Tough shit, she thought derisively. She picked up her purse and her briefcase and prepared to meet the press.

Instead, she realized that Nell was still there, waiting to say something. Her face was pinched; she looked very tired. She took Barbara's hand and looked up at her. Tears were in her eyes. "Whatever happens from now on," she said softly. "No matter what it is, I'm grateful. Thank you so very much."

Barbara felt nothing but confusion.

"He didn't stay away because he was tired of us, of me," Nell said in the same low voice. "She kept him. She made him a prisoner. And he escaped and came home. He was laughing, and happy. Thank you."

TWENTY-SIX

JOHN AND AMY Kendricks had gone home for the weekend; they would be back early Monday. Amy had insisted that they leave for the next two days. "Nell needs to have some time with her kids," she had said firmly. John had looked embarrassed. He had been willing to hang around, just to be there if Nell needed anything, and had not realized that their presence might become a burden. Nell felt ashamed for feeling that way since they had been so good, but she was glad they were gone for a short time.

Now she was reading to Carol. Downstairs, Travis was on the network on the computer, checking in, he said. And Clive was washing their dinner dishes. She tried to put him out of mind and concentrate on the words before her eyes, one of the *Just So* stories that she had loved as a child.

"'And the elephant child spanked his aunt. . . .'"

Carol giggled and then laughed as the elephant child went through the family, spanking them all in turn with his new trunk. Nell put the book down and plumped the pillow, straightened the covers, tucked in the blanket. "Okay?"

Carol pulled on her nose, held it, and said, "Oday."

Nell laughed and leaned over to kiss her. "Monkey. Pleasant dreams."

"Mom?" Carol said as Nell walked to the door. "Can I go to Michele's after school Monday? On the bus, I mean?"

"I guess so. I'll talk to her mother tomorrow. Is it something special?"

"No. She just asked me."

Nell hesitated, holding the doorknob, looking back at her daughter who was so pink and clean and blond. Slowly she went back to the bed. "Is something wrong, honey?"

Carol shook her head and pretended a yawn, but almost immediately she said, "You won't go to jail, will you?"

Nell sat down on the side of the bed and took her daughter by the shoulders, pulled her to a sitting position. "No way, José. I'm going to stay right here and finish reading that book and a hundred more to you." She watched Carol's face until it was relaxed again, and then drew the child hard against her breast and held her, stroking her silky hair, until Carol started to squirm. "And in the morning, waffles," Nell said. "With raspberry jam. Deal?"

Carol nodded, then yawned a legitimate yawn. "Deal," she said. She wriggled her way back under the covers; one hand reached out to pull a stuffed Pooh bear close, and she yawned again. Nell went to the door.

"Goodnight, honey," she said softly. She left the door

286

open about an inch, the way she always did, and moved away from it, but then she leaned against the wall with her eyes closed hard. The fear surged and ebbed and surged again.

After a few moments she went down the stairs, only to pause again, this time at the bottom, listening to Travis explain a complicated game to Clive. "You get to ask two questions, and everyone in the game gets to see them and the answers, so you've got to be careful what you ask."

The alien game, she realized. An alien was loose somewhere in the United States and the players were trying to find him/her/it. One of the players was concealing it. She smiled faintly. Travis could hardly wait until he was The Keeper, the one who tried to hide the alien. She entered the living room where Clive was standing at Travis's side at the computer.

"One down," she said cheerfully. "Any of that pie left?"

Clive had brought apple pie, made by Lonnie that afternoon. He grinned and went to the kitchen with her. "He's playing with kids from Atlanta, Chicago, who knows where else? I had no idea stuff like that was going on."

"I know. I was thinking that I should take them on a car trip, a long trip, just so they get an idea of the size of the real world. I don't think he suspects how far away Atlanta actually is, or New York." She cut a piece of pie; she had not wanted any after dinner, but, now, an hour or two later, dessert was welcome. They sat at the kitchen table where she could see Travis at the computer, intent on the game. So like Lucas, she thought. So very like his father.

"Doesn't it get pricey? Long-distance calls and all?"

"Not as bad as you'd think. He's on a budget, ten dollars a month, and after that, if he goes over, it comes out of his allowance." She looked at her son again, and the thought came, as clear as it was irrational, that he was using the computer to build a wall, that he was filling every waking moment with school, homework, and now computer games in order to erect a three-sided haven that was too constricted to admit her. After the first bite of pie, she realized that she didn't want it after all. Travis made one of those curious, incomplete gestures and snorted with laughter; he attacked the keyboard again.

"You didn't eat any dinner, and now you're just playing with the pie," Clive said in a low voice. "Lonnie said to tell you she picked those apples herself, and they've never been sprayed."

Nell took another bite.

"And she's picked out a new victim," Clive said. "Schumaker, and maybe Brandywine, too. But Schumaker for certain."

"Good!" Nell said. "If she needs any help, you know, with rat poison or something, tell her. . . ." She looked down at her plate when the realization hit her that she could not say something like that, maybe never again.

"I told her I'd be her accomplice, but she said it was to be a one-woman job or it won't count. I asked her if she planned to go to Denver, and she said she can wait for him to show up."

"He'll be sorry if he does," she murmured. "Barbara will slap him with a subpoena, too, I'll bet."

"Nell, will you marry me? Please," he said suddenly. His voice was husky, and he looked surprised at the words tumbling out like this.

"Shhh," she said. "Not now. Don't ask now. After this is all over, behind us, then ask. I can't think of anything now."

"But now is when you need someone. We can get married right away, and I'll file adoption papers. Now. Next week, as soon as possible."

She felt as if her little house had been set adrift on a storm-roughed sea all at once. The floor was rising and falling, the table was shifting, losing its solidity; even the air seemed to darken and thicken.

"Oh, God! Here, put your head down. This way." He forced her head down, and soon blood began to circulate again. She pushed his hands away after a moment and got to her feet, his hand on her arm, steadying her.

"How dumb can you get?" she muttered. "Me, I mean.

288

Not you. I want a drink of water. I'm okay now." But she felt moonbeam-light, as if she might drift up from the floor with every step.

They went to the sink, where she grasped the edge of the counter while he ran water and filled a glass.

"God, Nell, I'm sorry! I didn't mean to do that to you! I'm sorry."

"I know," she said, and drank the water. "It's all right. I'm just tired. Not quite enough sleep, probably. I'm fine now."

He looked agonized, and then he took her into his arms and held her almost too hard, nearly smothering her against his chest. She realized how much she wanted to be held and kept safe. She wanted desperately to be held and kept safe.

In the living room, Travis whooped gleefully, and Nell pulled away from Clive's arms. "Thanks," she said. "I needed that. You'd better go now. It's just about bedtime for Travis, and I'm going to bed the minute he packs it in. I'm really tired."

Clive touched her cheek gently, leaned forward, and kissed her lightly on the lips. "I'll come by tomorrow. Get some sleep."

After he was gone, she thought of the words "get some sleep" and didn't know which might come first, laughter or tears. She yearned for a night of sleep, of getting into bed as she used to, rolling over once, and slipping into oblivion the way a child does. Now, these nights, she slept, dreamed, and jerked wide awake, slept, dreamed, jerked awake, over and over and over, and in the morning when the alarm went off she felt leaden and groggy. Cry, she decided; that would be more appropriate than laughing. Crazy people laughed at the wrong times, she told herself; in her mind's eye there was Lucas on the ledge, laughing, happy. "Watch this!" Laughing.

Her mind reeled away from the image, the way it always did, even in her dreams, and she went to see if Travis was ready to call it quits for the evening. Sometimes, if he was in the middle of his own move, she stood by waiting, watching, understanding nothing of what he was doing. Tonight he was already out of the alien game. "He's in Wichita," he said. "I know he is, but I've got to think of the right questions to ask so no one else will guess, too. Got to be exactly the right questions."

"Well, sleep on it. Probably in the morning they'll come to you."

A light blinked on the computer; he grunted in satisfaction. "This guy has the Mandelbrot program. I gave it to him a long time ago, and he's getting some pretty good pictures. We're trading. I'll show you tomorrow, if you want."

"I want," she said. But *what* she wanted was for him to face her, to look at her directly, to smile his funny-little-boy, wise-old-man smile, to gauge her mood before launching into a fantastic scheme.

He turned off the computer, stretched and yawned, spied a book on an end table and went over to pick it up, and then bounded upstairs, calling goodnight. He did not look directly at her.

Saturday the fog lifted for the first time all week. The sun came out weakly, a drizzle fell, the sun returned, and altogether it was a pleasant late-fall day in Oregon. Barbara stood at the head of the waterfall gazing at the spray far below. She had not intended to come this far, but neither could she sit still and work through the words, the sentences, the paragraphs of her summation. She hoped that it would organize itself in her head while her feet moved. Now she looked at the waterfall, the gushing little Halleck Creek, the trail that twisted down to the ledge. Slowly she crossed the log to Nell's side and started downward again.

The forest was dense on this side, more so than on the other, and the trail was easier: more often used, kept in better shape. She spied a cluster of mushrooms and leaned against a tree trunk for a few seconds. Nell and Lucas used to gather mushrooms, she remembered. A bushel basket of chanterelles, Nell had said, and morels, puffballs. . . . She

290

pushed away from the tree and squinted her eyes when a mini-shower doused her head.

She became more glum as she continued down the trail. The image of Lucas was persistent: hungry, dehydrated, his feet so swollen he could not have put his boots on again if he had taken them off. Blisters, infection, agony with every step.

The trail wound around a mammoth fir tree and unexpectedly dropped five feet; she slipped in mud, fell to a sitting position, and slid another foot or two before she stopped. She just sat there for a minute, then finally heaved herself up again; now she looked back the way she had come. But it was shorter to keep going, she knew, and doggedly she went on, watching her footing more carefully. Now the trail was carpeted again with a deep mat of needles, and occasional rocks; the little mudslide had been a fluke.

She skirted the cliff that was the back boundary of the ledge; here, she knew, the trail was like stairsteps down, never in a straight line, but easy enough because it was so rocky. She stepped over a rivulet that had not been there back in the early fall when she had explored this whole trail, this approach to the ledge. She thought of the great heart of the Earth pumping its life-giving water in tiny rivulets that appeared only during the rainy season, and then joined the bigger creeks, like Halleck Creek, which rushed to the McKenzie River, which in turn joined the Willamette, and then the Columbia and at last made the tremendous flood that fed the great ocean. Fractals, she thought with a start of recognition. She was seeing them everywhere.

The trail had brought her to the side of the ledge; now when she paused she could step among the few trees that still hid the ledge from view, trees that would have hidden someone standing here, she added. She left the trail to make her way between the trees, only half a dozen or so steps, and finally she could see the entire ledge, the chasm that split the two parts, the edge where Lucas had stood laughing until the bullet struck him.

"Hasn't changed a damn bit," she muttered at last. The other time she had come up here, she had stepped off the trail at about this point, jumped down to the ledge, and finally had gone down the other part of the trail that Nell had used to climb up to the ledge. In irritation, she turned her back on the ledge this time and followed the main trail downward until it branched, with the lesser one angling sharply upward.

Ever-branching highways, roads, trails, paths, deer paths. Fractals again, she thought, like the ever-branching trees, or the ever-branching human arterial system. She had stopped at the fork, scowling at the path that climbed steeply, Nell's path. Abruptly she started to follow it, for no reason she could name, only to finish what was an exercise in futility, she told herself. Keep the body working, keep the blood flowing, maybe something will occur that will save the day, save little Nell, save the universe. She was breathing hard already; this section was steeper than the one she had left, and it was uphill. It also was muddy and treacherous; her foot slipped and she fell to her knees, clutching a tree trunk to keep from sliding again. Then, all at once, she saw the face of the cliff directly ahead; she took the next step upward, and another, and then stopped completely.

She could not see the right side of the ledge at all, she realized, only the cliff in front of her, and a log and several rounded rocks. To her right, obscuring the view, were straggly bushes and tree tops. She climbed the last foot or two very slowly, keeping a close watch on exactly when the edge of the clearing came into sight. At the top, she realized that she could see it sooner than Nell, because of the difference in their height. Nell would not have seen it even when she had reached the top, not until she had taken a few steps forward onto the ledge. Barbara stood without motion, remembering what Nell had told her. She had seen him, had closed her eyes for a second, then had taken the last step up in time to hear the shot, see him fall over the side. But she couldn't have seen him until she was already on top, several steps in. Slowly Barbara made her way to the tree trunk and sat down. The sun had come out again, and it was quite warm here in this protected place with its fine southern exposure.

She unzipped her jacket, tugged off her hat, and did not move again for a long time.

It was easy to believe she was the only living human being, up here with the trees and the sky and this sheltered clear spot. Not a sound penetrated, no wind stirred the needles of the endless forests, no animals scurried, no birds flew. The world had stopped. "Time to get off," she said under her breath.

She gazed at the far side of the ledge where Lucas Kendricks had got off the world, where he had been shot to death. Now she imagined Nell climbing up the trail, not the hard, steep part, but the wider trail that was much easier. She would have chosen the easier access since she was carrying a rifle, Barbara thought distantly. She looked at the trees beyond the ledge and imagined Nell leaving the trail up there, coming out from behind a tree to see Lucas, laughing at her. In the silent theater of her mind Barbara watched Nell raise the rifle and fire it one time, watched Lucas spin back, dead. And the angle of the bullet is no longer a mystery, Barbara finished silently.

Suddenly the sun vanished behind a mass of clouds that looked like snowdrifts, and the drizzle began to settle again. It was a very cold drizzle, not actually falling, but there, appearing all around her. She zipped her jacket, replaced her hat, and started down the trail.

"Goddamn it, Barbara, what happened?" Frank demanded that afternoon, standing at the door to the terrace where she was bundled up, leaning against the railing, staring at the river.

"Why is it so black?" she asked.

"It's fixing to snow."

"The river is trying to run away," she said with a nod. "And run away and run away forever." She left the railing and crossed the deck to go inside. "I can believe it's going to snow. It's turned frigid."

"Barbara, what's wrong? That's what I want to know." He

moved so she could enter the house, then closed the door firmly.

"I thought you had an unerring knack for recognizing when to push and when to pull, when to talk and when to be silent, when to ask questions and when to find your own answers." She intended to speak the words lightly, but they sounded bitter in spite of her efforts. She took off her down jacket and wool hat and ran her hand through her matted hair to fluff it again. She draped the jacket over a chair and continued on to the living room, where she stood close to the fire, rubbing her hands.

"You thought right," her father said, following her. "And now's the time to find out what the hell's going on."

"I went to the ledge today," she said. "Interesting place."

"And?" But he had become wary; he sat in his chair watching her closely over his glasses.

"She lied, that's all." She glanced at him, then looked at the fire again. "You've known from the start, haven't you? That's why you said you couldn't get her off."

"I went to the ledge very early," he said after a pause. "And I thought you had gone there early on, too."

"Oh, I did. But I didn't go by her path, Nell's path, and today I did. That makes a difference, doesn't it?"

"Barbara, sit down," Frank said then in a brusque voice. "I can't talk to your back."

She shrugged and sank into one of the fine leather chairs opposite him.

"When that girl first came to me I didn't think there was a chance in hell of getting her off, not a single chance. And you've given her a chance. Lundgren might pull the carpet out from under you on Monday, but there's still that chance that didn't even exist before. I don't know what happened up on that ledge, and neither do you, and I doubt that Nell does. But I think that crowd from Denver, Brandywine and Margolis and Schumaker, they killed Lucas Kendricks as surely as if they pulled the trigger, and they replaced him with a zombie. Lucas Kendricks has been dead for more than

294

seven years! And Nell deserves that fighting chance you've given her. She doesn't deserve getting thrown to the wolves."

"Oh, for heaven's sake!" Barbara said sharply. "I'm not going to bow out at this late date. Give me a little credit!"

"There are a lot of ways of abandoning a client," her father said slowly. "Ways you haven't even dreamed of yet. But the way you've found is a good one. You've banked your fires with ice water, and it shows. You go into court with that look of disdain, that suffering-martyr pose, that air of having been deeply offended and betrayed, you'll be saying, there's her neck, slash away at it."

She stared at him speechlessly; he stood up and walked out of the room without looking at her again.

It started to snow that evening by seven. Nell and the children were having a living room picnic. She had spread a blanket in front of the fire; they roasted hot dogs and had potato salad, and later roasted marshmallows. Then they stood on the front porch and watched immense, lazy snow-flakes drift to earth. "I hope it snows this deep," Carol said, holding her hand at waist level. "Where's our sled?"

"In the garage. We'll find it tomorrow if there's snow on the ground," Nell said.

"Maybe it'll be deep enough to ski," Travis said. "I better see if the skis need wax or anything."

When they were all chilled, they went back inside and roasted a few more marshmallows and talked about snow.

Doc Burchard stood on his deck with the snowflakes falling around him, wishing, exactly as Carol and Travis were wishing, that it would get deeper and deeper until the world was buried under a mountain of snow. He went back inside where Lonnie was making their dinner. She had to run, she said; it might start getting slippery soon. He told her to go ahead; he would finish and clean up later.

Doc and Jessie ate without a word. He had not spoken to her all week, they were both well aware. When they were done, as she was preparing to wheel herself out of the dining room, she said, "Lonnie says that Clive wants to marry Nell right away, adopt the children and all. Isn't that nice?"

He looked at her with hatred. "How long have you known?" he asked. His voice sounded harsh and strange to his ears.

"From the beginning, probably. I didn't make a note of the date."

"And never said a word, never let on. You treated her like a friend all that time."

"Oh, well, you know it didn't make a bit of difference. Not a bit. Not until she was a widow, anyway. Many widows would like to marry doctors. Haven't you found that to be true, dear?"

"Aren't you afraid to let me prescribe your medicine?" he whispered. "Aren't you afraid I might let you slip in the bathtub, or accidentally knock your chair off the deck, down into the river?"

She laughed and pressed the button on the arm of her chair. The mechanism hummed, and the chair turned smartly and headed for the door.

"You'd better call Lonnie back," he said in that strange new voice. "I'm taking a few things and going to town. I won't be back for several days, not until the snow is over, at the very least."

She turned to regard him from the doorway. "You're such a fool. Little boy running away from Mama, and so very angry. You're a complete fool." She sped down the hallway toward her room. The humming of her wheelchair was the only sound in the house.

Not town, he thought then. Not town. To Nell's house, but not this early. The children would still be up. Methodically he began to clear the table. Later, later. He looked down at his hands; the plates he carried were rattling because his hands were shaking so hard.

Lonnie Rowan was rocking, watching television, and dreaming. Her house was not as clean and neat as any of the others that she took care of, Jessie's, or Clive's, or Frank's, but

296

no one ever saw it but her, and it didn't matter. Her rocking chair had been her father's, and during his lifetime she had not dared move it even an inch from its place near the wood-burning stove. He liked things where he put them, liked to reach out his hand and take what he knew was there without having to look first. Now she shifted the furniture frequently and never put a book or magazine down in the same place twice. Sometimes, before she sat in the rocker, she would make a shooing motion with her hand, as if to make him get out. All the furniture was his and her mother's; she had never bought a stick of furniture in her life, never needed more than the house provided. But things were changing, she knew; things changed.

All those years he had said, "Now, Lonnie, don't you worry your head about the future. My little girl's going to be all right. You can trust the old man to see to that."

Then he was gone and the bills were her bills, and the future was here. She rocked and hummed under her breath, her face turned toward the television, an old black-and-white one that he had bought back in the sixties. But she was not seeing what was on the screen. She was examining a different future. In this one, she lived in the little house on Nell's place, and Nell and Clive and the kids lived in the big house, the way it was supposed to be. Her lips tightened, then relaxed again. *They* would go back to wherever they had come from, and Nell would be in the big house where she belonged. Nell and Clive, with no black people for miles around, the way it was supposed to be.

She, Lonnie, would do for them, cook for them, keep the house clean, do a little gardening. . . . She had watched how the kids were around their grandparents, full of laughs and jokes and hugs and kisses. That's how they would be with her, she had decided. She was a virgin; when she was still young enough to marry and have a family there had been her Ma to take care of, and later her Pa, and the years sped by. And the years sped by. There was no one for her, nowhere to go, no one to turn to. If she ever was going to have a family, she had come to realize, she had to make it happen.

She had watched Clive turn into a bumbling, tongue-tied

boy as soon as Nell was free, and she understood that he would marry her; he would make that happen somehow. And she would go with them, to the little house. She had watched him fussing with a bunch of flowers, a gift for Nell, and she had said scornfully, "Oh, she'll say they're nice enough, and they are. But you take her this plate of gingerbread for the kids, and see how she acts." After that he had carried her cookies, her cakes, her pies to Nell and the children; their love gifts, he had said, and blushed.

She jerked awake and sat straighter, tried to get back into the fantasy, but it seemed to swim out of reach now. Why would they welcome her? She heard the mocking question in her father's voice; it was how he always had mocked her when he drank too much.

Nell wouldn't welcome her, she admitted finally. Nell thought she was too gossipy, and Nell had got pretty mad when Lonnie voiced what everyone was saying over renting out her house to *those* kinds of people. Not Nell, she said to herself, but Clive. He liked her; he listened to her gossip and even asked questions. He knew that if she said it, it was so; she repeated things but she didn't make them up, and he respected that. But why would he welcome her into the little house? She rocked slowly, thinking hard. Gratitude, she decided, and the idea made her palms ooze sweat.

It meant that she had to tell on Jessie, and that meant that Jessie would cut her off without a backward glance, without a thought. She knew that bitch, and that's how it would be. Jessie and Doc were her main source of income. If she lost them, she would starve.

"Will you stop carping about money?" her father had yelled. "I told you, my girl won't end up in the poorhouse. I'm taking care of it!"

She rocked harder and harder. No poorhouse, not these days. Just out on the streets, sleeping under bridges, eating out of garbage cans. She began to cry softly out of frustration and fear, out of indecision. If Jessie and Doc split, she thought, they would move back to town, Jessie back to her sister, or her brother, somewhere away from here, and she would be out of that job anyway. But they probably wouldn't split up. They had had this kind of long silence before and patched things up again.

Her tears stopped and she got to her feet. A cup of cocoa, a bath, maybe something would come to mind about what to do, how to make certain Clive would want to hire her and let her live in the little house when he and Nell got married.

At ten the wind started to blow. Funneled through the river canyon, it whistled and howled and screamed, let up, and started again at a higher pitch. The television news featured the weathermen who grinned and acknowledged that they had been wrong again. The Pacific storm had been forecast to come inland up in Washington state, but here it was coming in hard and strong. Rain in the valley, heavy at times. Snow in the mountains, a foot in the passes overnight, blizzard conditions, a real Pacific storm front, the first of the season. . . .

A gust of wind backed some smoke up in the fireplace. Frank added another log to the fire. Fight wind with wind, he muttered to himself, make a good strong updraft. . . . He could hear Barbara in his study; his printer stuttered to life, stopped again, and she stamped out and upstairs. She had not settled in one spot for more than half an hour all evening. She had not spoken a word all evening, had looked through him in a disconcerting way when he spoke once or twice. He knew that look, that stamping around, that fretful stop-and-start routine, and he tried to keep out of the way, denying himself his own study that night, making coffee if the pot seemed too light when he lifted it, setting out crackers and cheese once, but mostly keeping as quiet as possible in the living room.

At twenty past eleven the phone rang. Frank scowled at the machine with its blinking green eye and did not get up to take the call. He detested answering machines. Now the light became frenzied and a hoarse voice said, "If you want the truth about the murder make Jessie tell what she knows."

299

The machine clicked, and the green eye winked at him one time a second as he sat without movement.

Finally he went to the table that held the machine, sat in the chair by it, and played the message back, listening intently. He started to play it again, and this time became aware that Barbara was inside the doorway, also listening.

"Just came," he said, and they heard the message another time.

"Recognize the voice?" she asked.

"Nope. Used the old trick of talking through a towel or something. What do you think?"

"I don't know. Everyone goes over there to her open houses on Thursdays, don't they? Could have been any one of her guests or Lonnie, or Doc himself."

"Probably not Doc. Not his style. Lonnie? Maybe, but she wouldn't want to choke the only real goose she has, would she? As you say, a lot of people turn up over there."

Barbara went to the machine and removed the tape. "Let's stash it away in a safe place. God, I wish this creep had spoken up earlier, before Jessie took the stand."

Frank was thoughtful for a few seconds, then shrugged slightly. "How I always thought of Jessie is that she's like a queen bee. All the other bees go out and gather the pollen and nectar, whatever it is that bees crave, and take it home. People take Jessie every tidbit, every scrap of gossip, rumors, announcements. She always knows exactly what's going on. She could have heard just about anything."

Barbara started to say something, when the doorbell rang. Frank went to open the door, and there stood Mike Dinesen, dripping wet, carrying his gym bag, grinning like an idiot. Barbara never had been so glad to see anyone.

TWENTY-SEVEN

NELL ADMITTED DOC into her house and stood aside as he took off a poncho that covered him down to the floor. Where it dripped, rivers were born on the foyer floor.

"I had to see you," he said. He looked frozen.

"Come in by the fire. Do you want something, coffee, tea?"

He shook his head, longing to touch her, to hold her, be held by her. The barrier was his handiwork, he knew; she never had distanced herself, never had denied him anything he needed. They walked into her living room; he drew near the fire.

"Nell, can you forgive me?" he whispered after a minute.

"You haven't done anything."

She sat on the couch and drew her feet under her, pulled an afghan over her legs. She looked like a precocious child.

"I'm going to leave her," he said then. "I can't stay with her, not now, not after what she did, tried to do."

"We must have hurt her terribly," Nell said softly. "I didn't realize."

He began to move about the room with jerky, short steps. He straightened a lampshade, touched a pillow on one of the chairs, moved Travis's sweater from another. His motions were abrupt, too quick, too nervous. All that energy, Nell thought watching. All that pent-up energy.

"I'll leave her," he said. "Next week. She'll go to Ted's house, or to her sister down in California, someplace. She has money, all the money," he said with bitterness. "She keeps reminding me that we live in her house, eat her food, drive her cars."

Nell knew all this. He had told her often that he couldn't leave Jessie, his debt to her was too great, he had too much pity, she needed him. . . . Jessie had put him through medical school, had set him up in practice, had bought the house they lived in. Nell watched him without interrupting. When he finally stopped his restless pacing, touching, and straightening and came to a halt before her, she shook her head.

"You do what you have to," she said in a low voice. "But don't pretend it's for me, or because of me. Remember when we knew Lucas was coming back? You asked me if I'd let him in my bed again, and I said no. I lied. If he had come back the way he was the last time I saw him, laughing, happy, the Lucas I always loved, he would have been welcome in my bed. I would have been the way I was with him from the start. What we had, you and I, I don't know what to call it. Not love, not like it was with Lucas. I don't know what it was with us, but it's over. Don't leave her for me, but for yourself if that's what you want."

A flush spread across his sharp face, and he wheeled about almost wildly. At the fireplace he looked at her again and cried, "I don't believe it! You said you love me. You can't change like that from one day to the next!"

"You told me to leave," she said. "I didn't want to, but you made me leave, and it was a good thing. The best thing. I needed you and you said to go away. Not one day to the next. Months, Doc, months. I learned something then. I learned something. I don't need you. I don't need anyone. I can stand by myself!"

He shook his head, shook away her words. "It's Clive, isn't it? Jessie said wouldn't it be nice if you and Clive got together finally. He's waited so long, and I thought what a good idea, to lull any suspicions she might have, to let the world see you with a man who was available, to make them all forget I even lived. We couldn't meet, not if people might be watching, and I thought yes, you and Clive, for now, for a short time. He's no good for you, Nell. He's a. . . . I don't know. Too rough. Too physical, not a real idea in his head, not a thought. Can you talk to him? Can he talk about anything that isn't woods and trees?"

She refused to look at him, to see him at all. She could feel her face tighten, and then tighten again. "Stop it," she said in a furious voice. "What did we have? Twenty minutes, an hour now and then. Did we talk? Did we comfort each other? All we ever had was sex, and we were both so lonely, so . . . empty. But that's not enough!"

"You've found someone younger with a bigger cock to stick between your legs. Is that it? You used me. My God, I wouldn't have thought it possible! You were using me all those years!"

She jumped up and flung down the afghan. "We used each other, maybe. It was safe. I told you from the start that I didn't expect you to leave Jessie. I didn't expect anything from you except what we had, and that's done with. I'm sorry, Doc. You'd better go now before I start to cry or something. Please, just go away!"

He nearly ran across the room but then stopped again, this time shaking all over. "Nell, I'm sorry. I'm sorry. I need you, Nell. I can't do this alone. Please. . . ."

"Go home, Doc! Don't try to lean on me. Not now. Can't you see that I'm barely able to stand up? If you try to lean on me I'll fall over and I may never be able to get up again. For God's sake, just go home!"

She did not follow him out to the little foyer, did not see him to the door, did not move again until she heard the door open and close, and the howling wind entered and died. Then she went to the door and turned the lock. She went back to the living room and added wood to the fire and stood hugging her arms about herself. She wouldn't sleep yet, she knew, not with the wind screaming like a demented demon. She approached the computer that Travis had set up in the living room months ago, for all of them, they had said, but it was for Travis, and they both knew that. She touched the monitor, a cold sleek surface, and touched the box, and she found herself sinking into the chair before it, blinded by tears. For the first time she wept for Lucas, for herself, for her children.

When she finally left the computer to wash her face and make a cup of tea, she realized that as much as she hated Ruth Brandywine, and it was a fierce hatred, she was also indebted to her. Ruth Brandywine had restored Lucas to her in some way. She knew that when she was a child, her belief that her parents had abandoned her had been a normal reaction to their premature deaths; she had read enough to come to understand that as an adult, even though her child-self never accepted it. Then Lucas had abandoned her and her grandfather had died, and finally Doc had tossed her away; the feeling had become overwhelming that there was no one she could trust ever again.

"Lucas didn't *stay* away," she whispered to her mirror image in the bathroom. Her eyes were bloodshot and puffy, her nose red. She nodded at herself. "He was *kept* away." How many times had she told herself that since hearing Ruth Brandywine's testimony? She couldn't say, but she would repeat it as many times as it took to make the belief sink in deep, to fill the void that Lucas had left in her so many years ago.

"See," Mike said at Frank's door, "they were saying on the news that there was a blizzard out here in the wilderness. It's just raining in town, but I thought if you get snowbound, it might be fun to be snowbound with you, and fight off the wolves with their gleaming fangs and their bloodlust-fired eyes. I'll distract them with the torch while you smack them with the shovel."

Barbara stared at him. "You've gone stark raving mad. How did you get so wet? Did you walk out?"

Frank took his jacket and held it at arm's length. He started for the closet with it but changed his direction to head for the kitchen. "I hope you thought to put some clothes in that bag," he said in a strangled voice, fighting the laughter that kept trying to erupt. "Maybe you can wear something of mine," he said then, eyeing the gym bag that was dripping. "You're the wettest human being I've seen in a long time."

"I walked the last mile," Mike said, still grinning. "I would have called, but there's no phone once you get through Turner's Point, so I just left the car and started to walk." They followed her father through the hallway into the kitchen. Mike squished all the way.

"Shoes," Frank said.

Obediently Mike sat down and started to remove his shoes. He was wearing running shoes; they were sodden.

"Why did you leave the car? Did you wreck it?" Barbara demanded, standing with her hands on her hips, glaring at him.

"Ran out of gas."

"Good God!" she muttered. "You still haven't fixed that gas gauge, have you?"

"Keep forgetting." He pulled off his socks; his toes were scarlet. "Forgot to put gas in the can last time I filled up."

"Well," Frank said, surveying the rest of his clothes. "Let's get you into a hot bath before you realize you're freezing. Come on, come on." He left; his shoulders were shaking.

A little later Barbara put down her yellow pad and looked at Mike, who was watching her and had been for many minutes. "Dad's gone off to bed in somewhat indecent haste," she said. "You realize that, don't you?" Mike was wearing one of her father's old terry robes and a pair of his slippers; he looked very comfortable in that room.

He nodded. "I was thinking. You know what I really like about you?"

"My intellect."

"That, too."

"My raven, cascading hair; my eyes like pools of inviting, unplumbed depths; my gazelle-like neck."

"I thought raven hair was black."

305

"It usually is; mine's different.

"All the above," he said. "But that's not what I was thinking about."

"So tell me already."

"Your ass," he said soberly. "I never thought of myself as an ass man, but there it is. I love your ass."

She sputtered with laughter and stood up, holding out her hands to him. He rose and put his arms around her; his hands slid down her back to trace the curve of her buttocks.

"Ah," he breathed.

"Ah, indeed," she murmured. "Let's go to bed."

In the guest room that had already become his room they made love with passion, but underlying it there was a quality of serene timelessness, as if they knew this act should not be rushed, and there was all the time in the universe awaiting them this night.

She would not go to sleep, she had told herself, a very long time ago, it seemed. But she fell asleep in his arms and came awake again at five in the morning. They were entwined, his arm over her, her leg over his. She eased away from his warmth with regret; it was time to get up, shower, have coffee, and go back to work.

When Frank came down, he found her at the computer typing furiously. "Did you get any sleep?" he asked at the door. "And do you want some breakfast?"

"Yes, some, and no, I already ate." She looked up at him without taking her hands from the keyboard. He studied her for a moment, then grinned widely and vanished again. She scowled at the vacated space. Some father! Where was the outrage? The shotgun? She began to grin, then reread her last words, and slowly her grin faded and she concentrated once more on the summation.

In midmorning Frank and Mike left to do something about his car and gas. Frank said he would drop in on Doc and Jessie, see if they had taken any storm damage. Barbara heard their words but paid little attention. She got stiff and

306

sore from sitting too long and went out to the terrace to stand under the roofed section and gaze at the river, which was steel gray. The wind was pushing it backward; the current was pushing harder in its determination to reach the sea. The battleground was marked by white froth; wavelets dashed frantically, larger waves rolled and churned. The rain drove in horizontally, the cycle nearing completion as the sea storm returned the water the rivers had carried to it all year. The lashing, wind-driven rain drove her inside again, back to the computer, back to the printout that was nearly finished.

Another time she stopped reading to listen; her father was laughing in the kitchen. She tried to concentrate again but finally had to leave the desk and walk through the hall to stand outside the kitchen, where silence had settled. Suddenly Frank said, "Listen up:

> *A nameless young lawyer cried, 'Sue!*
> *It's the civilized course for you.*
> *Don't fret about facts,*
> *My friend, just relax!*
> *By the way, my retainer is due.'"*

Barbara stifled her laughter as Mike said, "Oh, yeah? Well, take this:

> *A brilliant young mathematician*
> *Juggled sums like a maddened magician.*
> *When the numbers went screwy,*
> *He simply said 'Phooey.'*
> *And turned into a staid statistician."*

Frank snorted. "I don't get it." A dish rattled, a knife or something clattered. Then he said:

> *A judge from the bar fraternity*
> *Heard trials that dealt with paternity.*
> *He could tell at a glance*

307

Who had lowered his pants,
And screwed with no thought for maternity.

Barbara fled back to the study, where she stood grinning. Poor Dad, she thought then. How he had wanted a son. He never told her dirty jokes, and he cleaned up his language around her more than she did her own. "Not my fault," she muttered, and began to do some stretching exercises. Let him adopt Mike. Never too late to make a family any way he could.

Late in the afternoon Nell called and asked if she could come by. She looked dreadful when she arrived, sleepless, pale, so tired her hands shook when she tried to unbutton her jacket. The children had gone to play in the snow up at the Boy Scout camp, she said. It was a ritual that when it snowed up there for the first time in the season, and rained here, down five hundred feet, there would be a snow party. Friends had come by and picked up Carol and Travis.

"Can we talk?" she asked Barbara.

"Sure. Let's go to the study."

Nell glanced at Frank. "Will you come, too?"

Belatedly, Mike looked embarrassed. He said, "You guys go to the living room. There's something I wanted to do on the computer. If you don't mind, I mean."

They went to the living room, sat near the fire, and waited for Nell to begin. If Nell had noticed any change in Barbara, she was not showing a sign; she seemed so wrapped in gloom and unhappiness that she probably noticed nothing.

Finally Nell drew in a long breath and said, "I keep dreaming about Lucas up on the ledge. He's up there with my grandfather, talking and talking. In the dream, when I first go up to the ledge they don't see me, but then Grampa looks surprised and says, 'It's about time, young lady.'" She had been gazing fixedly at the fire; now she looked at her hands, which were clutching each other in her lap. She drew them apart and flexed her fingers. "Grampa is trying to tell

308

me something," she said in a very low voice, nearly a whisper. "I used to go up to the ledge with him when I was little, and I'd talk out a problem or something. He never told me what to do, but I seemed to know what I should do after we talked. I don't know how he did that. Then, after he died, I used to go up and pretend he was still back there, sitting on his log, and I talked to him. I told him about . . . things, and it was almost like before. Somehow I could come to some sort of decision that I hadn't been able to make before. It sounds crazy, doesn't it?" She trailed off; her hands had gone back to clutching each other again.

There was silence in the room. Now and again the wind made the fire sputter, or it drove a puff of smoke back down the chimney. Little of the sound of the wind penetrated the house, but Barbara felt that Nell had brought the storm in with her, and that it was raging in her head. She felt frozen by the icy winds that blew in her head. Finally Frank cleared his throat.

"Nell, what is it you think you should do?"

"Testify," she said in a whisper. "Tell them I didn't kill Lucas."

The silence this time was deeper; no one moved. Barbara realized she was watching her father, not Nell, and she jerked her gaze away. Again, she was thinking bitterly. Again.

"Nell," Frank said slowly. "You know we've been over that. You can't do your case any good by taking the stand, but you sure can do it a lot of harm." He took off his glasses as he spoke and polished them, peered through the lenses, and put them back on to look at her over the rims.

When Nell remained silent, Barbara stood up. "Wait a second," she said. The ice that had entered her was released in her voice, her manner. She hurried out and went to the dining room where she began to snatch papers away from the stacks that still covered the table. She found maps and drawings and carried them back to the living room. Her father was talking when she returned.

"We used to meet down at the store, or in the woods. Chatted a bit. He was a good man, and shrewd. He knew a

309

thing or two, he did. He wouldn't ever tell you to do anything that could hurt you in any way. Now you know that as well as I do."

"Maybe that's what he's trying to tell me, that it wouldn't hurt to tell the truth. He always said that."

Barbara swept a magazine or two and some newspapers from the coffee table and spread out the map, covered it with a few sketches. "Look at these, Nell," she said crisply. "These are preliminary sketches, but they're accurate. Look at them!" She waited until Nell's eyes turned to the drawing of the ledge. "If you came up this path, the way you said you did, exactly what could you have seen?"

"I told you all that. That's the path, and I saw Lucas. He said, 'Watch this.' Her voice faltered and she looked at Barbara. "I told you."

"So, pretend I'm Tony DeAngelo." Her voice deepened, became rougher and meaner with heavy sarcasm. "Mrs. Kendricks, what are these bushes in the drawing? Vine maples? How high are they? And you could see over them from down there on the trail? Were you on stilts, Mrs. Kendricks? Did you have a periscope, perhaps?"

Nell blanched, grabbed the drawing, and studied it.

Barbara went on in her cold, hard voice, "Weren't you actually over here, Mrs. Kendricks? On the edge of the clearing where the main trail is? Isn't that the only place where you could have seen the entire ledge, both sides of it? Isn't that the only place where you could have seen Lucas Kendricks that day? Didn't you choose the main trail that day because the other one is too steep, and you were burdened by the rifle you carried? Didn't you lift that rifle, aim it at Lucas Kendricks, and shoot him dead?"

"No!" Nell whispered, but not in answer to the questions that Barbara had fired at her. "No!" she said again, more shrilly. "I have to go." She stood up, a distant, staring look on her face.

"What's wrong?" Frank asked. "Are you all right?"

"*No!*" she cried, and ran from his reaching hands, ran from the room. "I have to go. I have to."

By the time they caught up to her she was already fumbling with the coats and jackets in the hall closet. Frank grabbed her by the shoulders and held her fast. "What's happened? Where do you have to go? What's wrong with you?"

A hard tremor shook her. She said, "I can't tell you. I have to go now." Her voice had become almost too calm all at once.

Baffled, Frank let go of her. She reached past him, brought her jacket out of the closet, and put it on.

"For heaven's sake!" Barbara said sharply. "You can't leave it at this! What do you intend to do?"

"I don't know," Nell said. She finished buttoning the big wooden buttons of her jacket, drew a wool cap from her pocket, and put it on. She looked from Barbara to Frank with a curious, almost helpless, expression; then she shook her head slightly, turned and left them standing speechless at the front door.

She had driven to Frank's house, no longer willing to cut through Doc's property and walk over. Now she drove home too fast and screeched to a halt outside her own garage. The rain was still very heavy, was still being driven in by the powerful storm front; she ignored it and walked around her house, toward the trail up to the ledge.

Within a dozen steps into the forest the wind abated, tamed by the massive trees. The trail had become a watercourse. Water swirled around rocks, plummeted down from rock to root to ground, roiled behind a dam of a fallen tree. She kept her pace steady; her feet knew this trail too well to be fooled by the camouflage of water and mud. As she climbed, the air grew colder, and presently she realized that the water underfoot had changed as well; it was not rushing as before. Pockets of snow appeared, snow was piling up behind rocks and logs. She made her way more cautiously. Water was navigable, but snow in the woods was treacherous, especially if ice had formed first. The snow deepened until the rocky trail was smooth and even; she moved very slowly

311

now, testing each step, holding onto trees where she could, but she kept climbing.

And then the top was level with her head, half a dozen more steps up, the steepest ones of all. Her foot groped in the snow for a safe place. She held a tree very hard, half pulled herself up that step, not trusting the foothold she had found. She did it again. Up here the wind was free; it howled and screamed and blew fine snow before it. The vine maples had been buried already, bent low by the wind, covered by the snow, simple mounds of white. She paused, catching her breath, and she knew she had not been able to see over the vines and bushes that day. A shudder passed through her; she slid her foot up another step, moved it until she felt a rock, and then pulled herself up again. The straggly bushes were all gone, all turned into white mounds. Snow blinded her momentarily. She stopped moving, waiting for it to ease up, praying it would ease up. When it did, she moved upward again, and now she was on top.

The wind shrieked, subsided, shrieked again, at times causing a whiteout, then visibility returned, then another whiteout. She blinked at the log. For a moment it had seemed that there was a figure on it, but she knew it was only snow, piled up behind the log, banked against the cliff face behind it. There was where she had seen Lucas, she heard herself say under her breath. Right there. She felt as if she had entered a dream state where the impossible was routine and no questions were allowed, or even necessary. She had seen Lucas there. She moved onto the ledge uncertainly, afraid of the blizzard wind, afraid of the capricious whiteouts.

She had to get to her rock, she understood, even if it was just another mound of snow. She also understood that she had to leave this place very soon and get down to warmth. Hypothermia could set in very fast, and she was wet. The wind screamed. She ducked as low as she could and still be able to move and made her way to her rock and sat in the snow on it.

"I came, Grampa," she said into the wind.

She could imagine his voice, remember his words in her

312

dream: "It's about time, young lady." She nodded. Yes, about time. Without more thought she stood up and looked about at the landmarks made alien by drifting snow and the blinding wind. "Lucas was right here," she said under her breath. "And a second later, he was over there, laughing."

Years ago they had come up here together. They had sat in the sunlight and talked about tomorrows, all their tomorrows. They had made love up here, and she had shown him her secret hiding place, the little cave behind the log. Moving in the dream state, shielding her face from the wind with her hands, crouching to lessen the target for the wind, she worked her way through the snow to the log and around it where the drift was two feet deep. She had to move the snow away with her hands. There was the round rock that was the doorway to her secret cave. She rolled the rock away and looked in, then reached in and pulled out a plastic bag. Lucas was here, she heard herself saying, and then again, "Lucas was right here!"

"Stop pushing," Nell said fretfully to her grandfather. "I'm moving. Don't push."

"Come on," Lucas called. "Can't catch me!" Laughing, he darted behind a tree.

She moved her foot another step. But she yearned for rest, to lean against a tree trunk and rest for a minute. No longer than that, just a minute. "Grampa, don't push," she moaned when he shoved her from behind; she stumbled, slid in the slush underfoot, and fell, clutching the bag she carried. She hit her cheek on a muddy rock and moaned again, and then rested her forehead against the freezing mud that no longer felt very cold.

"Come on, up on your feet. Come on, girl, get up!" Grampa said roughly.

Lucas was at her side, still laughing. "Hey, remember when we dammed Halleck Creek? Remember I kept saying the water was okay, not a bit cold? I lied, baby. God, was it cold! I could hardly talk because my teeth were chattering so hard."

313

She remembered. She had jumped in, finally, and they had wrestled in the frigid shallow water; she had tried to dunk him for pretending it wasn't cold. Lucas took her hand and pulled her upright, along another foot or two; Grampa nudged from behind, and suddenly she staggered out from the woods, to where the wind screamed. Lucas dashed water into her face. "Don't do that!" she cried. "Stop that!" He just laughed and danced out of reach, and she followed.

"We made it," Grampa said, stamping toward the house. He opened the door and went inside, and Lucas yanked her by the arm until she was inside also.

"Nell! My God, we've been scared to death. Where were you?"

Nell ignored the tall black woman who did not belong in her dream state. She watched her grandfather walk through the house, and Lucas was laughing and grabbing at the bag in her arm. "Give it to me," he said; she tugged back. "You can't have it. It's mine. I found it," she said. "Finders keepers."

"Nell? What happened? Nell!"

When Nell pulled harder on the plastic bag to keep it away from Lucas, it ripped open and tapes spilled out, clattering on the floor. Diskettes spilled out, too, but she saw only the tapes, Lucas's tapes. "I'm sorry," she said, weeping suddenly, her body caught in a violent tremor that she could not stop. "I'm sorry." She fell to her knees and tried to scoop the tapes up again, to keep them safe, but hands were on her shoulders, pulling her up, pushing her into a chair. Hands were taking off her soaked clothes; she closed her eyes and let it happen; finally she could rest.

TWENTY-EIGHT

"WHAT HAPPENED?" BARBARA asked when Tawna Gresham admitted her to Nell's house an hour later.

"I don't know. She was gone, and I got worried because the car was here, so I hung around. I was going to call you when she walked in, out of her head, hallucinating, nearly frozen. Doc's with her. I called him. She was crying for you to come, she has something for you."

Barbara ran up the stairs to Nell's room and stopped at the door. Doc was feeding her, talking in a soothing voice. "Come on, open up. You don't want to sleep just yet. First we warm up the insides. That's right, open. There you go." He glanced at Barbara. "She'll be all right, just a little too cold." He turned back to Nell. "Another spoonful, Nell. Come on."

Nell was almost completely hidden by covers. Her hair was damp. Barbara backed away from the door and went downstairs again. "He's giving her soup or something."

"Soup," Tawna said. "Just broth. Hypothermia, he said. It's a wonder she made it back to the house. Doc came equipped with heating pads and soup. I guess this isn't the first case of hypothermia he's seen."

"Where are the kids?"

"Up at the big house with James. He'll give them some dinner and play cards with them for a while."

Just then Doc came down carrying the bowl. "More broth," he said cheerfully. "She's almost up to normal again.

315

She asked if you'd go up for a minute," he said to Barbara. "If you want to talk to her, do it now, because in a while I'm going to give her a sedative, after she's warmed up. She's exhausted." He went on to the kitchen.

To Barbara's eyes Nell still looked frozen; her skin was pallid, her lips pale. "What happened?" she asked, going to the bed. She sat in the chair Doc had been using.

"I told you Grampa was trying to tell me something," Nell whispered. "It was the tapes. I found the tapes Lucas hid up there." She looked at the doorway nervously, withdrew her hand from under the covers, and reached for Barbara's arm. Her hand was cold. "I'm afraid those people will find out I have them. They might still be listening."

"Nell, what are you saying? You found tapes where?"

"On the ledge. In a secret cave. Lucas put them there that day." Her hand clutched Barbara's arm, and her gaze kept going to the door, then the window, back to Barbara.

"Okay. Do you want me to take care of them for you?"

Nell nodded. "For now. Until we decide what to do with them. Do you have a safe?"

"Dad has a safe. We'll take care of them. You get some rest now." She patted Nell's hand and stood up. "You went to the ledge in the storm?"

"It was snowing up there. Grampa and Lucas helped me get home. They were up there talking, I told you."

Barbara regarded her broodingly for another few seconds, then said, "Well, don't worry about the tapes tonight. I'll take care of them. We'll talk about them tomorrow."

Doc came into the room with a bowl of steaming broth. "Well, look at you, better and better."

He was a different person, Barbara thought in surprise. He was calm and competent, and yet her father had said earlier that Doc looked like hell, that he had a hangover, and Jessie had refused to see anyone at all. Domestic brawling, her father had said. This man feeding Nell soup was the idealized doctor from some golden past, making house calls, caring for the patient personally. Barbara left them.

She went to Tawna in the living room. "Nell said she has

316

some tapes she wants me to put away for her. You know anything about tapes?"

"She brought them in with her," Tawna said, nodding. "In a plastic bag that she managed to rip open. Tapes went out everywhere. I put them here." She pointed to two stacks of audio tapes on an end table.

Barbara stared at them, and slowly looked back to Tawna. "What did she say when she came in? What did she do?"

"She was incoherent," Tawna said. "Really out of it. She didn't even see me, but she was seeing something, or some things. She said something like 'You can't have it.' And then she said, 'Finders keepers.' When she tore the bag and the tapes came spilling she began to cry, saying, 'I'm sorry.' Then she passed out, sort of."

"Could she have taken something? You know, a drug or something? Alcohol?"

Tawna looked scornful. "Nell? Forget it. Besides, she was as cold a two-day-old corpse." She went to the kitchen. "I'll see if there's a bag around to put the tapes in."

"This is what you call being up the creek without a paddle," Frank said a little later. They were at the table where the tapes were fanned out neatly. Sixteen in all. There was not a tape player in the house.

Barbara regarded the tapes with bafflement and frustration. She had reasoned that Lucas had taken something that Brandywine and crew had wanted desperately to find again; she had gambled and said disks to lure Brandywine to Oregon. She had not for a second thought of tapes, regular music tapes that someone had recorded over. Only moments ago she and Mike had sat in his car with the rain beating on the roof and, using his tape deck, had confirmed the fact that a man's voice had been recorded over regular audio music tapes. The sound quality was poor, the rain and wind had made it nearly impossible to hear the words, but there seemed no doubt that Nell had found what Brandywine's detectives had been searching for. Sixteen tapes!

"I'll go buy a Walkman," Mike said. "I'll probably have to go in to Springfield. Take a couple of hours."

"Buy two," Barbara said.

"Make it three," her father said. "You think I could stand knowing you were both hearing what he had to say while I couldn't?" he demanded when Barbara looked surprised. He shook his head. "You know it's going to take as long to listen to them as it took to record them. Thirty hours? Thirty-two? Good God!"

"Mike, are you sure you don't mind? That rain's still pelting down like crazy. I'd go, but I really have to try out the summation."

"No big deal," he said. He touched one of the tapes. "Who could sleep tonight without knowing something about what's on them?"

"We'll eat when you get back," Frank said. "We'll plug in and eat. The American way."

After Mike had gone, Barbara stood at the table and regarded the tapes. "Goddamn it!" she said finally.

"That sums it up pretty cogently," her father said. "I suppose this explains why Lucas made that detour to the ledge. Nell finally remembered, or figured it out, or something."

"And she picked a blizzard and monsoon to wade through to get to them again," Barbara muttered. "Smart." Nell must have seen him just after he hid the tapes; when she closed her eyes, he moved out of her line of sight. Probably he had not wanted any connection made between his arrival and the hiding place. She scowled and cursed under her breath. Nell had remembered everything else about that day; why not this? Why not until now?

Frank turned his back on the tapes with a show of irritation. "You ready to try out your summation? Let's go to the living room."

When they got to the cheerful room with its welcoming fire, he seated himself in one of the overstuffed chairs, a legal pad on his lap. "What we used to do," he said with a faraway look on his face, "was have her sit and make notes if she thought of anything to question, and I just sort of moved around, peeking at my crib sheet from time to time. How's that sound?"

Barbara nodded, her throat too tight to say anything at the moment. She cleared her throat, placed her printout on an end table, and started. After ten minutes, she stopped.

"It's awful, isn't it?"

"Well . . . you seem a bit distracted, not concentrating exactly, I'd say."

"I'm out of my depth, Dad, and that's the truth. I don't know where I stand, where Nell stands. I don't know if she intends to testify. I can't stop her, you know. I'd like to get a continuance, but I doubt Lundgren would agree, not unless Nell is in the hospital, at least. I couldn't talk to her when I went over there; she was babbling like a loony. I don't even know if she intends to put on a psycho act from here on out. Tonight was a good start, if that's what's on her mind. I can't mention those tapes to a soul, not until we know exactly what's on them, and even then, so what? I just don't know what I'm doing any more."

"I guess that's what comes of trying to do too many jobs at once," he said thoughtfully. "Yep, try to do it all and you don't do anything."

"Meaning?"

"Well, it seems to me you've taken on a hell of a lot of hats. Judge, jury, prosecutor, investigator, defense attorney. Any one of them is a full-time job, in my experience."

She contemplated the fire. After several seconds she muttered, "You left out a few. Social reformer, theologian, philosopher, probably a couple of others that will pop into my head any minute now."

"All the above," he agreed. "And what you need for the rest of this trial is the actor's hat. You've done the defense attorney to the hilt. I'm very proud of you, Bobby. More than I can say. Assuming Nell will come to her senses, there's nothing you can add to your case. Not a thing. Lundgren won't grant a continuance unless you show cause that you simply don't have. So now you go into your dramatic act. The final scene, then curtain down, and the waiting starts."

Abruptly she got to her feet. "One more prop," she said, and hurried from the living room. She went to the kitchen and ran the water a few seconds while she thought. She knew how Tony would come on in court with his summation, filled with righteous indignation, demanding justice and so on. She had seen Tony work too many times not to know how his inflections would be, how his voice would rise and fall, the points he would make about law and the finality of death. All right, she told herself. All right. She knew more than Tony about this case, and she did not know if Nell had killed Lucas or not. That was the point, the only point, she said under her breath. No one knew except the killer, who was just possibly Nell, and Barbara could no longer trust anything Nell said. But she didn't *know*. Tony had *proven* nothing. She filled a tall glass and returned with it. Her father had not moved. "I'll save the histrionics for tomorrow. Now, where was I?" She sipped water, put the glass down, and began to move about the room, summing up the case for her client.

She went through the many steps thoroughly; now and then she caught a look of surprise on his face, now and then he made a note. Only once did she waver, when a memory surged through her mind. Not in this house, before they had this house. She had gone downstairs as a child and had heard his voice raised angrily, and, frightened, she had crept to the study door where she saw her mother in a chair with her feet drawn up under her, a legal pad on her lap. Her father had been pacing with great energy, shouting almost, his voice thick with anger. The memory ended there. She didn't know what happened next, what she had done, if she had inter-rupted, if she had continued to listen. Her mother had been beautiful. Her voice faltered, and she sipped the water, then went on speaking.

The memory had lasted only a second in real time, but in memory time it had been many minutes; the images it had brought were sharp and clear. Especially her mother's face, so intent on Frank's words, a little frown of concentration creasing her forehead, the tip of a pencil against her lip, pressing in on it.

When she finished, Frank grunted softly. "Okay," he said, and then he looked at the notes he had jotted, and they began to discuss the points he felt needed something. She listened carefully to his reasoning, and he listened just as carefully to hers. They were still at it when Mike returned.

"I bought two Walkmans and a tape player that will make copies," he said, lugging a large box to the living room. "And a lot of tapes. I thought it would be a good idea to copy everything and stash the originals in a safe-deposit box, something like that. I mean, if Brandywine's crew thought they had something important enough to hire those detectives and all, well, maybe we shouldn't take chances, either."

Barbara gave him a grateful look, and Frank patted his shoulder on his way out to put the finishing touches on their dinner and get it on the table. It was almost nine-thirty; they all seemed to realize at the same moment that they were starving.

"I was thinking," Mike said to Barbara, "we could divide the tapes among us and listen to enough of each one to see if the whole thing needs listening to right now. And if anyone finds something particularly interesting, we can play it on the machine so we can all hear it. Okay?"

"Good. Eventually we might have to hear everything, but that's a good way to start. I'm glad you were thinking of things like that. I certainly wasn't."

"Yeah, that's what I thought." Suddenly a distant look came over his face and he said, "Something I have to tell Frank. Be right back." He trotted from the room.

Barbara began to examine the many tapes. None of them was in a case; none was labeled. Maybe Lucas had removed the cases to save room, she decided, and wished he had thought to put numbers or dates or something on the tapes themselves. Then Frank whooped with laughter in the kitchen, and Mike returned, grinning. He looked like a little boy who knew very well that he had done something

321

marvelous and precocious. A dirty limerick, she thought with resignation. Determinedly, she did not ask.

Frank had made a casserole that might have been somewhat overdone and baked potatoes that very definitely were overdone. No one cared. They did not listen to the tapes during dinner, but immediately afterward they began.

Barbara listened to a disembodied voice that turned out to be deeper than she had expected. She had had no reason to expect anything, but when the deep voice identified himself as Lucas, she started, surprised. He was talking about some time in the past, and she had no way of knowing when the tape had been recorded, or how distant from that time the events he described had happened. Later, she told herself; she rewound that tape and inserted a new one.

Twenty minutes after they began, Frank made a grunting sound and held up his hand. Barbara and Mike took their headsets off.

"I think this is the first one," Frank said. Mike was using the big machine. He removed his tape and Frank slipped his into the slot. They all listened:

"September 14, 1982. Two days ago I told Emil I want to get out of all this and go home. Nell's right. This is all a piece of bunkum, and they're treating me like shit. Emil yelled at me and said to wait until he talks to Schumaker about my degree. He was sure it was just a technicality that kept it away from me. He promised to look into it ASAP. Today Emil said I should go to the lab and give a demonstration for Brandywine. They've been in conference day after day, hour after hour. I've never even met her yet. I didn't want to, but finally I said okay, one last demonstration, and then we talk about my degree, and he said sure. He thinks Schumaker needs a paper, for the committee, for the files or something. A simple paper, not a real thesis, he said. Notes about my work with him would be okay, fifteen, twenty pages, up to fifty or more if I want to go that high, but I don't have to. And then the master's degree. I don't believe it.

"I went to the lab. It's in the math building, a little room with a bunch of chairs with plastic seats, and a long table. I

322

have a special chair with arms and buttons on the right one. And there's a big screen, a computer monitor. There's a glass window, one-way glass, I know, because sometimes I help with other subjects and those times I'm on the other side of that glass. We just do one at a time in here. So, I take the chair and they're all behind the glass and it starts like always.

"I could go longer than anyone else, but even so after an hour or a little more I had to stop. It was tiring. Emil knew that, Schumaker knew it, and Margolis, but *she* didn't believe it. Go on, she kept saying over the microphone. Keep going, she said, as if she thought I stopped to prove a point or something. I told her my head was aching too much, and that was the truth. Sometimes it was my stomach that ached, but usually my head hurt too much to keep on. And I just wanted to take a nap.

"They came into my room and sat at the table. She said, why don't you go get a Coke or a cup of coffee, walk out in the fresh air to wake up. Take a ten-minute break.

"So I left, but I didn't want anything to drink, or to take a walk. I wanted to have a nap, so I went in the other room, the one we called the control room, and I could see them at the table talking. I put my head on my arms to go to sleep, but I kept hearing what they were saying. And she said I was resisting. Emil said I was cooperating fully, and she said, I don't mean that, I don't mean deliberately. You say the others all begin to have physical symptoms after a time? He said yes, and she said, they're all resisting. They meet a wall that terrifies them and gives them physical symptoms so they can retreat in good faith. I want to hypnotize him now, today, and see what that wall means.

"Schumaker said, does that mean you're in? And she said, I don't know. Not yet. But I have a few suggestions.

"I looked at them then and realized that Emil and Schumaker were treating her just the way they had treated Margolis when they wanted him to help with the computer programming. They were being very polite and acting like she was something really special, and she liked that. I could tell.

"I decided I wanted to pack up my stuff in the car and just go home, as fast as I could drive back. I started to leave, and then I saw my backpack in the other room by the special chair, and I knew I had to get it. My car keys were in it, and my apartment keys, my wallet even. So I went back in.

"She said, is your head better? and I said sure, it's fine now. She laughed and said, don't be silly. Sit down and I'll show you a trick to get rid of a headache. You can use it whenever you want. It's pain transference. I said no, I was okay, but she took my arm and sort of pushed me into a chair at the table. I said I didn't want to be hypnotized, and she laughed and said that since no one can be who isn't cooperative, there wasn't any danger of that. Keep that thought in mind, she said. Now where does your head hurt? I touched the back of my head without even thinking what I was doing, and she nodded as if she had thought so. Then she began talking about the pain, where it was, how it felt, on and on, and she told me to think of it as something I could see, something I could touch and move. She said, don't close your eyes, don't relax too much, just think about that pain. We're going to gather it up and start moving it. We'll move it down your neck, across your shoulder into your right arm and down into your hand. When it's all in your hand, you'll just throw it away. All with your eyes wide open. Simple pain transference.

"She never said a word about trance, or sleep, or relax, or close your eyes, nothing that I associated with hypnosis, but she hypnotized me anyway, and that's all I can remember of what happened in the lab this afternoon.

"Emil will tell me eventually. I know he will. It's night now, and I've tried and tried to remember and had to give up, but it's okay, because Emil will tell me. Now I have to get some sleep. It's going to be a long day tomorrow. We're going to start at eight in the morning and go through all the disks, everything. They're all excited. I know I planned to go home again, leave today, this afternoon, or tonight, but I'll wait until I find out what happened. Another few days won't matter, not after all these years.

324

"And I'm going to start making a record of everything I know about what we've been doing. Not the paper Emil said I need. That's bullshit. But a record, something to take away with me. I'll tape over my music tapes. Nothing now to make them suspicious of what I'm doing. I don't think any of them would like it if they knew I'm making a record of all this."

His voice stopped and the sound of Jimi Hendrix filled the living room. Mike turned off the machine.

"Oh my God!" Barbara breathed.

"He never had a chance," Mike said softly. "That poor guy never had a chance."

Frank stood up. "You want anything to drink? I'm having a glass of wine and then I'm going to bed. You can fill me in tomorrow." His face was drawn with pity.

Mike decided to make coffee; it promised to be a late night. Barbara got up to poke at the fire, but really, she understood, they all simply needed to move, as if to break the spell of that distant, dead voice. Poor Lucas, she thought. Poor Nell. All flip-flopped over. She had started out feeling only anger at Lucas for abandoning his wife and children, and sympathy for Nell, as well as admiration because she had handled it so well. Now the sympathy was for Lucas, and she was no longer certain how she felt about Nell.

None of this, she thought bleakly, had a thing to do with the case she had to sum up tomorrow. She glanced at her watch. Twelve-forty. Another twenty minutes and she would have to go to bed, or she would be a wreck tomorrow, she knew. The tapes would keep. They had kept for seven years, and then another six months. They would keep another few days. She remembered her fierce wish to destroy Ruth Brandywine along with her accomplices, and she thought, maybe we will yet. Maybe we will.

At five minutes before one Barbara found a tape Lucas had made in the woods on his way home. Frank had gone to bed; Mike had his coffee, and she was dead tired, but she and Mike listened to this tape together. Lucas sounded terribly tired:

"November was cold. I remember how cold it was day

325

after day, with a lot of snow up in the mountains, and a stiff wind that seemed not to let up. They were all fighting most of the time. Emil was making threats to take the work somewhere else if they all chickened out on him. Schumaker was threatening to blacklist him, and Brandywine was furious with everyone. No one was telling me anything by then, but I could see what was happening. Something had gone wrong with the kids Brandywine was hypnotizing, and they were all blaming each other. One of the parents was pretty upset, and the project was killed. Just like that, killed. Emil said he'd continue without their help, that he no longer needed anyone's help, that, in fact, he never had needed them, but that Schumaker had used him from the start. He was picking up street boys in Denver, taking them home, having them run the program, and testing them by himself.

"They didn't know what to do with me. Brandywine said that as long as I didn't know anything or remember anything, there was nothing to do, and that's how it was. I had no work, no classes, nothing to do. I read a lot during those last two weeks. Now it seems strange that I didn't just leave, but at the time I don't remember thinking of that. *Her* doing, no doubt.

"Then Emil called late in the afternoon. He was panicked by something, and I couldn't make any sense out of what he was saying. I got in my car and started for his house. The closer I got the more I was dreading getting there. I was really freaking out, seeing things, hearing voices, and one of the voices was of a kid, a laughing boy. He sounded delirious with joy, that's the only way I can think of him. He said he was hiding disks and showed me where they were, in my head. And I was scared, more scared than I've ever been. I must have been driving like a drunken driver, weaving back and forth, seeing things, the works, and I wasn't on anything. Nothing at all. So that's how I was when I reached Emil's house. The laughing boy said he would try to calm Emil down, in my head he told me that, but when I opened the door and went in, Emil was standing with a gun, and the boy was on the floor dead. There was blood everywhere. Emil saw me and shot at me, screaming something. Margolis came in right behind me and when Emil saw him, he shot again, and then turned the gun to his own head and fired it once more. Margolis and Brandywine put the gun in the laughing boy's hand, and they wrapped me in a blanket and carried me out and put me in my car. She drove me to her house, and I stayed there for weeks and weeks. I don't even know how long. No one ever questioned me about Emil's death, or anything else.

"That's the first time I understood what we were doing, what we had done, why the boy was laughing and laughing. I saw the web and the network and the pattern, all of it, and they knew I would remember this time. That's why they had to keep me under wraps for the rest of my life. I wonder now why they didn't just kill me and be done with it. But she thought it was under control forever, and for all these years it was. Then it came out again, and I know why the boy was laughing and laughing. I know why."

His voice broke; for a second, Barbara thought he was sobbing. A shudder passed over her when she realized it was laughter she was hearing, wild, joyous laughter.

Shakily she stood up. The laughter stopped and there was the music of Paul Simon. She stared at the tape player in horror.

"Brandywine wasn't lying," she whispered. "He was insane! She really was treating him for insanity."

TWENTY-NINE

AT LEAST NELL looked almost rested, not as if she would keel over any second, Barbara thought the next morning. She felt a twinge of jealousy, thinking about the sleep Nell had had imposed upon her by Doc while she, Barbara, had had vivid dreams in her broken sleep. She stood on the front porch of Nell's house waiting for Nell's answer to her question, what do you intend to do today? Clive's car was in the driveway; he had not come out of the house. The rain had almost stopped; the wind was gentle again, hardly present at all. The world smelled clean.

"Clive thinks I should go on record telling the truth," she said hesitantly. "He sounds like Grampa. You know, the truth can't hurt, and all that."

"Clive doesn't know diddly about law and criminal trials," Barbara said darkly.

"I know that. He says the truth would be best, or take the stand and say I just can't remember what happened. Count on them to pity me, I guess. He thinks that from an outsider's point of view, an observer's, what looks worst is not to say anything at all. I can sort of see it that way, too."

"And he's wrong. Let him stick to trees and woods and stay the hell away from the law," Barbara said. "What's *your* decision? Forget what Clive says."

"I won't lie about it. I didn't do it. I remember clearly what happened, and I didn't do it. But the truth is too fantastic to tell, isn't it? It's the least likely of the three. Your way, Barbara. I'll sit there and keep my mouth shut, and pray."

Barbara nodded and said briskly, "Okay. Clive will bring you in? What about the children? Have you made arrangements for after school? You shouldn't be distracted by worries about them today. Deliberation might take a long time." They both knew that what she meant was that if the verdict went against Nell, Judge Lundgren could order her into custody immediately.

Nell swallowed hard. "It's all taken care of." John and Amy Kendricks would cross the mountains some time during the day, but no one knew yet when; they were snowed in at the farm. "What did you do with the tapes? Will they help at all?"

"We made copies and they'll go in a safe-deposit box today. No help, I'm afraid. I haven't heard them all, of course, but that's how it looks. So, we'll see you in court. And, Nell, I wish us both good luck. See you later." She held out her hand to shake Nell's but abruptly she opened both arms and embraced her instead. Then she hurried back to the car where Frank was waiting, and they started the drive to town.

She had found Mike asleep on the couch that morning, too bleary to talk after being up all night. Frank had one set of tapes in his briefcase, Mike had the other. He wanted to get them in some kind of order, he had said, make some more notes. He would be in court a little late. Barbara wished the tapes had stayed hidden a few days longer. All night a Svengali figure had prowled her dreams; one dream had placed her against a rock, helpless in a charm, an onlooker while Lucas raped and mutilated that girl in the forest, and then threw back his head in raucous laughter.

Tony made only one point that Barbara had not anticipated. "Hired detectives do not commit murder," he said soberly, in his most mournful voice. "An agency is hired to do particular jobs that most of us find unsavory. They spy on people, they plant listening devices, they try to get copies of documents, they do many things, but they do not murder.

Because there's no need. They are paid for their time whether or not they produce results."

Point well taken, she had to admit to herself, as he continued.

"Ladies and gentlemen," he said eventually, "the facts are fairly simple and irrefutable. Nell Kendricks believed her husband was on his way to claim his share of property she had inherited and thought was entirely hers. She threatened to shoot anyone who entered her property. She did shoot at two men she thought were going to cut down a tree. She had reason to believe that her husband had hired them to do that. She sent her children away for the first time ever in anticipation of the arrival of her husband. When the computer system was delivered, she knew that Lucas Kendricks intended to move in again, to make that house his home again, to take up where they had left off years earlier. No one else entered that property that day. We know that. No one else had access to her gun. No one else had reason to kill Lucas Kendricks. . . ."

He began to talk about the ultimate crime, taking another's life, and the finality of death. He was nearing the end.

When it was Barbara's turn, she stood up slowly and approached the jury with her hands folded before her. "Ladies and gentlemen, yours is perhaps one of the most difficult of all tasks ever to fall to citizens of this country. There are many mysteries of the human heart and soul that we cannot fathom. There are mysteries of human behavior that we cannot comprehend. We can know only what our own senses tell us; all else we must take on faith. You can never know for certain what another human being thinks or feels. You can know only what that other person says. You can never know for certain what act another human being has committed unless you personally witness each act. And yet, you are required today to decide the outcome of a trial that involves murder, that will affect the life forever after of another human being and her children.

"As you consider the evidence that has been presented here, I ask you to keep in mind the question: Has the state done all it could have done, and all it should have done to clear up some of the mysteries that abound in this trial? Has the state proven beyond a reasonable doubt that the case it has presented is the only possible one? You have heard witnesses impeach their own testimony, recant their own words, confess to having lied. In those instances, did the state do all it could have done and should have done to find the truth of their testimony before accepting it as true?"

Slowly she tracked Lucas Kendricks's movements, and now and then she asked the same question: Did the state do all it could have done and should have done to find the truth?

"Placing the listening device in the tree was an illegal act. Recording conversations surreptitiously is an illegal act. Where are the tapes? Did the state make an effort to locate them and learn what they might reveal about what happened on the ledge that day? And if not, did the state do all it could have done and should have done to determine the truth?"

She sipped from her water glass and went on. She was keeping her voice pitched low, conversational, including each man and woman on the jury in her meditative summary.

"On that Saturday the listeners must have heard the UPS delivery man speak to Tawna and James Gresham. They must have heard him get directions to continue to the little house. There was time for one or both of them to get into the boat at their disposal and to approach Nell Kendricks's property from the river, dock at her beach, and get to her house without being seen. The second she left by one door, another person could have entered by a different door. They were looking for something Lucas Kendricks was said to have; they had been hired to track him, to find him, to recover something of value. Wouldn't it be possible that they assumed the something they were looking for had been delivered by UPS? So someone else did have access to the house, and to the gun that Nell Kendricks left on the couch when she went into the woods and up to the ledge. That it was someone other than Nell Kendricks is the only reason for the rifle to have been wiped clean of fingerprints. She had no reason to clean her fingerprints from it; the rifle was hers,

331

she had fired it recently. But someone had reason. If her prints had been found on it, no one would have thought that mysterious, but not to find any prints at all is very mysterious."

She walked to the drawings she had used before, and to the map that was enlarged to show both trails and the divided ledge clearly. "No one keeping out of her sight, following her, could have seen her take the right branch here," she said, pointing first to the map, and then to the drawing that included the large trees. "No one unfamiliar with that trail and the ledge would know about the small, steep path that goes up there. And anyone who kept to the main trail and ended up here," she said, pointing again, "would have had a clear view of the entire clearing." She turned to look at the jury; they were very intent. "Anyone standing here," she said with emphasis, pointing again, "anyone more than five feet eight inches tall, would have had a clear line of fire across the clearing. A shot from here would account for the angle of the wound, and we no longer have to assume a kneeling position, or that Lucas Kendricks might have leaned over, or any other odd position for him."

She walked away from the maps and drawings and continued her summation, again and again asking her main question about the state and its investigation.

"You heard the statement Nell Kendricks made to the investigating officers. She could add nothing to it in this court, and, ladies and gentlemen, it is not her obligation to prove her innocence. Her innocence is a given, just as it is a given for each and every one of us, unless proven otherwise. Has the state truly proven otherwise? Did they investigate the ranger who claimed to have seen Lucas Kendricks's car in the forest? Who told him it was there? Someone knew Lucas Kendricks was going home on foot. Who was it? The state has the resources to investigate; it is not the duty of a private citizen to launch such an investigation."

She moved in toward her conclusion at last. "Nell Kendricks was in no danger from Lucas Kendricks at any time, and she knew that. She had neighbors nearby. She had a car she could have got into and left in. She could have called the police. Any of these options were available to her. She did not have cause to want him dead. She could have divorced him at any time if she had wanted to. He was a poor, dehydrated, hungry man whose feet were so blistered and infected that every step must have been torment for him. He had escaped from his enemies and knew they were coming after him. He was afraid. He was not a threat to his wife, but he was a threat to others.

"Has the state proven her guilt? No, ladies and gentlemen, it has not. Has the state used its vast resources to investigate all the leads it could have followed to solve the many mysteries we have encountered? No, it has not. And until those other questions are answered, there must be doubt, more than reasonable doubt, indeed very grave doubt about who fired the shot that killed Lucas Kendricks."

When she sat down, she knew she had been inadequate. After all her preparation, all her notes, her practice, it was not enough, she thought in near despair. She felt Frank's hand on her shoulder; it was very warm. He squeezed and let go. Judge Lundgren called a ten-minute recess before he instructed the jury, and she let out her breath.

"You were so good," Nell whispered at her side.

Behind her, Frank growled, "Good work, Bobby. Top of your form."

The recess was agony. Nell was bewildered by the attitude of Barbara and her father; she had believed it over, but they were both more anxious than before, and neither one told her why. Barbara felt exhausted, hollowed out, with only a bunch of exposed nerves remaining now; she sat without moving. Frank paced. He saw Mike and shook his head slightly; Mike withdrew into the crowd of people milling about in the hall. Clive was in a seat looking tense. Frank nodded to him and paced the length of the aisle, back to the defense table where Barbara had not stirred, up the aisle to the hall door again.

Judge Lundgren returned to begin his instructions. He explained the difference between aggravated murder, murder in the first degree, and manslaughter. He explained the jurors' duty, and then he told them they could not consider any of Ruth Brandywine's testimony. They could not consider anything that had happened to Lucas Kendricks before he showed up on the ledge on his wife's property.

Barbara felt the hollow spaces within her filling with ice water as he continued talking about what was irrelevant and what was not, what could be considered, what could not. There would follow other investigations, he said in explanation; they were already underway, but none of that concerned the case they were to decide.

After the jury was led out and the judge left the room, Barbara again felt Frank's hand on her shoulder, but where it had been warm and comforting before, now it simply felt heavy.

When Barbara stood up to leave the courtroom, Tony appeared at the side of the defense table. He held out his hand, and after a moment she accepted the handshake.

"Good work," he said. "After this is all over, Larry would like to get together with you. He'll be calling." Lawrence Ernst was the district attorney.

She nodded.

"Barbara, the other day you asked who it was I wanted to see crying and begging. Remember? Good question. It really shook me up."

He could still do it, she thought in wonder; he could still look raw, strangely hurt, yearning. Instantly, with the recognition of that look, there came the response; maybe she could soothe that hurt, make it not hurt. Maybe she could make him well. She felt her hands tighten and said nothing.

"We've had a lot of time to think, you and I both," he said in a low voice. "Let's have a drink and talk. Not now, not today; when this is all behind us. Will you do that, just have a drink and talk?"

"I . . . I don't know," she said. "Let's find out later."

"Good enough." He turned, then paused and faced her again, this time with a small grin that came and went very fast. "I don't want to see you beg and cry, Barbara. My God, you look just fine on the white horse charging the castle walls." He wheeled and walked away quickly.

THIRTY

FRANK LED THE way to a small room where they could wait. He surveyed it gloomily when they entered; there were gray vinyl-covered chairs, a lumpy couch, and two tables, one with a telephone. "Many, many hours of my life spent in here," he said. "We won't have to stay here long today though. They'll announce the lunch break, and after that we can go to a more comfortable waiting room at the office. That's the routine."

"Do you have to stay with me?" Nell asked. She stood in the center of the room, hugging her arms about herself as if chilled.

"Don't have to, but you blow out of town and the attorney's neck is at risk. Remember a time, the Wesley Sims trial, remember, Bobby?"

She shook her head, distracted, pacing the small room that seemed to have been designed to deepen the gloom of a defendant.

"Well, Sims was my client, up on a charge of sticky fingers in the till, or some damn thing. He sat in each chair in here, tried the couch, and pretty soon said he had to leave for a minute or two, be right back. So off he went. And he didn't come back, and didn't. Finally the jury said they were ready, and still no Sims. I had clerks everywhere looking for the idiot, and at the very last minute in he waltzes, drunk as a lord. Really tied one on in about two hours. So we went in, and I had to prop him up all the way. Had a clerk stay right

335

behind him to hold him upright in court. The jury said not guilty and the silly clerk moved his hand, and down went poor old Sims. Out cold. The foreman asked the judge if they could reconsider." He laughed, and Nell managed a little smile.

There was a tap on the door, and Barbara rushed to open it. She knew it was too soon for a verdict, but still, she thought ruefully, there she was running. Mike stood there looking hesitant. "Can I come in?"

Barbara turned to Nell. "This is up to you, who waits with you," she said. "Anyone you want, or no one. Whatever you want."

Nell shook herself. "I forgot," she said. "I simply forgot that I told Clive he could wait. And you, too," she added to Mike. "I'm glad to have someone."

"I'll round up Clive," Mike said, but still hesitated. "I have a lot of notes about the tapes. Would you rather not go into any of that while you're waiting, or with Clive here?"

She looked surprised. "You heard them?"

"I'm sorry," Barbara said. "I should have told you. No time. No time. Anyway, there were so many, and I had to find out if there was anything we could use, so we all listened to them. Mike's the only one who got through the whole bunch."

Nell moistened her lips. "I want to know what you learned," she said. "I'll listen to them after . . . later. But I want to know. And Clive's all right. I've been telling him pretty much everything as it is."

"And getting rotten advice," Barbara muttered too softly for Nell to hear.

Frank caught her words and added, "Doesn't he have a job or something? And you," he said to Mike, "why aren't you in school? Clive already lost one job over this mess, and the way you're going, you'll both lose your jobs, and then who buys the Wheaties?"

Mike grinned. "In your day you had to walk six miles

through the snow to get to work, and you never missed a day. I'll go find Clive. Saw him a couple of minutes ago."

Nell sat at the table finally. "What do you mean, Clive lost a job?"

"He didn't tell you? Didn't Lonnie? She's the one who informed me, and everyone else in Turner's Point, probably. Said he messed up his last couple of estimates as soon as he knew you were a free woman. Just couldn't keep his mind on his work." He smiled at her. "And here he is doing it again. I'd say the boy's getting serious." He went to the phone then and ordered coffee. When he hung up, he added, "As for Mike, he seems to check in at his work when he's got absolutely nothing else to do, as a last resort."

The difference was that Mike never stopped working, Barbara thought. She found his scribbles everywhere, formulas, equations, strange icons that meant nothing to her, pages and pages of them.

The men came back together just as a boy brought in a tray with coffee. Clive went directly to Nell; he took her hand and held it. Frank paid the delivery boy and passed the paper cups around.

"Now what?" Clive asked.

"Wait," Frank said. "That's all, just wait. Some folks play cards, or read books, or knit sweaters, anything to keep the hands busy. Some order coffee that's undrinkable just to have something to stir, something to do."

"Remember Peter Neuberger?" Barbara asked Frank; he nodded. "He made quilt pieces," Barbara said. "Beautiful things. He had his clients furnish a piece of material, if they would, and he embroidered the charge—embezzlement, grand larceny, breaking and entering, whatever it was—and their names on each piece. His wife put them together."

Frank laughed. "One of his clients stole it."

Nell withdrew her hand from Clive and held her cup. "I'm glad we have something else to do," she said. "I can't sew or knit."

"Neither can I," Barbara said. "Okay, Mike, that's your cue. Where are the tapes now, by the way?"

337

He had put them in his safe-deposit box that morning, he said. He took out his note pad and laid it on the table before him, and then didn't touch it again.

"He made most of the tapes during a couple of weeks," he started. "Whenever he remembered something, he added it, and that makes the chronology out of synch, but I think I've got it more or less in order. The other difficulty is that Lucas never really knew what they were up to, not the theoretical end of the work. He had a gift of seeing, and they needed that, but he didn't have the training to let him comprehend the significance of the project." He looked at Nell apologetically; she nodded agreement. She knew; she had always known that.

"Frobisher was into chaos theory before it had a name," Mike said. "And he had his own theory that he never stopped pursuing, apparently. He believed in consensual reality, and he believed that we are trained from infancy to see the same world that our parents see, that almost everyone around us sees. He thought that wasn't the only way the world could be perceived."

Clive made an impatient sound and Mike said to him, "Did you know that babies make every known human sound in their babbling? The impossible French vowels, seventeen different clicks, the multi-tones of the Chinese, you name it. Babies produce them all, and they drop any that don't get reinforced. Extinction, it's called. They repeat the sounds they hear and lose the others, including some that can't be learned as an adult. Frobisher believed vision is exactly like that. And he believed he could retrain good subjects to see the world the way it really is, as a mathematical network that is altogether different, more complex and yet in some ways simpler than the one we see. That was his goal. Lucas was his means of achieving it."

"Jesus!" Clive said. "He was a nut case."

Mike grinned and spread his hands. "Maybe. From the beginning of history, as well as what we can decipher from the clues from prehistory, there have been those who claim that the universe is a mathematical formulation, that if we

338

can invent the right tools we can solve the problem. Mystics have described such a world; artists have painted it. It appears in poetry from the beginning of time." He shrugged. "Could be they're all nuts, as far as that goes."

Clive's expression changed subtly; he had looked angry and disgusted. Now he looked disbelieving. "You buy that, don't you?"

Mike's eyes seemed to unfocus; a curious, dreamy look crossed his face, and he said almost gently, "The world I'm talking about wouldn't be a lesser one, you know. There is great beauty in the perfect solution, elegance in an irrefutable proof, grandeur in a demonstrated truth. It would not be a lesser world, just different." He blinked, as if the inner vision had failed; his expression of wistful yearning became a faint grin of self-mockery. "The ultimate golden carrot: utopia. Anyway, Frobisher had the arrogance of almost knowing, and that's the worst kind."

Barbara found herself nodding at the phrase. The arrogance of almost knowing. It described those who harbored a doubt that had to be buried and reburied endlessly; they had to prove how right they were again and again. Those with real knowledge lost the arrogance and the need to prove anything.

Before Mike could go on, there was a knock on the door; the court clerk opened it and beckoned to Barbara. The clerk was a handsome, middle-aged woman with kind brown eyes and crinkly laugh lines. "Chambers," she said.

Judge Lundgren and Tony were waiting for her in the judge's chambers. Court would not reconvene, Lundgren said. They were free to go to lunch, and they should leave numbers where they could be reached after two. If no verdict had come in yet, court would reconvene at five-thirty. They were not to be more than fifteen minutes away from the courthouse until that time.

He looked tired; his manner was cold and distant, very formal, very proper. Today there was no offer of coffee in fine china cups, no pseudo-hospitality. He thanked them and dismissed them as soon as he had delivered his message.

"Well," Barbara said, outside his door. "That's it, just well."

"Right," Tony said with a grin. "His wife took off for Maui over the weekend and he got stuck here in the snow and freezing rain. I'd say the old boy's pissed."

"And blames us," Barbara said glumly.

"Oh, no doubt. I was willing to get on with it, you know."

"To hell with it," she said darkly. "Let him slosh through the slush like the rest of us." She strode away with her head high. But she could hear Tony's chuckle all the way to the large double doors that opened to the public areas of the courthouse.

They walked the few blocks to The Electric Station, a restaurant with refitted railroad cars used as dining rooms. No one else was in the section where their table was reserved; the waiter saw them seated, then vanished, to return very quickly with a pot of coffee and menus, which he left at Frank's elbow. Then he was gone again. Smooth, Barbara thought, nodding her gratitude to her father. Frank poured coffee, handed out the cups, and said to Mike, "You were saying?"

"I was," Mike said. "So there was Frobisher and his assistant doing his research, publishing a paper now and then, and Schumaker read one of the papers and got interested. That's when they took off for Colorado. According to Lucas, Schumaker had enough clout to see to it that Frobisher got a hefty raise, and that he was relieved of teaching duties in order to do his research. Later, he did the same thing for Brandywine, to get her to join them. Could be. Schumaker's a real draw for the school, endowment money, gifts, backing by the elite of the West, stuff like that. So they were set up, and for the next few years they continued the work, but now Schumaker was a coauthor of papers, and Herbert Margolis was brought in to do the computer end of the work. But things were going sour, or maybe the end of the road just kept receding. Whatever it was, Schumaker was getting bored with the whole project, and Frobisher was running scared that his funds would vanish. That's when Lucas took off and came home. None of the promises were being kept. He was no closer to a degree than he ever had been, and he was pretty disillusioned. He goes into some detail about the suggestions he made to get the work on the right track again, and apparently they decided to try one of them—to use younger people. They had gone to freshmen, and even a few high school students, but it seems they kept running into the same dead end, no matter what they did."

Nell was watching him as if entranced; her eyes were wide and unblinking, she was unmoving. Now she said, "That's when they called him, they told him they were bringing in the psychiatrist, Brandywine. They needed him to demonstrate what they were doing. They still needed him."

Mike drained his coffee cup and set it down, then moved it around and around in his saucer. He watched it when he spoke again. "They promised him the degree if he'd just write a paper, anything at all to show the committee, and agree to demonstrate what they doing for the new team member, Brandywine. That's when he started to make the tapes; he knew it was a lie this time, and he planned to leave, but he agreed to do the one demonstration first, and she got him. After that one time he never mentioned leaving again. And some days, he says on the tapes, he had no memory from the time he entered the lab until he was back in his apartment that night. No memories of anything that happened. But they were excited, and now they were rushing into the idea of using young teenagers, thirteen, fourteen at the oldest."

He was turning the cup around and around. Barbara reached out and moved it; at the same moment, Frank touched Nell on the arm, then shook her arm slightly. She jumped as if awakened from a dream.

"Let's order some food," Frank said briskly. He handed out the menus. He waved the waiter over and began asking about the various seafood entrees and making suggestions to

341

the rest of them, things he knew were excellent. For the moment they were just like any other group of people who had leisure time, who could stretch out the lunch hour to any length they chose.

The waiter came back with hot rolls and butter, another pot of coffee, and now the talk was only about food. The waiter had become supremely efficient; he served them swiftly, gave the table a professional glance, then left them alone. For a time they were all silent as they ate their lunches, all but Nell, who only played with the salad before her.

Barbara said, "You might as well go on with it." She put her fork down and rested her chin in her hands. Nell nodded and put her fork down also, and made no further pretense at eating.

Mike buttered another roll first and took a bite. "Okay. I'll fast forward a bit. This is still September, remember. Things were moving along at a pretty good clip, apparently, but then there was some trouble. Two of the kids they had tested, and kept testing, went joyriding in a stolen car and ran off a mountain road. One dead, one paralyzed from the neck down. Called a simple accident, but it panicked our crew. It gets a bit hazy here, but I think another kid went insane, and that's when the whole project was killed, the first week of October."

Nell picked up her water; her hand was shaking so hard the ice rattled in the glass. She stared at it and made a deliberate effort to hold it steady enough to drink, and then set it down too hard. She was ghostly pale. Clive put his arm over the back of her chair and rested his hand on her shoulder.

"Go on," she whispered.

"Yes. Well, Frobisher wouldn't give it up. They had fights and he said he'd finish alone, get his own subjects, and handle everything by himself. Schumaker said not at the school, their reputations were at risk, so Frobisher decided to continue at his house. He began to round up kids from the streets, nameless boys who could use five or ten dollars. Lucas couldn't do it, whatever it was, any longer; Brandywine

342

had left a suggestion apparently that he would not allow himself to be tested again. But he helped Frobisher set things up, run the computer program, do whatever was required as an assistant."

His voice was very low, and he spoke more slowly as he went now. "They were into late October. Lucas could see what was going on in Frobisher's house, and he was convinced that modifications they had made were working, but he couldn't seem to focus on them. Also, he was having wild dreams that scared him. Then, in November, Frobisher found a new kid, a Chicano whose name Lucas didn't know, but he called him the laughing boy. And whatever was going on was working with this boy. Frobisher was wild with excitement because the boy wasn't being hypnotized, and it was still working. He had found the way around the dead end that had stopped him for years."

The waiter came back then and asked with near anguish if anything was wrong with the food. Would they like to order something else? Frank reassured him that it wasn't the food. "They're all dieting," he said. "Just more coffee." They remained silent until he had cleared the table and departed.

Mike looked at his watch; it was one-thirty. "Okay," he said, and went on briskly. "That last day. Frobisher called Lucas; he sounded desperate and said come right now. Lucas got in his car and headed out for his house, but he says that he was hallucinating all the way. He kept hearing the laughing boy, laughing, talking to him. The boy said Frobisher was crazy, trying to kill him. He hid some disks and said he had to try to calm Frobisher down. When Lucas went into the house, Frobisher had the gun, the boy was dead, and they were both cut up and bloody. Frobisher shot at him, and then Margolis arrived and Frobisher killed himself. Brandywine was there by then. Margolis and Brandywine set the stage to make it look like the boy had shot Frobisher, and they hustled Lucas out of there and hid him, and from then until he woke up last June he had no memories of himself as Lucas Kendricks."

Nell made a muffled sound and ducked her head quickly and kept it lowered.

Clive looked bewildered. "Why would they do that?" he demanded. "It doesn't make any sense to me."

"To hide the fact that there was research going on, or had been, that led to insanity, or even murder, maybe," Barbara said sharply. "I'm just surprised that the police bought it."

Frank nodded thoughtfully. "Not so surprising. It could have been a combination of things, the big one being Schumaker. If he said Frobisher had a yen for boys, and there would be a terrible scandal at the school if anything of that sort came out, that would have been distracting, I suspect. Small, expensive private school like that probably brought in lots of big bucks that you wouldn't want to scare off. And since they were both dead, Frobisher and the boy, it probably didn't make much difference to the cops who pulled the trigger. Two gays out of the picture; let them all shoot each other. I've heard more or less that kind of statement often enough to believe I might have heard it back there."

Remembering the night that Clive had voiced pretty much the same sentiments, Barbara nodded.

Frank took the bill and fished out his credit card. When Clive and Mike offered to share it, he shook his head. "Don't mind at all," he said. "But I prefer to buy food that people actually eat." Then it was time to walk to his office. The jury would be back at work in the deliberation room.

It was a pleasantly cool afternoon; the sun appeared, vanished behind clouds, appeared again. As soon as it came from behind the clouds the temperature rose by several degrees; when it was hidden, the temperature plummeted. Clive and Nell walked ahead of the others, talking in low voices. She looked almost childlike beside the large man.

"What did Lucas say about the girl in the woods?" Barbara asked Mike, glad that he had stopped when he did. Nell didn't need any more of this today. Barbara knew that Lucas had sat under the trees in the forest and had talked into a tape recorder; it was one of the images that had haunted her dreams last night, that aching, hungry, tired man speaking in the silent woods, alone in the black forest.

"He said he left her at the washed-out section. He started to go back with her, but he was sure that Brandywine would be waiting on the highway somewhere for him, so he worked at turning the car around and gave her the key, and he started to hike home. She was taking pictures, he said."

Mike took her arm and slowed her pace a bit more, giving Nell and Clive more distance. "He was pretty bonkers toward the end," he said softly. "Second or third night, he stopped making any sense whatever. You'll have to hear it yourself. I'm not so sure she should." He nodded toward Nell.

"Eventually she'll have to decide," Barbara said. It occurred to her that she could work up a good case of jealousy if she put her mind to it; every man who met Nell seemed to want to protect her sooner or later. She shrugged the thought away, and said, "You mentioned disks. That the laughing boy said he was hiding disks. Was there more about that?"

Mike looked troubled. "What he actually said was that the boy showed him where he hid the disks in the barn. How, I don't know. Or even if it's true. But that's what he said."

Barbara shivered, although at the moment the sun was shining brilliantly and the temperature had risen again. "All this gives me the creeps," she muttered, and told Mike what Bailey had reported about the people who now lived in Frobisher's house. Their little boy had seen Lucas leave the barn carrying a bag.

"Damn, but that makes more sense than having Brandywine and crew search for the tapes. They could claim he was a raving madman, and anyone listening probably would agree. But Frobisher's disks!"

"Yeah, but where are they?"

He scowled at the sidewalk. Frank had been listening silently. Now he said, "Maybe Nell left them in the same place they've been all along."

Barbara looked up. Nell and Clive had come to a stop outside the office building, waiting for them. When they drew near enough, Barbara asked, "Nell, is there anything else in that secret hiding place? Where you found the tapes?"

She shook her head. "I'm sure not. I reached in and felt around." Her eyes widened then and she said quickly, "There were some disks, computer disks. I forgot about them. They must still be at the house. I just wasn't interested in them, only in the tapes." She looked from Barbara to Mike, back to Barbara again. "Do you want them? I can get them tonight when—" She suddenly paled and looked as if she might faint, as if she remembered again at that moment that she might not be allowed to go home that night, or for many nights.

Barbara took her hand. "Hang in there, kid. Just hang on. But, yes, we should round them up. How about if one of us goes to pick them up? Where are they?"

"I don't know. I forgot all about them. Maybe Tawna picked them up when she picked up the tapes. I don't know."

"I'll go have a look for them," Mike said. There was a strong undercurrent of excitement in his voice, in his expression. When Barbara started to object, he said quickly, "You can't go, and Frank should hang around with you, and Clive's place is with her. Doesn't leave much, does it? I'll go. Will I need a key?" he asked Nell. "Is your house locked up, I hope."

Nell found her keys and handed him the one to the house.

"You go on up," Barbara said to Frank. "I'll come in just a minute."

Frank took Nell and Clive into the building, and she turned to Mike. "Listen, we don't have a clue about what's on those disks, but something big, or something Brandywine and her crew think is big. You'd better make copies of everything and stash them away in the safe-deposit box." She looked at her watch and groaned. "There isn't time for that today, is there? Do you have a safe place? Maybe at the university? Somewhere?"

"Don't worry," he said. "I'll think of something. And I'll

make copies before I come back. See you later." He kissed her lightly and trotted off.

She started to call to him, to say something, but instead, she watched him until he rounded the corner, remembering the day she had met him, and he had been wearing his jogging clothes. How comfortable he had looked in them, how comfortable he had been with her from that first moment. She realized that what she had started to call after him was, *Be careful.* She bit her lip in exasperation with herself and entered the building to join her client in what she knew would be one of the longest afternoons of her life. It was twenty minutes after two.

THIRTY-ONE

THE LOUNGE WAS large and bright, with big windows and good oak furniture, book cases, a television. A coffee maker was on a side table. Frank made coffee. Barbara looked over an assortment of magazines, everything from *Time* to *Architectural Digest* to the *New England Journal of Medicine*. There were magazines on high fashion, home decorating, gardening . . . something for everyone; people awaiting verdicts ranged across the board in taste, wealth, interests. There was a case with a chess game, checkers, cards. . . . She turned away from them all and went to the window to watch people entering and leaving a café across the street. Frank left the lounge, returned, sat down, got up and left, only to repeat the sequence again and again. Nell held a magazine; whenever she felt anyone's glance on her, she turned a page, but she saw nothing. Clive found an interesting article. He tried to show a photograph to Nell, who smiled politely at him and looked at the picture; she could not have said what it was.

At four forty-five John and Amy Kendricks rushed in; the roads were plowed out, mountain passes open, traffic moving again. Barbara and Frank left the lounge to the family.

"What the devil are they doing?" she muttered, stalking through the corridor to his office, maintained for his infrequent days in town.

"They're hung," he said grimly. "Got the word from Joyce." She was the court recorder who always knew everything happening at the courthouse.

"Jesus," Barbara said.

"Could be worse," he said.

"Right." Worse would be the verdict, guilty as charged.

Mike should be on his way back with the disks, she was thinking. Back in town by five-thirty. He knew they had to be in court again by five-thirty. But he would need time to copy the disks and put the originals in a safe place. She should have told him to come here to the office, use the office safe overnight. Would he think of that? Maybe he would call here when he got back in town, about five-thirty? Six? She found that she couldn't focus on the problem. How many were there? How long would it take to copy them? Whose equipment would he use? His own, no doubt; he would go home, then, not go to court. She had to give it up.

There was a soft tap on the door. Frank opened it to one of the clerks standing in the hall, looking puzzled. He was Stevie Postel; he had been with the firm as long as Barbara could remember, a small, gray-faced man with big dark eyes magnified to raccoon proportions by thick eyeglasses.

"There's someone wanting to see either one of you," he said. "Ruth Brandywine. Isn't she the one whose toes you toasted in court?"

"For God's sake!" Barbara exclaimed. "Not now!"

348

"Wait a minute," Frank said. "Maybe I should see what's on her mind if you'd rather not."

Barbara looked at her watch again. Five after five. "Dad, we have ten minutes at the most. Sure, let's have a go at her. Ten minutes' worth. I thought she'd hop on her broomstick and head back to Colorado. Okay, Stevie. In here."

No matter what else, the lady had good taste in clothes, Barbara had to admit when Ruth Brandywine entered the office. Today she was wearing a jade-green velvet suit with a creamy silk blouse. Frank was standing behind his desk, Barbara at the window. Frank nodded toward a chair opposite his.

"Please," he said. "What can we do for you?"

She ignored him and the chair, and looked at Barbara. "I have to talk to you. I know this isn't the time, but I was afraid you would refuse a phone call, so I came in person. After court adjourns, will you meet me then?"

"Talk about what?" Barbara asked bluntly, with no more show of manners than Brandywine was displaying.

"The disks. The research. You're in over your head, and you have no idea of the danger. Will you meet me?"

Slowly Barbara nodded. "Are you staying in town?"

"Yes. At the Hilton."

"Leave your room number," Barbara said. "When we're through today, I'll give you a call. We'll find a neutral place, not in your room, not here."

"That's fine." She drew out a card from her purse and jotted down her number. "I'll go back and be in my room until I hear from you." She handed the card to Barbara, then turned and left without another word.

Snow Queen, Barbara thought distantly. Even the card felt cold; it seemed to send a chill through her hand, up her arm.

"Well, well," her father murmured. "Having Roy White-horse tell her he had disks paid off, I'd say. What the devil does she want?"

"Would you buy a used car from that lady?" Barbara asked. "Time to head out, I guess. You want to explain to them what a hung jury means? Damn, this could go on for days!"

He patted her arm and went out ahead of her. In the lounge, as they all put on their coats, he said, "The judge could accept that the jurors aren't going to be able to agree and it all ends now. Or he could sequester them and make them continue tomorrow. Not a thing anyone can do at this point, except the judge."

"If they are hung, what does that mean for Nell?" Clive asked. He looked almost as haggard as Nell; his voice was dispirited.

"Well, the district attorney could drop the charges and it's really finished, or he could start all over and try the case again, hoping to do a better job next time. That's in his hands."

"Oh, God," Clive said in despair. He looked at Barbara. "Isn't it a good sign, that they're having trouble deciding? I think that's a good sign."

She started to answer, but her father's voice stopped her. "Sure it's a good sign. One of the best. Come along now, time to be on the way. You all right, honey?" He looked closely at Nell, who nodded silently. "Good, good. Here we go then."

Amy Kendricks took Nell's arm, and they left the offices and went back to the courthouse. It had grown dark; street lights and traffic lights, automobile headlights and taillights were like Christmas ornaments. Some of the windows they passed already had Christmas decorations; with a start, Barbara remembered that Thursday was Thanksgiving. It was time for decorations and celebrations.

Judge Lundgren was frostier than ever; he looked martyred when he said the jury would be sequestered to resume their deliberation at nine-thirty in the morning.

Before Nell left with Clive and her in-laws, Barbara drew Amy Kendricks aside. "See if you can get her to eat something. I don't think she has all day. Maybe you could get Doc to prescribe a sleeping pill for tonight. She needs food and rest."

Amy nodded; her eyes were filled with tears. "That poor child," she said softly. "Our poor little child. Thanks, Barbara. We'll bring her back in the morning. Thank you."

And Goddamn it! Barbara thought with a flash of anger; she, Barbara, was doing it too. Protecting Nell.

"No answer," Barbara said slamming down the telephone in the courthouse lobby. "Where is that son of a bitch?" It was almost six; Mike should have put in his appearance by now. "Look," she said to Frank, "you call Brandywine and set up something for six-thirty. In the Hilton, the lounge there. Okay? I'll go out to Mike's house and leave him a note to meet us there when he gets back. I don't know what else we can do."

"Stew, worry, fret, curse, stamp our feet, cast the yarrow stalks, put out an APB, hire a bloodhound. . . ." Frank stopped at the look of wrath on her face. "Calm down, Bobby. You're tighter than a pregnant sow's belly at term. Go on and leave your note. See you at the Hilton." He waved her away and started to walk.

She knew it was futile to speculate, but her mind refused to stop. Accidents, traffic snarls, out of gas. She gritted her teeth. Out of gas, caught up in running the disks on his computer, or someone's computer, involved in copying them. . . . His house was dark and empty. She turned on the light in the living room, walked past the garish rattan sofas, the cushions scattered on the floor, glanced in the bedroom, where the bed was neatly made, and went on to the kitchen, where all the dishes were washed and put away. He was neat, neater than she was. Finally she sat at the table to scrawl the note. She propped it up there and left.

Ruth Brandywine and Frank were at a window table when Barbara entered the lounge. Frank had a scotch and soda, she saw with surprise. Ruth Brandywine had mineral water. Frank stood up and held a chair, questions in his eyes; she shook her head and sat down. The lounge was busy; at the far end a piano was going; waitresses were scurrying, people laughing, talking too loudly. Just right, Barbara decided. When the waitress paused in midflight, she ordered a bloody mary. She really wanted a good stiff straight bourbon, or something equally to the point, but she knew that would be a mistake. Frank had said it; she was too uptight. A quick surge of alcohol might act like a pinprick; she suppressed a giggle at an image of dozens of squealing piglets tumbling out.

Ruth Brandywine was surveying her as if she were a specimen, she realized. No one spoke until Barbara's drink was placed on the table and the waitress had flown away again. The piano started a jazzy Scott Joplin. The bloody mary was just peppery enough.

"Did that man lie about the disks?" Ruth Brandywine asked then. "How did anyone know about disks?"

"I guess you're kidding," Barbara said. "I'll give you the benefit of the doubt, anyway."

Ruth Brandywine shrugged. "You're right." She gazed out the window at the moving lights of the city. "I really did treat Lucas Kendricks. He was mad, paranoid schizophrenia; when he wasn't tranquilized and maintained in that state, he was out of control. A danger to himself and others, apparently, although that was not clear at the time. It was my treatment or institutional care. No alternatives would have sufficed."

She looked at Barbara. Her black eyes reflected the colored lights of the lounge like bits of polished onyx. "It's really immaterial whether you believe me. Nothing can be proven at this late date. I just wanted to get that in. I had nothing whatever to do with his death, nor did any agents of mine. That needs to be stated, also. If I had wanted him dead, don't you think that over the years many opportunities existed to accomplish that? I did not want him dead at any time." She sipped her mineral water and narrowed her eyes in thought. "It seems very clear to me that his wife shot him. After killing that poor girl in the woods, he must have appeared totally out of control to his wife, and perhaps he *was* totally out of control. That surprised me, I admit,

352

because I fully believed that his violence was directed inward, not toward another person. But that's beside the point now. I really don't care about any of that. I understand that you have a job to do, to protect your client. I can sympathize. However, Lucas took something that did not belong to him, and it is imperative that I recover that material."

"You said disks," Barbara murmured. She knew it was irrational to be as angry as she felt; she had stated very nearly the same thing to herself, to her father: She had a job to do, to protect Nell from the heavyweight apparatus of the state. It sounded different when this woman said it.

"Yes, disks. Computer disks. Either you know about them and told that man to mention them in order to lure me here, or you made a lucky guess. I don't believe in lucky guesses."

Barbara glanced at her watch and bit back a curse that formed. Instead, she looked at Ruth Brandywine coldly. "Exactly what do you want? We're simple folk here. You have to spell it out for us. If I find such disks you want me to hand them over, help you get your name in neon lights, win a prize, get on the cover of *Time*? What do you want? And why do you think I give a damn?"

A wintry smile crossed Ruth Brandywine's face and vanished again. "You should not care any more than I should care about you and your problems except for the fact that our fates have put us in a confrontation at this intersection, and neither of us can move until we satisfy certain conditions." She studied Barbara openly and frankly for a minute, then said, "You are a very clever young woman with a great gift for discerning the truth. Body language, the ways in which eyes shift when a lie is being told, the odors given off by a person in stress, something else. Whatever it is you perceive you probably are unaware of, but you believe in your intuitive sense of truth, or lying, as the case might be. I know," she said, and the icy smile appeared again, just as fleetingly as before. "Look at me now, Barbara Holloway, and know that I am telling you the truth. I do not want the disks for myself. I would refuse to keep them longer than it would

353

take to destroy them. If you produced them this instant, I would take them to the parking lot and set fire to them. I would do it here at this table, except for the fact that I do not relish the thought of another cross-examination concerning my motives."

Looking at her in the silence that followed, Barbara thought simply, *Yes*. She was startled when her father made a strangled sound and leaned forward at the small table to demand, "What the hell's on those disks? What were you people up to?"

"They," Ruth Brandywine said firmly. "What were they up to?" She finished her mineral water and made water rings on the table, overlapping them again and again. "There's a famous experiment in which the subjects are given eyeglasses that invert the world they see. Have you read about it?" She didn't look up from her rings within rings to see how they reacted. "It's strange, but within forty-eight hours people adapt to existing in a world that's completely upside down. Nothing changes for them after the initial period of adjustment. No one on the outside can tell what they see, because they behave normally. When the experiment ends and they stop using the inversion spectacles, there is another period of adjustment, like the first. They have to relearn how to see the world the way the rest of us see it." Now she looked up at Frank, then Barbara. "I wish I knew how much you have already learned."

"More than you've told us so far," Barbara said evenly.

Ruth Brandywine hesitated only a moment, then said, "Good. Emil was trying to train people to see the world in a particular way, and the images he put together to be run on a computer were designed to help toward that end." She spoke deliberately, as if choosing each word, deciding as she went how much to say.

"And what difference would that make to you, me, anyone other than the person being experimented on?" Frank demanded. "So people see the world upside down, or crossways, or in black and white. So what?"

She looked old and bitter suddenly; the fire in her eyes

354

seemed dampened so that they became black holes that reflected nothing. "I wish I knew," she said in a low, intense voice. "I wish I knew." She raised her glass and appeared surprised to find it empty. "I'll have that drink now, if you can get the waitress over."

She ordered a double Jack Daniels on the rocks. Barbara shook her head, as did her father. Barbara's drink was watery with melted ice; she had hardly touched it, after all. While they waited, Ruth Brandywine said, "Let me tell you about another classic experiment. There is a hallucinogenic plant in Peru that the Indians use to concoct a potent drink that gives them hallucinations that involve black panthers, leopards, flying snakes, the typical images that keep turning up in their art. Someone began to wonder what outsiders would see if they ingested this drug, and they tried it on naïve North American students, people who knew nothing about it and its effects and the images. They saw black panthers, leopards, flying snakes." The waitress brought her drink; after she was gone again, Ruth Brandywine lifted the glass and said, "Many hypotheses have been suggested, but no explanation that satisfies has come yet. Cheers." She drank.

"You can't make me believe that just looking at images on a computer monitor can have any lasting effect," Frank said harshly. "What are you leaving out?"

"You're partly right," she said after a moment. "There was no effect whatever with me. Emil was unaffected, as were Walter and Herbert. But Lucas Kendricks became psychotic, and at least three other boys did also. There's no way to predict who will be affected, and to what extent, by the training sequence of those disks. And that's why we, not just I, but also Walter and Herbert, want them absolutely and totally destroyed without ever being run again. I don't know what all is on them. No one does, I suspect. They were Emil's work, of course, and he continued to modify them right up to the end. But they are potentially dangerous to anyone who tries to run them."

Frank was not even trying to mask his disbelief. "We've got a client on trial for murder. Do you honestly think that we'd turn over anything that might possibly be of help? Or burn them unseen? Dr. Brandywine, I ask you again, what are you leaving out?"

"No, I don't believe that," she said softly. "But consider, Mr. Holloway. Worldwide—nationality aside, religion aside, belief systems aside—the same images turn up in the art of children. The same images turn up in the art of psychopaths. Would you see snakes and large cats under the influence of that Peruvian drug? Probably. We have the same latent images in our psyches, archetypes, if you prefer, the same pattern of behavior under certain conditions, all of us share them, and there's something in Emil's work that is psychoactive, that triggers behavior that is indistinguishable from paranoid schizophrenia. But you are correct, not everyone is influenced. If you find the disks, Mr. Holloway, if you decide to investigate them more thoroughly, let me suggest that you be the one to view them. Not her," she said, indicating Barbara. "But you. You see, Mr. Holloway, you know what you believe and you are less likely to suffer consequences. If they affect you at all, you probably will simply suffer a bit of amnesia, the way Lucas did, and the other boys, until I hypnotized them to find out what they were experiencing, why they were going mad. That was why they asked me to participate in the studies, to find out what was happening in the heads of those boys. That was my only part in the project. What I told them put an end to the research, all but Emil's. I stopped it, Mr. Holloway, just as soon as I fully realized how dangerous it was. But I predict that you will see only a series of beautiful pictures, and the world has enough beautiful pictures, it doesn't need these. Destroy the disks, Mr. Holloway. Look at them and then burn them. Or give them to me and watch me burn them."

Her voice was low, but she had lost the hard control she had shown earlier; she spoke with a passion that was unmistakable, a passion that demanded belief. Abruptly she stood up and nodded, then left them at the table.

"I'll be damned," Frank said fervently. "What the hell was that all about?"

Barbara pushed her glass back. "Dad, I'm scared. Where's Mike with those disks? I'm going back to his house, see if he's come home yet."

"Me too, I guess," her father said. "Murk, murk! By God, I hate murk!"

At first Barbara thought he had returned, but when they entered the house she realized the light was from the lamp she had left on. Her note was still on the table; the house was empty. Wordlessly she searched her purse for her address book and then called his office at the university. After twelve rings she hung up.

"Okay, sit down while I make a call or two," Frank said. She went to the kitchen, where she sat at the table staring at her note, listening to his voice in the living room. When he finished and said, "Come on," she followed him out of the house silently. He drove them to a restaurant and explained, just as if she hadn't heard: "I told Billy I'd call back in half an hour, see if he knows anything, and give him the number where we'll be for the next couple of hours. That damn fool's out of gas somewhere, that's all. He'd think nothing of striking out on foot, just leaving the car wherever he happened to go dry."

In the restaurant, after he checked in with Billy Whitecomb at the sheriff's office, he ordered steaks for both of them. She still had not said a word.

"Honey," Frank said, "he's a big boy. He's been around. He can take care of himself."

She nodded. "We shouldn't have let him go get the disks," she said at last. "I shouldn't have talked about the case with him, included him in any part of it."

"Ah, Bobby, don't start the should have, shouldn't have loop. It doesn't go anywhere and you just get tired. You trusted him, you still trust him, and so do I. Don't beat yourself over the head about it."

"You don't understand," she said fiercely. "He's a mathematician, like Frobisher and Shumaker. Do you think he can resist seeing what's on those disks?" In her head she heard

357

the infectious laughter of Lucas Kendricks, the way she had heard it on his tape, the way Nell had described it the last time she saw him. She blinked hard. Not Mike, she wanted to cry out. Not him.

Frank was called to the telephone a few minutes later and came back to report that there was nothing to report yet. Mike had not been admitted to any local hospital; he wasn't in the slammer. Nothing.

"I told Billy we're going home," he said. He eyed her steak morosely. "I don't like to pay for food that gets left on the plate. Come on, I'll make you an omelette or something."

"You don't have to baby me," she said sharply.

He chuckled. "Honey, don't you know I just want to? Come on, let's get moving."

He made a detour to drive past Mike's house. He had turned off the lamp on their way out; it was still dark.

THIRTY-TWO

DRIVING, FRANK ASKED, "How much of what the lady shrink said do you suppose is anywhere near the broad general truth that we all revere as such?"

Barbara had to pull herself back from a void. "Some of it." She surprised herself then by adding, "A lot of it, actually. Even it if is pretty self-serving. I guess the truth can be self-serving at times."

"Um. She's one scary lady. One hell of a scary lady."

He passed a truck. He was a good driver. When Barbara

was a child they had driven hundreds, thousands, of miles during summer vacations. She remembered how bad a driver her mother had been. They always joked about it: She couldn't drive and talk at the same time, or drive and listen to others talking. Frank had not allowed her to drive very often when he was in the car. He joked about that, too, said he was too susceptible to nervous breakdowns to deliberately put himself in harm's way.

Now, having maneuvered around the truck and pulled away from it, he said, "I think she was leveling about a few things, anyway. One of them just could be that the disks should be burned. Will you promise blind, honey?"

"You know I won't."

"Yes, I guess I do. Okay, let's compromise. If those disks turn up, let's do it her way, let me have a peep at them first. Deal?"

"First after Mike," she said bitterly. "Let's decide if they turn up." She glanced at his profile, dimly red in the lights from the dashboard. "She said you would be safe because you know what you believe. Do you?"

"Tough question, honey. Real tough. Maybe she sees a realist in me, more than in you. Over the years I've lowered my expectations so often that I finally reached a level where I got from people pretty much what I expected, and that's the end of illusion and disappointment, maybe the end of childhood. Pragmatism, realism, whatever it is, maybe that's what she sensed in me."

Suspecting that she would not get more than that from him, she did not persist. But it was more than that, she was certain. He did know who he was, what he believed, and he was not afraid. That made the difference. He was not afraid. When her mother had been dying, he had provided the strength she needed to die with courage and even grace. Over the years Barbara had thought of him as simply lethargic or even fatalistic in his acceptance of what was happening at any moment, but now she thought it was not just like that. It was more as if he was able to say and believe, that was last year, or yesterday, or an hour ago, and this is

359

now. She remembered what he had said about lowering his expectations, but that was not just right either. He had an acceptance of people that she lacked; their goodness, their evil, whatever he saw in them did not surprise him. He was unsurprised by Mike's betrayal.

Barbara realized that she had come to view it as betrayal; the terror had subsided, leaving a dull ache in some part of her that was so deep that she didn't know if it had a name, if it could be removed and examined. Not the heart, she felt certain; the heart had become an organ that could be seen with instruments as it pumped, that could be dissected and examined for the fatal flaw when it ceased. The pain she was feeling would not show up with the instruments of science, she knew. What then? The soul? The soul, she thought, exactly that. She felt certain that Mike had taken the disks to a friend's house, or to his office, someplace where he had run through them all and realized that he needed time alone with them in order to understand the work, to follow it step by step.

Also, she told herself, he would be in no more danger than Brandywine or Schumaker. Young, naïve people might be at risk, but not scientists or mathematicians, or elderly lawyers. No, Mike would be fine, happily at work. When he was finished, when he had made it his own in the realest sense, then he would show up again with his engaging smile. And then? She could not say what then. Her previous reactions to betrayal had been to immerse herself so deeply in work, or school, or something, that she had no time to spend on disaster; or else to run away.

She knew she was to blame. She should not have sent him, used him, and again it came back to that, people using people for their own purposes. The people in Colorado using naïve boys, using Lucas, using one another. She was as guilty as any of them. She had been willing to use Mike, to use Clive with her attempt to disprove that the forest ranger could have seen what he claimed. And *he*, the ranger, had tried to use circumstances that could have had deadly results. That still could have them. But that was how it worked when you used people, she went on inexorably; the consequences were of no importance. She had even used Ruth Brandywine, not with any real hope of changing the outcome of the trial, but rather to raise such clouds of dust that no one would be able to see clearly. She had tried to manipulate the jury, the judge, the spectators, Tony, everyone, because she had decided that her ends were worthy.

She felt a great bitterness thinking again about Ruth Brandywine's dismissal of the mutilation and death of the girl in the woods, her dismissal of Nell and her children, of Lucas and his ruined life, his death. Brandywine had said she, Barbara, had a gift for discerning the truth. She could have laughed at that.

She gazed straight ahead; lights appeared, drew even, vanished; red lights appeared, were passed, vanished. Truth, she was thinking; she had believed Nell Kendricks was telling the truth. She had said that to her father, who accepted that Nell had shot and killed her husband. She had believed Nell was innocent. Her intuitive self had believed until her rational self had started the "Yes, but" routine and killed the belief.

They were driving along the winding shoreline of the reservoir. The surface of the water was black, as if a hole had opened there and the little bit of world bounded by its outline had dropped into it. She rejected that image immediately. It was like the black center of a Mandelbrot set, she thought then. If you turned the magnifying glass to any segment of the border there would be the complexity, the mystery, the ever-expanding patterns that were unique and were also nearly like all the other patterns that might emerge at different places. She and her father were segments of one of the patterns, swirling about each other, touching, withdrawing, flying off in opposite directions, returning. And at Turner's Point there would be a hundred, two hundred other similar patterns; people in the houses that rode the ridge above the point generated their own similar yet different patterns. All held together, and kept separate by invisible links.

361

The links that bound them were the same that had bound humans from the beginning of time: love, hatred, jealousy, greed. . . . Nothing changed even while everything was in the midst of change.

She had flown out of this set, determined never to return, but the pull back was stronger than the pull away, and she had come home, just as Lucas had. Suddenly she realized with startling clarity that Judge Lundgren had been mostly right in limiting the scope of the trial. She had not really thought that hired detectives would gun down a man, but if she renounced that as a possibility, she had to eliminate Brandywine and her colleagues as suspects in the death of Lucas Kendricks. With this admission, she accepted that the pendulum had swung again; she had returned to her original belief that Nell was innocent. Something in Nell's recounting of her story had made Barbara say, *I believe*, even though she had to admit later that the impossibilities had outweighed the probable truth. Her rational self had silenced the irrational believer, and now she could curse herself for offering up Brandywine and company, for casting suspicions that she, Barbara, did not entertain instead of trying to find a plausible alternative.

But even if the judge had been right in saying no, he also had pulled the sides of the box too close. This particular box had to include the death of that poor girl in the woods. Janet Moseley belonged inside the box. Janet Moseley was not irrelevant.

They drove through Turner's Point, where at least half the lights were already off; people took sleep seriously out here in the country. Then Frank turned onto the private, gravel road; when the fir trees closed in about them it was as if they had entered a singularly dark tunnel that their headlights could not penetrate. The only light was directly ahead, now on a wall of tree trunks and undergrowth, now on an open space that was too restricted. It was as if the darkness had to remind them that they were limited creatures in spite of their attempts to penetrate beyond their range with high beams. And then they were home again.

Frank kept his word and busied himself with an omelette as soon as they entered the house. She called Mike's number, his office, and finally Bailey Novell. His machine took the call. With nearly savage fury she told the machine to tell Bailey to get his ass in to Frank's office at ten the next morning. When she stamped back to the kitchen, Frank began to whistle tunelessly. Good, she thought at him. Just don't say it, anything.

The next morning when they arrived at the courthouse, Doc was in the corridor. He looked almost as wretched as Nell.

"Will they decide today?" he asked.

"Probably," Frank said. "You look like hell, by the way."

Doc drew himself up straighter. "I want to talk to you, Frank. Just you. Not about Nell or this trouble. But, first, if they come in with a verdict, will you have someone give my office a call? I can be over here in five minutes. She's . . . she might go to pieces. I'm concerned. What it is, is I'm really frightened for her. If they are hung, will there be another trial? My God, she can't stand to go through it again."

Frank took Doc's arm and shook it slightly. "You're babbling, you know? Go on to your office. Don't do any heart surgery today, okay? Go on. I'll call you when they call us."

They started to enter the courtroom but were stopped again, this time by Clive. "I have to check in at work," he said. "I'll be back as soon as I can. Will you be at your office again, like yesterday?"

"Yep," Frank said. "You still have a job to check in at? I'm surprised."

"I'm taking sick leave," Clive said. "I'll be back in half an hour." He hurried off. He looked as if he qualified for sick leave.

This time when they started to move again, they actually got inside the courtroom. Ten minutes later they were dismissed with the same instructions as yesterday.

Back in the corridor, Nell said, "We want to hear the tapes, if that's all right. I brought a tape player. It's in the car." She looked as if she had not slept at all; the skin was tight across the bones of her face, and her eyes seemed to get larger and larger as she lost weight week after week.

"I'll bring them around," Frank said. "Is there anything else I can get you?"

She shook her head.

"Did Mike get over and pick up the disks?" Barbara asked, trying to sound offhand but aware of a stridency in her voice.

Nell did not register surprise, or interest either. "Yes. Travis was still home waiting for James. He said Mike was there and left again right away."

John and Amy Kendricks, who had stayed back a few steps, now drew near. With a heartiness as false as amateur theatrics, John said, "We'll walk over. We can use the exercise, isn't that right, girls?"

Barbara and Frank watched them walk away.

"I think Doc's got a point about another trial," Frank said. "That girl's really at the edge."

The whole issue of how to plead would arise again, Barbara knew. The thought occurred to her that the district attorney might even suggest a lesser charge, just to be rid of this, especially now that there were far bigger game fish in the waters. Could Nell resist? What hope could she, Barbara, hold out if she did resist? The next time, she also knew, she would not be allowed to bring in what had been declared irrelevant this time. Tony would see to that. But the odds were stacked against her being called upon to defend Nell a second time. The family, Clive, Doc, Nell herself, all probably would want someone else, and she could not blame them a bit. She felt tired and dejected as they started to walk toward the office. It was all falling apart, the way everything she touched always fell apart.

Nell and her family sat in the lounge listening to the tapes. Tears ran down Amy Kendricks's face; she was obliv-

364

ious. Nell looked like a sightless wax doll. Clive had returned; he sat across the room with a tortured expression, watching Nell. Barbara fled to Frank's office. Bailey would not arrive until eleven; he had left a message, and until then she had nothing she could do. She had tried Mike's house, his office, the department secretary, everyone she could think of. She sat behind Frank's massive desk and stared out his window at the life of Eugene, surging this way and that. Frank had said he would just mosey back to court and see if he could get in on the scuttlebutt about what was going on in the deliberation room.

Early on, Barbara had written a list of questions; many, even most of them, were still unanswered. Now, every time her thoughts whirled back to Mike, she denied that the flutter she felt was fear but called it anger instead, and she forced herself to consider the questions. Why had anyone dragged Janet Moseley across the lava bed to the creek? Who had called the ranger to report the car, and why? What did Jessie know, if anything?

If Mike ran the disks, she thought clearly then, and if the disks made people crazy, what form would his madness take? Would he be dangerous to himself, to others? Should she call Brandywine?

She dropped a pen she had been twisting around and around and forced herself to consider Jessie Burchard. After a moment she picked up the pen again and this time began to jot notes. At eleven Bailey and Frank came in together.

"Anything?" she asked her father.

"Rumor is they're at seven to five and have been since yesterday afternoon. Seven guilty."

"Rumor," she said with a dismissive wave. "Hello, Bailey."

Frank shrugged; he knew how the rumor mill worked as well as she did. "You look pretty good behind the big desk," he said, and took a chair opposite her, a client's chair. Bailey took a second one.

"Hi," he said. "You sent, I came."

She described Mike, his family, his work, his house, everything she knew about him, and told Bailey to find him.

"I don't care how much of a stink you make, either," she said grimly, her anger stronger than her fear at the moment.

Bailey grinned. "I can take that two ways, you know. You're telling me I don't have to pussyfoot around, or you're telling me I should make noise. Which?"

"Make noise. If you can't flush him, maybe one of his colleagues or buddies will pass the word that you're making noise." He nodded. Then she said softly, "And, Bailey, I have another small job, and this time I don't want you to so much as peep about what you're doing. Really QT. I want to know if Clive Belloc got fired from his last position, or if he quit. And if he was fired, what jobs he messed up during the last week or so that he worked for them, where those jobs were, when he did them, everything you can rustle up. He worked as a timber estimator for one of the big lumber companies. I don't even know which one." She glanced at her father, who was regarding her as if watching a horn emerge from her forehead. "Do you?"

He shook his head. "He might have mentioned it, but if he did, I wasn't paying attention. One of the big ones is all I know."

"So there you have it," Barbara said to Bailey. "And I want it yesterday."

"Jesus," he groaned. "Give me a break. When did he leave the job? Do you have that much?"

"Oh, yes. A week or so after Lucas Kendricks was killed. In June."

Now Bailey looked interested. "Yeah? Okay, that's something. You got priorities here?"

"Both ASAP."

As soon as Bailey was gone, Frank said, "Clive, huh? You want to enlighten an old man just a bit?"

"I was brooding about what Jessie could know. I kept thinking of the scenario I painted in court, about the private detective going around to Nell's beach, up to the house, and so on. Okay, I admit I don't think either of them did it, but I think that must be how someone did it."

"You're back to believing her story?" His voice was filled with wonder.

"Yes, I'm back to that. Let's assume she's told the absolute truth as far as she knows it. I was thinking Jessie might be protecting Doc, but if Nell told the truth, and I think she did, he was home when she called that Saturday, so it couldn't have been him. Besides, I just can't put him on the other side of the mountain the day Janet Moseley was killed. And I can't bring myself to believe there are two killers hanging out around here." She paused, thinking, then said, "I tried James Gresham. Tawna would lie for him, I guess, but I can't place him on the mountain road, aware of the creek up there. And they both say he's never fired a gun in his life. And, finally, there wouldn't be anything for Jessie to know, or to hide, about him."

Frank shook his head hard. "Whoa, honey. You're going too fast for me. Where does Jessie fit in?"

"She was on her deck that Saturday, watching the search for the body of that girl. She could have seen someone—Clive, for example—head the wrong way, and put two and two together later. It probably amused her to think of him winning Nell after murdering her husband and letting her stand trial for it. I kept thinking there was something about the binoculars that I should pay attention to. Jessie had them on the deck; I saw them. But remember that day when Clive was supposed to go to the Forest Service road and let me find out if anyone could really see that far? I saw him, and I shouldn't have. Not ten miles. But I saw the flag, and a man's figure. He faked it. He must have been much closer than ten miles, no more than three at the very most. I got sidetracked when I realized that the ranger couldn't have seen any chrome on the car, and then I forgot about the whole thing. But why would Clive have faked the scene, unless he didn't want anyone to question the ranger's story? He didn't want any questions asked about who else might have known the car was down there."

Frank considered it with a distant look on his face. Finally he nodded. "Could be. But, God alive, it's not much."

"I know. That's why I want to find out if he was in the area where that girl was killed. He would have known about the creek being there. That really has bothered me. Who knew it was there, and why drag her body to it? The second part I don't know, but the first is Clive. He probably knows the forests better than anyone in the state."

Again her father was silent, thinking. "If the police had picked up Lucas he would have taken the rap for the girl's murder. Aggravated murder, death penalty sure as hell. Lucas couldn't have beaten it. Not over in Deschutes County. Probably not anywhere."

"Suppose that was the plan, but then he saw Lucas laughing, his arms outstretched as if about to hug Nell. I don't know. Maybe he went crazy. Maybe he thought Nell and Lucas would go back together, that she would stick by him. Otherwise it just doesn't make any sense not to let the law take care of Lucas. I think that was his one second of real passion; everything else was absolutely cold-blooded."

Her father walked to the window and stood gazing at the street below. He shook his head. "Boy, oh, boy, do you ever need one piece of hard evidence. It's all could be, maybe, probably, no doubt. And finding hard evidence six months after the crime is just about as likely as finding an ice rink in hell. What are you going to do?"

"I don't know. Wait for Bailey to check in. And then, I just don't know."

Neither of them mentioned Tony, or anyone else in the district attorney's office. Pointless, they understood. Once the prosecutors said black is white, they stuck to it. Too much was already invested in proving black was white; too many egos were at risk. Any unproven theory at this time would simply be written off as yet another defense attempt to get a client out of deep trouble. Barbara had no hopes now of the jury's bringing in a not guilty, not after this long a deliberation. If they brought in guilty, there would be the appeals procedures to initiate. The best she could hope for was a hung jury, and then find whatever it took to indict Clive before the district attorney's office announced if it would

368

retry. After they were committed again, it would be just as difficult as it would be today to make them consider alternatives. It came down to a matter of saving face, she knew, and she also knew that image was far more important than substance to men like Tony DeAngelo.

Frank jammed his hands into his pockets, paced back and forth a minute or two, and then cursed softly. She looked across the desk at him and waited. "It's going to take hard proof," he said darkly. "They could indict the first time on circumstantial, but to disprove that, and to get someone else, is going to take proof, and I don't see how the hell we can get it."

"Me neither. But thanks, Dad." When he looked blank, she added, "You said *we*. I needed that."

No one could face a restaurant meal at lunchtime; they had food delivered to the lounge. Frank joined the family there, and Barbara went for a walk. At three, Bailey called in.

"Barbara, you won't like it. The guy flew out this morning, to Denver. You want someone to go after him?"

She shook her head numbly, then said no. She stared at the phone a long time without moving. Then she called Brandywine's hotel and learned that she had checked out. Denver, she thought distantly. He had gone to Denver. Like Lucas.

At four-thirty the call came telling them to return to court. And by five they knew they had a hung jury. Snagged, Frank said, at seven to five. They got there and never budged again.

THIRTY-THREE

THE WAY THEY all hugged her, anyone would have thought it was really over and Nell home free, Barbara thought sourly. Amy Kendricks was weeping again, and John was blowing his nose hard too often. Clive kept grinning and grinning, and Nell looked ten years younger than she had minutes before.

"Can we talk tomorrow?" Nell asked. "When the kids are in school? Did Mike give you the disks?"

"He put them in a safe place," Barbara said. Probably that was as true as anything she could have said. Nell and her family and Clive left together, once again with Frank acting the good shepherd. They stopped at the door to the hall where the press was waiting, and now Doc appeared; he went up to Nell and kissed her forehead, then quickly walked away. She watched him until Frank took her arm with one hand and Amy's with the other and propelled them into the crowd.

Tony came over to shake Barbara's hand. "You pulled it right out of the fire," he said. "Didn't think you could do it. We'll be in touch."

She nodded. Yes, she knew they would be in touch. Then she steeled herself and she, too, left the courtroom. She smiled and waved and said nothing at all as she pushed her way through the reporters and camera crews.

"Home?" Frank asked, when they were both inside the car.

"Home."

She put her head back and closed her eyes. She did not have to think of a thing right now, she told herself. She did not have to plan out the next day, try to anticipate what anyone might utter, damaging or helpful, did not have to put on stockings and makeup, did not have to say a single word. If she could blank out her mind, how pleasant that would be. No words, no pictures, no memories, no fears, just a comforting blank. But her thoughts kept circling around Mike and the disks and Denver and Ruth Brandywine and Schumaker and Margolis. Around and around.

After a while Frank murmured, "Too hard to decide what to keep, what to file away."

"What are you talking about?" She did not open her eyes.

"Your cross-examinations. Some of them have to go in the book, of course, but which ones is giving me a problem. I want them all."

"You won't when you think of the transcription costs."

"Ah, won't be a big problem. Taped just about everything, you know."

"You what?" Now she sat up straight and stared at him. "You didn't! Lundgren will have your head if he finds out."

"I reckon I don't aim to tell him," he said cheerfully. "Can't say I noticed a budding relationship forming between you and old iceface, either. Did I ever tell you about August Tremaine and the time he had his secretary take down everything in shorthand?" He chuckled and launched the story without waiting for an answer.

"So anyway," he said presently, "there they were with hundreds and hundreds of pages of shorthand notes, and she started to type them up for him. But funny thing was, she didn't know shorthand, you see. For four years he'd been dictating letters, you know, party of the first part, all that, and she'd been typing up beautiful letters, literate as hell. Old Gus couldn't have dictated those letters if his life depended on it, and he was giving himself pats that could have broken his arm, but he couldn't admit that the letters

371

weren't his. Not old Gus. So when the girl began to transcribe her notes, she was filled with creative energy Shakespeare would have envied. The people began to talk in rhymes, in iambic pentameter, in Faulknerian sentences, and it was lovely. Oh, it was lovely."

"Did any of it touch upon the trial at all?" Barbara asked, laughing.

"Absolutely not. She sort of lost sight of what the trial was all about early on. Now, old Gus was a lazy son of a bitch, and his memory was pretty much shot, so when he started his cross-examination using her transcriptions, everyone in court thought they had slipped sideways in time and space to fall into a loony bin."

That evening at dinner, once more at the kitchen table, Frank scowled at her plate. "Getting just a little bit pissed," he said, "at people messing up perfectly good food."

She looked down guiltily; she had made little mounds of food: a hill of peas and carrots, an island of chicken breasts with mushrooms, a cliff of scalloped potatoes. . . .

"Honey," he said, "he could have a perfectly good reason, you know. Sometimes people get a wild idea and they have to go wherever it takes them. Not as if they really have much choice, sometimes."

She smiled briefly. "It's okay, Dad. I'm a big girl now. It's just that . . . that—" Nothing else came. Sometimes they have to go wherever it takes them, she thought then, and abruptly she pushed her plate back. "I'm going back to town, to Mike's house. If he isn't back by morning, I'll go to Denver and get him."

Frank blinked in surprise. "That's not exactly what I was getting at," he said mildly.

"Goddamn it to hell!" she muttered then. She had forgotten that her car was still in the shop. "Look, either I take the Buick and leave you stranded, or you have to drive me in. Want to toss a coin?"

"Bobby, you don't even know where he is."

"Oh, yes, I do. I don't know the address, but I can find it. Walter Schumaker's place in Denver. I'll find it, and him."

"Damn it, Bobby, slow down. Mike's a grown man, after all. He might not take kindly to being rescued, especially if there's nothing to rescue him from."

"He's as naïve as a child," she said softly. "You know he is. Smart, intelligent, and dumb. As dumb as Lucas was. Those people are dangerous, and he doesn't know that. He thinks his brain is enough, and it isn't."

"You think you're a match for them?"

"You betcha." She stood up. "I'll toss a few things in a bag. Ten minutes. You can decide if you want to be without a car or be chauffeur again."

He grumbled for the first few minutes of the drive back to town, but when she did not respond, he subsided. There had been a flight in from Denver at seven that evening, and Mike could have been on it; there would be another flight at eleven-thirty, and another in the morning at six forty-five. And no doubt Mike either was home already or he would be on one of the other flights. She did not respond to that, either.

By the time they reached Franklin Boulevard and the university area, a misty rain was falling. It was just enough to smear the windshield. He cursed under his breath. "Don't eat or drink anything they offer," he growled.

"No way," she said at that. "Brandywine can't fix my headache, or backache, or anything else, either. Don't worry, Dad. I've read a book or two about hypnosis. I'll be careful." She added rather grimly, "I'll tell them I promised to report in frequently."

He drove through the university district where many young people did not seem to realize that it was raining; they were out on foot, on bikes, milling about generally. On Mike's block he had to drive nearly to the corner before he could park.

"I'll go to the door with you. Damn silly business. I'm warning you, he won't like you to come charging after him. Not a bit."

"Dad," she said softly, "what if it happened to you and Mother? Would you go charging off after her?"

"That's different."

"I know. Come on, let's see if the wandering boy's home yet."

When they approached the house, she stopped, her hand hard on her father's arm. At the front door one of the orange cats was clawing to get in; the other one was pacing back and forth. "Saber Dance and Ditto," she whispered. The cats would be asleep in the flower boxes if Mike was not home. "Didn't you turn off the light last night?"

He nodded. Although the drapes were drawn, they could see light in the living room. "I told you he'd be here," he said gruffly.

"But something's wrong," she said in the same whisper.

"I don't see Mike's car anywhere."

"That's wrong, too." She relaxed her grip on his arm. "Let's go see. We'll have to play it by ear." She had her key out already, but when they went up to the door, she knocked, and then again. The cats stropped her legs and whined. She knocked one more time, and then used the key and opened the door. Both cats streaked inside past her.

A big white-haired man was at the computer; he had blanked the screen and was facing them. He looked alarmed and somewhat angry. Mike was sprawled on one of the sofas, his eyes closed.

"Hey!" Barbara cried, "What's going on? You guys deaf or something? Mike? What's wrong with him?"

She ran to the sofa and took Mike's hand. He opened his eyes part way, sighed, and closed them again.

"He's just passed out," the man at the computer said. "Drunk. Who are you?"

"Dad, I think we might need an ambulance, or the police, or something," Barbara cried. "What's going on here? Who are you? What's wrong with Mike? I'm his fiancée, and this is my father."

Another man appeared in the doorway from the hall then. "Please," he said, "don't be frightened. There's nothing

374

much wrong with your friend. He simply drank too much at dinner, I'm afraid."

His head was large and appeared even larger because of his thick, long hair, which had started to turn gray but was still brown with light streaks. Walter Schumaker, Barbara realized, remembering his face from the covers of several magazines over the years.

Frank had stayed by the front door. Now he pulled it open, and called out, "Bailey, call the police. Quick!"

"Shit!" the man at the computer said. "Who's out there?"

"Bailey Novell, a private detective. We were going to let him get some names and numbers to start tracing Mike's whereabouts," Frank said. He glanced outside, waved, and pulled the door closed again.

The two men exchanged glances. The one at the computer stood up. "That's it. Let's get out of here."

"He's lying," the other one said, studying Frank closely. "Let's finish what we started."

"You finish. I'm leaving." He grabbed a raincoat from a chair and pulled it on as he stalked to the door. After a moment the second man followed him. He picked up a coat on his way through the room. They went out together.

Frank locked the door after them and hurried over to Barbara at the sofa. He knelt by Mike and looked at his eyes, felt his pulse, and then said, "I think he's okay. Doped, maybe. Not drunk."

"Who's a doctor nearby? Someone who will come over here. I don't want to put him in the hospital if we don't have to. Too many questions." She smiled fleetingly. "And we don't know any of the answers yet." You never ask a question that you don't already know the answer to, she thought distantly.

Frank nodded and looked around for a telephone.

The doctor had come and gone again. He had looked at Frank with a sour expression. "I thought you retired," he muttered. And he said that Mike had a lump on his head and was sleeping off a sedative. Without urinalysis and/or blood

375

tests, that was as much as he could say about that. "Let him sleep. See someone tomorrow if the head gives him any trouble, could be a concussion."

"Not here! He can't sleep it off here," Barbara said as soon as the doctor was gone. She had fed the cats and looked through the house, but nothing seemed to have been touched except the computers. She could not tell anything about either of them, the one turned on in the living room, or the other one in the bedroom. Both had been in use.

"Right," Frank said heavily and sat on the second sofa, regarding Mike. "On the other hand, we don't know what those guys were looking for, if they found it, or if they'll be back."

"Let's call Bailey and have him send someone to spend the rest of the night here. By tomorrow Mike should be able to take charge again." The question was if he had put the disks in a safe-deposit box. She bit her lip as she glanced over the many boxes of disks on his computer desk.

Frank called Bailey and talked soothingly, denied that it was very late, and arranged for someone to come by and guard the house overnight. It was after twelve when he started the drive home again, a young associate of Bailey's in the house, Mike asleep in the back of the car with Barbara holding him.

"What the hell did Frobisher find?" he murmured as he drove. "What the hell is on those disks, and where the hell are they now?"

Barbara's sleep was troubled by dreams that left her feeling fearful, but with no memory of the contents, just a vague unease. She told herself to remember one of them, even as she drifted away again. She came wide awake twice thinking each time that she heard Mike's voice; when she roused herself enough to get up to investigate, it was to find him sleeping quietly in the guest room. The third time it happened, she turned over, pulled her blanket higher, and went back to sleep. Pale light was seeping in around her drapes by then.

When she went downstairs, it was nine-thirty. There was a note propped against the coffee carafe. *Gone to get Mike's car. Back soon. 7:15.* The last time, she thought bleakly, she really had heard voices the last time.

She had coffee and read the note again, and now she realized that they wouldn't have gone off for the car at that hour; it could wait until later in the day, wherever it was. Not the car. The disks? She sipped the coffee and nodded. It had to be the disks. And Mike must be okay, she added, or her father would not have gone off with him. The unease her dreams had brought made her too restless to sit still, or to consider breakfast.

She started to clear off the dining room table, stacking the maps, the drawings, all the material she had gathered. For what purpose, she pondered glumly. Her father had been afraid he couldn't get Nell off, and she hadn't been able to get her off the hook, either. And the next time it would be even harder. She went to the outside door then and looked at the deck, and the river beyond, gray and still today, as if it had no movement of its own. Deceptive river, as fickle as a teenage lover.

Nell called and asked if she could come over, and Barbara was relieved to have something to do while she waited. She had no illusions about what she was doing: puttering, waiting.

Nell was very pink from the cold air; she had walked, she said. Not by way of Doc's property, but all the way around. Something she had been missing, just getting out and walking. "Where do I stand?" she asked at the kitchen table, holding a coffee mug with both hands.

"It could go several ways," Barbara said. "A new trial is as likely as anything else." She regarded Nell for several moments, then said, "If you want another attorney, we'll understand. I'd cooperate in any way possible."

Nell shook her head vigorously. "No. But I'm worried about Travis. He's twelve, old enough to understand what's happening, as much as any of us can. We're going over to John and Amy's for Thanksgiving, but we'll be back Friday.

They asked us to stay the weekend and I said no. Travis needs . . . something, I just don't know what. Talk maybe." She sipped the coffee, staring past Barbara. "He likes Clive, I think."

Very carefully, Barbara said, "Travis probably needs to have you home with him for a time. It's been hectic for everyone."

Nell nodded, still looking at something else. "I guess that's part of it." Abruptly she shook herself and looked at Barbara. "I don't believe any of us could stand another trial. Not John and Amy. Not my kids. Maybe not me."

"You're tired. That's to be expected. I'm tired, too. We all are."

"Clive would be willing to adopt both children. Did you know that? That's good of him, isn't it?"

"Nell, listen to me. You've been through the wringer and you're feeling desperate, but the worst is behind you. Don't make any decisions too soon. Rest first. Relax. Take walks, play with the children, do all the things you used to do with them, and don't try to see too far ahead. Not just yet. We don't know yet what the DA will decide, and we haven't given up, not by a long shot. There are some things we're still looking into."

Nell smiled at her, a strangely gentle smile, the way she might smile at her daughter if she was being ridiculous. "If I say what happened, I won't be believed ever. I don't believe it myself. And if I can't believe that, maybe I really have amnesia for what happened. Maybe I actually did take the rifle up there. Maybe I was startled and scared when he appeared so suddenly, and before I could think, I fired. Then I forgot it and made up an incredible story. Not expecting to be believed, really wanting to be challenged, to be forced to remember." She nodded. "When the children are older, they could accept that. Travis could accept it now, I think. Accidents happen. No one has suggested I planned it. An accident."

Barbara felt icy all over. She leaned forward. "For God's

378

sake, Nell, is that what happened? What did you do? Climb up on a rock to shoot him?"

"That's no more incredible than the story I've been telling," Nell said softly. "I don't know the details, or why I cleaned the rifle afterward. But none of that matters. Can't you understand what I'm saying? None of that matters because no one will ever believe the actual truth. They'd believe a lie." She stood up. "Maybe truth is more relative than we ever suspected. Maybe it takes a believer to make something true. It can't exist independently of at least one believer. Maybe there's no way ever to know what's true. I don't know what I believe any longer. I used to think that if you told the truth everything would work out." She laughed without humor and left the table, left the kitchen.

Walking away, she continued to talk. "I have to go now. I wanted to tell you this. That I don't think the kids could go through it again. Carol is so afraid she's having bad dreams and has gone back to thumb sucking. Travis. . . . He hardly even speaks to anyone these days. He can't force himself to look straight at me! What do you suppose they're saying to him in school? On the bus? Kids can be so cruel. I was thinking that if they had a mother and a father, if we all lived as a family, and if I have to be. . . . If I'm gone for a time, there would be some kind of stability for them." She found her jacket in the foyer and pulled it on, took a wool cap from the pocket and put it on. Her short, curly hair stuck out all around it like a soft fringe. "Children need a father," she said vaguely. "They never knew theirs."

Helplessly Barbara walked to the front door with her. "Please," she said, "just don't do anything too soon. Let it rest a few days. Give us a chance to follow up some of the lines we're looking into. Will you? Please, Nell, will you let me know the minute you decide anything? Anything."

Nell shrugged. "A few days. But I don't dare wait too long, you see. Everything takes time."

Barbara watched her walk away until she was hidden by the big trees. Then she slammed the door. The telephone was ringing.

She stood by the answering machine when she heard a deep voice ask first for Mike, and then for her, or her father. She started to lift the receiver, then drew back and listened.

"This is Walter Schumaker. I should like to have a conference with Barbara Holloway, Frank Holloway, and Mike Dinesen. This afternoon, if that is convenient. I shall be at this number for the next several hours. Please let me know." He gave the number and hung up. She played it back again, frowning. Then she shrugged. That, at least, could wait until her father returned with Mike. Let them decide about Schumaker.

The immediate problem, she admitted then, was that she didn't blame Nell. Not a bit. She could walk into a judge's chambers next week, Frank at her side, Tony there being professional and cool, and it could end, sentence passed, sentence begun almost instantly, the future settled. Nell's future, the children's future, Clive's future. Indecision was more stressful than a bad decision; hadn't she read that somewhere? If not, she should have, she thought grimly. She couldn't even tell her she suspected Clive, not without some proof. But neither could she let Nell marry him, not if he actually had done it. No matter what, she promised herself silently, she would not allow that wedding to take place.

Her mood was deep and black when Frank and Mike arrived later in their separate cars. Frank came in first; she looked past him to Mike who was entering the foyer. "What the hell did you think you were doing? Where were you? What happened to you? How are you?"

He looked at her as if his eyes were not focusing properly; his expression was puzzled. He reached out, but stopped short of touching her, let his hand rest in midair momentarily, and then made a curious motion, as if tracing an outline.

"Mike! What's wrong?"

Abruptly he seemed to shift to wakefulness from a near dream state. He put his hand to his head. "I think I have a concussion or something. It's okay now." He drew her into his arms and held her.

It was wrong, she thought almost wildly; this was not the reassuring embrace of someone trying to prove things were all right, but rather this was like the clinging embrace of a child coming out of a nightmare, pleading wordlessly to be held *here*, to be kept *here*, not to be allowed to slip back into the frightening dream.

THIRTY-FOUR

THEY SAT IN the living room before a brisk fire. Mike was sprawled in one of the soft chairs, his legs stretched out before him, his eyes closed. Frank was in the matching chair, as stiff and tense as an expectant father; Barbara huddled on the couch.

"Just tell us what happened," she said in a low voice. "Mike, please snap out of it and tell us what happened to you! Do you want to see a doctor?"

He laughed but did not open his eyes. "No way. They'd stick me in the equivalent of Bellevue, whatever it is out here. As long as I don't move and don't open my eyes, I seem to be okay."

"For God's sake, how did you mange to drive out?"

He looked thoughtful, his forehead gathered in furrows; then he said, "I don't know. I seem to have a screwed-up time sense, among other things."

Barbara looked at her father helplessly. Frank said, "He was in the kitchen when I got up. He seemed about as normal as he ever was, and he wanted to go home to see what they

381

did to his computers, and to the airport to collect the disks he had stashed in one of the lock boxes, and to get his car. That seemed reasonable enough. He kept his eyes closed most of the way, said he had a headache."

"He drove home with his eyes closed?" she cried. "This is crazy!"

"Well, not closed, not like now. We started to drive, with him out front, and he was a bit erratic. Just a bit erratic. So I pulled around him and stopped and we had a little talk, and he said that if he kept his eyes on a fixed object, he was okay. He tailed me, I guess with his eyes fixed on my license plate or something. That's what took so long. I never went more than thirty."

She stared at him in disbelief. "You let him drive in that condition? Why? Why didn't you get a doctor? Or leave his damn car somewhere and keep him in yours?"

Frank was watching Mike so intently that his eyes had started to tear. He wiped them with his handkerchief and then fished his glasses out of his pocket and wiped them carefully. "Bobby, I don't know why, and that's God's truth. I don't know."

She was startled then by a deep sound from Mike; she realized he was chuckling softly, low in his throat. He did not open his eyes.

"I got the disks," he said. "I took them home to copy them, and to see what they had. Sometime later, I knew what Frobisher had done, and I had to talk to Schumaker and Margolis, Brandywine, too, if she was around. I was in Denver, calling Schumaker. You see, my time sense is messed up. Sorry about that. I was doing one thing and thinking I should do something else, and there I was doing the something else." He was laughing under it all, she knew; it was like the subdued mirth of a child at Christmas.

"Then what?" she asked. Her voice sounded unfamiliar, too shrill, trembling.

"I think I got erratic in Schumaker's office, or somewhere. Erratic. Nice word. Off the straight and narrow, veering, unpredictable. He kept saying the work was over

382

with, done, destroyed. He lied. I think they probably re-strained me, and then gave me something to calm me down. It worked just fine. Then we were home, my home, and they were looking for the disks, to see if I had loaded them into my computers, saved them under some other name, hidden them under the laundry. He brought Margolis because he's the computer genius. The disks can't hide from him." The laughter broke out this time. It vanished almost instantly. "Hey, Barbara, don't cry. It's all right."

Tears were running down her cheeks. But he had not opened his eyes.

"I'm going to get us some coffee," Frank said, hurrying from the room.

"I'm sorry I scared him," Mike said softly. "And you. I can't seem to help it right now. Listen to me, Barbara. Listen. I have to go through the disks one more time. I can't stop where I am, you see. I can't keep my eyes closed forever, but if I open them, I'm not really sure what I'll see. That's how it is right now." He was laughing again, not openly, but under his words laughter seemed to ripple and bubble.

"No! Where are they?"

"Frank has them. But, Barbara, I need to go through them again. I really need to. I feel like a flickering light bulb, on and off, on and off. I can run the copies on Frank's computer."

She shook her head. "Tell me what's on them. What they did to you. You act as if you've been brainwashed or something."

"Brainwashed. In the washing machine, churning around and around. That's exactly right. In the Whirlpool. That's a brand name, you know. Apt. In a whirlpool you get spun around and around and finally thrown out. There are a lot of places where you can land, a lot of places where you can be thrown free, some of them places you don't want to hit, because you won't leave them again. In the whirlpool, spinning, spinning. That's where I am, Barbara, spinning around and around. You can't guide me out and neither can Frank. The disks can, I hope."

383

"You're tripping," she whispered. "My God, they must have given you LSD or something like that. A hallucinogenic drug."

He laughed. "I want the disks, Barbara. Come on in, Frank. And bring your briefcase. That's where you put them, isn't it?"

Frank walked into the living room. "I think we should call Doc, or take him to the hospital if Doc's not home yet."

Barbara nodded miserably.

"And have another Lucas on your hands?" Mike murmured. "That's what they did to him, you know. He was caught in the whirlpool and they didn't know what to do, so they kept him on tranquilizers for years and years. No way, Frank. Not me." He drew his feet in and started to rise from his chair; when he opened his eyes he went dead white, swayed, and then clutched his ears with both hands, closed his eyes again. "God!" he whispered. "Oh, God!"

Barbara got up uncertainly and took a step toward him, then another. He raised his head, but his eyes did not focus on her; his face was twisted, in pain or fear was impossible to tell. She stopped.

"I have to finish," he said hoarsely. "I didn't know enough to go all the way through them. Don't you understand, I can't stop here!" He raised one hand before him and made a sweeping gesture, as if brushing away cobwebs. He did it again and turned his head aside, brushed his cheek.

"Mike!" Barbara screamed. "Look at me! I'm here! Look!"

He kept brushing at his face, at the air before him. Desperately she snatched up the crystal candy dish and waved it in front of his eyes. "Look at this! You concentrated on Dad's car and drove home, you can concentrate on this! Look at it!"

Slowly he stopped his motions, his eyes fixed on the dish as she moved it back and forth in front of him. He drew in a deep breath. "Frank," he said tiredly, "don't."

Frank had been moving toward the telephone. He stopped.

"You know what Brandywine's solution was," Mike said in a voice that sounded as if it were coming from a deep tunnel. "You know Schumaker and Margolis went along. They didn't know what else to do with Lucas. They don't know how to control this, none of them. No doctor would have any better solution than they do. I need to finish. Lucas finally came out of it, remember. That's the only way."

Barbara felt Frank's arm about her shoulders. They stared at Mike. A smile crossed his face and he said almost mockingly, "I am quite lucid at the moment. Lucid, from the Latin *lucere*, meaning to shine. And they made it mean sane, or rational. Wrong. It means to shine. And I am quite lucid. You see, what has happened is that all the synapses have been disconnected, and now when they fire, it's rather random, but brilliant, with shining patterns, and new ways to see and hear. Like, I hear the river singing a melancholy dirge. It's cold—the river, I mean—and it's unhappy, thinking about the spring and the summer and the quickness of the fish then. Now they are sluggish. Is that lucid, Barbara? I never thought of the river that way before, you know. Never. But the trouble is I can't seem to keep the river out there. If I open my eyes it might be in here with us. Or I might be out there in it. And you, Barbara, I can't tell where you stop and start, where your edges are. Or mine. Especially mine. Where are the boundaries? Where do you start and I end? I'm spread too far, too far. And I don't know how to pull in again. I need the disks, Barbara. The whirlpool will throw me out sooner or later, the synapses will reconnect in a new pattern, the turbulence will end and there will be different linkages, but what kind, what will they mean? The light goes on and off, on and off, but it has to stop one way or the other." He grimaced and his hands clenched, his eyes squeezed shut even tighter. When he spoke again, his voice was so distant, it was hard to make out the words. "This world will kill me, Barbara. I need to be guided back. Is that lucid enough?"

"Yes," she whispered. Frank's hand clutched her shoulder convulsively, and she said it again, clearer, louder. "Yes."

"Good," Mike said quietly. "Let's start."

He directed her without opening his eyes. Occasionally a grimace passed over his face as if he was in pain or in terror, and at those times his voice stopped. Once she had to shake his arm to get his attention in order to proceed. She got the program loaded and running before Mike attempted to join her. When he did, he walked like a sleepwalker, keeping his gaze fixed and staring, keeping one hand on the wall as he moved. Then he sat at the desk and breathed in deeply. "Don't watch," he said; after that he ignored her and Frank altogether. Presently the screen was filled with patterns that danced and writhed. Barbara backed away. Her mouth was very dry.

Frank took her by the arm and led her to the kitchen. "I really did make coffee," he said.

"I'm so afraid. Dad, I'm so afraid!"

"Me too, honey. Sit down. I don't think we had much choice in the matter. Sit down."

She sat down and wrapped her arms about herself and rocked back and forth. Frank came to her side and held her, stroking her hair gently.

Barbara had made sandwiches that neither she nor her father wanted. From time to time one or the other went to the study door to gaze at Mike, who was transfixed before the monitor. His fingers on the keyboard—jabbing, pausing, jabbing again—were the only sign of consciousness, the only sign of life. An hour passed, another.

"How many disks are there?" Barbara asked in desperation, returning again from the study door.

"I don't know. Eight, ten. A stack."

They both jumped when the doorbell sounded. Frank went to see who it was, and in just a second or two, he came back with Schumaker and Margolis and a third man who had a revolver. They were all dressed in business suits and topcoats, like three stockbrokers, or realtors out to close an important deal.

"This is our private detective," Walter Schumaker said.

"Only ours is quite real. Mr. Holloway, please join your daughter over there. I want my property that Mike Dinesen stole. Mr. Claypole here is our insurance that there will be no violence."

When it appeared that if Frank did not join Barbara, Claypole would assist him, he walked stiffly across the kitchen. Schumaker nodded to Margolis. "Why don't you have a look down that hallway?"

"No!" Barbara cried, and started to run toward the study.

Schumaker stepped in front of her. "Don't be tiresome," he said.

"You can't come in here with an armed man like this!" she snapped. "That gun makes it deadly assault!"

Schumaker shrugged. The detective and Margolis had gone into the study. Frank walked across the kitchen, out to the hallway. Schumaker did not try to stop him. At the study door the detective blocked entrance. Mike, at the computer, appeared unaware that Margolis had come to his side and was reaching past him. When Margolis turned off the monitor, Mike roused, started to rise. Margolis put his hand on Mike's shoulder, pushed him down into the chair; with his other hand he picked up the disks that were by the side of the computer. He slipped them into his pocket. Mike had become as passive as a zombie.

"They loaded the whole thing onto the hard drive, it looks like," Margolis said.

From the hallway Schumaker said, "Well, erase it or something. You're the computer expert."

Suddenly Mike started to jerk away from Margolis's hand, and this time the detective moved into the room and grabbed his arm, jerked him from the chair, and held him with his arm twisted behind him. Mike winced and groaned and tried to swing at the large man, who simply twisted his arm higher. Without warning Mike slumped and would have fallen to the floor if the detective had not caught and held him. Claypole looked bewildered.

Barbara was already at Mike's side, feeling for a pulse.

"What did you do to him? Bring him to the living room couch. For God's sake, what did you do to him?"

"Get on with it," Schumaker said to Margolis, then turned and led the way back through the hall to the living room.

"You can go now," he said to Claypole as soon as he had deposited Mike on the couch. The detective shrugged and left without a word. Schumaker walked to the couch and stood over Mike with a brooding expression. "He'll sleep for hours, more than likely," he said. "They mostly do after a session." He took off his topcoat, folded it precisely, laid it carefully over the back of a chair.

Barbara glared at him with fierce hatred. She had been kneeling on the floor by Mike; now she got up stiffly and walked to the telephone. "I'm calling the police. Forced entry. Assault with a deadly weapon. Theft. Vandalism." She lifted the phone.

"They will wake him up and have a raving madman on their hands, and two incoherent witnesses." Schumaker sank down into the chair, careful not to lean back against his coat. "Ms. Holloway, you and your father are in something you can't start to comprehend. Don't exacerbate the situation more than necessary by bringing in additional outsiders. You know we can burn the disks and destroy everything on the computer long before police arrive. Let's talk first."

She looked from him to her father, who was ashen-faced. Wordlessly he nodded and sat down in his own chair. She put the phone down.

"Talk," she said, not moving yet from the table.

"Sit down," Schumaker said wearily, and then waited until she went back to the couch and sat on the floor by Mike. "If you bring in the police this is that I shall tell them. Yesterday, this man, a complete stranger to me, forced his way into my home and made wild threats. He was in possession of work I assisted with seven or eight years ago; how he obtained that work, I don't know. He made insane accusations and demanded explanations for work that I have not even thought of in a decade. At one point we had to

388

subdue him, and then he fled. I called my associate who had been involved with the work from long ago, and we agreed to meet at the airport to try to talk the young man into surrendering the disks that are ours. He admitted that the work was ours and said that we could have it if we chose to accompany him to his home and collect it. We chose to do that. However, you two interrupted us in the middle of our task. Today, fearing more violence, I hired a bodyguard to accompany us here to collect the remaining copies of the disks." He scowled and shook his head. "It isn't pretty, and not altogether believable, but accept this, Ms. Holloway: Your friend is in no condition to contradict a word of it. He did threaten me, and he did say I could collect the disks."

Frank had listened with an intent expression. He said, "Tell us, Dr. Schumaker, what is on those disks that's important enough to bring all you people up here from Denver, to resort to such means to recover?"

Schumaker nodded gravely. "You deserve that much," he said after a pause. "Very well. Frobisher discovered a perfect tool to induce insanity. Believe me, it was not what he was looking for, but a by-product that he could not eliminate. It takes only a few hours, and it appears that no one is truly immune. Think what such a program would be like in the hands of unscrupulous people. It could be watched in small segments and still retain its effectiveness. A minute or two during a half-hour television show. A few minutes during a special of two hours. That would be enough eventually after continued refinement. Anyone could reproduce and broadcast his material. That's what's so important, Mr. Holloway. For a very brief time I assisted in his project, before I realized exactly what he was producing, at which time I severed all connections with the work and the man. I thought he had abandoned it, also, right up until his death at the hands of one of his subjects. I had no idea that he had continued, and that the disks were still operable, until Ruth said someone had recovered them here. Yesterday your young friend convinced me that indeed the program is still powerful, still deadly. At least four young people were driven mad by it,

389

Mr. Holloway, five counting Dinesen here. Four of those young men are now dead. As soon as we know your computer has been cleansed of the material we shall destroy the other disks, in your presence if you like, and that will end the matter." He gazed at Mike, pityingly now. "As for how he will be, I have no idea. Lucas Kendricks was salvaged enough to lead the rather dull life of a maintenance man. He was the lucky one of the four we knew about. And Frobisher is dead. There's no one to punish, no one to blame. Ruth, Herbert, and I tried to eradicate the menace. We didn't know there were disks, and as soon as we did know, we tried to recover them." He spread his hands wide and shrugged. "If you had turned them over to Ruth, this young man would not have exposed himself as he did. Who is to blame, Mr. Holloway? Where is the axe to fall first?"

They all turned to look when Herbert Margolis entered the living room. "Done." He pulled a bunch of disks from his pocket and held them up. "This is the lot."

"Let's add a log to the fire, make sure we have a good updraft, and then finish," Schumaker said. He got up to kindle the fire, and when the new log was blazing, he stood back and watched as Herbert Margolis tossed in the disks one by one. It did not take very long; no one moved as the disks curled, caught fire, and burned fiercely for a second or two, and then turned into black ash.

"And now it is really over," Schumaker said and drew in a long breath. "At last."

"No," Barbara said softly, still on the floor by the couch where Mike slept. "It isn't over. I don't know what Frobisher thought he was doing, but he succeeded with Lucas finally. He succeeded with the last boy he worked with, and he killed that boy because he succeeded. Didn't he? Isn't that what really happened?"

Margolis looked startled and began to shake his head vigorously. "That isn't what happened! The police said the boy killed Frobisher!"

"Shut up," Schumaker said coldly.

Barbara went on. "What if it worked with Mike, Dr.

390

Schumaker? Would you want him dead, too? Is that why Lucas is dead, because it worked?"

Schumaker picked up his lovely gray topcoat and pulled it on. The look he gave her was pitying and contemptuous. "You know as well as I do that Nell Kendricks killed her husband. And you should be grateful, young lady, that the process did not succeed with your lover. Because if it had, he would be the loneliest man in the world. Better he should be mad and content than the only one of his kind on Earth."

"He's a mathematician, like you," she said softly. "No, that's not quite right. Not like you. He doesn't think you're very good. He said you peaked twenty-five years ago and haven't been able to do any original work since, but he's as brilliant as you probably thought you were once." A deep flush suffused Schumaker's face. She got to her feet, speaking in the same low, intense voice, "He knows what's on those disks now."

"You're a fool!" Schumaker snapped. "If the process worked with him, he wouldn't care if anyone else knows or not. But it didn't, simply because it can't. The process itself is impossible. Frobisher tried the impossible and failed. Dinesen will appear quite mad, my dear. Raving mad. For how long, I can't predict. Schizophrenic, perhaps paranoiac. He may suspect and dream that there was something wonderful on those disks, but it will forever be out of reach, as impossible to attain as the rainbow. There will be no financing. Until he recovers, no teaching. No job of any sort. He won't even be able to hold a conversation with another human being. I saw those boys: gibbering maniacs, every one of them. Lucas was a raving madman when he wasn't sedated. I wanted to let him go to an institution, to let him go anywhere. He would have been killed in a day, in an hour, out in the real world. Two boys drove off the road. Probably thought they could fly or something. That's what the process does, Ms. Holloway." He started for the door.

"What did Ruth Brandywine find out when she hypnotized those boys?" Barbara demanded.

391

This time Schumaker was taken aback. "She didn't tell you that," he said. "She never said anything like that."

"What did she learn from them?"

Herbert Margolis nearly ran from the room. "I'm leaving," he said.

"She learned something that frightened you all into stopping the work, didn't she?" Barbara demanded. "That's when you quit, not because some unfortunate boys were driven mad, or died, but because you learned something that frightened you. What was it, Dr. Schumaker? Was it that the process actually worked the way Emil Frobisher hoped it would? And you had something on your hands you didn't know how to handle? Was that it?"

Slowly Schumaker pulled kid gloves from his pocket and started to put them on, studying her all the while. Then he said in a quiet voice, "Leave it alone, Barbara Holloway. You may know the law, but you've bumbled into an area where you are as ignorant as a school child. The work is gone. It cannot be reproduced. Dinesen will be in no condition to reproduce it, and you know nothing about it. I will give you just this bit of advice. If you bring in a psychologist, try hypnosis with him, you will simply confirm that he is mad, that he is out of touch with reality; he may even talk about a strange, alien world view, but nothing about the work, the process. Just leave it alone."

He turned and walked out of the room. Frank followed him to the front door, closed and locked it after him. When he got back to the living room, Barbara was standing at the couch, gazing at Mike, who had not stirred once. Frank put his arm around her and held her for a moment.

"Ah, Bobby, what a hornet's nest we've got ourselves into."

She drew back. "Right. Did you tape it all?"

"Jesus, how did you know that?"

"I saw you fiddling with your pen, and I remembered that junior G-man kit you used to have, with the microphone that looks like a pen. Is that how you taped the trial?"

392

"Yep. Works just fine. Just fine. But damned if I know what good it will do us."

She looked down at Mike again. She should get a blanket, she thought vaguely. Or restraints? Straitjacket? The tape recording wouldn't do a bit of good, she thought in despair. Not a bit of good.

THIRTY-FIVE

AT FOUR DOC called to see if he could drop in. Frank glanced at Barbara, who was sitting with a book in her hands, not reading a word. She shrugged. Mike was sleeping on the couch, covered now with a blanket. She had removed his shoes. He was sleeping as peacefully as a baby.

"Sure, Doc," Frank said. "I'll be here."

"No point in having him see Mike, I guess," she said. "No point in my seeing him."

"We'll talk in my study." Now and then that afternoon he had gone to the couch, felt Mike's forehead, or his pulse. When he sat down, he had not even pretended to read. He had gazed at the fire, or out a window, or at his daughter, or Mike. He welcomed Doc, welcomed an interruption.

He left Barbara baby-sitting. He thought of it that way, baby-sitting. At the thought, a pang of grief swept him. He never had even breathed to her how much he longed for a grandchild, a whole passel of grandchildren. He would have been overjoyed by a grandchild by way of Tony as much as he disliked him. But his genes were probably okay, he had

393

told himself, and he damn well knew that Barbara's were just fine. The moment of grief passed when he took a last look at Mike on the couch. Then he closed the living room door and went to the kitchen to wait for Doc.

At first Doc turned down his hospitality. "It's a business call," he said almost primly, taking off his long, heavy jacket. He was as jerky and jumpy as always, not sitting still long enough to warm a chair.

"Damn it, we can talk business over a glass of wine, or a cup of coffee," Frank growled.

Doc agreed to coffee and went to the sliding door to the terrace. The river was nearly black in the late-afternoon light. It was getting dark already, the clouds low, threatening rain again, heavy snow in the mountains.

"I want you to divorce me," Doc said suddenly, and with nervous energy he paced the kitchen as Frank made the coffee.

"Um. Have you both discussed it?"

"No. No. I wanted to talked to you first. But she knows, just not when. Now is when."

"Sit down, Doc. You're making me twitchy." Frank came around the counter with the coffee tray and indicated one of the chairs at the table. Doc sat down. "Now, let's have it." He poured for them both.

"Nothing to have! I want out. I've wanted out for a long time, but it seemed, oh, I don't know, indecent, I guess. Now I don't care. Out."

"Is there someone else?"

Doc jumped up so fast he nearly knocked his chair over. He caught and steadied it, and then sat down again. "Not like that. I mean— Not like that."

Frank regarded him morosely. Barbara had told him about Doc and Nell, but that was over, he was certain. "Okay," he said. "But you should see a marriage counselor, you know. Differences can be reconciled if both people want reconciliation."

"I don't! Christ! I said I want out. That's all."

"Do you expect her to fight it?"

394

"Oh, sure. Tooth and claw."

Frank's sigh was mournful. It would be messy, nasty, dirty, filthy, all the things he hated. "You'll want to talk to one of my associates, then. Sandra Seligman would be good. You know I don't do divorces, myself."

"Come off it, Frank!" He ran his hands through his thin hair and nearly knocked his cup over with his elbow. Frank grabbed it and moved it away from him. "Anyone can do a simple divorce. I could get a kit and do it myself. I took care of you through a lot of stuff that's not my specialty."

"Kicking and screaming all the way," Frank snapped back at him. "And you could have turned me over to a specialist at any time, you know."

"Well, I didn't. I don't want Sandra whoever she is."

"This isn't going to be a simple divorce, you idiot! There's property, and investments, and insurance, and your earnings, today's and in the future. What kind of picture will she make in a divorce court in her wheelchair? She'll clean you out down to your holiest socks!"

"I know all that," Doc said almost meekly. "I just don't care. Help me, Frank. I want you to do it. I'm taking her down to her sister's place in Palm Springs this evening. For Thanksgiving." He laughed, a short, bitter sound that was almost a sob. "Thanksgiving. I'll tell her Friday, down there. We'll talk on Saturday, and I'll fly home Sunday. She won't come back with me. Not yet. She'll have her sister to comfort her and scheme with her and plan revenge, whatever. That's all right, too. After that, I don't know. Probably I'll stay in town. I just want to know you'll take care of things. I don't expect you to work miracles. Just try to keep my skin intact. That's acceptable."

"Goddamn it all to hell!" Frank muttered. "I might not even be able to do that much for you." He drummed his fingers on the table for a minute, then said deliberately, "Listen, Doc, when I was sick you did some pretty damn embarrassing things to me. My turn. And you sit in that chair and answer, or I'll toss you out. I know about you and Nell. Goddamn it, I said sit still!"

Doc was up and out of his chair faster than Frank could reach out to stop him. He ran to the sliding door and stood with his shoulders hunched looking out.

"Okay, answer from there. I don't give a damn, just tell me what I need to know. Is it over with you two?"

Doc nodded.

"Since when?"

"Late summer, early fall. I don't know."

"Did Jessie ever indicate to you that she knew?"

"Never. Not until she testified. I never guessed." Abruptly he swung around and returned to the table. He put both hands on it and leaned forward. "She knew. God knows how long, but she knew. It was her idea for Nell to start going out with Clive. She said it was unnatural for such a pretty young woman not to date; the police would find that suspicious. And everyone around here knew she never gave him the time of day until after Lucas was dead; no scandal could possibly be attached to that pairing. I believed her. God help me, I believed her, that she wanted to help Nell. But she was taunting me all the time, and she was afraid after Lucas died, afraid I might. . . . I don't know, do what I'm doing now, I guess."

"Oh, Moses in a basket," Frank muttered.

"But she wouldn't admit it for a million dollars," Doc said fiercely. "She's too arrogant to admit a younger woman came along, that her husband might have played around, that she wasn't the only star in his universe. She won't admit that." He smiled crookedly, a mirthless grimace. "It would hurt her more than me, and she knows it. I've reached the point where I don't give a shit who knows what, and she knows that, too."

Frank did not bother to tell him that many people undergoing a filthy divorce would step gladly into the pit if they knew the recently beloved would end up there, also. Instead, he sighed. "Okay, give me a call when you get back in town. And think about it hard before you start that little talk with her, will you?"

Doc shrugged. "I told her I was coming over to give you

our key, so you can have a look around now and then. Here it is. No lies. Thank God, no more lies after this rotten weekend is over." He snapped a key off his chain and put it on the table.

He left soon after that, as jumpy as he had been on arriving, but with a new determination that made all his motions seem more directed, not simply the aimless, blind restlessness of a desperately unhappy man.

Frank opened the living room door to see Barbara kneeling at the side of the couch, holding Mike's hand. Shaking her head, she placed the hand back under the cover and stood up.

"I thought he was coming awake. He was moving, but that's all, just moving. It moves, it breathes, it's alive!"

"You need a drink. And I can use a drink. Come on, let's see to that, and I'll fill you in on Doc's new backbone. Interesting Filipino doctor got hold of him and inserted it without drawing a drop of blood, far as I could see."

When he told her what Doc's plans were, she cursed. At his questioning look, she said darkly, "Nothing. Just another little thread snipped off, that's all. If Jessie leaves without telling anyone if and what she might know about Lucas's death, we'll never find out. I'm with Doc in that. She probably won't come back here. Too proud."

"Honey, she wouldn't lift her little pinkie to help Nell, no matter what. You know that as well as I do."

After dinner, Frank dozed in his chair; Barbara tried to concentrate on the book she had been trying to concentrate on all day. She tried rephrasing what she had read: The normal human heartbeat is not regular. There is a random irregularity that is now recognized as healthy. Good. She nodded at the book. When the heartbeat becomes very regular, a heart attack might follow. When it becomes chaotic to an extreme, fibrillation can cause death in minutes. Then the author had gone on to discuss the brain and its waves, also randomly irregular. The flicker effect can synchronize the brain waves in a regular pattern in some people, and the

397

result can be a sudden swing into turbulence, a chaotic electrical activity: a seizure. Good, she told herself again.

All God's children got irregularities, she thought. Irregularity, the bane of Western civilization.

Abruptly she was remembering one of the articles Ruth Brandywine had written, one not dealing with adolescent learning patterns. This had dealt with channels. Synapses. All open at birth, receptive, and then one after another closing, to become inaccessible, out of reach forever. Unless someone like Emil Frobisher found a way to open them again, Barbara thought then.

Physiological changes occur, Brandywine had claimed, irreversible changes that also affect the chromosomes. Mutagenic changes. Drugs can cause mutagenic changes, ionizing radiation can, and synaptic realignments of the brain.

Barbara closed her eyes hard, trying to visualize again the accompanying diagrams and pictures of brain tissue and chromosomal studies from children who had died before and after the acquisition of language, before and after walking, before and after reading skills were mastered.

Brandywine's critics had said she was talking about the process of maturation, nothing more than that. She had claimed that infants could focus their eyes at birth—an incontestable statement—but that most of them rarely did, not until there had been sufficient reinforcement. After they learned to focus them in approved ways, they could no longer perceive whatever it was they had been seeing before that. What caused infants to have night terrors? she had asked, and answered: a turbulent brain system receiving too much data, all contradictory and overwhelming. The brain was sent into a state of turbulence that was the proximate cause of night terrors that persisted until reinforcement of some synapses made connections that overrode other connections that were then severed, not to be joined again. Throughout childhood the channels continued to close, although not at the same rate as the two-year period of turbulence. Children with eidetic memories lost that ability when they learned to read. Children who had a telepathic

398

rapport with their parents—most children, she had claimed—lost that ability when they became socialized.

And each change, she had written, was accompanied by a distinctive physiological change and an alteration in the chromosomes.

Barbara slipped without transition into a dream. She was ice skating on the river, which had frozen solid from bank to bank. The ice was incredibly clear, to the point of invisibility; below, she could see the fish peering up at her with eyes like buttons, never blinking. She sped over the clear ice, exhilarated by the freedom, by the swiftness and ease of motion. She was flying, she thought joyously. Although she knew that ahead, beyond the next curve, or the next, the river churned and boiled, she skated with the abandon, the happiness of a child who has no future, only the immediate now. She laughed.

Her dream laughter woke her. She jerked upright in her chair; the book slid off her lap, and when she reached down to retrieve it, she glanced at the couch and cried out. Mike was sitting up, looking straight ahead with a preoccupied expression.

"Are you all right?" she asked uncertainly. She was immobilized by fear, her voice hoarse, strained.

"I think so," he said after a hesitation. He brought his gaze in from where it had been and looked at her. "I think so," he said again.

Frank was sitting rigidly on the edge of his chair. Mike glanced at him and shook his head. "I don't think I'm dangerous," he said.

Frank grinned, but it was a faked expression that did not reach his eyes. "You must be hungry," he said without relaxing a single muscle.

"Yes, I suppose I am."

Still no one moved. Then Mike said, "I had a friend in college who had epilepsy. After a seizure he would sleep for hours; when he woke up he always said he felt peaceful, but very tired. That's how I feel, very peaceful, and very tired. I suppose I must be hungry. What time is it?"

399

"After nine," Frank said. He glanced at Barbara. "Why don't you go make him some scrambled eggs and toast. Something light and quick."

She caught in her breath with the realization that her father was afraid to leave her with Mike, who had that strange, preoccupied expression again, looking off into the distance, as if he had forgotten they were there. Wordlessly she got up and walked out to the kitchen.

When the eggs were ready, Mike ate a bite or two, then put down his fork. "Guess I was wrong." Abruptly he stood up and looked around the kitchen as if seeing it for the first time; he rubbed his eyes and sank into the chair again. "I have to go home," he said.

"We can't let you go off alone," Barbara said. "My God, what happened to you? How are you? How do you feel?" Her voice rose with anger suddenly, and she slammed down a cup of coffee; most of it splashed out, a mini–tidal wave racing over the table. She ignored it. "Answer me! You were asleep all day. They burned the disks. Do you even care? Say something!"

He regarded her almost thoughtfully. "They had to burn the disks," he said. "I understand why Emil Frobisher killed that laughing boy. Not because the kid was able to use the process, make it work, but because Emil Frobisher couldn't, and he knew he couldn't. It must have been like giving the thumb to a fellow ape, knowing you could not have a thumb, that you were going to stay in the trees the rest of your life while he learned to make fire, make tools, write books. Evolution doesn't ask if you want it or not, it happens or it doesn't. Frobisher made it happen, and then made it unhappen, and then killed himself. He must have known he was a blind man with the power to create a one-eyed king."

She shook her head, aghast. "What happened to you?"

"I got glimpses," he said slowly. "Another world. Like going from the dun-colored Kansas plains into the techni-color of Oz. There's another world within reach, here, there, all around us. We've always known it was there, but there was something in us lacking; the ability to attain it failed. Most who kept trying went mad, some reached out and felt a wall as cold and forbidding as steel, and they rebounded in denial, in anger. People tried to reach that other world with meditation, prayer, fasting, drugs. . . . Frobisher learned how to retrain the brain, to free a latent ability; he learned how to open the gate, but he couldn't go through. He must have got glimpses, enough to know what he couldn't have. You talked once about the veil of ignorance, but this is the opposite. The veils are gone. In that other world there aren't any more veils." His voice broke and he turned away; awkwardly he got up and left the table to stand with his back to Barbara and Frank. "I have to go home. I really have to be alone."

"I'll drive you to town," Barbara said. "I'll sleep on your couch tonight."

He shook his head. When he spoke, his voice was muffled and thick. "I don't want anyone near me for a while. I'll drive in. I'll call you in a day or two."

Barbara looked at the table, where she had made a mess with her coffee. It had run all the way across. She saw the key to Doc's house in the puddle, and she said, "Not home. You could go to Doc's house, house sit for him a day or two. Will you do that? Please, Mike, you'll be alone. They won't be back until Sunday. You can't drive by yourself now. Not tonight."

"Good idea," Frank said, and stood up. "I think there's an extra poncho in the hall closet. You get them and I'll go find a flashlight and walk over with Mike, show him the guest room over there, make sure there's coffee, little things like that."

When Mike did not protest immediately, Barbara hurried out to get the ponchos. She returned with two of them. Mike was very distant, very calm. His eyes were reddened. Briskly she began to clean up the coffee on the table. Frank came back with the flashlight, and in another minute he and Mike left. No one spoke again.

She stood in the silent house, her arms wrapped about her, shivering. She had never been so cold.

* * *

401

Frank was making dinner for three, Barbara realized the next afternoon. She had a headache and felt as if she might be catching a cold, or the flu, or something, and even when she thought this, she knew she was simply exhausted. Bad night? Frank had asked that morning, and she had glowered at him, had continued to glare throughout the morning, and early afternoon; now her glare was even fiercer as she watched him preparing three game hens.

"What's the use? He wants to be alone. Remember?"

"I intend to haul his ass over here for dinner," Frank said cheerfully. "Now, let's see, sweet potatoes. Did I get sweet potatoes?" He wandered off to the pantry.

She paced the house, too restless to sit still, too tired not to feel every step she took as painful. At the sliding door she gazed at the river, silver today under a sky that couldn't decide if the clouds should lift altogether or not. Although the sun came through, vanished, appeared again, the river remained silver, not at all reflective of the abrupt changes in the heavens. The new storm front had evaporated.

How could anyone see it any differently? she wondered, as she had over and over that day. This was the way the world was, clouds, trees, river, people, bridges, garbage dumps. . . . Suddenly, looking at the silver river, she remembered what Nell had said about her dread at the idea of that girl's body being dragged over rocks in the river. It was as if she had caught an echo of the actual event when Janet Moseley had been dragged over the lava, Barbara thought then. She tried to shake away the thought, but it persisted.

What would it be like, she wondered, to be the one-eyed person in the world of the blind? Would you scorn them, pity them, ignore them, use them? Use them, she thought darkly. If the way people used people now was any indication, if anyone had that kind of edge, life would be hellish, at least until everyone had one eye, when it would all even out again. Would the blind hunt down and try to kill off the one-eyed? She nodded. They would have to. Self-preservation would demand it. The power of numbers against the power of superhuman abilities. It would be bloody.

Why, then, her thoughts continued, did Schumaker and company permit Lucas to stay alive? She sat at the table thinking and was only vaguely aware when Frank began doing things in the kitchen again, then not at all aware of him until he touched her arm.

"Wine," he said. "You drink wine. Me cook. You wake up and drink wine."

She blinked at him. "Dad, Lucas must have appeared absolutely normal until the night Emil Frobisher was killed and they began drugging him. He said he was hallucinating, remember? In the tape, he said he was seeing things, hearing voices and the laughing boy. He knew where the boy hid the disks. They were communicating somehow. But it started that day, not before. Why?"

Frank had come to a stop halfway back to the cooking area. He swung around to look at her. "Go on."

"He knew Frobisher killed the boy. Afterward they drugged and hypnotized him, and after that he was always controlled until he ran away. But he appeared normal after he ran away, he was able to shop, drive, do whatever he had to do. I can't believe those girls would have got in his car if he had seemed insane. The people in the café in Sisters would have stopped it, or at least they would have remembered if he had been acting crazy in any way. No one mentioned anything like that. His father said he was afraid of being followed, but that wasn't crazy. It was very real."

Frank was watching her closely. "What are you getting at?"

"Why did Schumaker assume that Mike would be insane, appear insane?"

Frank poured himself a glass of wine and came to the table to sit opposite her. "Bobby, what are you getting at?"

"They don't know as much as they think they do," she said. "They must have thought that Lucas was driven mad when maybe it was their own interference that made him that way. As soon as he was free, he was okay, and according to his last tape, he said he knew why the boy laughed. Remember? And he laughed. Nell said he was happy, laughing when she

403

saw him. Frobisher must have altered the program more than they realized. The last boy he tried it on apparently didn't go insane in the slightest, but it took with him. Maybe it took with Lucas in spite of what they believed about their control of him, making him forget all about it. That's why he bought food and camping stuff. He must have intended to spend time alone listening to the tapes, trying to remember what had gone on before they started treating him. He must have remembered finally, and that's why he was happy and laughing at the end."

Frank gulped down most of his wine. "I tell you this, honey. I'm just real glad those disks are gone, burned up, the research gone, done with."

She was paying scant attention, her eyes narrowed in thought, frowning. "What if Schumaker has that detective keep an eye on Mike for a time, a couple of weeks, say? Maybe not around the clock or anything like that. But to check up on him now and then. What if they begin to wonder if he's insane, or why he isn't, if that's the case? Frobisher was the only one of that bunch who actually saw an unqualified success, apparently, and he killed the boy. You saw Herbert Margolis, how he reacted; he knows the truth about those deaths. Dad, they can't just walk away from Mike now; they're too frightened of what they've let loose. What will they do if they suspect the process affected him the way Frobisher meant it to?"

"Christ on a mountain!" He stood up and went to the other side of the kitchen.

He had no answer, she knew, any more than she did. In a little while he said he was going to go collect Mike now because later he would be too busy finishing the meal, and maybe she could shake herself enough to set the table. He sounded very cross.

Although the dinner was excellent, the dinner party sank without a ripple, Barbara thought later at the table, with not a thing to say. Mike was like a schoolboy whose ears still rang with his mother's admonitions: *Sit up straight, mind your P's and Q's, speak when spoken to, be polite and taste everything, laugh at your host's jokes.* . . .In between obeying without hesitation all the orders, he sat silently, withdrawn, preoccupied, mired in whatever it was that had possessed him and turned him into an expressionless stranger.

Finally Frank laid down his fork carefully and leaned on his elbows, regarding Mike. "Son, either you tell us what you're going through, what's on your mind, what happened to you and how it's affecting you, or I'm going to pour the gravy on your head. Hear that?"

Mike looked puzzled at first, then belatedly he smiled. The smile was short-lived. He folded his napkin and put it down on the table. "I think I'd better go now," he said. "I'm sorry, Frank, Barbara. I shouldn't have come, not yet. I can't say anything about it. I don't know what to say. I don't know what's happening, or even how to talk about it. It's like hearing music for the first time and trying to describe it to the deaf. Do you talk about it in mathematical terms, in emotional terms, as a force, resonances, sound waves, as a reminder of yesterday, all the yesterdays? See? I don't know how yet. Or even if there's anything to talk about."

He stood up and looked at Barbara with an expression that was quickly banished and replaced by one of friendliness. "I'll give you a call," he said, and left them at the table. In a moment they heard the door open and close. Neither moved.

That look, she thought distantly, trying to hold her awareness far away from herself, as if to cage it, contain it, not feel it at all—that look had been one of pity.

THIRTY-SIX

TIME PASSES, BARBARA thought sometime during the night. Whatever it is, it passes. You think it won't, that it got stuck somewhere, and then you see the hour has changed after all. She felt this was a revelation worthy of great discourses, discussions, debates. She stifled a giggle, moving from her window back to the bed, which she had torn up so completely that she had to remake it before she could crawl back under the covers.

Four o'clock, she realized a bit later in wonder. She had thought it would never leave the three hour. Three o'clock, three-fifteen, three-eighteen. . . .

She tried to arrange the coming day, but the pieces eluded her. Instead, she kept thinking of the nature of violence, and how once more she had stepped into the cage with the violent ones. In spite of all her protests, her yearning to be free of it, her determination to participate no more in a system that was irreparable, she had walked inside the arena again. Now she was committed to see Nell through it. And then? Then, she knew, she wanted to destroy Ruth Brandywine and Herbert Margolis, and most of all, Walter Schumaker. The self-knowledge filled her with despair.

Well, she told herself sourly, you tried to be saintly, and you failed. Sainthood's not for you, kiddo.

Or anyone else, she added, looking at the clock again; this time she pulled herself from the bed. Trying so hard to

406

relax was more exhausting than being up doing something. Sweep the kitchen, wash windows, read the almanac, read the cereal box, anything was better than the kind of physical struggle it was to remain in bed.

What had Frobisher offered and then taken back? Unexpectedly, the question welled up again, like Old Faithful gone erratic, she thought in the kitchen, waiting for the coffee. What would it be like to hear music in the land of the deaf? To see in the land of the blind? Evolution, Mike had said, offered, withdrawn, destroyed. Yet the feeling of change was rampant. She had seen all the new age magazines, the psychic bibles, the ads, the workshops announced. Had the apes sensed change? Had they stared at their hands without thumbs in wonder? Had Neanderthal Man glimpsed Cro-Magnon across the valley, and felt fear and wonder? She shook her head sharply and poured the coffee.

Maybe humans didn't have time to wait for nature's evolution, she thought at the table, her hands cradling the hot mug. No time, no time. The Earth is threatened; we're all threatened. No time to wait. *They* had set themselves up as Titans, but unlike Prometheus, they had not been willing to pay the price, the agony of the rock. They had found something, and then destroyed it. Something evil, deadly? Something wonderful that they couldn't have themselves? Or just something so different that where it would lead could not be predicted, nor what changes it would bring about? That would be the most fearsome of all; to change the world with no idea of what the changes would ultimately mean. But wasn't that exactly what the miners, the forest levelers, the dam builders, the chemical companies were already doing? Making changes on a scale inhumanly large, with unpredictable results. A butterfly wakes up, and someone in a corporate office says *do it*, and the world changes.

Even as she thought this, she accepted that it was different when it was human nature itself that was being changed at the level of chromosomes. Not just a new cure for an old disease, a one-to-one cause-and-effect process, but a process that could be passed on and on.

407

Where did Mike fit in? What happened to him? How was he now, this morning, this minute?

Abruptly she stood up and went to find a note pad. No matter where her thoughts started, they always came back to those same few questions that she could not answer.

"Ah, Bobby," Frank said when he entered the kitchen at eight-thirty. He rested his hand on her head for a moment; she reached up and patted it.

"Dad, it's all right. I'm all right. Get some coffee."

"You look all right, all right," he said and shuffled over to the counter.

"Well, I am. Look, someone has to get in touch with Tony today, or Larry Ernst, if necessary. We have to get them to agree not to announce a new trial for a few days at the very least. A week or two would be even better."

"Honey," he protested. "House rule, no business before breakfast. Kee-rist!"

She nodded absently and glanced over the page of notes she had made. "Okay. And I've about decided to give Clive to that Deschutes sheriff, not Tony. I'd like to discuss that, though. It could be I'm just being bitchy. I know I'd like to see Tony with egg on his face."

Frank groaned and set about making himself scrambled eggs, muttering under his breath as he moved back and forth from refrigerator to stove.

She looked up. "I'm sorry. What?"

"Not much," he said. "Just that you can't give what you ain't got."

"I'll get him," she said, and looked down at her notes again. "I'll tackle Nell. She has to put off telling Clive anything, making any decision about confessing. I'll see if I can get her in line for now. Don't quite know how since I can't really tell her anything, but I'll do something."

Frank banged a spatula against a pan. He was scowling ferociously when she looked at him again. "How long you been up?"

"I don't know. Hours."

408

"Showered yet? You haven't even got dressed yet. Why don't you go do some of those things and let a man eat breakfast?"

She did not go to town with Frank that morning. He took the car and planned to drive in to Eugene after picking up his paper. He would see Tony, or the district attorney, Lawrence Ernst.

"Make it good, Dad," she said, and kissed his cheek.

He had recovered his equanimity; it comes with food, he had said. Now he searched his pocket for car keys and said with a straight face, "I'll be good. They know I'm the one who cuts deals. One way or the other I'll buy us a little time."

She put her hands on his chest and gave him a little shove, then went back to the kitchen and her notes. The garage called to say her car was ready, could she pick it up? She said no way, and, grumbling, they agreed to send it out with a driver and a following car to bring him back. The price they were charging her, she thought, they should be happy if they had to send out a parade.

The next time the phone rang, it was Bailey.

"Got something pretty interesting," he said, and she caught her breath. What to anyone else might be earthshaking was merely interesting to Bailey. "I'd better come out there with it," he went on. "Couple of hours. And, something else, you know that guy you got your eyes on? If you can round up a picture, that would come in handy. His ex has a pretty interesting job with the city, by the way. Thought you might like to know that, too. Clerk in the DA's office. See you around noon."

She sat down trying to sort it out. Eugene was a small enough city, she thought, that it wasn't really surprising to find Clive's ex-wife in the DA's office, or anywhere else. Frank said it had been a friendly divorce; they kept in touch. Early on, she remembered, Clive had said he asked around about her and her father. She nodded. He had a contact, after all, someone who could answer his questions, keep him informed of what was going on. Today's visit by Frank? She

409

nodded again. He probably would find out about that, too. It was quite likely that Frank would hint that with a little time he could get Nell to cut a deal, but that she, Barbara, was being difficult.

She shivered, suddenly remembering the rock smashing through her windshield. Just another dimension, she told herself, another little interesting quirk in a case that was filled with them. Briskly she stood up and began to pace. A picture of Clive. Not here, probably not at Nell's house. Then she remembered Jessie's snapping her picture on her deck. Possibly she did that with everyone who visited.

It was not raining, not very cold; the woods were misty and a vibrant green. Everything was saturated with green, the trees, the needles, mosses, ferns; they all seemed to glow and pulsate. Everything was dripping, or airing drops as if they had been hung out like tiny ornaments. It was very quiet; even the river was muted by the trees. The river song was such a ubiquitous melody that its absence gave an unfamiliar alien quality to the woods now.

At the edge of the woods, with Doc's house sprawling before her, she paused, then straightened her shoulders and walked forward. She tried the front door, locked, then she tried the door to the service area, locked, and finally went around the house to the glass doors of the living room. Mike stood there.

"Open up," she called.

He shook his head.

"I don't want to talk to you, or even see you. I'm after something."

He started to walk away, back into the room, and she hit the door with her fist. "Open this door or I'll break it!"

Now he came back and released the lock and slid the door open a few inches. "You just can't leave it alone, can you?" he said bitterly.

"Don't flatter yourself, buster. I told you I'm after something. Just go hide under a bed or something and let me get on with it."

After he pushed the door open, she stalked past him

410

without a glance. In the center of the room she stopped, considering where Jessie might keep photographs. At a sound from Mike she glanced over her shoulder, and then spun around, staring. He was laughing. His laughter was raucous and unchecked; He clutched the door and held on, nearly doubled over with laughter.

She shrugged and turned away from him, denying the panic that seized her. Pretending an oblivion that would have been superhuman if true, she started to move toward the television room, den, whatever they called it here. Once more a strangled sound from Mike stopped her.

She faced him, her panic, fear, faked calm all giving way to fury. "Either I put my nose on upside down this morning, or it's a private joke that I couldn't possibly understand, or you're wacko. And at the moment, I don't give a damn which."

He closed the door all the way and moved to a long white sofa and collapsed on it. "You're wonderful," he said as soon as he caught his breath. His mirth was so close to the surface that he had to gulp in more air before he could go on. "I've been wrestling with ghosts and demons and spirits and wraiths and shadows, and you come in with absolute hard-edged reality and pass right through my tormentors without a flinch, without a glance, and scatter them off into never-never land."

"Wacko," she said, and then more critically, "You look like hell!" He looked as if he had not slept even as much as she had, and she knew that was too little by far. He had not shaved; his hair was wild with too much handling. Probably he had not eaten.

"I have a right. What are you after?"

"First, how are you?"

"You said it: wacko. But getting better."

She nodded as if the answer satisfied her. "A picture of Clive."

His expression was completely blank. Then he glanced about the room and said, "Here?"

She nodded and went on into the hallway to look for the

den. She had not been past the deck before and was impressed by the luxury of the interior. Everything was white or gold, the wood pale; here and there a lovely dark blue in a cushion or a drape was all the contrast there was. A good decorator had done it all, she decided; all very handsome, expensive, precise, and inhuman.

She began to open drawers in a desk, and went from there to a sideboard with a single drawer, and then on to a table and finally found a drawer with a photo album, and eventually she found a Polaroid of Clive. She let out a sigh.

She had been aware of Mike's presence throughout her search; he had stood watching her with his arms crossed over his chest. He moved aside when she walked from the room, back into the hallway, toward the glass doors again.

At the door he caught up with her and touched her arm. She stopped moving. He reached out and touched her cheek very gently, ran his finger along her chin, all the time studying her face intently. His touch was the most arousing she had ever felt; she was confounded by the wave of eroticism that swept her, made her feel lightheaded. He looked as startled as she was by the blatancy of the sexual need his touch had awakened. He looked frightened. He pulled his hand back and stepped backward, just as she was drawing away. They both stood motionless, staring, until she took another step away, and then another.

She shook her head hard and closed her eyes hard; when she opened her eyes and looked at him again, it was over, whatever it had been. "I have to go," she said, surprised that her vocal cords responded normally, that her voice sounded normal.

He nodded.

"You know where to find me if you decide to come back," she said, and turned quickly and ran out across the deck, back over the lawn, and into the healing woods.

As soon as she was deep enough into the woods that the trees hid Doc's house, hid her, she stopped her stumbling flight and leaned against a tree trunk and breathed deeply.

"My God," she whispered, after a moment. "My God."

They kept meeting on new grounds, the same two people creating ever-new patterns. At first it had been as if they had known each other for centuries, old friends, comfortable together, comfortable making love. Exciting, but comfortable, with few surprises. Then they had turned into shy adolescents, discovering sex, discovering mutual attraction, discovering the other, and through the other the self. But this. . . . She had no word for what had happened. Lust. Passion. She shook her head. Shopworn words that meant nothing. She had gone through a period of lust and passion in her early college years when sex had equated with life, and the partner had been whoever the current turn-on was. Each time it ended, she had been heartbroken, but even then, at an age that now seemed terribly young, she had known that endings were part of the game, accepted, looked forward to in some perverse secret way because each ending implied a new beginning, a rekindling of the excitement that went with the new other. Then Tony had come along, and brought new excitement, new passion, but never ease, never comfort. Never that. All lust, never trust, she remembered telling herself when she left him at the end. He had brought a sense of danger that had increased the excitement to a higher level than she had known, and she had mistaken that for love. Her first love lost, she had thought at the time, her first real betrayal. Since then, she had allowed no one to touch her, not in any real sense. Not even Mike.

She had set rules: He had to do this first, say that first, make the first move. . . . She had set up a testing program. She bit her lip when she felt her eyes burning with tears. "Goddamn it," she muttered under her breath. She pushed herself away from the tree and started to walk again, her eyes downcast, watching for rocks on the trail, but no longer seeing rocks or anything else. Goddamn it, she thought again, she didn't have time for this, not today. She rubbed her eyes with the back of her hand and trudged through the woods.

Bailey arrived before twelve. He grinned when Barbara let him in the house. "You want a smoking gun, I deliver a smoking gun. How's that for service?"

413

"Wonderful," she said dryly. "Show me."

"The old man home?"

"No. You'll have to put up with just me. Coffee?"

"Always. Never turn down a potable, that's what my father taught me. Only thing he ever taught me, but if you get only one lesson, make it good." He pulled off his jacket and handed it over. He was carrying a rolled map.

They went to the kitchen table, where he unrolled his map and anchored the ends while she got the coffee. He took three spoons of sugar and heavy cream. How could he drink what he did, coffee, booze, whatever was available, and still run marathons? She waited impatiently until he had everything to his liking and then sipped his coffee before leaning over the map.

"Here," he said finally, "is where the girl was killed, on the Forest Service road. Red *X*. Okay?" She nodded. "Okay, and down here, outlined in red, is a two-hundred-acre tract that was supposed to be cruised that week. And up here is seven hundred acres ditto. And finally, here, one more piece of woods, three hundred forty acres. Your boy had them all on his list, due in before the fifteenth of June when bids were due or something like that. He filed his report on this one first, Squaw Canyon." He pointed to a tract fifty miles north of his big red *X*. "He reported on the evening of June sixth," he said smugly. "The day Janet Moseley was killed. Then on June eighth, he turned in this one, south of the scene of the crime, Shadow Rock. And finally June twelfth, this one, Three Creek Meadow, that abuts the Forest Service road where they found the car. But, Barbara, sweetheart, all three reports were scrambled. They had to do them all over."

"Give me a break, Bailey. I'm not a descendant of Paul Bunyan, you know. What does that mean?"

He drank his coffee and set down the cup before he explained. "How I see it, he never made it to Squaw Canyon that day and just turned in an estimate based on experience, but without knowing there's a really big burned-over section in there that doesn't have any trees. He was off by five hundred thousand board feet. His Shadow Rock estimate is closer, off a couple hundred thousand board feet, and his Three Creek one is exactly the same as Shadow Rock. All wrong."

She shook her head and then studied the map. "You said the Three Creek one was first on the list? He could have been in there the day Lucas drove in with Janet Moseley? Is that what you mean?"

"I don't mean anything. Just found it interesting. Say he was in there, and then hightailed it out again, up the highway to the area of Squaw Canyon, but didn't go all the way in. Getting too late by then. So he pretended he had done that one first. But he turned in a bad estimate, and he was too good at his job to make a mistake like that, three times yet."

She was tracing a possible route from the Forest Service road, back to the highway, north, back into the mountains again. She nodded. "If that's what he did, he probably made sure people up there saw him," she said then.

Bailey chuckled. "See? That's why I want a picture. I talked to Roy Whitehorse, who knows exactly where to go to show people a picture. Okay?"

"You're a damn genius, Bailey!"

"I know. I know," he said, but he flushed with pleasure. "Roy said something else pretty interesting. He said if your boy turned up with red lava dust on his truck, they would have noticed up there. They notice things like what you're driving, if you have a gun rack, what kind of mud you've picked up. There isn't any red lava where he was supposed to be that day. Just good old black lava rock roads and dirt roads, all through those canyons."

"I think we've got him, Bailey," she said softly. "And if we do, I think your pal Roy and Sheriff LeMans should be the ones to take him. Or should I send Roy a bunch of roses?"

Bailey laughed. "Okay if I breathe a word of that?"

She nodded. "Oh, yes. And that bastard was telling everyone he began messing up his reports after Lucas was killed. Hah!"

415

When Bailey left, she put away the map and thought about lunch, but did nothing about it. Instead, she put on a sweater and went outside to stand at the rail, gazing at the river, thinking about Mike Dinesen and the new dimension that had suddenly appeared in their relationship. Relationship, she thought then, with almost bitter intensity; that's what people called it now. Never love, but a relationship. Meaningful relationship, casual, friendly, whatever it was between two people had been neatly labeled and somehow sanitized.

As she gazed at the river her mood changed again, and she found that alarming also; quicksilver mood changes were not part of her usual pattern. But she relaxed with the new change and found herself thinking how fine it would be to be the river, to flow endlessly. Or a tree, to stand in the wind and rain and sway with their rhythms. Or a rock. She smiled at herself and went back inside. So this was what it was like to be in love, she marveled.

The phone rang a few minutes later. Nell was calling to say she was back home, that she was going to take Carol to town to shop a little and see the Christmas decorations, and just spend a little time with her.

"I wanted them both to go," she said, "but Travis. . . . He's reached an age where he thinks shopping is women's work, I guess. Anyway, he'll be here, but I told him not to answer the phone. I just wanted to tell you."

"Thanks. I'm glad you did. Buy yourself something pretty and silly, okay? The more frivolous the better."

Poor Travis, Barbara thought when she hung up, he was old enough to stay home and not answer the phone and make himself a hot dog or something if he got hungry. But he wasn't old enough to deal with the fact that his mother was accused of killing his father. Soon, she promised him silently; we'll settle this soon.

Frank returned, looking tired and cranky; he had not slept well either. "We've got a week, at least," he said, hanging up his coat. "But they intend to go after her again if she doesn't own up to it voluntarily. Tony's words. I stopped by

416

the bank and got the Lucas tapes. Might as well have them here, listen to the whole bunch of them. I went by the bakery and got some decent bread."

She told him about Bailey; he nodded but didn't comment. He was regarding her closely when she started to talk about Nell and her plans for the afternoon. He waved that aside.

"What is it you're not telling me?" he asked, going past her to the kitchen. He went to the refrigerator and brought out cheese, placed it on a board, and the bakery bread on another one. He was starting to cut the bread when he looked up at her and said, "Well?"

"Nothing," she said helplessly. Then she blurted, "I'm in love."

The knife stopped sawing; he did not move for a moment, then started to cut again.

"Dad? I thought you'd be pleased."

He barely glanced at her as he cut another slice. "'Course I'm pleased," he said darkly. "Have you seen him today? How is he?"

"I think he's all right. He needs time to straighten things out, that's all."

When Frank finished cutting bread and arranged the slices on the cheese board, he glanced at her. His expression was stony. "You think. What if you think wrong?"

She was deflated so quickly she gasped. All day she had not thought of that, she realized; she had denied the possibility ever since seeing him at Doc's house, but now the fear was with her again, deeper than ever.

THIRTY-SEVEN

"YOUR MOTHER WAS a very fine cook," Frank said at dinner. "And I'm an excellent cook. Where did we go wrong with you?"

She had insisted on making dinner. "Fair's fair," she had said, and then burned the pork roast, underbaked the apples, and forgot to salt the peas. The baked potatoes were fine. Although she had set the table for two, she had cooked enough for three; Mike had not showed up. She scowled and cut another bite of meat.

With coffee, Frank said, "Way I see it, you've solved the wrong murder. Good reason, I guess, for turning him in to LeMans. Maybe you can talk the sheriff into booking Clive for both murders. Tony sure as hell would raise a stink."

"I know. There's not even enough for LeMans at this point. And I don't see any way to get any hard evidence, any proof. He'd be a good client right now for a shyster criminal lawyer."

They were both studiously avoiding any mention of Mike. She remembered what Bailey had said about Clive's ex-wife and told Frank. He cursed.

"So he'll find out what I was up to today," he said savagely, "and then what? Another rock through your windshield? A bullet through your head. Goddamn it!"

"Well, I didn't put her in the D.A.'s office, or see to it that they had a nice, friendly divorce," she snapped. Suddenly she became very still, thinking hard.

"What?" Frank asked.

"I'm not sure. Wait a minute." She sipped her coffee and then said, "Remember that I asked you who Nell was sleeping with when all this first came up? I never thought to ask the same thing about Clive. But he's a healthy, virile young man, divorced for what—four, five years? Is he celibate? I doubt it. You would have heard from Lonnie if he was dating. Was he?"

Frank thought for a few seconds, then shook his head. "In fact, she tried to push him in that direction, from what I heard, and he joked it away."

"He's terrified of AIDS, really spooked about promiscuity, about gays. It came up at that dinner party at his house. He was pretty vehement about the whole thing."

"Too vehement?" Frank asked softly.

"Maybe," she said, just as softly. "Maybe he was."

Frank reflected about what he had seen of Clive, what he had heard, and then said, "He's the perfect Stevenson hero, noble, waiting patiently for the one woman he loves, worshipful from afar, never touching her. Everyone's been genuinely moved by his devotion, his open love for her. A real Leatherstockings type. But is that enough, and if it is what can you do with it?"

"I don't know," she said tiredly. "Just another datum. Another check in another column."

There was a soft tapping on the sliding glass door; Barbara jumped up and covered half the distance to it before Frank got out of his chair. She pulled the door open.

"Hi," Mike said.

"Come in."

He took a step forward, inside the house. "I love you."

"Will you marry me?"

"Yes. Yes, and yes," he said.

She was frozen, afraid to touch him, be touched by him, afraid to reveal herself again, afraid not to. He reached out and took her into his arms. The fear vanished with the kiss, when she knew it was not only her desire but also his that had

419

sprung up around them like a physical bond. Not just desire, but a need so fierce that she ached from it and knew he felt the same hurting. When she at last drew back from his embrace, she heard her father at the doorway, clearing his throat. She did not look at him.

"We're going to be married." Her voice was almost unrecognizable to her ears.

"And not a minute too soon, from the looks of it," Frank said. His footsteps receded down the hallway, his study door closed.

"I love you," she whispered then. "I do. I really do. I love you."

"Let's go to bed."

"Yes. Yes, and yes."

They made love with abandon, and again with tenderness. They got up and wandered hand in hand downstairs, sat hand in hand before the fire. They ate cheese and bread and drank wine, and made love again. They talked sporadically.

"It's always new again," she whispered once during the long night. "How can that be?"

"We're working past so many layers," he said. "Self-protective layers on layers. I don't think I have any left."

"I know I don't. I didn't even know this me was in here." She shivered; his arm tightened about her shoulders. "No more defenses," she said. "It's scary. Almost scary."

"Scary," he agreed.

Finally they fell asleep entwined, then woke up again after nine in the morning. She opened her eyes to see him looking at her, smiling. She reached out to touch his cheek, and this time she saw the startlement on his face, saw his eyes widen. She laughed.

There was a note on the table from her father. He had gone to town for the newspaper. "So," she said. "I make breakfast. Eggs? Fruit? Cereal?"

"All the above. I'll help."

"I thought you never cooked."

"Breakfast doesn't count," he said seriously.

"Okay. Skillet. Eggs." She bent down to get the skillet from a cabinet, groaned, and very slowly straightened up again.

"What's wrong?"

She felt her face go hot. "Sore. My God, I'm sore!"

They both laughed. "You go sit," he said. "I'll feed you. This one time only, mind you. No habits are to be assumed from a one-time occurrence."

Gratefully she poured coffee and took it to the table and watched him searching for things, putting things together in a way that seemed strange to her. Scientist at work. First assemble everything you'll need, then proceed. That was his method apparently, and never hers, at least not with cooking. But that was exactly how she preferred to practice law, and why Nell's case had been such a bitch, she thought. She had not been able to line up things at any time; too much had been out of control, out of her control. Unpredictable, even unknowable events had intruded too often. She realized with a start that not once since his return had she thought of Mike's experience with the Frobisher program; not a single time had she considered it, much less asked about it.

He was whistling tunelessly, and now stopped and began to chuckle. He became serious again quickly and finished turning sausages, finished the eggs and toast, and brought everything to the table.

"Excuse me a sec," he said and left, to return with one of the legal pads. He jotted something and passed it over to her, and began to eat.

She read his scrawl with difficulty:

> *There was a young lady of law,*
> *Who, they said, was unlikely to thaw.*
> *When love made things muddle,*
> *And she turned into a puddle,*
> *He laughed, because he held a straw.*

"Oh," she cried. "Of all the arrogant, self-satisfied, egotistical. . . ." She ripped the page off the pad; he reached across the table and tried to grab it. When she pulled away, he came around the table to retrieve it, and then Frank walked in.

Hurriedly Barbara folded the sheet of paper and thrust it down into her pocket. Mike took his place at the table with a guilty expression. Primly Barbara sat down again and picked up her fork.

"And good morning to you, too," Frank said.

When Barbara glanced at Mike, he was grinning, and she began to laugh, and then said good morning to her father.

Ignoring them both, he got coffee and brought it to the table. "Got some interesting calls this morning," he said. "You in the mood for business, or is it still children's hour?"

"Tell us," she said, pleased at how natural the *us* sounded.

"Right. First, I made a couple of calls and got an answer. What you were speculating about last night, about our mutual friend, is true."

She shook her head impatiently. "Anything you have to say to me, you might as well just go on and say. You mean Clive?"

"Yep. Not generally known, but there it is. He's discreet. One long-time relationship with one very respectable person who happens to be married, all very quiet, orderly."

"Ah," Barbara said, but she still didn't know what she could do with the information. "What else?"

"Sheriff LeMans called. Said he'll be passing by this way and would like to drop in around three. No doubt he wants to know what you have, how good it is." Then Frank looked at Mike and said very deliberately, "Now, how about you? I trust my daughter's judgment more than that of most people I know, but I learned a long time ago not to trust anyone in love where the loved one is involved."

Barbara put her fork down hard, but Mike nodded.

"Fair enough," he said. "I believe I'm normal, as normal

422

as I ever was, anyway. No lasting effects that I can discern. But I wanted it!" He stared off past Frank for a second or two, then brought his gaze back. "I wanted it," he said quietly. "I tried to will myself to accept the program the way a kid might will himself to grow another inch or two, or to sprout wings. You will it and will it, and when you check the mirror you almost convince yourself that nubbins are forming, that it's working, but you know it isn't and can't. That's how I was. I wanted it more than I've ever wanted anything in my life. I would have given my soul for it to succeed. I thought it was taking, willed it to take, and then. . . ." He shrugged. "The door closed with me on this side."

"Are you able to leave it alone?" Frank asked bluntly.

"That was Frobisher's problem," Mike said after a pause. "He couldn't have it. Was he willing to let anyone else? He said no at the end. I don't blame him. It would be inhuman to give all that to someone else knowing you were forever banned yourself. I can even sympathize with Frobisher for killing the boy who made it work. In the end they all turned their backs on it, Frobisher killed himself over it. I'll leave it alone." His voice had turned ragged and harsh. He sounded grief-stricken. Abruptly he stood up and walked across the kitchen with his coffee cup, filled it at the counter, and stood with his back to them for another minute. No one spoke until he lifted his shoulders, let them sag, and faced them again. "So, quiz over? What is this about Clive and the sheriff? What have I been missing?"

Frank began to fill him in, but Barbara was thinking what it would be like to hear music in the land of the deaf, to see in the land of the blind, to fly in the land where people crawled. Although she wanted to weep for Mike, she was glad that it had not worked for him. If it had worked, he would not be here, not be hers. For a moment, she too had sympathy for Frobisher, who had seen however briefly the glorious handiwork of a demigod, who had known the power of creation for a brief moment, who had been a god denied the Eden of his own creation.

* * *

"For crying out loud!" Mike exclaimed while they waited for the sheriff. "Just tell Nell what you suspect and get her away from him."

Frank shook his head. "Bad move to show your hand before you have all the cards. He could become dangerous to Nell. He could just take off for Alaska. He could come after Barbara."

"Most likely he would simply get a lawyer and bluff it out," Barbara said. "Any kid fresh out of law school could get him off with no more than we have at this point."

"He can just get away with it," Mike said in disgust. "That's what you're saying. But when do you warn Nell? After the wedding?"

"Now, Mike," Frank said. "We wouldn't let it go that far. But now's too soon. We need just a smidgeon of hard evidence, which we ain't got."

"And if you can't find that hard evidence, he gets away with it." Mike's disgust and disbelief were both undisguised.

"That's how the system works," Barbara said. "And how it has to work, damn it! The state has to prove guilt and assume innocence, every time."

He threw up his hands. "That sucks!"

"We need a crystal ball, infallible, indisputable, ever-ready to show what really happened. We need people who are genetically incapable of lying. We need people who would die before they would hurt anyone else, who would die to prevent any harm to anyone else. And until we get that world, the system stinks and always has and always will. We tinker here and we tinker there, but it stinks. And we don't know how to fix it." Barbara's anger was as deep as Mike's, her helplessness more frustrating because she knew better than he that Clive could walk away from it unscathed and that Nell might have to face yet another trial. Also, she knew the torment Nell was suffering trying to weigh the certainty of a plea bargain against the uncertainty of another trial.

"I'm going back to Doc's and make sure I didn't leave anything," Mike said, still angry, helpless. "I know there's an unmade bed, and probably a mess in the bathroom. Let me know when the sheriff's gone again." He left with an angry expression.

"Way it goes," Frank said. "System stinks, but it's the only system we have."

"Right. Let's not preach to the choir, all right?" In her head she was crying, *Out! I want out!*

Sheriff LeMans was late. At twenty after three Barbara stood at the glass door, looking at the river, which was hiding today under a thick white cover of fog. The fog would creep up the banks later, hide the fishing camp, the store, insinuate its way up to the house, test the windows, the doors without a sound. Under it the river was invisible, secretive, silent. The fog's touch was icy, she knew, like death. She shivered and returned to the living room.

"Who is Clive's lover?" she asked. "Anyone I know?"

Frank raised his eyebrows. "I told my informant it would not be bandied about," he said. Then he added, "Bill Meyerson. Explains why Clive moved out here. Meyerson has a ranch a couple of miles up the highway."

"Good heavens! Our golden boy in the state legislature? Are you sure?"

"Who can be sure of anything? It's what I was told."

The doorbell rang then, and she went to admit the sheriff. He was in his full cowboy outfit. She almost looked past him for his sidekick, Tonto, or at least a white horse.

She took his sheepskin coat and his wide-brimmed hat, which she handled gently. Two hundred dollars, she decided, at the very least. They exchanged pleasantries as she put his things in the closet and then led him to the living room.

"Sorry I'm late," he said, shaking hands with Frank. "Found myself overshooting your place and ended up down at Mrs. Kendricks's instead." His eyes twinkled just a bit as he added, "'Course, I was curious about her setup, how easy it would be to get up from the river without being seen. Had a little look around while I chanced to be in the neighborhood."

"What can I get for you, Sheriff? Bourbon, scotch, coffee?"

"No, no. Nothing." He glanced over the array of bottles that Frank had put out, and then said, "Well, maybe just a touch of that Jack Daniels. To take the chill off. Pretty part of the country around here, but God, it's too wet. Too damn wet."

Barbara understood the rules very well, but she was growing impatient with the good-old-boy act; she sat down in her chair and made herself wait until the dancing ended and the business began. It was not long, after all. As soon as the sheriff had his drink and was in his chair, he turned his full attention to her.

"Your man, Bailey Novell, and my man, Roy White-horse, seem to have struck up quite a friendship. Real pals, from the looks of it."

"What have they found?" she asked, surprised to hear the bluntness of her father in her own voice.

"Well, Roy took him to a bar or two, up around Red-mond, his stamping grounds, places where the rangers and loggers like to hang out when they're off duty. They can put Belloc in the wrong place at the wrong time with the wrong kind of mud on his truck, pretty much like your man, Novell, suggested they might. It's not enough, though. What else is there?"

She told him what little there was, and he shook his head in disappointment. "I know," she said. "Not enough."

"Well, we can get on it, go up and down every back road out there, try to find someone who saw him that day, but it's been a long time. Lots of dust has got blown around since then."

"Sheriff," she asked slowly, looking at the fire, "is there any chance that that girl was not penetrated by a man at all, that he used an object of some sort altogether? Was there even a trace of semen?"

It was a while before he answered. "Could be, I guess. No semen. The pathologist said the river could have washed it away."

426

"Maybe. Maybe there never was any to start with. I don't think he would have touched her; he was too afraid of contact. If he was afraid of making contact with her blood, or any fluids, that would explain dragging her that way, too. Would the laboratory have made an AIDS test?"

"Yes, they did; nothing there." He was watching her very closely, his eyes narrowed, his drink disregarded.

"But no mention has come out about the test, has it?"

"Nope. No reason to report the negative." He glanced at Frank, who was sitting motionless, watching Barbara. "Why don't you just come out and say what you're thinking?" the sheriff asked then, and finally sampled his drink.

"Thinking out loud," Barbara said. "Everyone made note of the fact that Lucas had not marked his hands in any way. But if someone hit that girl hard enough to break her jaw and break teeth out, chances are good that his hand was marked, the skin broken. And he's terrified of AIDS. Just a thought."

"You're grasping at straws," Sheriff LeMans said sadly. "Even if you show us an injured hand, that's still not enough. He works in the forest; lots of injuries in the forests. I wouldn't want to go up with a case like the one I can make, not with you defending." He drained his glass, set it down, and shook his head at Frank, who made a motion toward it. "Best be getting on," he said. "That fog's not going to get any better."

They all had stood up and started to move toward the doorway when the bell sounded again.

"I'll get it," Frank said.

"We'll work at our end," Sheriff LeMans said, "but I don't feel hopeful, Ms. Holloway. Not at all."

She nodded, listening to Frank at the front door. Nell and Clive?

"We wanted to tell you first," Clive was saying.

She felt a knot of fury gathering in her chest and held up her hand to the sheriff to silence him. Clive was going on.

". . . don't want to interrupt if you have company."

She stepped into the hall then and called, "Hey, come on

in, you two." Then she turned to the sheriff and motioned him back to his chair. "Please," she whispered. He did not look pleased, but he sat down again and picked up his glass.

"Hi, Nell, Clive," she said when they entered the room. Nell looked miserable and cold; she evaded Barbara's eyes. Clive was smiling broadly. "You remember Sheriff LeMans, don't you?" She waited until they all said the expected greetings, then asked, "By the way, where are the kids?" If they were tagging along, this would be just another little social hour.

"Tawna's letting Carol paint jewelry, and Travis and Celsy are playing a game or something," Nell said. "Celsy's home for the holiday."

Barbara nodded. "Why don't you take that chair close to the fire. You look frozen. That damn fog's impossible." Nell went to the chair and huddled in it, holding her hands out toward the fireplace. "Actually," Barbara said then, "we were just talking about you two. Nell, this is a terribly impertinent question, but I have to ask. Have you had sex with Clive?"

Nell gasped, and Clive made a deep-throated noise.

"No!" Nell said.

"Of all the damn busybody—" Clive started, but Barbara cut him off.

"Oh, shut up. And sit down. You have to hear this, too. You see, that girl in the woods, Janet Moseley, had AIDS, and whoever raped her was possibly infected."

"Nell, let's get the hell out of here." Clive was on his feet, reaching for Nell's arm.

"Why don't you sit down?" Barbara said. "I repeat, you should hear this, too. Even if the guy used a condom, or even if he didn't penetrate her, if he so much as scratched his hand on her jaw, it's possible that her blood was enough to infect him."

Clive jerked his hand back as if it were scalded. His left hand cradled his right hand for an instant. "You're crazy," he said. "What the hell is this all about? What does it have to do with us?"

Sheriff LeMans had set his glass down softly; he was

tense, poised. Frank was still standing near the door. Nell stared wide-eyed at Barbara, very pale, transfixed.

Deliberately Barbara said, "I think all sexual partners should be told if there is any danger of infection, however remote. In Nell's case, I think she should be aware before she announces any wedding plans that her future husband is gay and quite likely infected with AIDS. And I think his other sexual partners should also be told. Bill, for example."

Clive lunged at her; she jumped aside as the sheriff leaped up, grabbed Clive's arm, and swung him away. Clive turned to him. "She's a crazy bitch! What's she saying? This is crazy!" He was livid, and shaking.

"Let's just sit down and discuss it," Sheriff LeMans said almost soothingly.

Clive jerked free of his grasp and yelled at Barbara, "You can't do this to me! You're crazy!"

"Maybe. But who tells Bill? You or me?"

"There's nothing to tell! I don't know who you're talking about. I don't know what you're talking about."

"Or," Barbara said coolly, "we can leave him out of it altogether, never mention his name again, and you just tell us what happened. Someone very discreetly can advise him to get a medical test. Routine checkup, that's all anyone would know. Maybe he would appreciate that you kept his name out of it, maybe he'd wait for you, the way you offered to wait for Nell."

"This is blackmail," Clive said hoarsely.

"No, it's plea bargaining before the fact. It happens all the time. It's how the system works."

Clive turned to the sheriff. "You're a party to this kind of blackmail?"

"I'm an interested spectator," Sheriff LeMans said. "Listening."

"He doesn't know the last name," Barbara said. "And there's no reason to tell him, unless we have to string out an investigation."

"Let me think," Clive muttered; he put his hands over his face. "God, this is crazy."

429

Suddenly his arm lashed out at the sheriff, caught him across the chest, and threw him back onto the chair. Clive spun around and ran; he hit Frank in passing and knocked him down, and then he ran out into the hall, slammed the door behind him, on out the front door, and slammed it shut. Sheriff LeMans ran out after him, but before he even reached the door, there was the sound of a car engine, tires spinning on gravel, and the roar of acceleration.

Sheriff LeMans returned grim-faced. He scowled at Barbara. "Where's the phone?"

She pointed; she was on one knee at Frank's side, helping him up. "Are you all right?"

"Sure, sure. Nothing broken, I think. Good God, Bobby, why didn't you warn a fellow?"

"What kind of car is he driving?" Sheriff LeMans asked at the phone.

"We walked over," Nell said.

"Jesus Christ," the sheriff snarled. "He left in a car. Whose?"

They had to go out to see that he had taken Barbara's car. She remembered that the man who had delivered it earlier had said the key was in the ignition. She described it to the sheriff, and gave him the license number. Nell was sitting as if stunned.

After the sheriff was finished phoning, Nell asked, "Can I go now? I want to go home to my kids."

"Sure, honey," Frank said. "I'll drive you over. I won't be more than a few minutes," he added to Barbara. "Hold the fort."

"I'd better go collect Mike," she said.

The phone rang; the sheriff scooped it up and began to talk again. He waved them all out.

On the deck outside, Barbara pulled on her cap and turned up her jacket collar. The fog had crept up the river banks to create a new earth form, joining the land that the river had bisected. The fog appeared solid enough to walk on. She began to walk toward the woods, toward Doc's house, benumbed by the last half hour, not elated over Clive's collapse, not jubilant at beating him, not at all victorious. *Benumbed* described it, but even with the word in her throat, she knew it was wrong. Soiled, dirty, that was how she felt.

In the Buick, Nell huddled, staring straight ahead. Frank glanced at her, back at the road, at her again, stymied for anything to say to her. She broke the silence when he turned into her long driveway.

"He wanted me to go to his house, after we saw you and Barbara. He said he had champagne that he's been saving for months, for this day. We would have . . . would have. . . ."

"Honey, it's over. You can relax. It's really over," Frank said, and then he caught his breath. Barbara's car was in the driveway near the little house.

Nell choked back a cry; her voice was like a sob, "He's gone. He took his truck. That's all, he just came for his truck." Then she looked at Frank and whispered, "He keeps a rifle in his truck. He'll have that, too."

THIRTY-EIGHT

ENTERING THE DEEP woods was like stepping out of time, Barbara thought as she walked slowly. The trail here was so narrow that too little light penetrated for undergrowth to take hold; the trees closed overhead, creating a perpetual twilight out of time. Ten thousand years ago, it was like this: Trees grew, died, fell; and new trees rose, always the same in the midst of change. Moss was on everything, hanging from lower limbs, layer upon layer on tree trunks and rocks,

431

velvety, moist, deeply green, fragrant. Even the silence was uncanny, unworldly; distance, trees, fog muted the voice of the river, turned it into a ghost river, also out of time, frozen under the spectral robes of fog.

Then she heard a sound on the trail ahead somewhere. "Mike? Is that you?"

The silence returned, more profound than before. She strained to hear anything and had to give up. Nothing. The trail was crooked; no trail in the deep woods was straight. Trails twisted around living trees, snaked around fallen tree trunks, circled boulders. She could not see more than ten feet ahead, and could hear nothing now. She realized she was holding her breath, unmoving, and breathed again, took a step. A bird, she thought. A squirrel or rabbit. Coyote. Cougar, bear, elk, deer. . . . She walked faster, making no noise on the carpet of endless cycles of needles, and she heard a sound again, the snapping of a branch, a foot scraping a rock, something. This time it was to her left.

To the right, fifty yards away, thirty, twenty, somewhere, was the edge of the cliff, the river below. To her left, at about the same indeterminate distance, was the gravel road. She must have covered half the distance to Doc's house, she thought. And then. . . . Then she would have to cross the cleared space, be out in the open. . . . The sound came again, to her left, behind her, between her and the road, between her and home. She started to run.

"Run, Barbara," Clive said mockingly, still behind her, off to her left. "Run, run."

She ducked off the trail, behind a tree. He laughed. Slowly, she edged away from the tree, darted to another one, only to hear his mocking laughter again.

"Don't do this, Clive. Go back to the house. Let's just talk about it. You can plead your case, you know."

"Shh," he said. "You know, it's funny in a way. I didn't want to kill Lucas. I saw the rifle and I got mad that Nell left it where one of the kids could pick it up, fool around, get hurt. That's all. I picked it up, and the shells, and I wasn't thinking about shooting anyone, until he began popping up here, there. But I want to kill you, Barbara. Not too fast, not from behind so that you don't know what's happening. Oh, I want you to know. I've had you in the cross hairs at least twice already, and I waited, you see, because I wanted you to know. And now you know."

"What about that girl? Why did you kill that poor girl?" she called. As soon as he spoke, she moved again, behind the next tree.

"I saw Lucas and her going up that dead end road, and I got curious when they didn't come out again. Then she said he was walking home, and I thought she was kidding me, mocking me, trying to be funny." He stopped moving, stopped talking; she didn't move a muscle. Then he said, "You guessed right about her, Barbara. I wouldn't have touched that little slut for all the gold on Earth. I used a stick. Crazy Lucas, let them think crazy Lucas did it. I didn't want him dead. In jail, the booby hatch, Nell ever faithful. I would have been her good, loyal friend—good to her, good to the children."

As soon as he spoke, she moved again, froze again; the eerie silence returned. This was his world, she thought desperately; he knew how to move, how to hunt down his prey. She was not even sure how far from the trail she had drifted, how close to the edge of the cliff she was now, and she could hear nothing.

His voice sounded very close, amused when he said, "You'd better breathe, Barbara."

"You can get a good attorney who will handle the case," she cried, and ran again, stopped again. "You could say you found the car and no one there. You were ready to blame Lucas; you still can. A good lawyer would raise doubts in the jury's mind." This time she held her breath, listening.

The silence was prolonged. She pulled off her cap, a light blue wool cap that would be visible a long way in the darkening woods. She looked around and saw a spike sticking out from a tree, a broken branch, head high; she dropped down in a crouch.

He chuckled, and she ran in a crouch to the tree with the

433

spike. "Thank you, Barbara. Good defense. I just didn't want to get involved. I had no idea a crime had been committed. I assumed it was just hikers out in the woods. Very good, Barbara, very good."

She still had not seen him; his voice carried in a way that did not yield a real clue about how far away he was. But he could see her every time she moved, she knew. Predator and prey, prey and predator. Only one had need to see the other. She wedged the cap on the spike so that most of it was on the side of the tree where she was, with an edge that Clive could see, if he was still behind her and to her left. She bent over as low as she could get and still move, and this time she crept away from the tree to take shelter again behind another one. No sound followed.

"Breathe, Barbara," Clive said softly. "Don't just wait for me. I like it when you run. Run, Barbara."

His voice was farther away; she was certain it was farther away, that he was talking to her cap. She looked around in desperation; the trees were not as big now, and there was the beginning of underbrush. She was coming to the edge of the woods. The light was fading, twilight and fog settling over the forest. Already the tree trunks and shadows merged and looked like a solid wall. But in the open, she would be clearly visible.

"I said move, damn you!" Clive said then, clearly, too loud.

She was shaken by the sound of a shot. She raced to the nearest underbrush and threw herself at it. He shot again. At her cap, she realized, when he began to laugh.

"Hey, Barbara, good trick! Really good thinking." He shot again. "Problem is, Barbara, you've run out of woods to hide in."

I know, she thought despairingly. I know. She kept her face down, her hands under her, not to let anything pale show in the shadows. Soon it would be too dark for him to see her; if she could be a shadow among shadows until then. . . .

"Clive, knock it off."

434

Barbara gasped. Mike! She lifted her head to look for him. "Stay away from him!" she yelled.

"I was thinking," Mike said easily, in a conversational tone, "Lucas must have scared the hell out of you."

"You, too," Clive said, and fired again. "I didn't come looking for you, Dinesen. But you, too."

"Yes, it must have been a shock. What did he do, appear and vanish, take a giant step to the edge of the clearing? Must have scared you pretty bad."

Clive shot again.

"Like this, I suppose," Mike said.

"Goddamn you! Damn you!" Clive screamed, and shot again.

"Over here," Mike said. "Let's walk, Clive. This way. Go on to the house, Barbara, now."

"Like him," Clive whispered. "You're like him! Devils!" He fired the rifle again.

Mike's voice kept moving, Barbara thought in terror. She drew herself up to her knees to look out over the top of the brush she had landed in. She saw Clive aiming, saw Mike disappear behind a tree. Beyond him the trees were a solid mass of darkness where wisps of fog curled and retracted, rose and fell. Clive spun around, facing her for a second, then away, and shot again. His face was livid with fear and insanity.

Barbara got up and ran across the clearing to Doc's house. She was trying to punch in the numbers of Frank's phone when he appeared and took the telephone from her hand. He held her at arm's length examining her, then drew her in close in a hard embrace. The sheriff was beside him.

"Where is he? Are you hurt?" LeMans asked.

"He's in the woods, over there! Mike's in there!"

"We've got him," LeMans said grimly. "I radioed for help as soon as we heard the first shot. There's no place he can go."

"Mike's in there!" she screamed at him.

"Well, it's getting dark. If he can stay out of sight just a little longer. . . ." There was another shot from the woods.

Then a car pulled in at the house; the state police had arrived.

They had a bullhorn and lights, and many men who milled about for a time. Barbara sat unmoving. No more shots came from the woods. No sound at all came out of the woods.

"We'll go in from all three sides," LeMans told her father. "We'll bring them both out."

She shook her head. "Mike took him out on the fog and let him drop off in the middle of the river. And Mike just kept going, laughing. He was laughing." Her voice came out thick and strangled, as if she were fighting her own insane laughter, or sobs. She clamped her lips together.

LeMans looked at her father and said, "You'd better take her home. I'll come around when it's over."

"Yes," Frank said heavily. "We'll go. Come on, Bobby. Come along. We'll go clean up those cuts and scratches."

She went with him without protest. It didn't matter where she was.

Later, she sat in the living room. Now and then she shivered until Frank brought down a blanket and wrapped it around her shoulders. He put a drink on the table by her chair and then sat down opposite her.

Still later, the sheriff came back and talked to Frank in low tones in the foyer. She could hear every word. They had found blood. They had found Clive's rifle, about fifteen feet from the edge of the cliff; they must have fought there, must have gone over the cliff together, down into the river. It was too dark and too foggy to continue the search tonight. They would resume in the morning. They would bring in skin divers in the morning. She did not move.

In the little house Nell said, "Aren't you kids tired of that game yet?"

Travis shrugged in that gesture that was wrenching to

her every time she saw it; she turned away. Tawna stood at the door.

"Come on, Nell. Leave them to it. They had hamburgers and stuff. If they get hungry, they can come up to the big house." The two women left Travis and Celsy at the computer.

"Let's see what's on this other program," he said. They had killed the dragon, rescued the princess, escaped the alien space ship. He keyed in a command and the screen cleared, then a brilliant Mandelbrot filled it again, all electric blue, silver, flaming pink.

"Rad!" Celsy said softly. "What is this?"

"More of Mike's Mandelbrot stuff, I guess. The disks turned up, so I copied them. I haven't checked it out yet. Let's watch."

Barbara stood in her room. Since she wasn't hungry, she must have eaten. Since she was in her room, it must be bedtime. Since the house was deathly silent, Frank must have gone to bed already.

"The door didn't close," she whispered to herself. "Not all the way. He was mistaken about that. It was a swinging door after all." She nodded and mechanically began to undress. Then, in her warmest robe, she stood at the window. The world was utterly black and silent out there. The river was silent, revealing nothing. She dragged a chair to the window and sat down staring at the blackness, just as if she could see through it, and she tried to recapture every word, every glance, every touch from the first day that she had seen him in his running clothes.

In her room in the big house, Celsy was at her window, also. She reached out tentatively, curled her fingers in the air, as if about a physical object, and she laughed without making a sound. In his room in the little house, Travis was reaching out, laughing soundlessly.

The fog had become visible again, a luminous, motionless world of fog pressed against her window. An illusion,

Barbara thought; not fog at all, but a cold steel wall. A butterfly flapped its wings and the wall had parted for Mike, but it was still there, unyielding, invisible, and real.

She groped in her jeans for the yellow paper she had folded and jammed down into her pocket, thinking, "There was a young lady of law. . . ." She found the sheet of paper and smoothed it out, and then she opened her window wide and breathed in deeply. As if her breath were a signal, a murmur stirred high in the fir trees. The wind was starting to blow. Now she could smell the air filtered through the millions of fir needles. Soporific, she thought. Finally she went to bed, put the yellow paper under her pillow, and she wept, and, weeping, fell asleep.